Defenders of Myth
~Beginnings~

Michael Gisman

The characters and events portrayed in this book are fictitious. Any similarity to real persons, living or dead, is coincidental and not intended by the author.

Cover art by: Allen Morris
Cover design by: Allen Morris
Printed in the United States of America

Copyright © 2021 Michael Gisman
All rights reserved.
ISBN: 978-1-7375988-0-0

DEDICATION

For Holly
My best friend and most patient wife

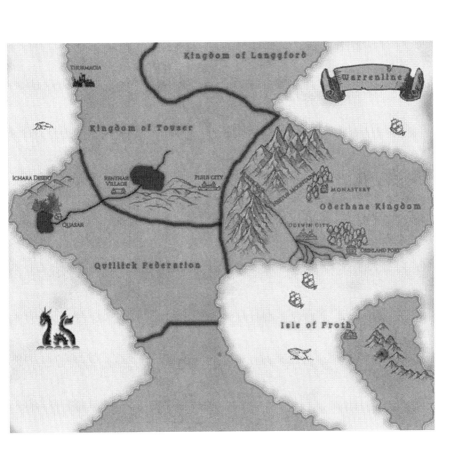

PROLOGUE

The morning air was crisp with cool air and smelled of new growth; sunlight poured down onto the courtyard but did little to relieve the cold that seeped into the old man's bones. Old but not decrepit, a tall man, burly with large, calloused hands that spoke of seasoned strength, he walked with a purpose of both familiarity and ritual. Bred from a lifetime of service to a greater good, a passion that still burned but tempered from his sixty years of life, he pulled his cloak tighter about him as he made his sure and steady way to the gate. The gate stood closed, its double doors secured by a thick square beam running horizontally across them. As he reached for the crossbar, he cocked his head as though listening to something. It was muffled, but the noise could be heard, a soft cry as though from a hurt animal.

The old man hastened to open the gate, lifting the bar and setting it against the side wall; he pulled the doors open. Peering down into the dawn light, he saw two bundles of cloths and rags, the crying coming from the one on the left. He bent down to one knee, parted the rags of the crying bundle, and found a baby's face looking up at him. Turning to the other pile and opening it, he found another baby looking at him, this one smiling and reaching for him. The old man smiled, reached out with a hand, and let the baby grab his finger. Looking up, hopeful for some clue to the two infants' abandonment, he scanned the surrounding area, which revealed little but dappled sunlight and trees just starting to bud. His gaze returned to the two bundles, and he took his finger back; picking both up with a care and gentleness that belied his age and strength, he rose to his feet, turned and reentered through the gate, and strode into the courtyard beyond.

CHAPTER ONE

It was raining. A slow, steady drizzle coated the forest and monastery, leaving the air heavy with its dampness as the old stone blocks wept with water. The kind of day that lay heavy on the heart and slowed times passage. Fires could not take out the chill; candles were not bright enough to edge out the dull gray afternoon. It seemed everyone was despondent and waiting for a break in the weather. This was especially true of the youngest guest of the monastery.

The room where he sat had cold stone walls covered in cheap tapestries depicting battles from ages past; iron sconces held flickering candles that lined the walls in the breaks between them. To his right, a large bay window overlooked the Hestur Mountains, which appeared hazy and indistinct in the distance. The young man sat at a wooden desk, wearing a grey robe that hung loosely around his developing frame; wavy blond hair flowed to his shoulders and edged his face while bright blue eyes gazed dreamily out the window.

"Kalend!" the teacher rumbled. "I do not talk to hear myself, young man. Listen, and you may yet learn something."

The young man, Kalend, turned back to his teacher, sighed, and responded, "Yes, sir," with an air of resignation. However, as soon as the teacher began to instruct again, he turned back to gazing forlornly out the window.

Shaking his head, the teacher stopped and asked, "Maybe we should take a break, and you can visit the Martial Master?"

Kalend perked up and replied, "May I, sir?"

The teacher looked at him sternly and said, "Yes, but you cannot shirk your duties to study other things besides fighting. Someday, you will need this knowledge and be grateful for it!"

Kalend rushed out the door with a backward, "Thank you, sir!"

The teacher sighed and mumbled, "You better be grateful," to the now empty room.

Hurrying down the hall, Kalend felt some small guilt about rushing out on his teacher, whom he generally liked, even if the subject matter sometimes bored him. Thought of training was too much for him; it had been a week of what felt like nothing but scholarly study with little weapons practice. The Martial Master had been on a trip to the nearest village to help with new constables' training. Being the only true master of both hand-to-hand and weapons combat for many leagues, he was often called upon to help finish the training and prepare the new force for its protection duties. He was due back this morning, and Kalend was eager to continue training at his mentor's hands.

Kalend turned left at the end of the hall, pushed through the door, and entered the courtyard. The monastery was built in the shape of a square, with all the buildings joined around the center opening. One wall had a large double door that served as the gate and was customarily left open, as it was today, for there had been peace in the surrounding area for as long as Kalend could remember. Look-out towers were positioned on each side and gave an expansive view of the surrounding countryside, which was occupied by farmhouses, crops, and orchards.

As Kalend hurried into the courtyard, he slid in the gravel to a stop and stared wide-eyed at the scene before him. The Martial Master was in a furious fight with another man. They moved back and forth, striking blows with their long swords, neither having a shield; they blocked, parried, and dodged, unmindful of the steady drizzle. With mouth agape, Kalend could only marvel at the speed and grace with which they fought. After the initial shock wore off, his next impulse was to help his teacher, but something held him back. He then realized they were both grinning, and even as they fought hard, it became apparent they intended no real harm to each other. Next, he noticed a crowd had gathered and watched with appreciation and awe; this was a spectacle to be enjoyed, but in Kalend's case, to also learn.

With the two combatants wholly focused, Kalend watched closely to try and get a glimpse of what was really happening, for he rarely passed up an opportunity to learn the art of fighting. The men's swords were a blur, and he was sure that he missed many of the nuances, but still, he saw much to emulate. The dancing and weaving and knowing the attackers' mind, he tried to anticipate what the attacker's next move would be, with limited success. So, it came as a shock when the fierce action came to an abrupt halt. With broad grins and heaving chests, the two turned and faced each other for several moments before raising their swords and saluting in unison. The crowd seemed to gather its collective breath with a quiet stillness, then all at once burst out in a loud cheer. The two turned sharply towards the throng and bowed deeply in appreciation.

The Martial Master gravely looked around at the cheering audience and asked, "Isn't there work to be done?" Those gathered quickly fled in several directions as they went to tend to their original tasks.

Kalend was left alone with them both. The Martial Master was an imposing man, medium in height but bulky, with muscles hardened from experience and a daily routine that saw him frequently on the go. He wore dark brown trousers with a black shirt that clung to his torso and accentuated his physique; he flipped his light brown ponytail behind him as he looked upon Kalend. He had a direct and piercing gaze that could see through a person, as though reading one's thoughts and at the same time being aware of all that was around him. Kalend knew this was from years of training and meditation, and someday, he hoped to emulate that ability. When the Martial Master spoke, everyone listened and jumped to do what he asked, not out of fear but in total trust and respect.

He beckoned for Kalend to come forward. "Kalend, come, my boy; I have a special person I would like you to meet."

Quickly crossing the few yards that separated them, Kalend took stock of this stranger. He was tall, well over six feet, slim with a willow-like torso, long legs, and wavy jet-black hair that cascaded around his shoulders. He wore dark green pants and a matching doublet with a long sword on his left side and a short sword sheathed on his other. He had a peculiar mustache that swept from the middle into two curly Q ends that quivered when he smiled, as it did now with Kalend's approach.

"And this is the young man I told you about; his name is Kalend," the Martial Master said by way of introduction.

"Pleasure to meet you, sir," Kalend responded while shaking the stranger's hand.

"Well met my young friend. My name is Louquintas; your master has told me much about you."

"Hopefully, good things, sir," Kalend replied with a smile.

Turning to the Martial Master, the man laughed good-naturedly and said, "He has good manners, unlike you, Tosrayner."

The Martial Master smiled at them both and said, "Come inside, both of you, and we shall find food and drink."

***** *****

A fire burned merrily within a fireplace against the far wall, and groups of candles lit the long table where the three sat. Spacious with bare walls and a tall, dark wood vaulted ceiling, this was the meeting room. Kalend had never been in this room before, as it was used to plan events that he was not old enough to participate in. He would later recall this room with fondness, as much that would transpire in his life started within it. But at that moment, his attention was riveted on the two men before him.

With wine in hand and a platter of cheese and bread before them, the two spoke in serious tones about politics in the neighboring city of Odewin. Then, they switched to more trivial matters as they laughed and chuckled over the exploits of a local farmer's daughter and the subsequent drama associated with it. It became apparent that the two knew each other quite well and had a long history together. There was an ease and familiarity amongst them that bespoke of old friends who had not seen each other for a long time but seemed to pick up right where they left off some time ago. They talked passionately about some things and smiled about others while laughing at things that Kalend did not understand or missed entirely. Still, it was a pleasure to see old friends get acquainted again. A half-hour passed before they ambled over to refill their goblets from the pitcher resting on the stand beside the door. Kalend found their attention had turned to him as they sat back down.

Louquintas asked, "So, my young friend, what do you think of your master's sword work out in the courtyard?"

"Amazing! I have never seen such a display of skill; my master has never looked better." Kalend replied excitedly.

Louquintas smiled as his mustache quivered and asked another question, "Who would have won, do you think?"

"My master," came the quick reply.

Laughing outright now, Louquintas said, "Your loyalty is commendable, and you could be right. However, I am not so sure; we may need a rematch."

The Martial Master smiled and replied to his old friend, "Maybe someday, but for now, we have important matters to discuss."

"Right as always," Louquintas said as he tipped his goblet to Tosrayner.

"Shall we tell him then?"

Louquintas shrugged and looked at Kalend appraisingly. "May as well, the sooner we can be on our way."

The Martial Master looked to Kalend with a kindly but sad smile and said, "Kalend, your training here at the monastery has come to an end; we have other plans for you now."

Kalend's jaw dropped, and he stammered, "Excuse me, sir?"

Sighing, the Martial Master said, "Your training with us here is over; you have learned much. However, fate has decreed another path for you. You shall accompany Louquintas on a short journey to a small group of elderly women in the mountains. There, your training will continue under the ladies and Louquintas."

"But all I know is here, you, my friends; why must I leave?" Kalend responded in shocked disbelief.

"That is a long and complicated tale. One best told tomorrow in the morning."

"But I want to know now," Kalend pleaded, "You can't just send me off with some stranger!"

"Louquintas is not a stranger to me; he is a friend, a compatriot, and someone who can better serve your need for training." Tosrayner replied sternly before softening his tone, "Plus, I can and will send you off; for better or worse, your care was left in my hands, and now it's time for me to pass that responsibility on. You will obey me in this, will you not?"

Crestfallen, Kalend looked up at him and said, "Yes, sir."

Louquintas placed his hand on the boy's shoulder. "Have no fear, boy; we shall practice together, and you will grow and develop into a fine fighter someday."

Shaking his head in dismay, Kalend asked, "May I be excused, sir?"

The Martial Master responded, "Yes, but plan to meet us at first light tomorrow, and we will answer many of your questions."

Kalend woodenly stood up from the table and stumped dejectedly toward the door.

"Oh, one more thing, Kalend."

Turning back to the Martial Master, Kalend asked sullenly, "Yes, sir?"

With a slight smile on his face, the Martial Master told him, "On your way to bed, why don't you stop by the stable and pick out a horse for yourself. Speak with the stableman; he is waiting for you. Be careful which one you pick; he will be yours and your responsibility but will also see you through much that is to come."

"My own horse?" Kalend stammered.

Louquintas laughed. "He seems kind of addled, Tosrayner; this may be more shock than he can handle."

Blushing, Kalend turned to leave again. After the door clicked closed, the two old friends grinned at each other.

"That didn't go so bad. What do you think?" asked Tosrayner.

"Not bad at all; he took it well," Louquintas responded, then rose and strolled over to help himself to another pouring of the dark wine they had been drinking. As he returned with a full goblet, he asked, "Are you sure this is the right thing to do?"

Tosrayner sighed. "I don't think we have much of a choice. We are too visible here. If your information is correct, then they have some clue that the missing children may be found in our neck of the woods."

Settling back into his chair, Louquintas said, "Yes, but they don't know where, plus they were but babes when found, and there is no way they could know what the children look like now that they are older."

"The problem is the story of their finding is known to everyone around here, at least the finding of the boy. It makes me happy we split them up and kept secret where we sent the girl."

Louquintas nodded, "It's your call, and I am more than happy to help." After taking another pull from his drink, he smirked and said, "Now that I have met the boy, I can perceive some fun to be had training him."

Laughing, Tosrayner responded, "Keep your instincts under control, you bandit; he has much to learn still. Hone his weapon skills, but do not neglect his mental training as well.

He is just starting to understand how meditation and the mind can play such a big role in his performance on the field of battle."

"Don't worry so much. Remember, we had the same master's in training; what had been taught to us, I shall try and pass along to the boy."

"You were always the more reckless of the two of us; you got me into a lot of trouble," Tosrayner said with a smile.

Louquintas laughed and responded, "Yeah, well, you followed right behind and helped out in the trouble. I just kind of led the way, is all."

"Be that as it may, just train him well and protect him."

Louquintas put his dusty boots up on a nearby chair and said, "So be it. Me and witches will teach him."

Tosrayner grunted and retorted, "Call them witches to their face, and you may find yourself as a carrot for the rest of your days!"

"I know better than that!"

Tosrayner smiled and then turned more serious. "Their powers will help hide you and the boy from prying eyes, and it being so remote shouldn't hurt either."

"We will take good care of him."

Tosrayner rose to his feet, fought a yawn, and said, "It's late and been a long day; time for some shut-eye."

"I plan to finish my wine and watch the fire for a bit; sleep well, and it's great to see you again."

Tosrayner replied, "You too," then quietly headed out of the room.

The door silently closed behind his old friend as Louquintas stood and positioned his chair in front of the dying fire. Mug in hand, he leaned back and spread his feet before the warmth emanating from the fireplace. He took a sip and contemplated all that was to happen in the days to come. Much was to be planned in a short time, and he wondered how life had taken such a turn. So serious things had become of late. Where was the fun? He chuckled and murmured, "Still, excitement will be had shortly…with the witches!"

***** *****

Kalend hurried noisily down the hall, his mind awash with excitement at the prospect of owning a horse! He was to be given something only adults usually had and then only those with power, money, or influence. A rare and unique privilege, this was indeed, especially for someone his age. But then it hit him: why was he given this privilege? His pace slackened as he mulled over all that had transpired in the meeting room. Yes, he was getting a horse, but at what price? To leave all that he knew and loved? He was not sure owning a horse would be worth it. He always wanted to explore the world, see the sights his teachers talked about, and have adventures like some of the heroes of ages past. But now, now that he faced the reality of leaving, he found the whole idea both scary and exciting at the same time. He thrust his way through the doors leading into the courtyard as those emotions threatened to overwhelm him. He paused and drank in the cool evening air, and another question flashed within his mind: who are these "elderly women in the mountains" the Martial Master spoke of? Having never heard of such a group, he could only speculate, which led to more questions. Why was he being sent to them? What could they teach about fighting? His pace took on a determined stride as he decided that these were questions that needed to be answered tomorrow.

As he crossed the midpoint of the courtyard, his thoughts strayed to Louquintas. An interesting man, quite different from his master in many respects, he seemed to be more jovial, brash, and less disciplined in some ways. However, with the display of swordsmanship he put on, less disciplined may not be the right word. He shook his head; more carefree would be a better way of seeing him. Overall, he found it hard not to like the man, even with that outlandish mustache.

The double barn doors soon loomed before him, and Kalends' mind snapped back to his original purpose. As he entered, he was greeted with the heavy scent of fresh straw mingled with the damp muskiness he had come to associate with the stables. He strolled down the aisle lined with stalls on either side, patting the occasional horse between the ears, at least those curious enough to have poked their heads over the low wire and wood-framed enclosures. He found the Stable Master within a stall midway down on his left, attending to the grooming of one of his charges.

Looking up but continuing to diligently brush the deep black mane of a tall stallion, he asked, "What can I do for you, young sir?"

Kalend had always liked and gotten on well with the Stable Master; with his country drawl and vast knowledge of horses, he had found the man to be a contradiction. An intriguing combination of infinite yet straightforward wisdom in the field of horses.

"I was told to come and get a horse," Kalend responded while trying and failing to control his excitement.

"Well then, we best see what we can find for you," the Stable Master said as he set his brush down on the nearby shelf. Moving out of the stall, he motioned for Kalend to follow him. "There are some good horses in the last few stalls. They are young but ready for owners."

"Have I ridden any of them before?"

"No, these three are just out of training."

Coming to a halt at the far end of the aisle, they stood before three stalls. The Stable Master motioned for Kalend to have a look. "These be them; you may have your pick." Starting at the closest stall, he looked the horses over, each in turn, slowly taking their measure. He pushed his excitement to the rear of his mind; he knew this was a serious matter and that care must be taken. The first horse was medium in height but with a large barrel chest, a dark chocolate brown, and a fine coat. The horse glanced at Kalend with disinterest and then went back to its feed. The second horse was taller and had less mass but exuded a lean strength. Deep creamy black mixed with brown, his shiny coat glistened with the torch light; he peered at Kalend for a long moment, then gave a whinny that ended in a high-pitched whistle. With a raised eyebrow and a short laugh, Kalend asked the Stable Master, "What was that?"

The Stable Master shrugged. "He had an illness when he be younger and left him with that whistle."

Turning to the last stall, Kalend inspected the third horse. A pure black with a ruff coat and rugged appearance, this horse did not bother to look up from the hay it munched. Taking a step backward, Kalend reflected on all three; each was different, each one unique, and each would make for a fine companion. "Which one would you pick?" Kalend asked solemnly.

"Depends on what you are looking for. The first is tough as nails and can take a pounding but not very swift of foot. The second is fast, very fast, not as hardy as the first, but with a hidden strength all its own. The third is just plain hard and aggressive."

Assessing each of them again, he found himself drawn back to the second horse, the whistler. He stepped forward and reached out a hand; the horse nestled his hand and gave another whinny-turned whistle. Suddenly, Kalend knew this was the one, and he said with conviction, "This is the one….and I will name him Whistler."

The Stable Master nodded. "Very good, young sir. I shall have him readied for you."

Kalend thanked the Stable Master, and as he turned to head down the aisle, something occurred to him; he paused, then asked, "Did you know I was coming to get a horse tonight?"

With a small smile, the Stable master said, "Yes, I did. Tosrayner told me to expect you and give you any help you needed in picking one." Laughing, he went on to say, "I don't just hand out horses to any boy who walks in and asks for one; that would be a good way for me to be put out of the monastery."

Kalend bowed and said, "Thank you for the help and the horse."

"Take care of him, and he will take care of you, young master."

Taking his leave of the Stable Master and his new horse, Kalend walked out the barn doors into the refreshing night air.

He paused to gaze up at the clear sky for a moment, then closed his eyes and took a deep breath, calming his mind and body as he had been taught. Letting his mind relax and swirling thoughts slow so he could take in all that had transpired. He found it interesting that the Stable Master knew beforehand that Kalend would be there that night; did he also know Kalend would leave soon? That then begged the question, how many people knew? So many questions that had no answers! It was not much consolation that tomorrow would bring those answers when your whole life was turned upside down in one night. Sighing, he slowly began to make his way to his room, which was located on the far side of the monastery. With his feet crunching loudly on the gravel of the courtyard in the otherwise still and quiet evening, he figured it was time to get some sleep. If that was possible after an evening such as this, he was unsure, but he knew he needed to be at his best tomorrow.

***** *****

"Wake up, Kalend," a whisper bubbled up from deep within his well of sleep. "Wake up, Kalend," it came again with more urgency.

"Damnit boy, wake up," it came yet again…but this time with a shaking that rattled his teeth. Kalend groggily came awake to find a dark silhouette hanging over his bed. "What? Who??" he asked with confused irritation.

The dark silhouette straightened and snapped, "Need to get up; time to go."

Forcing himself more awake at that pronouncement, the boy squinted at the dark shadow hovering over him, and he noticed a strange wiggling above the mouth of the shadow. "Louquintas, is that you? What's going on?"

"It's me. We have a slight change of plans. We must leave. Now. Tonight!"

"Tonight? Why?" Kalend asked as he flung his blankets off and shook the last vestiges of lethargy from his mind.

"Something has come up. We need to get out of here; I will explain on the way. Grab your stuff." Louquintas responded urgently.

Kalend hastily rose from the warm confines of his bed and stumbled about while he pulled on his dark green hunting pants and matching tight-fitting shirt. Then, he began to scoop up the rest of his belongings in the darkness. He was thankful for his inability to fall directly asleep last night; it had given him time to begin packing; some good had come from it, after all, he thought ruefully. Then, all the memories of why he had had trouble falling asleep came rushing back. All those questions that needed resolution, what was going on? He needed answers, now, before he went any further.

Stopping in the middle of his room, backpack in one hand, sheathed long sword in the other, he turned to Louquintas. "What is going on? I must know. Before I go any further, I need some answers!" He pleaded.

Facing him, Louquintas responded gravely, "Alright, the short answer is, your life is in danger, and we must get you out of here."

With an incredulous look, Kalend blurted out, "In danger? From whom?"

Shaking his head, Louquintas admonished, "We need to go. I told you I would explain on the way."

Grumbling, Kalend finished gathering his few belongings and then followed Louquintas through the doorway. Kalend noticed Louquintas was dressed in dull black chainmail that hung to his knees, with equally dark chausses protecting his legs, armor he had not been wearing when they had first met. His pulse quickened as he realized its implication. They moved quickly down the hall and passed out into the courtyard, where Tosrayner stood waiting for them with two horses. One was Whistler, saddled and ready to go. Louquintas went to the other horse, mounted, and looked at Kalend, who had stopped in front of his Martial Master.

"Sir, what is going on?" Kalend asked Tosrayner.

Putting his right hand on Kalend's shoulder, Tosrayner looked him in the eye, "Listen, my young pupil, follow Louquintas. Follow him as you would me. He can explain on the way. Much is happening faster than I thought, and I can no longer protect you here." Putting up his other hand to forestall any response, he continued, "I know you have questions; I wish I could be the one to explain it all. There is no more time. Remember all that I have taught, and know that my thoughts are with you. Now, quickly, on your horse." Once Kalend was seated, he shook his pupils' hand and warmly said, "Good luck."

Louquintas had quietly watched the exchange but now said, "Let's go!" and put his heels to his horse. Heading out the gate and into the night, he did not bother to look back. Kalend reluctantly trotted after but looked to his Martial Master and received a fist-to-heart salute while he passed through the gate.

He galloped closely behind Louquintas, past the farmland that surrounded the monastery, down the cobblestone road, and onto the dirt track beyond. Headed from all he had known and cared about, the path before him was clear in the predawn light, but the path of his life was now hazy and indistinct. All those questions he had were now compounded by many more.

CHAPTER TWO

The two riders slowly emerged from the dense forest; they stopped at the shadowy edge and took in the view before them. Small rolling hills stretched for many leagues, covered in lush green and brown grass, which waved and bent to the slight breeze that blew from the West. The sun was setting and would soon be lost and swallowed by the dark mountains in the distance; the remaining light poured onto the grass and made it shimmer, a counterpoint to the darkness looming over them. The Hestur Mountains, the destination for which they had been riding for two days, could now be seen for the first time. This unobstructed view made them smile, and they took deep breaths of air, clearing their lungs of the cloying dampness of the forest they had just left.

Turning to his companion, one rider asked, "Well, Kalend, what do you think, shall we make camp here?"

Looking around, Kalend responded, "Looks good to me, Sir."

"No need to "sir" me. Just call me Louquintas."

"Yes, sir Louquintas!" Kalend said with a smile.

Laughing and shaking his head, Louquintas dismounted, then asked, "Why do you think this is a good place to set up camp?"

Kalend gestured to the grass before them, "Out there, we would be visible and stick out like a sore thumb; here beside the forest, we will blend in."

"Very good." Louquintas nodded while he started to unpack his horse.

The two weary travelers spent the next hour in silence while setting up camp, making sure the horses were cared for, and then prepared dinner and ate, the latter consisting of beans and the last of the meat all cooked in a pot over the fire. Having finished his meal, Louquintas put aside his dish, picked up a nearby stick, and proceeded to spread the ashes in the fire pit. He had dug it deep, but he hoped to diminish even more of the light it gave off. Once the fire died down to a dull red glow, he reclined against a nearby tree stump and looked at Kalend.

"Time now for some plain talk and questions answered, don't you think?" he asked.

"Yes, please!" Kalend responded in earnest.

Louquintas pulled and twirled his mustache with one hand, then looked to his young apprentice and began, "The whole tale is long, but I will try to condense it down to the more important parts. So....to start with, you were not born in the monastery; you knew this, yes?"

Kalend nodded. "I know I was found and taken in and have been there ever since. I have no idea who my parents are or who left me."

"What we know is your parents were members of the court at Odewin City, and you were left with the monks because it was feared your life may be in danger. They had many powerful enemies. Politics in the city can be -interesting."

Leaning forward, Kalend asked eagerly, "Are my parents still alive?"

Looking at him with pain in his eyes, Louquintas answered softly, "We are not sure. They were last seen on the way to the palace; they never arrived, but a message was sent to their loyal servants back home, who were caring for you. It said you should be sent away, and since it had your family seal on it, they took it seriously."

Kalend looked away, sighed, and stared up at the twinkling stars that filled the cloudless night sky. The soft radiance of the fire warmed them both as they each became lost in their reflections. I wanted answers, and now I get some Kalend thought. Not the answers he hoped for, but at least there was some glimmer that he may, someday, get the rest of the answers he needed. Louquintas eventually continued, "It was later rumored that your parents had been chased into the desert by some hired assassins. The note confirms they at least escaped for a while."

Looking back at Louquintas, Kalend asked quietly, "These same assassins are now after me?"

"Maybe not the same people exactly, but the same group who hired the assassins. It all amounts to the same thing: they are after you, and if they find you, it won't end well."

"Why me? I was a babe and know nothing of all this! Never even knew my parents; how could I be a threat?" Kalend pleaded.

"Your family is old, well respected among certain groups, and has many friends who would rally to you if they knew of your existence," Louquintas explained.

Kalend sat quietly and thought through it all before asking his next question, "Why do I get the feeling there is more to this than you are telling me?"

Louquintas stared into the fire for some time before responding, "Yes. There is some I know but much more that I don't. Some things will have to wait to come from people who have a better head for all this business. What I can say is that I will answer the best I can any questions you have in the days ahead."

"What were their names…my parents?" Kalend asked solemnly.

"Rashana and Parson Hylund."

"Hylund, so that is my surname," Kalend mused.

Louquintas nodded. "They were good people by all accounts and big supporters of the old king; it was only after

King Olbert passed away that your family's enemies had the guts to go after them."

Standing up, Kalend went over to the pile of wood they had collected earlier, picked out a branch, and threw it on the fire. Watching it ignite, he thought about all they had talked about so far. It was a beginning, with much more he wanted and needed to know. His past was starting to come alive before him, a cohesive picture forming of where he came from. He would need time to sort it all out and decide what else to ask; for now, his thoughts went to their current predicament.

Kalend sat back down, looked to Louquintas, and asked, "So what of these women you are taking me to?"

Louquintas laughed and responded, "Hmmm, what of these women? First, know that they are trusted friends, not just of myself and Tosrayner but also of your family. Second, they are powerful and can protect us."

"Protect us. How can a bunch of old women protect us?" Kalend inquired.

Louquintas hesitated and continued, "Those old women have power, for they are sorceresses."

Kalend shook his head and laughed, "Sorceresses. Really? Turning people into toads and talking with trees. How is that going to help? It's all tricks to fool the gullible!"

Louquintas looked to Kalend with a severe expression. "It's more than that, my young friend; their power can conceal us from prying eyes. We could walk right past them and never know they were there. I have seen them in action; do not underestimate what they are capable of."

Still smiling with disbelief, Kalend said, "If you say so. Otherwise, I will believe it when I see it."

"Well....just don't do anything to irritate them, or you may find out the hard way!" Louquintas said with a twinkle in his eye. "Either way, they will help, and your training will continue there."

Shaking his head again, Kalend asked, "Ok. Let's say they really do know magic; what does that have to do with my training? I know nothing of magic."

"Your enemy's families have warlocks to help them, so the better you understand how it all works, the easier it will be to evade them. Remember this: there are many sorts of power, and one of those is information. Those with knowledge have the edge over those who don't."

Kalend gave Louquintas a direct look. "This is another of those things you know more about than you're telling me, isn't it?"

"Yes. It will all work out; time and training will give you most of the answers you seek." He stretched then and yawned expansively, "It is late. Let's get some sleep, and we can talk tomorrow while we ride."

They wrapped themselves in their cloaks, settled in as the fire died down, and soon fell fast asleep. Kalend dreamed that night of shadowy figures chasing him, magic filling the air, and his unseen parents calling out to him. One shadow hovered over each of his dreams, a ghostly figure. It stayed just on the edge of his vision and floated in and out of each consecutive one. Appearing to watch over him, never calling out but a constant presence nonetheless. As the night wore on and the dreams became more convoluted, this figure started to take shape. Not a child, yet not having reached adulthood, it became obvious this was a girl on the cusp of becoming a woman. Near the end of a more vivid dream, he finally called out to her, but she turned away, took a step, and vanished. Then he awoke drenched in sweat.

***** *****

The next day found the two travelers atop their horses and moving quickly through the tall grass in the mountains' direction. The wind blew unimpeded across the wide-open land, cutting into them as they pulled their cloaks tight to keep the chill at bay. It was cloudy, and the days were getting colder with old man winter just around the corner; soon, they would have to keep a weather eye out for snow. The promised chat did not happen as they moved from hill to hill; keeping their heads down and out of the biting wind had taken priority.

Their journey, though cold, was uneventful and fast over the rolling hills, and at day's end, they reined in their steaming horses at the foot of the mountains. Wrapped with spruce, pine, and firs and caped with a mantle of gleaming snow, they loomed above them like giant white-haired guardians. From what Kalend could recall from his geography lessons, they acted as a formidable barrier between the Kingdom of Odethane and the rest of the world. He could only remember one central passage over or through them.

"Will we be taking the Norry Pass?" Kalend asked.

"No, we will be taking a game trail I know; I just have to find it first."

They headed northeast, and Louquintas stopped periodically to examine the dense forest surrounding the mountains' edge. It was close to an hour before he cheerfully announced he had found what he was looking for, a small opening between bushy hemlocks that marked the beginning of a trail. They decided to set up camp at the trailhead and wait until dawn to tackle the mountain.

As Kalend took his saddle off Whistler, he paused as he lifted it; something felt odd. A feeling crept over him as if the mountains called to him. Like tentacles had reached out, penetrated his mind, and pulled him toward something deep in the forests above them. He gazed up into the canopy of timber and determined, no, not something, but someone. He realized that it was not malevolent; whatever it was that tugged at him, it was more like a warm, comfortable, and oddly familiar presence that urged him onward. The feeling quickly passed, but yet he keenly felt its sudden disappearance. He shook his head and wondered if all the excitement had finally gotten to him, first a strange dream and now this. He decided it would be best not to tell Louquintas about the whole experience.

Even after taking turns keeping watch through the still and quiet night, the following morning found them both feeling refreshed and eager to see what the day would bring. As they made ready to continue their journey, Kalend took some time to check on his new mount. The ride so far had done little to tax Whistler, and he seemed to be in good spirits, but Kalend had been taught that your horse was a responsibility one did not neglect. As he checked Whistler's coat for burs and hooves for damage, he realized he was beginning to understand the curious whistles and noises the horse made. When hungry, he gave a fast-low-pitched wheeze; when he wanted to run, a high-pitched snort. It was coming to the point that Kalend was unsure who was training whom. He shook his head in denial of the silly thought. But he admitted a bond forming, which he assumed was just a natural occurrence of caring for and depending on the horse.

As Louquintas prepared to lead the way onto the trail, he took one last glance back to the hills they passed over yesterday and stopped. Standing still as a rock pillar, he peered due east for several seconds. Kalend followed his gaze, but not seeing anything, he started to turn away. Then something flashed. Just on the periphery of his vision, his gaze snapped to that spot; it came again, a glimmer of movement on top of one of the hills. There for a second, then gone.

Louquintas quietly said, "They come."

A shiver ran down Kalend's back. Someone really is after me, he thought. This was the reason for his flight from the only home he ever knew. That movement became a lightning bolt to his subconscious mind, a part that had still been in denial about everything he had been told so far. He felt a wave of emotions: fear, curiosity, anger, and denial. They pummeled his mind, each one crashing over the next. He turned to Louquintas and asked with a snarl, "How do you know it's someone after us?"

Seeing the conflict that passed over his young pupil's face, Louquintas responded evenly, "Anyone else and we would see them more clearly; they have some type of cloak which helps to mask them. If they are not after us, then they are fleeing from someone, for they move fast. We should move on; we don't want a part of them either way." Not waiting for a response, he stealthily slid through the bushes that hid the trail.

Kalend gave one more glare at the last spot he had seen movement before leading Whistler onto the trail behind his teacher. As the forest swallowed them, his mind returned to what he had seen. Maybe it had nothing to do with us? It could have been outlaws trying to escape justice or any number of things. This thought did nothing to console him; in fact, the more he reflected on it, the more convinced he was that they were after him. It just felt like they were; it was odd, as though he could feel them moving on the edge of his awareness.

Staying behind Louquintas, he hoped they would reach their destination soon. If the witches could hide them, they would need it; those in pursuit could not be far behind. "How far till we find the camp?" he nervously asked.

"Not too far…I'd say maybe one hour in, then we will be close. We will not find the camp; we will get close, and the ladies will find us, or someone they send will," Louquintas responded.

"You think those following us saw us go in?"

"I doubt it. I never can tell, though. Don't worry; all will be well." Even with that statement, Kalend noticed that over the next hour, their pace quickened.

As Kalend thought, the hour had passed, and with nothing to be seen but trees and the stray squirrel, he was about to pester Louquintas again when a figure suddenly materialized. Like a ghost, it flowed from the forest to block the trail. Tall and lean, it wore a dark green hooded cloak that covered the mysterious shadow from head to toe. A long arm stretched forth from the cape, beckoning them to follow it off the trail. Louquintas nodded at Kalend and followed the cloaked figure into the woods. They moved along a different path now, a narrow one; Kalend did not consider it a trail, so small and insignificant it appeared. He tried to ask a question, but Louquintas quickly shushed him, shook his head, and mouthed, "Not now."

They slipped through the forest for two silent hours, and then the path suddenly opened before them. A clearing appeared, complete with two huts along the right side, a large fire pit in the middle, and what looked to be a cave entrance into the mountainside on the left. A fire burned merrily within the pit, casting a warm glow about the camp, and as early evening settled about them, the sun dipped behind the mountains. A chipped and pitted black cauldron hung over the blaze by a tripod, and as steam poured over its edges, an old woman wearing a battered brown cloak stooped and peered down into its depths. The three paused on the edge of the camp for several seconds before the crone coolly straightened and, without surprise, nodded her head to their guide, who quickly moved off to the cave and disappeared within. Kalend felt his hair stand on end before her piercing gaze as she began to speak.

"About time, Louquintas. I understand you were followed; how could you let that happen?" she demanded with a gravelly voice.

"Even the best of us slip from time to time," Louquintas shrugged.

"They are going the wrong way now. So, come here and give this old woman a hug!"

Louquintas crossed over to her and gave a giant but gentle hug, then held her at arm's length. "You look well, Yarguri."

"Not too bad for being one hundred and two, eh?" she rasped.

She looked over at Kalend, who stood without moving while trying to take it all in. "What's with the boy? His feet work?"

"He's fine, just overwhelmed by everything; come over and say hello, Kalend."

Kalend hesitantly walked over to stand before them. His nerves felt on fire from both trepidation and the feeling of raw power emanating from the ancient woman; he knelt to one knee before her, bowed his head, and stated, "At your service, my lady."

She reached out with both hands and gripped his shoulders, then pulled him to his feet with a firmness that belied her age and admonished, "Rise, no need to bow to me…..and please call me Yarguri."

"As you wish, Yarguri," he responded with humility.

It was not just fear that guided him to show such respect for her; it was the realization that this so-called witch was much more than that. Yes, she had power, that was very palpable, but it was her demeanor and the way she put him at ease. She exuded a calmness that radiated around her and settled over him like a cloak. Even Louquintas did not seem to be immune, as he stood looking more at peace than he had the whole trip to the mountains.

As his wits slowly returned, he became more aware of the surrounding camp. Movement caught the corner of his eye, and he turned toward the nearest hut as a young woman was exiting the doorway. Wearing a long, deep green dress with fiery red curly hair that descended to the middle of her torso, she paused to study the three of them huddled together. As their eyes met, her face lit up with a large, beautiful smile. She gathered her skirt together in one hand, and with her hair streaming behind, she rushed toward them. While never losing that dazzling smile, she threw herself into his bewildered arms and blurted out, "So good to finally meet you, my brother!"

CHAPTER THREE

The initial days at the witches' camp passed quickly for Kalend after that first meeting. The shock and overwhelming feelings from that night of revelations had dissipated but not disappeared entirely. To know he was no longer alone was something new for him; feelings of elation would course through him when he thought about his sister. Of course, this brought even more questions to his already overflowing mind. Why had this been kept from him? Who all knew? Over the following days, he did manage to get some answers, even if, as usual, they were not always to his liking.

He learned his newly found sister's name was Hollilea, and it seemed they all knew of their kinship, at least those closest to him. Tosrayner and many of his teachers at the monastery, Louquintas, the witches, of course, and even his own sister! Not him, however; no, he had been deliberately left in the dark. When he angrily asked why, the answer was that it had been "for your protection." Louquintas explained they had been afraid he would leave to find her before he was ready. He privately had to admit he may indeed have gone to find her if he had found out. However, it still made him surly to know they had not trusted him enough.

He thought the surprises and major shocks were over, but shortly thereafter, the witches calmly informed him that they were not just brother and sister but also twins. This added even more complexity to the whole new arrangement of his life. They even alluded to some mysterious "connection" between them, a connection that he and his sister would learn to utilize in time. Having no idea what they were talking about, he thought it best to just go along with it for now.

Those first few days were also spent getting acquainted with his new life, home, and people. Their guide had turned out to be a man, Karl by name; he seemed to be the witch's caretaker. He did most of the manual labor, fetching wood for the fire, fixing the huts, hunting for food, and even helping to prepare dinner. And there were actually three witches that occupied the camp; besides Yarguri, two other witches were introduced to him; Yootuk and Queshan. Yootuk was short and stocky; she did not mince words, and he learned to always jump to obey when she spoke. Queshan was tall, quiet, and reserved, but when she did speak, it was with an iron resolve. The three acted like sisters, but they were not. Having spent the better part of eighty years together, they had grown to become much closer than average friends. With a common purpose in life and living isolated with only each other, Karl and the relatively more recent Hollilea had created a deep bond.

The days quickly drifted into weeks. Kalend had weapons practice with Louquintas in the morning, lessons on how magic and the world worked in the afternoon, followed by chores in the evening. Little time was left to get to know his sister. She had her training separate from his, which seemed to entail much time making things smoke and sputter. Some very non-lady-like words would sometimes accompany those displays when he saw them, and they were usually followed by an admonishment to be more demure and ladylike. Never mind that none of the witches ever showed any lady-like tendencies. In general, the three tended to be a crude and crusty lot.

One evening, after all the lessons and chores, he finally found himself alone with Hollilea by the fire. They sat quietly, staring into the flickering flames, unsure and shy around each other still; she looked at him and asked hesitantly, "So, how is your training coming along?"

"Fine, I suppose," he responded quietly.

"I am so glad to finally meet you," She blurted. "It seems like we just met, but Yarguri has been trying to keep us so busy we haven't even been able to talk."

He smiled and said, "I know. Don't worry. As soon as they see us chatting here, I am sure they will rush out to break it up."

She laughed merrily. "We will run away if they try!"

"That would irritate them," he grinned.

Hollilea became more serious and said, "I am sorry you didn't know about me. I have known since I was just a little girl. They told me someday we would meet and be reunited, just not when."

"It's ok; it's not your fault. I'm still not happy about it, but I do understand the reasons for it."

As the conversation continued, Kalend found himself more at ease with this young woman, who was his sister. It became natural for both to express what they felt, and neither hesitated to ask the other questions. Their youth and natural curiosity came to the foreground, and Kalend thought she was just as eager as he was to know more about the other.

Hollilea continued, "Yarguri has been working with me to try and reach out to you even before you got here. When I focused my entire mind, I could almost feel you moving closer to me. There was even one night that I thought I had found you. It seemed like you were in a dream, and near the end of it, you looked as if you saw me, but then I lost you. Yarguri said I must keep my focus and not get distracted."

He sat staring at her, pale and trembling, unable to find his voice.

She cocked her head and exclaimed, "You look like you saw a ghost!"

He gathered his wits, took a deep breath, and asked with a trembling voice, "I thought I had…..was that two nights before we met? When you tried to find me with your mind?"

"hhmmm....yes, I believe it was," she mused.

"I saw you then!" he blurted out. "You kept coming in and out of my dream; just when I could see you more clearly, I called out, but then you vanished."

Her eyes had gotten wide as she looked at him. "By the gods, it did work then," she whispered.

"It would seem like it did." Kalend paused for a moment in reflection, then continued, "But I think there is more going on than just that dream. I think I have felt you out there, somewhere, most of my life. It's been like a tiny warm ember in the back of my thoughts. And before we started on the trail up the mountain, I was sure I felt something pulling me toward this spot. As if that ember had blazed to life for a brief moment."

Hollilea smiled. "Yootuk said we have this special bond that will allow us both to make a connection. With time and practice, we will even be able to speak to each other in our minds over vast distances."

He shook his head. "Both of us? I have no idea how to do the stuff you do. Yarguri and Queshan have been teaching me to read signs of magic but not how to use it."

"Yes, Kalend, but what they teach will help you learn to form that connection. You are still early in your training." They heard Louquintas respond directly behind them.

They both turned to face him as he came around the fire and sat down opposite them. Kalend asked, "How long until I get to try?"

"Not long, I would expect. That is the province of Yarguri; she will have the final say when you are ready."

Hollilea looked at Louquintas with a raised eyebrow and asked, "So, what is your place in all this?"

Chuckling, he said, "Well, now, I was friends of your parents many years ago. It was just after I had become a man when I met them. I had joined the guard that was assigned to protect them with a good friend of mine."

Kalend smiled and asked, "Was that good friend Tosrayner?"

"Yes, it was; we both had trained together under the same weapons master and then appointed to guard your parents."

Hollilea looked at them both and asked, "Who is Tosrayner?"

"My teacher at the monastery," Kalend told her and then asked Louquintas with a hint of anger, "If you were assigned to protect them, where were you both when they were attacked?"

"Your parents had many guards; some traveled with them while others stayed to guard their home. That particular day, we were the ones left on home duty." He smiled gently at them then and added, "It was Tosrayner and me who dropped you both at that monastery so long ago. Several years later, Tosrayner went back and eventually became their weapons master."

Hollilea asked, "So….we were split up; when was this? And why was I sent here?"

"You were not so much sent here…Yarguri showed up around a week after we dropped you off and demanded you be given over to them. The old weapons master resisted at first, but….Yarguri can be VERY persuasive when she wants to be."

Kalend shook his head and said, "It seems everyone has had a hand in our lives, which is everyone except us!"

"We had our reasons, and the alternative is both of you would most likely be dead if we hadn't done what we had to…..remember that." Louquintas responded firmly.

"Still feels unfair," Kalend grumbled.

"Time to grow up, my young bull!" he responded gaily.

They all turned as Yarguri hurried out from the witch's hut and headed over to them, "Someone has broken through our defenses; the magical barrier that conceals us is down." She said with urgency, "You must all leave; we will slow them down. This includes you, Hollilea. Guide them to the Othurean; we shall meet you all there."

Worried about leaving Whistler, Kalend asked, "What about the horses?"

"Never mind them; we will bring them to you. Now, quickly get your stuff; we don't have much time."

The three jumped up and raced to get their belongings from the huts and passed a grim-faced Karl armed with his staff. They gathered their packs and met back outside. Yootuk and Queshan had joined Karl and Yarguri at the edge of the clearing; facing east, they stood still while looking for whoever approached.

The wait was not long; a massive ball of fire came hurtling out of the woods, and with a roar, it engulfed the four. They disappeared; the fire wreathed around them, shooting upward; it rose higher than the tallest pine. The light blinded Kalend and his friends, and as they shielded their eyes, Hollilea called out, but the crackling blaze drowned out her voice.

One minute, the witches were surrounded by flames, and then the fire began to shrink, faster and faster, collapsing downward until Yarguri could be seen standing in the middle with her arms raised above her head. Blue light flowed from her hands, pouring over the four of them, protecting them, and putting out the fire. As the last of the flames winked out, three grumpy-looking witches and one angry-faced man stood staring into the forest.

Two groups of armed men came charging out of the foliage. One group went straight for the witches and Karl, while the other headed for Kalend and his friends. Louquintas drew his sword and met the lead man with an overhead strike; Kalend, who had drawn his sword a second behind Louquintas, engaged another. Five men quickly had them surrounded, and they found themselves back to back, defending themselves and each other. Constantly moving, weaving with each other, they fought hard but purely defensively. Both received many minor cuts and nicks as their attackers pressed them. Kalend, being the least experienced fighter, took the brunt of the blows.

Hollilea had taken a few steps backward, tripped, fell, and sat watching, unnoticed and unsure how to help. She realized that her two friends could not hold out for much longer. She glanced over at Yarguri and saw they were in the middle of hurling bolts of ice and lighting into the other group of attackers. They would not be any help for a few minutes. Minutes that Kalend and Louquintas did not have, she had to do something. Surging to her feet, she urgently raised her hand and, speaking words she had practiced many times, unleashed a barrage of lightning that hit two of the attackers. They crumpled to the ground in spasms of pain. Hollilea was thrown backward as the lightning left her fingers, landing hard; the breath exploded from her; never had she felt that much power flow from her.

Louquintas's sword flashed out to the two men twitching on the ground with one slash each; they ceased to move, and then he spun to parry the attack of a third. Kalend took advantage of the slight surprise and pressed his attack, taking one down with a thrust to the gut. Pulling the sword out of his attacker, he whipped around and slashed at another; not taken off guard, this one parried the strike. They traded blows, each feeling the other out, looking for an opening.

Having dispatched the third man, Louquintas came up behind the one Kalend was fighting, waited for a few seconds until he had a clear view of his back, and then plunged his sword until it exited the unfortunate man's chest. He pulled his sword from the dying man, made eye contact with Kalend, and gave him a nod. Kalend felt dazed, excited, and disgusted all at once. Then, both turned their attention to the attackers the witches and Karl were engaging with.

Two men were down, and Karl was in a fierce fight with the three still standing, his staff a blur as he parried blow after blow. Another assailant had appeared, cloaked and standing at the edge of the forest; one hand thrust toward them, it was hurling a steady stream of fireballs at the witches. The three were alternating between defending and counter-attacking. Even with the blinding display, Kalend noticed something odd about the arm protruding from the cloaked figure; he squinted, trying to make out what it was that he saw. He was not sure, but he thought the arm looked covered in scales!

Yarguri had turned to Louquintas and growled, "Get them out of here. NOW!"

"Come on," Louquintas yelled to Kalend and Hollilea as he picked up his pack and headed into the woods opposite the battle that still raged around the witches.

They quickly followed him. The three plunged into the woods and down a game trail they had frequently used to move around the forest. They started in a half run, but mindful of the dark and unable to see clearly, they slowed to a brisk walk. Kalend had taken the rear position and followed closely behind Hollilea, keeping her backside in plain sight. It was a dark, cloudy night with no moon to light the way, so they relied on Louquintas's ability to read the forest by whatever means he had. Kalend kept his ears tuned to what was behind him but did not hear anything that sounded like pursuit.

About a half-hour into their flight, Louquintas stopped, gathered them together, and asked Hollilea, "So, who, what, or where is the Othurean that Yarguri told you to lead us to?"

"They are a group of nomads who live not far from here. They are…….not exactly human," she replied.

Kalend, already a little unnerved from the events of the evening, asked sharply, "What do you mean 'not exactly human'?"

"They are a small group of beings who call themselves the Othurean. Much smaller than humans and covered in fur, they have some resemblance to large monkeys; however, don't let their looks throw you; they are very smart. Staying hidden deep in the forest, they live in the trees and sometimes caves."

"Do you know the way from here?" Louquintas asked.

"I think so. As long as we are still on the trail we started on?"

"We are."

"Ok, then we need to follow this one until we reach a fork, then go right. Follow that for a while, and we will come to a batch of odd-looking trees; they shouldn't be too hard to spot."

Louquintas snapped his head around to look behind, "Shhh, someone comes!"

Kalend stood quietly with his head cocked and listened, and then he heard it too. Whoever it was, they were close. "Off the trail, hide," Louquintas hissed as he led them into the woods.

They hunkered down behind some thorny bushes to watch the trail. Two shadowy figures soon passed them with swords leading the way. Louquintas tapped Kalend's shoulder and motioned for him to follow; rising silently, they moved onto the path and came up behind the two.

Louquintas reached out with both hands and gripped the head of the first shadow; he twisted violently and fast and broke its neck with a loud snap. The second shadow whipped around and, with its sword, struck a diagonal slash at Louquintas, who quickly stepped back as the strike barely missed him. Kalend unsheathed his sword and thrust at the shadow all in one move; the shadow brought his blade around and parried the blow. Kalend used the parry's momentum to spin around and land a decisive blow with his free fist to the face of the shadow. As the figure stumbled backward, Louquintas, who had come along beside it, used a powerful roundhouse strike to take its head off.

Hollilea came out from the trees and joined the two as they stood looking down at the fallen figures. Louquintas bent over and flipped the first one onto its back; it was a young man with dead eyes staring out into the night.

"What should we do with the bodies?" Kalend asked.

"Leave them. Let's get our packs and keep moving." Hastily, they gathered their belongings and headed back onto the trail.

A couple more hours passed, with Louquintas leading and Hollilea giving directions when needed, giving ample time for Kalend to relax and reflect on all the happenings of that evening. Having never actually fought anyone when his life was at stake made this his first authentic battle experience; it was an exhilarating feeling! He thought he handled himself well; he had no significant injuries, and they all survived the attack, which made him smile with pleasure.

Reflecting on the physical aspects of the fight, an image appeared in his mind of the first attacker he killed, his first ever. He could still picture the look of agony on the man's face as his sword slid into the man's gut. The smile of self-congratulations faded fast with that memory; he had almost felt the life fluctuate and ebb as it had coursed down his blade. Kalend stopped in midstride, leaned over to the side, and was violently sick.

Hollilea turned to him and asked worriedly, "Are you alright?"

"Yes," he panted between bouts of retching.

Louquintas had turned and walked back to them, saw the look on Kalend's face, took the situation in, and grunted, "He will be fine; he just needs some time and a large drink of ale."

She looked from one to the other, then shrugged. "If you say so."

After a small break for Kalend to recover, they trudged on into the night, all of them feeling tired physically, emotionally, and mentally from the night's activities.

Coming around a bend in the path, they noticed it was not as dark as it had been, for the sun was rising, and dawn was fast approaching. They came to a small clearing with towering trees that were quite different from those they had been passing. Much taller and broader, with large branches spread over a wide area, the trees radiated out from the clearing.

They stood awkwardly looking around at the scene, unsure what to do next. Hollilea said they would be noticed and found. Just as she finished speaking, a small object fell from the closest tree and rolled toward them. A small figure popped up and nonchalantly approached the tired group.

"Greeting my friends," it hailed them.

Covered in fur and standing around four feet tall, this was the strangest creature Kalend had ever seen. The fact that it talked was very disconcerting; who had ever heard of such a thing? An animal that talked? He could only shake his head and stare, unable to find any words to reply.

Hollilea stepped forward and bent down to embrace the creature. "So good to see you again; we are in need of your help."

The little ball of fur studied the group, then nodded his head. "Come this way; we have food cooking and places for you to rest."

Strolling back to the tree he had dropped from, he gave a small whistle and a rope ladder unrolled from the branches above. Looking at the group, he motioned for them to follow as he began to climb.

Hollilea noticed Kalend's apprehension. "Don't worry, they are friends, and the view from up there is fantastic," she exclaimed, then headed toward the ladder and quickly scampered her way up. Louquintas patted him on the shoulder and moved to follow her.

Hollilea had disappeared into the foliage above, and Louquintas was halfway up before Kalend found the nerve to move. Exhausted and numb from the whole evening, he mumbled to himself about how this whole thing was madness, getting attacked by a scaly-armed warlock and now following a fur ball up into a tree. He could only continue and hope this all made sense at some point.

CHAPTER FOUR

Winter had come to the mountains. For days, the snow had been falling and now covered the forest in a white blanket; Kalend stared into the softly falling fluff and wondered where Yarguri was and hoped Whistler was alright. Three days should have been more than enough time to make the trip. Surviving the attack was not his worry as much as traveling through the snow for three old women. He had seen firsthand how powerful their magic was when attacked, but how helpful that would be while traveling in challenging weather was another matter. Even though he knew Karl was there to help, he worried for them. With a deep sigh, he hoped they would arrive soon or that Louquintas would relent and allow him to go in search of them. Knowing that the latter would not happen any time soon, he could only sit and keep watch.

Looking around at the Othurean village, Kalend was struck yet again by its strangeness. Huts thirty feet above the ground, built into the trees and made from some form of light plaster, they looked like cocoons wrapped around the trunks with large branches sticking out. A ragged hole on one side was used for a doorway, and most had a small porch attached, which was given additional support from below by beams running from the trunk to the edge of the platform. It was from this perch that he sat with his feet dangling over the edge.

On the other side of each hut was another hole, this one higher up and smaller, which allowed smoke to leave and acted as a chimney. Inside, lightweight clay formed a fireplace used for cooking and heating. So far, the couple of homes he had been in had contained two levels. The first held the living and eating quarters, while the second was reserved for the sleeping chambers. Kalend and his friends had each been given over to different families, who became their caretakers. After receiving shelter, food, and drink, they soon felt refreshed from their harrowing flight.

Kalend's gaze returned to the winter scene before him, and he noticed movement along the path leading into the village. At first, it was just a ripple in the falling snow, a shadowy movement that caused the snow to swirl in odd patterns. Shapes began to appear; one bent-over figure ambled out from the forest, and then another one led a horse. These two were quickly followed by a third leading another horse. Then, a taller, leaner shadow strolled out behind them all. As they approached the hut, Kalend recognized the last horse as Whistler, with Karl, the lanky one, bringing up the rear. Elation poured through him as he stood to bid the witches a happy welcome, but the joyful shout died on his lips as another silhouette emerged from the forest to their right and made straight toward them. The witches stopped, turned, and appeared to shout a greeting to the stranger. But that greeting was lost to Kalend in the swirl of snow and wind. He hesitated and watched as the stranger closed the gap to the women, who stood calmly and patiently as they waited.

Kalend noticed something odd about the stranger; it took him a few minutes for his mind to work out what. Then it hit him; the snow was falling through the figure! Shaking his head, he leaned forward to get a better view and see if his eyes were deceiving him. He could clearly see right through the stranger, and he or she was not leaving any footprints in the snow. As he watched the stranger greet his teachers, he felt the hair on the top of his head start to stand on end, and a cold pricking sensation crept down his spine. He was too far away to hear what was said, but it looked as though the witches mostly listened. Kalend watched intently for several minutes, and then the stranger lifted its right hand and held an object out to them, which appeared solid and not as ethereal. The lead witch pushed her snow-covered cowl back, and it was Yarguri who reached out to take the object and quickly slipped it inside her cloak.

The stranger bowed to the three before heading back toward the forest and quickly disappeared into the falling snow. Yarguri looked up at Kalend and raised a hand in greeting as if she had known he had been watching all along. He returned the gesture, kicked the rope ladder over the edge, and began to descend to greet them better.

After some initial hugs, Kalend went to check on Whistler. As he approached, he reached out a hand to gently stroke him and received the now familiar whinny-turned whistle at his touch. Kalend laughed and patted him affectionately on the head.

"Thank you," he said to Queshan as she handed the reins over.

"The horse has been eager to find you," she quietly responded.

"Eager?" he asked.

"Yes, it seems he knew we were heading to you, and the closer we got, the more agitated he became. I had to slow him down constantly."

"You sure it was me he was looking for?"

Queshan gave him a direct look and raised an eyebrow.

"Ok, ok, you know way more about this kind of thing than me," he relented. "I am just happy to see him well."

Yarguri cleared her throat and asked, "Where is everyone else?"

"Right above you," Louquintas responded from high in the tree Kalend had just left.

Without any show of surprise, Yarguri looked up. "Good, get everyone together; we have much to discuss."

Louquintas nodded and moved off to gather the others.

*****   *****

A half-hour later found them all gathered in the hut Kalend had been staying in, warming themselves by the fire with mugs of hot spiced cider in hand. Two of the Othureans had also joined them, Turol and Tyber; they were brothers and the village's informal leaders. Kalend had yet to understand the place's politics, but there did not seem to be too much hierarchy from what he had seen so far, just the two brothers.

Louquintas moved from the fire to sit on a short chair and proceeded to ask the witches, "How did you escape from the attackers?"

"We finally overwhelmed Pouluk, which was the warlock; he escaped into the woods along with one of his men. Two others had slipped around us and headed down the trail you went on."

"We had some fun with those two; they are now of no concern," Louquintas said with a grin.

Shaking her head, Yarguri continued, "We figured that much. We took a day to gather some belongings and clean up. And then the storm struck, and we waited another day, but we did not want to chance waiting anymore, and here we are. Foul weather to travel in, but we are made of sterner stuff than we look."

Kalend moved to a seat near Louquintas and asked, "This Pouluk, I saw something odd about him. He had what looked like an arm covered in scales?"

"Hmm, yes," Yarguri responded. "That was due to some accident he had with his power getting away from him several years ago. We don't know the particulars of the event, however."

"ok....so you know him then?"

"Yes, we have encountered him before. He has a brother who is also enormously powerful; I am surprised he was not with him."

Yootuk grumbled, "We need to move on to other matters; we do not have much time."

Kalend frowned and asked, "I have another question. Who or what was that person I saw you meet with before you reached me? Also, what did he give you?"

"We do not have time for this!" Yootuk exclaimed.

Yarguri frowned at Yootuk and said, "He has been through much. We can answer a few more questions from him." Turning back to Kalend, she continued, "Those are complicated questions you ask, more so than you realize, but in answer, that was Thora, my Wiccenda."

"What's a Wiccenda?"

"They are the ones all sorcerers, and sorceresses derive their power. Our power is not just pulled from thin air; we form a bond with our Wiccenda, who then allows us to draw strength from them. The bonding usually takes place when we are very young."

"Was he really there? I could see right through him like he was a ghost!"

"He was not here in person but in spirit."

"All the training I have had so far, and yet you have never mentioned this part?"

"It was not time for you to know about it."

Kalend drew breath to ask another question, but Yarguri held up a hand and said, "We do need to move on to other matters. I am sorry and wish I could answer all your questions, but we do not have the time, and they shall have to wait."

She stood and moved to stand before the fire, then turned to face them as she warmed her backside. "We need to make some decisions. It would be best if Louquintas and Kalend continued from here, over the mountains and to the nearest city, Pleus. You have some friends there, do you not, Louquintas?"

"Yes. Several, in fact."

"Good. We have received word from Tosrayner that you should make your way to the Ickara Desert. From Pleus, you can get any supplies you need and then head out from there. Oh, and someone awaits you in the desert."

Kalend perked up and asked, "Who waits?"

"Tosrayner didn't say. Only that you should make your way there."

Hollilea pushed off from the rear wall she had been leaning on, walked to Yarguri, and asked, "And what shall be done with me?"

Yarguri looked at her with kind and gentle eyes. "You, my girl, shall remain with us to continue your studies."

Putting her hands on her hips, Hollilea said, "Why should I have to stay behind? I finally meet my brother, and now you are splitting us up again?"

"Yes, we are. Once you have completed your training, you can rejoin him, and with powers, that will be helpful. Until then, you must both go your separate ways."

Turol and Tyber, who had sat quietly during the whole meeting, abruptly stood together. Turol cleared his throat. "Much more is going on here than meets the eye. Yarguri, you and your sisters have been good friends and neighbors, so we think it's time we involve ourselves more."

Yarguri regarded them both briefly and then asked, "In what way?"

"Well, for starters, we can send someone with Louquintas and the young chap."

"Whom would you send?"

They grinned, looked at each other, and laughed. "We have just the person," Tyber said. "His name is Trealine; he is something of an adventurer. He has traveled more than any of us and knows how to take care of himself. He could be a good scout. Also, we are small but can fight well when needed."

Yarguri paused a moment, then said, "If Louquintas approves."

Louquintas looked at the furry beings and responded, "Fine with me, as long as he follows my lead."

Yarguri nodded in approval, "One last piece of business then." She reached into a pocket on her dress and pulled out an intricately carved leather bracer. She presented it to Kalend. "This is for you; it will help you on your journeys."

Kalend sat up, accepted the bracer, and asked, "What is it?"

"It is a bracer of power; it will allow your sister and you to communicate, plus some other things as you both will learn. It will also make it difficult for magical prying eyes to find you. No more questions for now!"

Kalend slipped the bracer on his arm and knew better than to ask anything more.

Yarguri looked around the room at everyone and snapped, "Let's get to it."

CHAPTER FIVE

One week later, Kalend and his friends stood on the edge of a road leading to the city of Pleus. The journey through the mountains had been uneventful; outside of the bitter cold, they had gotten lucky, and no more snow had fallen during the trip. They traveled single file, with Louquintas in front, Kalend second, and Trealine bringing up the rear. Due to the mountainous terrain, they had been trekking on their own feet while Louquintas and Kalend led the horses. It had been decided that Trealine would ride with Kalend when the time came.

Kalend had gotten to know Trealine along the trip. He was quite different than the other Othurean he had met; he was more serious and taciturn but had a sarcastic wit. Dressed in forest-colored attire with a small axe hanging from each hip on a wide leather belt and a crossbow slung over his backpack, he strode along with casual ease. His awareness of the mountains and the forest was unmatched by anyone Kalend knew. He was born to them, and it was obvious. Several times along the way, Louquintas would miss a trail, and Trealine would quickly point out the right way. This made the trip faster and easier than they had thought.

They moved out from under the forest canopy at the base of the mountain and gazed upon the dull grey city walls in the distance. Trealine whistled for them to stop and said, "Time for me to find my own way around the city."

"Find your own way?" Kalend asked.

"Yes. The people in that city would not welcome me and make life difficult for all of us. Most of them are probably not overly fond of Othureans."

"Will you be safe out here alone?"

"Don't worry about me."

Louquintas spoke up and asked, "Could you perhaps take the horses as well?"

Trealine grumbled under his breath, "Yes, just go through to the other side, and I will find you." With that, he quickly gathered the horses and vanished into the woods.

Kalend looked to Louquintas and raised an eyebrow in question.

"I have no idea. He will find his way. Let's get a move on; I need a drink, a bed, and maybe some companionship."

"Companionship? How many people are going with us?"

Louquintas laughed and clapped him on the back. "I was thinking of the female variety!"

"Ohh," Kalend responded somewhat nervously.

"Are you not acquainted with the fairer sex?" Louquintas asked with a smirk.

Kalend blushed and stammered, "Not really." Then he cleared his throat and defensively grumbled, "Not many girls at the monastery."

Laughing harder, Louquintas strode onto the gravel road toward Pleus and answered gaily, "Not to worry, my young pup; we can fix that. It's time for you to become a man."

***** *****

The gates to the city were wide open, and the four guards who stood watch looked bored and, for the most part, ignored the travelers entering and leaving. Kalend passed under the substantial stone blocks that formed the gate wall and got his first view of a city's interior. With his mouth agape, he stopped in amazement and took in the scene before him. People moved everywhere, into and out of buildings that lined the two cobblestone lanes leading from the gate. Everyone looked to be in a terrible hurry without really seeing those around them.

Louquintas noticed his young friend had not followed him down the lane to the right, so he swiveled around to see Kalend looking about in astonishment. Walking back, he grabbed his student by the shoulder and said, "Come on, you look silly standing there and are irritating those trying to come in."

That is when Kalend noticed the dirty looks directed his way as people flowed around him as they entered the city.

They quickly moved on down the street, going deeper into the heart of Pleus. Kalend saw much that was new and alien to him. People of all shapes and sizes, dressed in a riot of colors, he came to realize that you could tell how wealthy a person was by the way they were dressed. Or at least how they wanted others to perceive them. It seemed the more colorful and outrageous the dress, the more pompous and arrogant they were. While those in more modest clothing, basic smocks of drab browns and forest greens, the more meek, timid, and even fearful they appeared. Kalend attempted to ask Louquintas about these differences but was silenced and told not to ask questions like that while still on the streets.

Louquintas soon led them down a more muted alley, with fewer people, where only a smattering dressed as if they were wealthy. The look and feel in the air was more that of wary caution; everyone gave each other room to pass, and many kept one hand on their coin purse. Striding with a purpose and look that said no one should bother him, Louquintas moved to a building on their left. A large weather-beaten sign hung above the doors leading in; it read "The Punchers Inn" in red letters, and two men in a boxing stance were carved below.

Louquintas, with Kalend trailing close behind, shoved the not-so-sturdy oak doors wide open and strode inside. The interior was dank and smoky; a fire burned low in the hearth on the left wall, and tallow candles lined the one to the right, all of which provided a dim light. A battered bar ran opposite the doors, with stools placed unevenly and sparingly before it. The room was filled with mismatched tables and chairs that looked to have been thrown together from pieces that had been someone's cast-offs. Kalend thought the furniture might have been high quality at one time, but now it all looked very used and abused.

Few patrons graced the Inn with their presence. And those glared at them suspiciously as they made their way across the room. A large, tall man stood behind the bar; with arms crossed, he looked at them with a scowl plastered on his face. Kalend, already nervous from the stares from those seated at the tables, hesitated and stopped about halfway. A skittish silence descended over the room.

"Who are you?" the big man rumbled at them.

"I?" Louquintas asked while pointing to himself.

"I don't see no others I don't know."

"Maybe you should look a little harder then," Louquintas responded with a smirk.

Kalend placed his hand on his sword, and with that, several of the men at the nearby tables pushed back their chairs and stood. For what seemed like an eternity to him, everyone glared at them, and he became anxious things were beyond even Louquintas's ability to control.

A door on the far-right wall that Kalend had failed to notice suddenly opened. A man stumped through and froze when he saw the standoff taking place. His gaze moved to Louquintas, and after a small frown, he threw up his hands and laughed roughly. "Well, well, looked what the dragon dragged in," he said to the man behind the bar.

"You know this man, boss?" the big man asked.

"Yes, I do. Nothing to worry about here; he is an old friend."

"If you say so," the barman mumbled after giving Louquintas one last hard look.

The other patrons returned to their seats and conversations with only the occasional glance in their direction.

Louquintas gave the barman a dismissive wave and turned his attention to the other man. "Well, Jacob, how's it going?"

"Not bad. Could be worse. Then again, could be better."

"At least you're still alive; that's a surprise," Louquintas said jovially.

Chuckling, Jacob responded, "Heh, I can say the same about you!"

"Very true!"

"Why don't we chat in the backroom, and you can inform me as to why you have invaded my humble establishment," Jacob said as he motioned for them to follow.

Going through the door he had just exited, Jacob led them into a dimly lit kitchen. Against the far wall was a brick oven with counters running from either side of it; pots and pans littered the surface, and it looked none too clean, like the rest of the place, Kalend thought grimly. Along a side wall was a square oak table with four chairs where a scrawny, unkempt man sat casually peeling potatoes.

Jacob motioned to the man and gruffly barked, "Get out."

The man mutely stood, grabbed his basket of potatoes, and hobbled to the side door.

"Oh, and bring us some ales," Jacob bellowed to the man's retreating back.

The man bobbed his head and squeaked, "Yes, sir," then changed course to exit through the door leading to the bar.

The three sat down, and Louquintas proceeded to give a quick summary of the past few weeks, keeping it simple without divulging much in the way of specifics. Jacob leaned into his chair and tapped his chin thoughtfully with one finger as he listened patiently.

"So, we could use some information and supplies, and I was hoping we could hold up here for a few days," Louquintas said as he finished the tale.

"No problem there. I have a room for you to use," Jacob responded.

"Thank you, my friend. I knew I could count on you!"

"Heh..you still have to pay me, of course," Jacob said with a smile

"Don't worry, you bandit, you will be paid!"

Jacob turned his attention to Kalend and said, "You have fallen into questionable company here with this character. However, I assume you already know that."

"Nice to meet you, sir," Kalend responded politely.

"Please, just call me Jacob."

The door to the bar banged open, and the potato man scurried in with their drinks and set them down before them. Kalend promptly grasped his mug and took a long pull from the frothy contents. This was his first taste of ale, and he did not want Louquintas to stop him, for back at the monastery, they would not have allowed him to drink until he was older. He found the taste bitter and sharp and that he liked it. Louquintas, who had been watching amusingly, smiled and nodded his head.

The talk turned to local happenings and issues that Jacob had with hired help and other mundane topics. Kalend decided that he liked the ale more and more as he drank. By the time he could see the bottom of his mug, he felt a slight warm sensation at the tip of his nose, and his head felt a little fuzzy.

Jacob rose and said, "Come, let me show you to your rooms, and then you can rest, go out for supplies, or whatever else you want."

Kalend and Louquintas followed Jacob, and as they passed through the side door, Louquintas asked, "Have any idea where we could find some companionship of the fairer quality?"

Jacob laughed. "Yes. I will give you directions to a place that should have some nice…companionship."

CHAPTER SIX

Walking down a dark alley at dusk was not the ideal time to let your mind wander, Kalend thought as they walked briskly to their next destination. That destination had Kalend thinking of things other than what lay around him, so he put his trust in Louquintas to be aware for them both. He knew that was not good, but he couldn't shake the thought of what awaited him next, which had his mind scrambled with emotions. He found that he was nervous. Very nervous.

The evening air was brisk and cool, which helped calm but not stop his racing mind, so he still felt flushed and jittery when they arrived at the house Louquintas had been searching for. Going up the small flight of stairs that led to a landing and a single door, Louquintas paused, glanced at Kalend, gave him a wink, and then rapped his knuckles on the door.

A woman opened the door and spoke briefly with Louquintas, then pushed it wide to allow him to enter. He motioned for Kalend to follow and slipped through the doorway.

Kalend hesitated at the foot of the stairs, and the woman stepped out onto the landing. She was tall with long auburn hair, which she tossed to one side with a flick of her head and then looked down at him with a warm smile and said, "Don't worry darling, we don't bite."

Kalend blushed and hurried up the stairs, and as he did, he heard Louquintas's laughter float out to the alley. "Unless you want them too!"

Once through the doorway, he found himself in a long rectangular room with low ceilings. The wall to his left held a roaring fire within a marble-sheathed fireplace, which cast flicking shadows over the whole ensemble. Scattered about the room were plush chairs, love seats, and divans, many of which held men and women in various stages of undress. Some women were sitting in the men's laps, and there was much whispering and many a naughty giggle.

The lanky woman who had opened the door took Kalend's hand and guided him through another doorway to their right. This next room was smaller and had a dark wooden bar running along the right side. Lined up before the bar was a bevy of young women; some smiled and looked eager to see him. A couple had naked hunger in their eyes, while others eyed him with a cool appraisal. His heart skipped a beat and then sped up.

His guide looked to Louquintas, who had been standing off to the side appraising the women, and asked, "What's your pleasure tonight?"

Kalend found her voice to be smoky and smooth. For some reason, it made his pulse quicken even more. His heart pounded in his chest as he watched Louquintas glide over to the farthest woman, a long blond-haired beauty with ample bosoms. Louquintas bowed and then held out his hand; she giggled, pushed his hand away, slithered into his arms, and kissed him full on the mouth.

The woman with the smoky voice turned to Kalend and asked, "And, who would you like?"

Kalend stood in a trance-like state, so it took a moment or two before it sunk in; she was speaking to him. Fumbling for an answer, he looked to Louquintas for help but saw his mentor was already heading up some stairs at the back of the room, giggly blonde in tow.

"It's ok, young sir. They all know what they are doing, and you will enjoy yourself, I promise."

As Kalend gathered himself together the best he could, one of the young women stepped forward, took his arm, and said, "If it's ok, Madam, I'll look after him."

The Madam looked at Kalend and asked, "Will she do for you?"

All he could do was nod his head and stammer, "Yyes."

The young woman smiled and led him to the same stairway he saw Louquintas disappear through. Once at the top, she whispered, "Don't worry, we will have fun. My name is Francine. What is yours?"

He stammered, "Kalend," as she guided him down the hallway.

*****   *****

Francine was a polite, gentle young woman who did not get pushy or judgmental about Kalend's nervousness. They sat on the bed and talked for almost an hour before she moved closer and kissed him. At first, he just let her lead, and then he began to return her kiss, finding his nervousness melting away under the heat he was feeling. Her hands wandered to his shirt and began to undo the buttons; after the last button was deftly released, she opened the shirt and ran her fingers along his bare, muscular chest. A shiver ran from his head to his toes with that touch, not a cold shiver but one of delight. He moaned into her mouth as their tongues danced, his whole body responding to his need.

A scream ripped through the building. It was a scream of pure terror, and Kalend's heated blood cooled instantly. He leaped from Francine and the bed and quickly buttoned his shirt as more screams tore through the night. As he reached for his sword to buckle it back on, the door burst open, and an armed man charged through and swung directly at Kalend's head.

Not having time to unsheathe his sword, Kalend blocked the attack, driving the attacker's blade downward. He punched with his other hand, and the man stumbled backward. Shaking his sword free from his scabbard, Kalend stood in the ready position as another strike came at him, this time low and at an angle. He parried, but before he could counterattack, the man lurched to the side, crashed into a side table, and fell on the floor, out cold. Kalend looked up and found a terrified Francine standing before him with the remnants of a vase she had smashed over the attacker's head.

Hurried footsteps came to the door. Louquintas popped in, paused to scan the scene in the room, and announced, "Time to go."

Kalend grabbed his sheath and raced to follow Louquintas but abruptly stopped, whirled to Francine, kissed her, and said, "Thank you."

With Louquintas leading, they rushed down the stairs, taking them two at a time. In the bar room, they found a furious fight raging; men with various weapons were grappling with creatures from a nightmare. The nightmarish beings had horns protruding from their heads, bushy beards, pointed ears, and goat-looking legs; Kalend had never seen or heard of their kind before. Quickly, they waded through the area, dodging and weaving those caught in death struggles, making their way to the main room. Bursting through the doorway, Kalend found the once lurid setting was a mess of overturned couches and chairs. Bodies, both human and other, littered the floor. At the far end, a man in a gray cloak stood with a group of the two-horned creatures; he paused when he took notice of their entrance, pointed, and screamed, "That's them, kill 'em."

Louquintas turned to the door they had entered the building from, kicked it open, rushed down the stairs, and sprinted into a side alley. Kalend heard others exit the building and give chase, but he did not want to slow down to look back. Racing through the city, Louquintas shot down another alley to their right, then one to their left; Kalend thought he heard their pursuers losing ground. He finally glanced back to see how far away they were and felt a hand grab his shoulder and yank him to the side while another hand clamped over his mouth. Louquintas had slipped into a shadowy nook between buildings and had pulled him along.

"Sshhh, quiet now," Louquintas whispered into his ear.

They stood still and strained to hear over the frantic beating of their hearts. Running footsteps surged in their direction and then abruptly halted directly before them.

A raspy voice whispered, "Which way?"

An equally raspy voice answered, "This way…. I think," and footfalls hurried down an alley leading away from them.

Sighing with relief, Louquintas released Kalend, looked around, and said, "I have no idea where we are."

Kalend looked at him with exasperation and shook his head. "I thought you knew this city?"

"I know some of it, but this is an area I don't know well. I have a general idea of which direction to go, so let's get moving. And keep your eyes open!"

Kalend once again closely shadowed Louquintas, his eyes darting from side to side, alert for any sign of pursuit. They did not encounter anyone and heard nothing for almost half an hour as they moved stealthily through the alleys. Just as he began to relax, a masked figure appeared directly in front of them, motioned for them to stop, and, with a muffled voice, said, "Your pursuers are close by. Come with me, and I will lead you away from them."

Louquintas stopped in mid-stride and, with a hand on his weapon, asked, "And who the hell are you?"

"I am a friend of Yarguri. She said you may be headed this way, and if I could give aid, that I should."

"How do I know you're her friend?"

"She said to tell you; I know of the bracer on the young man beside you that she gave him."

Louquintas visibly relaxed, cocked his head to the side, and with his usual smirk, said, "Ok. But you will excuse me if I am still wary."

"That's fine, but please, let's leave now. Follow me; we don't have far to go."

Following the masked man down another alley, Louquintas made eye contact with Kalend and silently mouthed to be careful. After a few minutes and several more turns, they ended at the door of a three-story building that sat alone at the end of a dimly lit street. Quickly, the masked figure unlocked the door and ushered them inside. The three of them passed down a short, narrow hall that opened into a cobble-stoned courtyard surrounded on all four sides by balconies on each level of the house. A five-foot fountain stood in the middle, and three concentric circles led upward to a figure of a woman holding a jug that poured clear water into the top circle, which then drained over the edges into the lower ring and then into the bottom one. Kalend paused to watch the fountain and could not see how the water got into the jug.

"Do you like it?" rumbled the masked man as he stood behind Kalend.

"How does it work?"

"No idea. A friend from another place put it here, and it has been flowing ever since. I know magic but not science." He shrugged and continued, "He said it was some type of suction or some such."

Louquintas stood nonchalantly off to the side and asked, "Interesting, but not as interesting as who are you?"

"My name is Jarlwo, and you are Louquintas. The young lad is Kalend. As I said, Yarguri told me of you both. Let's retire upstairs, and we can talk some more."

He led them up some stairs to the right, which zigzagged upward toward the roof. Taking the last step to the top, Kalend paused as he overlooked the city. A four-foot wooden wall lined the roof, and a table with several chairs around it stood off to the side under a covered open-aired pavilion. He moved to the nearest wall and leaned against it with his hands, taking in the curious scene of the city's flickering nighttime lights. They came from one and two-storied homes, some windows open to the night air and others shuttered with light peeking out around the edges. Oil-based streetlamps lined many of the avenues, casting wavering shadows along the buildings' walls. Some sections of the city had more lights than others, and one section seemed devoid of any. It gave him a sense of calmness and serenity after the evening's roller coaster of emotions.

"Come, join us," he heard a muffled voice call to him.

Turning to the table, Kalend saw that tall, tapered candles had been lit, and the masked man and Louquintas had sat down and were looking at him. He moved to join them, pulled one of the high-backed chairs out from the table, and sank into it; he quickly discovered it felt good to sit and that his legs felt a little shaky.

Louquintas asked their host, "So, how do you know Yarguri?"

"I also am a practitioner of the arts. We have worked many times together."

"Heh. I have to say thank you for your help. Those things trying to find us didn't have our good health in mind."

"You are most welcome. And no -they did not."

Kalend cleared his throat and nervously asked, "Sir, do you mind if I ask why you wear that mask?"

"Not at all. I like to conceal my identity from the general public. There are times I need to do things with my powers, and when I suspect I may use them, I wear the mask. This way, I can go about my affairs as a…" he paused, smiled wanly, and continued, "more normal person the rest of the time."

Louquintas ignored the pause and asked, "What kind of things?"

The man reached up and pulled the mask away to reveal scars that crisscrossed his face. It looked to Kalend like he had been mauled repeatedly by a big cat. He pushed back the cowl of his cloak, and long silver hair fell to partially cover the disfigurement. Emerald eyes stared at them; he leaned back into his chair and interlaced his fingers, the two index fingers coming to rest just above his top lip. He appeared to contemplate the question and eventually sighed, "That is not so easily answered, my new friends."

"Then, what can you tell us?"

"First, that those pursuing you are coming from the same source as those who attacked you at the witch's camp," he held a hand to forestall Louquintas as he was about to speak, "And yes, I know of the attack, from Yarguri."

"How about the horned creatures? What do you know of them? And how the hell did they get inside the city without anyone noticing?"

"They are called Panes. The reason they can move freely in the city is that they can cloak themselves with an illusion such that they look like men. However, it's a difficult illusion. So that in battle, they can't maintain it."

"That's why we saw what they looked like then," Louquintas said as he looked at Kalend.

Kalend nodded and asked, "What about the men with them?"

Jarlwo replied, "One would have been their handler, a person who controls them. The others, I suspect, were just mercenaries there to help." He paused, then continued, "There is much to tell you, so if you can hold off on the questions till after, I will fill you in on what I know; it would be faster if that is ok?"

Kalend and Louquintas nodded their heads in agreement.

Jarlwo stood and, with his hands clasped behind him, began his narrative. "The first thing is, I know Kalend has learned much about magic but not so much about where it comes from," he stopped and looked at Kalend. "You do know of the Wiccenda?"

Kalend nodded and replied, "Yes, Yarguri told me some."

"Good. Good," Jarlwo said as he paced to and fro. "That is helpful. They come from another place and time but can send, let's call it a shadow, of themselves to us. This other place they come from is alien to us; however, they speak our language and seem to know some about us, whereas we do not know much about them. Some help those who want to do good with our powers, and some help those with more sinister designs. Two of the more evil warlocks are Pouluk, whom you have already bumped into at the witches' camp, and his other not-so-nice half, Tworg. They are constantly vying for more power and are at odds with those of us who are trying to keep the peace; both currently work for the king of Odethane, Kourkourant."

Jarlwo moved to the wall and peered out over the city for a minute, then turned and made his way back to the table and sat down. He looked to Kalend, sighed, and said, "Well, my boy, another truth you shall learn tonight is that it was the King, Kourkourant, who had your parents killed or at least made them disappear. We are still unsure which."

"The King!" Kalend exclaimed, "Louquintas told me they were influential, but my god, the King himself?"

"Yes. He thought the only way to remain king was to get rid of his most ardent opposition. That would have been your parents. He is now sure that a son survives, and he is sending everything he can after you without letting too many others know of your existence." Jarlwo looked directly at Kalend and continued, "That is why you must stay on the move."

Kalend shook his head. "Where are we to go next?"

Jarlwo leaned forward in his chair and said, "Renthar village, then take a boat to Quasar." He abruptly rose to his feet and continued, "Come with me. I have a few things to show you and a map you will find interesting."

CHAPTER SEVEN

Hollilea felt the sweat roll down her neck and crawl down her back; it was not a pleasant experience. With her dress sticking uncomfortably beneath the thick layer of clothes she wore to ward off the chill, she slowly floundered her way up the snowy mountain. Karl plowed ahead through the drifts and banks, creating an easier path for them, but Hollilea looked forward to the promised fire and new home they headed toward. She already missed her brother and still wished she had been permitted to join him, but at that moment, as her body perspired while her nose froze, she just wanted to rest and relax near some heat.

The witches had assured her they knew of a place in the mountains they could hold up in, and once new wards were established, they would be safe. Karl rounded a bend in the path, stopped, looked about, and said, "I believe this is it."

Yarguri trudged up beside him and proclaimed curtly, "It is."

They stood and stared at a frozen creek that ran through a snow-covered glen. Hollilea grunted as she scanned the area; it did not look very promising regarding a shelter or, more importantly, a fire. However, with the sun glistening off the pristine snow that blanketed the area, she did find the place beautiful and peaceful. It was like a winter dream that seeped within, eased her soul, and soothed her aching muscles with its charm. Then she smiled despite the cold; she could almost feel the place call to her and say…home.

It was not long before Karl had a fire blazing, which the party gathered around and soaked up. Plans were made to create shelters, and after they warmed themselves enough to shake off the chill, they set about making them with determination. Using heavy canvas provided by the Othureans and saplings cut down by Karl, they quickly had three passible lodgings up.

The following days put the finishing touches on their campsite, or at least as much as they could while winter lasted. Hollilea then was back to learning about her magic, but now with renewed focus and renewed purpose. It was no longer an ability she was told to learn because of some possible abstract future need. The need was here, now. Helping her brother and reuniting with him drove her to dive into her studies with a passion she had never had before. Knowing he was out there, coupled with the knowledge that others looked to harm both of them, gave her a purpose for all the hard work.

Yarguri grunted as the ball of fire that Hollilea had conjured above her palm hissed, wobbled, and winked out. Hollilea grimaced and, with a tinge of frustration, said, "I had it under control, then I could feel it begin to break up, and as I tried to regain control, I lost it completely."

"Your concentration, like the flame at its end, flickered and wavered." Yarguri sighed. "Drawing power from your Wiccenda and then redirecting it into the flame cannot waver at all. If you do, unfortunate things can happen. You must continue to train your mind to block out any distractions."

Hollilea brushed a tendril of wind-blown hair from her face and asked, "But what about if I am also in danger? How will I know if someone sneaks up on me while I am so engrossed in the conjuring?"

"Let your subconscious mind be your guide for what is around you. The deeper you relax and focus, the more your mind will pick up and see without you even being aware of it. In time, your sub-conscience will be your protector."

Hollilea smiled. "As I am protecting others, my mind will be protecting me."

Yarguri nodded, then admonished, "But only if you train your mind!" She turned to head back down the trail to their campsite, looked back at Hollilea, and said, "My teaching is done for today. Stay and meditate; work on letting go."

Hollilea grimaced ruefully; she was not surprised at the abrupt departure, but it still amused her how one moment they would be training rigorously and then told to just stop and meditate. Then again, she guessed it was a combination of the witch's blunt personality and training methods. After training with such rigor, being asked to meditate was a sudden, unwelcome change requiring concentration and a letting go. Perched on a fallen log, she inhaled deeply and exhaled slowly, letting all her tension drain away with the air as it exited her lungs. She settled into a comfortable cocoon within her mind, allowing the quiet stillness surrounding her to cover her like a warm blanket. She sank within the blankness of a calm void.

A whisper rippled across the serenity she inhabited, one that spoke of a disturbance. Hollilea allowed that ripple in to make it one with her meditation, and she could feel someone or something approaching from the woods. Whatever or whoever came with stealth, she relaxed some more and let her subconscious mind see more clearly.

Hollilea opened her eyes just as the creature drifted out of the woods to her right. She sat calm, relaxed, and looked upon the newcomer with a smile. She felt no menace from the creature and found it beautiful, a graceful being that glided above the ground to hover before her. A flowing gossamer of colors that undulated yet maintained the basic shape of a human female, it smiled at Hollilea as its face firmed and became more substantial than the rest of its body.

Hollilea smiled back and hesitantly said, "Hello."

The being nodded and replied in a lilting soprano voice, "Hello, Hollilea. My name is Vetleena." With a slight shake, it glowed brightly, and the rest of its body firmed to match its face and gently settled onto the ground before Hollilea. A lush woman with a knee-high, loose-fitting lavender dress and long raven hair stood before her and asked courteously, "May I sit beside you?"

"Yes," Hollilea responded, motioning for Vetleena to join her on the log. "I felt your presence coming toward me, but it was an odd feeling. Like you are a dream....is that what you are? A waking dream?"

Vetleena gently responded, "No, my dear. I am very real. However, I do occupy a different reality than your own. One that is part of yours yet remains unseen...usually."

Hollilea laughed softly. "That is the sort of non-answer I would expect from my teachers."

"I could see that. In fact, I have seen it. We have kept an eye on your training for some time. There are many forces looking for you and your brother. I wanted to introduce myself and let you know you are not alone. The world is changing, myths and legends of yore are awakening, they can feel a change in the very earth."

"What changes?"

"You will find out in time. For now, you need to know that the changes are occurring, and you and your brother will help usher them in. These changes will affect not just your world but others as well." Vetleena smiled at Hollilea. "Aaahh, my dear. You are young, but trust your training, your instincts, and your brother. Hold them tight, and you will see unimaginable things."

Hollilea shook her head in mild frustration; the calm void slipped some as she said, "Again, you evaded giving a direct answer." Then she sighed and continued, "But I guess that this is all part of my training, part of who I am. To find those answers myself."

Vetleena laughed gaily. "Yes, it is! You see some things clearly. We may not see each other again, but then again...we may. Just know that we are out there."

"Who is this 'we'? These myths and legends you speak of?"

Vetleena smiled, stood, shimmered back into her amorphous state, and silently disappeared into the woods. Hollilea shook her head after the strange being left; what had happened to her life, she thought? So much had changed, so many questions. She knew that living and training with three witches was not natural or what ordinary people did. But to her, it was ordinary, like her use of magic; it was just a part of who she was. Now creatures watched her, and powerful men threatened harm; what was she to do?

After a long, restful night's sleep in their new lodgings, Hollilea decided not to tell her teachers of the visitor she had. She felt no ill will from the creature or experience and wanted to keep it her secret. Even though Vetleena said they may not see each other again, Hollilea felt sure they would; she was just not sure when. So she threw herself back into her studies, and the memory of the meeting faded.

The next day, Yootuk invited Hollilea to join her in the woods as she placed protective wards around their new camp, and Hollilea eagerly accepted. A bright, cheery, but cold blue sky peeked out from the canopy of pine and naked oak branches above them as they slowly and cautiously made their way through the snowy landscape. Yootuk instructed and, in careful detail, outlined how she would place her wards. A small gesture, a few mumbled words, and a light touch was all Yootuk needed to leave a ward upon a scabby pine. There would be a small flash, and a dull glyph would appear briefly and then disappear. Hollilea learned that the glyph was a conduit for the True Source and that it could hold its essence for a short period of time. But that vigilance would still be required, and periodically resetting the wards would be necessary.

They settled into a routine of Yootuk setting a ward and Hollilea asking questions between the trees they marked. Eventually, the conversation turned to Hollilea's brother and the bracer he wore. She wanted to know about it, how it worked, and how her brother, who had no ability with magic, could use it. Yootuk explained the bracer itself had a more permanent glyph upon it, and that glyph was tied to both of them. The Wiccenda had other such artifacts, but they were rare, and for them to give one to the siblings spoke of their commitment to them. Hollilea would need to learn to use it to talk with her brother directly; she grimaced at the thought of yet more training but then smiled at the reward of being able to connect with him.

    Later that evening, after enjoying a steaming helping of rabbit stew that Karl had prepared, Hollilea sat contently before the fire and thought about her brother. The sun was just dipping into the tree line above them, and dusk would soon settle over them as she reached out with her mind towards her brother. Unlike her previous attempt, which had resulted in him seeing her in a dream, she now searched for both him and the bracer. She soon felt a vibration, faint and distant, but she was drawn to it, like a moth to a flame, and her mind flew unerringly toward it. The bracer acted as a bright beacon within a vast darkness; she hurried toward it, eager to establish a link with Kalend. As her mind settled over him, she paused as she sensed a presence near him. One that filled her with dread, one that caused fear to flush through her veins, and one that made her fear for his safety. She felt her grip on the connection slip with that fear. She pushed it aside and let her happiness at finding him overcome that fear; the connection strengthened, and she reached out with her mind and nudged the bracer. She felt him briefly fiddle with it, which sent ripples across the connection, but she received no direct response. She prodded it again and, once again, received nothing. Feeling somewhat exasperated and ignored, she gathered herself, then gave a hard mental stab at the bracer.

CHAPTER EIGHT

Louquintas rushed through the Punchers Inn's front door, and with Kalend a step behind, they hurried through the main room to the bar. It was still early morning, and the sun was just peeking over the horizon; it seemed like no other guests had arisen yet or bothered to grace the bar with their presence. Kalend guessed this was due to the early hour and that most of the inhabitants and guests were more of the night owl variety.

Louquintas dragged over a stool, motioned for Kalend to do the same, and then withdrew some folded papers from his inside shirt pocket. Placing them on the bar, he neatly unfolded them and spread them out so they could get a good view. The first sheet appeared old with a burnt browning around its edges, and faded lettering was scrawled along the top in a language Kalend was unfamiliar with.

Pointing to the words, Kalend asked, "Can you read what it says?"

Louquintas nodded. "Yes, it is an old language, not much used anymore. Actually, I'm not sure where it was ever used." He shrugged and continued, "I learned it long ago. It says Physical and Topographic Map of the City of Pleus. The next line is too badly worn, but the first word is Federal."

"What does Topo..gra..focal mean?"

"Heh...not sure what that word means either," Louquintas grimaced. "Doesn't matter." He pointed to some lines on the map. "These lines are the sewer routes under the city, and as you can see, one is directly under us, and it appears there is an entrance found here at the inn."

Kalend peered closer and traced the route with his finger. "Seems like it comes out on the other side of the city. Right where we want to be anyway."

"The old man was correct. This map is interesting. Just what we need to avoid the surface streets, which will soon become very hazardous to our health."

The kitchen door swung open as Jacob strutted out with a wooden tray full of clean mugs and made his way behind the bar. "Hope you found your evening's entertainment to your satisfaction?" he asked as he placed the cups on dirty shelves that lined the rear wall.

Louquintas gave Kalend a quick glance and a shake of his head to indicate not to say anything. "It was good! Not long enough, but you know how that goes."

Jacob put the last cup away, turned to them, and gave Louquintas a deliberate look. "I heard something bad went down last night. I don't want to know what. I'm only glad you both made it back in one piece."

"No. You don't want to know."

"I just said that." He smiled, shook his head, then looked down, noticed the map, and asked, "What's this?"

"A map."

"No shit. Stop being a wise-ass, and maybe I can help," Jacob replied in exasperation.

"Ok, take all my fun away." Louquintas sighed and then asked with a smile, "Do you have a sewer opening under this pest hole?"

"Pest hole?"

"Alright, this fine luxury hotel and most fantastic eatery!"

With arms crossed, Jacob just stood there and glared at Louquintas.

Kalend, having had enough of the banter, snapped at them both, "Stop it," and looked to Jacob. "Sir, we don't have much time and could use your help and any information you may have?"

"Sure thing, for you kid, I will. Yes, there is an entrance to the sewers; it's on the lower level. I keep it tightly closed and locked. However, it is useable, as I have had on occasion to....hhhmm shall we say, let people leave in such a way as not to be seen."

"Perfect. Will you show it to us?"

"Yes. When do you want to leave?"

Louquintas gathered the maps together, looked at Jacob, and before Kalend could answer, said with a more honest voice, "Now, if we may? And thank you again. I owe you one."

Jacob snorted, "You owe me more than one, my friend. But get your stuff, and let's get you out of my pest hole."

*****   *****

The stench was overpowering. Slogging their way through the sewer was a smelly and wet trip Kalend would have gladly missed if they had had a choice, which they did not, so he kept breathing through his mouth as much as possible. Trying to lessen the effect. It did little good.

Louquintas led the way with his usual determination and aplomb. As they slowly twisted and turned through the warren of passages, Kalend kept getting distracted by the bracer on his left arm. It was alternating between itching like mad or quivering lightly. He tried to scratch under it, twist it around, and move it so as to make it stop. Nothing seemed to do any good, and he thought about taking it off and putting it away to get some peace, but just as he went to remove it, the irritation stopped.

They came to a large opening that revealed an intersection with three different options. Louquintas swore quietly, came to a halt, and pulled the map out of his shirt. Kalend moved closer so that the light of his torch, the only one they had, could fall onto their only means of direction. After a few seconds of study, Louquintas grunted, "This way," then headed down the passage on their left.

As Kalend entered the new passage, his bracer gave a hard jerk as if someone had kicked him in the arm. It kicked again, and this time, he stopped and let out an "ouch." Louquintas halted and asked, "What's wrong?"

"I don't know. This bracer just kicked me," Kalend replied in exasperation.

"Stop playing around. I want to get out of here; I don't like it any more than you."

"I am not playing," Kalend responded angrily as the bracer kicked yet again.

Running his finger along the top of it, he traced the runes that marked it. As he did, they began to glow faintly, and then he heard a feminine voice snap, *"Stop playing with it and talk to me!"*

Taken aback, Kalend stumbled a pace and then responded hesitantly, "What?"

Louquintas looked at him with a puzzled look. "I didn't say anything."

The feminine voice also responded, *"It's your sister. Don't tell me you forgot about me already?"*

Kalend, still confused, asked out loud, "Hollilea, is that you?"

"Yes, but I'm in your head, silly. We can talk through the bracer you have, oh, and no need to use your mouth. It's just in our minds."

Louquintas looked closely at Kalend. "You sure you're ok? I know it smells bad in here, but don't let it go to your head!"

Kalend focused his eyes on Louquintas. "Hang on; it appears that I can speak to Hollilea through the bracer."

"Hmmm…Ok. At this point, not much surprises me, but don't take too long. I am beginning to get used to the smell, and that can't be good."

Kalend returned his attention to his sister. *"I don't have much time; we are in kind of a hurry."*

"I know. Once we made contact, I could locate you and sense what was going on."

"*You know where I am?*"

"*In a general way, you are underground in a passageway, under what I think is a city.*"

Kalend grunted, "*Not bad.*"

"*You do know that some creatures are following you?*"

He stiffened up and glanced back the way they had come. "*No! What creatures?*"

"*I don't know. They have horns and don't seem to have real feet.*"

"*Damn. Alright, we had a run-in with them before. Any idea on how many there are?*"

"*Nope. I just sense there is more than one.*"

Louquintas noticed the new tension in his student and asked, "What's wrong?"

Kalend held up a hand for a moment for silence and asked, "*Sis, we need to get out of here. Is there anything else you can do to help?*"

"*I don't know. Just leave this gateway open!*"

"Gateway? Open? I have no idea how I opened it, to begin with, let alone close it!"

"*Just think of me and speak my name in your mind if you need anything else.*"

Kalend turned back to Louquintas, who had been waiting impatiently, "We need to hurry; those Pane creatures are behind us."

"Perfect," Louquintas mumbled. "Let's move. You can explain to me this whole talking to your sister when she isn't here a little later."

Sloshing quickly down their chosen path, Kalend kept an eye out behind them for any sign of pursuit. He saw and heard nothing. This did little to reassure him. He trusted his sister, so, therefore, he was confident they were back there somewhere. Keeping track of time in this hellhole was almost pointless, he thought, so he had no idea how long they traveled in the oppressive darkness, ever watchful for the unseen creatures behind them. His nerves became raw, and he found himself more and more on edge. He started to imagine he heard or saw something behind them every few moments. When he thought he could not take anymore and might go mad from the pressure, a light appeared before them. Louquintas abruptly stopped, and with Kalend's mind tightly wound, he stumbled into the back of his mentor. Louquintas either did not notice, which Kalend doubted, or he chose to ignore his student's lack of awareness.

"Looks like the way out," Louquintas whispered. "But let's be careful; we don't know what's out there." Then, a loud clank reverberated off the walls behind them. A muttered curse, sounding shockingly close, quickly followed.

Unsheathing his sword, Louquintas barked, "That tears it. Let's go!"

Kalend yanked his sword from his scabbard and hurried to catch up with Louquintas, who had not waited for his apprentice but had immediately sprinted toward the light and exit. The light loomed larger and brighter as they swiftly made their way to freedom from the darkness. The sounds of pursuit were now pronounced as their pursuers had given up all pretense of stealth.

Louquintas burst through some scraggly brush into the light and skidded to a halt. Kalend stumbled out soon after and came breathlessly to stand beside Louquintas. They were alone beside the base of a hill; trees and shrubs surrounded a small clearing before the cave entrance. The sun was dipping below the trees and bathed the clearing in a dusky light. The sudden crunching of gravel and jangle of weapons from behind caused them to whirl back toward the cave with raised swords. Two Pane creatures stumbled forth and faltered in surprise at the weapons pointed at them. Louquintas took advantage of their momentary shock and thrust his sword cleanly through the first Pane's chest. It died with a look of shock still plastered on its face. The second Pane recovered quicker and took an overhand swing at Louquintas. Kalend stepped over and blocked the blow to the side. The Pane spun around with the force of its deflected blade and ended up having it pointed at Kalend. With a sneer on its face, it laughed. That laugh abruptly morphed into a look of puzzlement when an arrow sprouted from its chest. It grabbed the feathered shaft and plucked at it weakly with its empty hand, and as blood started to ooze from its mouth, it fell over with a gurgle and died.

Kalend stared at the body a moment or two and then heard a voice from behind, "That should take care of it for sure." He turned around with a raised blade to see Trealine standing at ease in the clearing, holding a crossbow at his side and a grin on his face.

Louquintas laughed and said, "About time!"

Trealine grunted, "You're welcome." Then, he beckoned them to follow and slipped into the trees behind him.

Kalend looked to Louquintas, who just shook his head and motioned to follow the Othurean. They traveled for some time when Kalend suddenly remembered his sister. Hurrying his hand over the runes of his bracer, he imagined his sister and called out to her in his mind, hoping this would connect him to her.

"I am here. Are you two alright?" Hollilea asked anxiously.

Kalend quickly filled her in on their escape from the sewers and Panes.

Hollilea sighed. *"I was so worried."*

Kalend laughed. *"No worries, Louquintas was here!"*

"I know, but I still worry. I don't want to lose my brother and only family; we haven't had time to get to know one another properly."

The three emerged from the forest to find a small clearing where a fire was burning cheerfully among a ring of stones. Trealine leaned his crossbow against a nearby pine tree and crossed to the fire, where he plopped down before the blaze. With outstretched hands, he sighed as he warmed his fingers. Kalend stopped at the edge of the clearing to say goodbye to Hoillilea. *"Sis, we are at the campsite. I need to go for now, but we need to talk about this bracer thing, and soon."*

"Yes, we do. I am still learning what all I can do with it, but I think I will be able to give even more help in the future through it. Bye for now!"

"Hope to talk to you soon," Kalend responded as he moved to join the others.

They settled in around the fire while the daylight faded around them, and Louquintas swiftly got Trealine up to date on all that had transpired since they had last seen each other. When the tale was complete at last, Trealine just shook his head and grunted in understanding.

Kalend looked around and asked, "Where are the horses?"

Trealine pointed toward some dense bushes where a couple of horsebacks poked above the hedge. As if they sensed them looking in their direction, both raised their heads over the broad leaves, and one gave out a whistle as if in greeting. Kalend laughed and asked, "How are they doing?"

"They have had it better than you these last couple of days," Trealine responded while he poked at the fire with a stick. "It twas Whistler who led me to that cave. Strange, but the whole time you were gone, it was as if he knew where you were. After a while, I picked up clues on how he behaved; he would glance toward the city and whistle. This morning, he kept pulling me in this general direction until I found the cave entrance. Then I made camp here and waited in the trees to see what would come out."

Kalend looked over his shoulder at Whistler. "How odd!" he exclaimed. "I knew this horse was different."

"He is that."

Louquintas, who had listened to this exchange quietly, looked at Trealine and asked, "Any chance of some food?"

"Yes. I have a couple of rabbits I caught earlier today; they are over near my pack."

"Good. I'm famished!" Louquintas exclaimed as he stood and walked over to fetch the rabbits.

Kalend stretched his legs before the fire, leaned back onto his elbows, and let out a sigh as relief spread over him. The excitement and adrenaline had been slowly fading, and now he felt content, especially with the idea of food to be had soon. With his mind relaxed, he was able to put much of the recent past together, which eventually brought him around to the near future.

"Where too next?" he asked.

Louquintas, who was busy skinning the rabbits, didn't look up as he responded, "Well, our next stop is Renthar village. From there, we take a boat to Quasar."

"How far is Renthar?"

"Hmmm... shouldn't be more than a week. It's mostly grasslands and hills. But this assumes we can manage to make it without pursuit, which I am not so sure of."

Kalend sighed again, this time with resignation. This adventure was not what it seemed, but then he grinned and admitted he would not want to be anywhere else, even with warlocks, Panes, and a king after him. It all just felt right, like this was his destiny, and he was born for this. He realized that this sounded a little arrogant, but deep down, he knew it was right and that his part to play was just beginning. He found himself looking forward to whatever lay ahead but also knew he should be more afraid than he was. It was not that fear had left him, not at all, just that the fear was tamped down with the realization that he was exactly where he needed to be in life. This helped him cope with the anxiety and the unknown. He mulled all this over as they silently ate, his thoughts twisting and turning over his destiny and where it might lead. Later, he would find himself falling asleep with a smile.

CHAPTER NINE

The journey to Renthar village took almost two weeks. Much longer than Louquintas had estimated, Kalend thought, but he noted this was mostly due to the horrendous weather they had experienced the whole trip. It seemed as if the heavens had opened and unleashed all the water of the oceans on them. Granted, Kalend had never seen an ocean; therefore, he had no idea how much water that could be, but he figured it could not be more than what had been dumped on them the past thirteen days. Weeks later, he would ruefully smile in remembrance of his ignorance this day. It seemed to be nothing but rolling hills they crossed over, a soggy wet mess with abysmal visibility, while each peak appeared the same as the last. If he did not know better, he would have sworn they were crawling up and over the same one, over and over.

The rain had started to finally let up as they crested yet another mound, and with less rain in the air, they could see that fallow fields covered the land around them as the hills had finally ended. They could make out a small cluster of buildings that resembled a village in the misty distance. Two main roads led into the middle of the town and crossed over each other before going out on different sides. One of those roads passed close to where they sat astride their horses.

Louquintas nudged his horse toward the road and said, "Come along now; I don't know about you two, but a dry, warm taproom is what I am needing."

Kalend glanced at Trealine, who was perched behind him on whistler, and asked, "Will you be going around again?"

Trealine paused, frowned, then said, "No….. I don't think so, not this time; let's see how the villagers react to me. Most likely, they have never heard of my race. Even if they have, hopefully, they won't have the same prejudices as in Pleus."

Louquintas heard the exchange and added, "Yes, I think we should stay together. If there are problems in the village, we can get out fast."

They reached the road, and Louquintas urged his horse into a canter as they made their way down toward the village. The road's cobblestone surface was wet but held them up well so they could make better progress than when going through the grassy hills. The fields covering the land on either side held the occasional farmhouse, but they saw and heard no one. Kalend was not surprised; what with the dreary weather they had experienced for days, it would have been more of a surprise if they had seen someone.

As they approached the village, they could make out drab square houses with smoke twisting into the air above their chimneys. Other buildings were much more extensive, and Kalend thought those were most likely inns or other businesses. But before he could get a better look, the drizzle they had been traveling through suddenly morphed into a downpour, and visibility dropped to a few feet. The deluge swallowed the buildings, and the three pulled their hoods tightly over their heads as they muddled on.

Lightning split the darkened sky, and thunder crashed around them as the wind picked up, driving the rain at an angle and stinging them along any exposed flesh. Kalend kept his head down, but his eyes glued to Louquintas's back. They did not get very far before Louquintas yanked his horse to a stop and squinted straight ahead. Kalend nudged Whistler alongside his mentor and tried to pierce the gale around them. He saw nothing but rain and wind until a lightning bolt briefly lit the sky. Then he saw them, two ghostly figures plodding along the road toward them.

They had long black robes with hoods pulled up so Kalend could not make out any features, and they each held a staff that they used to walk. Then, just as quickly, the light winked out, and he could see them no more. Louquintas urged his horse to slowly back up, but a light flashed again as he did. This time, the two hooded figures were illuminated by the staff of the stranger on the right, the tip of which seemed to have burst into flames and hissed spitefully in the rain. The other pointed at them and shouted something, and a moment later, wind and rain slashed into Kalend. He felt Whistler rear up in fright, and he and Trealine tumbled off his back. Kalend felt the breath blasted from his lungs from the fall; he gasped and rolled onto his knees. He looked for Louquintas and found him off his horse as well. But with sword drawn, he was already up and stalking his way through the driving rain toward their attackers. Kalend then noted Trealine had rolled off to the other side and drawn his axe, and with head bowed into the howling gale, was also making his sluggish way toward the pair.

Kalend rose to one knee, paused, and sensed these two attackers were different and more than mere swords would be needed. That gust of wind had not come from just anywhere; it had manifested at a shout. He quickly placed his hand on his bracer and called out Hollilea's name. She responded urgently, *"What's wrong?"*

"Someone is attacking us with magic!" he replied as he ducked a ball of fire that went roaring over his head.

"Hold your bracer up and think of a shield, as you would use with your sword."

He brought up the image of an old round shield he used to practice with at the monastery; nothing happened. *"It's not working!"* he mentally shouted.

"You must concentrate; try again!" His sister urged.

He closed his eyes and bent his whole mind to the task, trying to reach that meditative state he had practiced for so many years, blocking out all the noise and rain around him, focusing everything on that round shield. A moment later, he felt a presence in front of him; he opened his eyes, and a shimmering round disk of what looked to be hardened air was floating before him. Another ball of fire came careening toward him; he put his hand up to block it, fearing it was futile, but as he did, the floating disk moved as well, and the fireball slammed into it, bounced off, and shot upward. The fire sizzled into the air above him before it petered out as it succumbed to the rain.

"Well done!" he heard Hollilea shout in his mind.

Kalend peered into the downpour for the others and saw Louquintas had managed to make it within a few feet of the attackers. Trealine had also gotten within range and was preparing to engage the two. The strangers had been so focused on him that they did not detect Louquintas and Trealine until almost too late. At what appeared to be the same time, they turned toward his friends, raised their hands, and lightning hurtled out of their palms at point-blank range. Kalend yelled out in fear, but the lightning stopped in midair right in front of them; the bolts shivered for a moment and then winked out. All four stopped in amazement; Louquintas and Trealine recovered first and lunged forward at the same time, but they never connected as, with a loud pop, the warlocks disappeared.

The three remaining looked at each other in amazement and then around them, making sure they were alone. They were not. Off to the side and slightly behind Kalend stood another figure, this one also cloaked, but with the hood flipped back, a mask covered the person's face.

"Jarlwo?" Louquintas hesitantly asked as he raised his sword.

"Yes. Tis I. Looks like I made it just in time." Came a muffled response.

Louquintas lowered his weapon. "Yes indeed. Thank you."

"My pleasure. Shall we move off to the village and out of this rain?" Jarlwo asked nonchalantly.

***** *****

The Renthar Inn was a comfortable and warm place and moderately filled with people. With the weather being as it was, it appeared that many a farmer was in attendance. Several surly patrons complained bitterly about their soaked fields and work not getting done. Kalend heard much of this as they stood at the bar and looked around; Louquintas finally eyed a table in the far corner next to the fireplace that seemed satisfactory. He led the four of them over to it, and they each plopped into the sturdy oak chairs that ringed it.

Jarlwo sat with his back to the wall and sunk into the corner's shadows. He had taken off his mask and pulled his hood up to cover his face as best as possible.

A waitress had been watching them and came over to inquire about drinks as they settled in. She was fair of complexion, plump but in a curvaceous way, and a bosom that heaved when she breathed; for some reason, she made Kalend's face flush.

"What would you' all like this day?" She asked in a folksy way.

Louquintas gave his customary grin and answered, "Ale for each of us, my dear."

She turned and headed back to the bar with a smile and a giggle. Louquintas grinned even larger as he watched her saunter away, seeming to admire her ample rear, then he turned to the table and looked at Jarlwo. "Well, it seems we owe you our thanks. That's twice now; you have saved us! But how in blazes did you know where we were and needed help?"

Jarlwo bent forward, looked conspiratorially around, and they all leaned in; after a dramatic pause, he proclaimed, "Dumb, stupid luck!" He laughed and leaned back into his chair.

Kalend and company sat still for a moment as that soaked in, then the three laughed, and some of the tension left the table.

"The reality is that I was traveling for other business close by, felt a magical disturbance of significance, and came immediately," Jarlwo continued.

The barmaid sashayed back to their table with mugs of ale on a wooden tray and, with more heaving bosom, proceeded to hand them out. Louquintas gave her a light pat on the bottom as she turned to leave. With a crooked smile, she stopped and said to Louquintas with iron in her voice, "Do that again, sir, and you will have to live with the consequences."

Louquintas looked as if to make some quip, thought better of it, bowed his head to her, and responded with humility, "I apologize, my lady."

She laughed gaily. "Apology accepted, good sir," then gave him a wink and moved onto another table of waiting customers.

Jarlwo frowned at Louquintas. "I do have a message for you."

Louquintas raised an eyebrow, "And that would be...?"

"Yarguri and the witches, along with Karl and Hollilea, are on the move. I spoke with them as we came to the inn and told them of the attack. They are trying to evade Tworg, who, up until this attack on you, had been a pain in the witch's behinds." Jarlwo laughed and continued, "But I am sure they gave Tworg fits; he is no match for them. They also said to keep moving and get to Quasar as soon as possible. They now know which direction you should head once at the desert, Northeast, and find what they call Frok camp. "

Kalend leaned forward and asked, "Why Frok camp? Who is there?"

Jarlwo looked to Kalend and responded, "I honestly don't know. They just said for you to head there. On the other side of this village is the Hessporr river, you can get a boat and take it down to Quasar. There are barges headed down that way all the time, as there is a fair amount of trade between the two towns. You should be able to find a barge or two that can accommodate you and your horses."

Louquintas sighed and said, "I guess that's the plan. What about you? Are you coming with us?"

"No, I am afraid not. I have other things to attend to."

"Then I guess we should get some sleep and see about a barge tomorrow."

Trealine grunted and, with a gravelly voice, said, "Not until after I get something to eat."

The group ordered food and talked for a while about the trip ahead and other matters. Kalend had become less focused on the discussion around him and more worried about his sister, and he hoped that she was safe. Knowing the witches and Karl was with her was a comfort and gave him some peace of mind. Plus, it was becoming increasingly evident that his sister's powers were growing. The help she had provided twice now was incalculable, and for her to be able to wield power through him spoke of her increased strength. He made a mental note to contact her soon, when he was alone, to ask her more about how they could best utilize this newfound power.

Kalend's thoughts drifted from his sister to the journey ahead and who could be at Frok camp. There had to be a reason that everyone wanted him to go there. But it seemed as if no one wanted him to know. He was once again being left in the dark for his own good. Even though he knew they had his best interest in mind, it was irritating and frustrating. He just hoped they would soon recognize he was getting older and becoming a man and no longer needed to be protected from everything. With a yawn, he pulled his mind back to the conversation at hand. It seemed that Louquintas had talked to the serving girl and reserved a room for them all. With another yawn, Kalend stood with everyone else and gratefully followed them to their waiting beds.

CHAPTER TEN

Kalend stood leaning against the rail of the barge and watched as the land slowly slipped by on either side of them. Finding the barge that morning had been relatively easy; getting the horses on board had been another matter. He glanced at them, and they seemed at ease now, their eyes covered with cloth to help them stay relaxed; Whistler was the lone exception to the blindfold. He had walked onto the barge as calm as a daisy. After a handler had tried to tie the cloth around his head, he quickly decided, after almost being bitten, that it was not needed. Kalend grinned at the memory and thought the horse handler had made the right decision.

The barge was a simple flat-bottomed river boat with a large deck, complete with railing on all sides and a small cabin perched in the middle. The cabin was where everyone would cram if the need arose, such as in times of harsh weather. Kalend avoided it; the smell alone was reason enough, but he also wanted to see where they were going. Even if there was not much to see, he wanted to be sure he did not miss anything. Being on an adventure turned out to be many things, all of them vastly different from what he had imagined, but at times like this, he found tranquility in the journey. So he took these moments to reflect on what had transpired and what was yet to come; this allowed him to realize a calmer state and to open his mind to the world around him, which allowed him to see and sense things he may otherwise have missed. Like that bird high in the sky, to his left, soaring effortlessly along the currents of air, banking and wheeling with abandon. Or the slight movement amongst the trees that lined both sides of the river, an activity that spoke of an animal scared off from their approach. Even the flow of water as it lapped the edges of the barge as they floated and bobbed their way along could also be heard anew, with a more full and pristine melody.

A bend in the river ahead brought a new sound. Kalend shifted his gaze forward and leaned over the railing; this new sound was different, not in harmony with the land, air, and water around him. As they slid around the curve, he spotted something thrashing in the water ahead. He focused his gaze on the turbulence and recognized arms and hands flailing about, slapping the water unevenly. A head appeared in the middle of the splashing water, then it disappeared, only to reappear after a moment. Kalend could clearly hear gasping and coughing each time the head popped above the water as they drifted closer. He also noticed the head was appearing less frequently, the splashing becoming less animated, and then it ceased altogether. Better do something, he thought as he unbuckled his sword and let it drop to the deck, then heaved himself over the rail.

Kalend landed unceremoniously with a splash; the shock of the cold water nearly took his breath away. He swam toward where he had last seen movement, his breaths coming in gasps from the cold. Once at the scene of the last ripples, he took a deep breath and dove. Visibility under the water was dismal, at best, so he reached out with his hands blindly as he kicked with his feet to propel himself downward. Just a couple of seconds under, and then he felt something; he grabbed hold, pulled back, and kicked toward the surface.

Breaching the surface with a gasp, he pulled his prize closer and found that he had hold of the arm of a young woman. He wrapped his arm around her waist and swam on his side back toward the barge. The captain had watched him disappear over the rail and had called to his crew to halt its forward progress with long poles that they buried into the silt of the river. He swam to the gate as Louquintas opened it and called down, "Pass her to me, my young fish." Doing as he was told, he passed along the unconscious woman, then clambered aboard and flopped onto the deck, gasping as he tried to regain his breath.

The captain strolled over to inspect who was brought onto his barge. He gasped and blurted out, "Throw her back in!" Louquintas, who was kneeling over the woman, trying to see if she yet lived, looked up in puzzlement and asked, "Why?"

The captain opened his mouth to respond but cursed instead as an arrow suddenly appeared between his feet. Buried deep into the planks, its feathers quivered as he backed up with a frightened expression. Several more arrows silently rained down onto the barge, killing no one, but some came close enough to draw slight scratches on a few of the crew and several more curses from their captain.

A loud voice rang out, "DO NOT MOVE!"

Everyone froze and looked toward the shoreline for the originator of the shout. Several forms with drawn bows stood with arrows pointed toward the barge; one figure had an arm stretched toward them, and his voice rang out once more, "Do not move, and no one will be hurt; we want the woman."

Louquintas raised his hands above his head and yelled out, "We mean no harm. We saved her from drowning and will gladly return her to you."

The shoreline figure dropped his hand, and the others along the banks slowly lowered their bows. The barge rocked suddenly as several beings sprang over the railing and landed with soft thuds. Catching everyone by surprise again, these newest strangers stood still and glared at Louquintas. After a brief pause and appraising look, one came forward with his hand extended in greeting, "Thank you. We also mean no harm."

Louquintas clasped his hand. "Well met stranger."

Kalend observed this all from his prone position on the deck; he was captivated by the strangers, as he had never seen their like. They stood tall and lean, and most had short braided hair, but what was so remarkable was their skin, which was a mosaic of colors: blue, green, purple, and red, all mixed, so as they moved, their skin seemed to shimmer. They wore tight-fitting forest-colored garb, long leggings that stopped mid-way down their calves, sandals that matched, and short-sleeved shirts laced up to their necks, all of which, when added with their exotic skin, made them almost disappear with the forest behind them. Their eyes were a deep brown and much larger than any human eyes he had seen before. Kalend thought they moved with grace and an assurance of confidence that was imposing.

The Stranger looked down at the unconscious woman. "She will live and does not need your attention."

Louquintas stood, nodded his head slowly, and asked, "How can you tell?"

"We heard her get bitten by the river Shartook. That is when we came running, but you had already reached her. The Shartook bite causes a temporary paralysis of the lower limbs; this is how it normally drowns its prey. However, we of the Barnasea are of hardier stock and can stay underwater much longer than humans. She was not down that long."

Louquintas raised an eyebrow. "Barnasea? I have heard of you but know little."

The stranger laughed. "That is not surprising. We have spare contact with humans and prefer to keep our distance. This is a special occasion." He paused, then continued, "By what name do you go by? I am Weelay."

Louquintas nodded his head and responded, "I am Louquintas. The young man lying on the deck who saved your friend is Kalend."

Weelay offered his hand to help Kalend up. Once on his feet, Kalend bowed to him and said, "Pleasure to meet you, good sir."

"The pleasure is ours, and thank you for saving Juliet; that is a kindness not often seen by humans toward us."

The captain, who had been standing off to the side while watching these exchanges, cleared his throat and snorted. "Yes, it is. For all our sakes, I believe it best if we put you all to shore so you may go about your business."

Trealine grumbled under his breath and then, with a quiet murmur, asked, "Why the rush, captain?"

"They are odd folk, tricksters, and not to be trusted."

"And you have first-hand knowledge of this?"

"Well.....not me, but everyone says so around these parts."

Trealine had moved closer to the captain, all the while fondling the axe handle at his belt. "You shouldn't trust this, everyone; they may be the real tricksters."

Weelay moved and touched Trealine on the shoulder and gave it a squeeze. "It seems you may know of how those of us who are different can be treated with suspicion. In this case, it matters not to us."

Trealine looked up at Weelay and stared at him momentarily, seemed to come to some conclusion, then said, "Your call," as he shrugged and moved away from the captain.

Weelay looked to the captain and, with a smile, asked, "Could you please take us to the shore now? We mean you no harm or distress and have no wish to remain any longer than needed."

The captain nodded, turned to his crew, and bellowed instructions to move the barge toward the shore; they responded quickly as they appeared eager to be rid of the captain's unwanted guests.

Kalend knelt beside the still unconscious woman and felt for a pulse in her neck; he wanted to be sure she yet lived. It was all well and good that these strange folks said she would be fine, but since he had done the rescuing, he wanted to be sure himself. He quickly found that her pulse was strong and vital. As he moved his finger away from her throat, her hand shot up and, with a steely grasp, pulled him back down. She looked him in the eyes and whispered, "Thank you."

Kalend kneeled there, face to face with the woman, and was enchanted by her large brown eyes. His breath was taken from him, and all he could do was stammer, "You're...welcome."

She released him, sat up, and looked around; when her gaze fell on Weelay, she nodded once and stood. Kalend was captivated by her beauty as he looked up at her; long bluish-white hair hung down to rounded shoulders, lean and lithe. She displayed a grace of presence even while soaking wet and having just been rescued. He rose to stand before her, and she gave him an appraising look. Then she impulsively hugged him and said, "Thank you again; you were most kind to risk yourself for me."

Kalend blushed and managed to croak, "You're welcome again as well."

Juliet pulled away, giggled, and patted him on the cheek. "Such a nice boy."

That made him blush even more.

Louquintas and Weelay laughed simultaneously and looked at each other knowingly. Weelay admonished her, "Juliet, don't tease him."

Kalend felt relief pour out of him when he felt the barge bump to a halt along the shore.

Weelay moved to the side of the barge and motioned for his three companions to follow; they all grabbed the railing and, with graceful ease, leaped over the edge to land on the embankment. He turned back to look at Juliet, who had not followed. After a few solemn moments, he firmly asked, "What are you thinking?"

Juliet stepped toward Weelay and away from Kalend and stood a little taller as she addressed the question, "I believe I would like to travel with these folks; it's time for me to see some of the world. Besides, I now owe a life debt to the young one."

Kalend flinched at the words 'young one.'

Weelay nodded his head and looked to Louquintas. "A life debt is not something we take lightly, but I know our ways may not be yours. Would you mind taking her with you? She is of age to travel and can handle herself in battle and in hunting."

Louquintas looked to Juliet and back to Weelay, ran his hand through his hair, sighed, and solemnly replied, "I know of your people, and unlike our captain here, I have an appreciation for your hardships and life. I, too, take a life debt seriously. However, our journey is fraught with utmost peril; she would then be a part of that. There is also my concern that I do not know you or her personally and need to look to the welfare of those whom I lead."

Weelay nodded his head. "I appreciate your concerns; if you know of our people, do you happen to know of some of our customs?"

"Yes, a few of them," Louquintas smiled. "I take it you are referring to a particular one?"

"We are a cautious people and have learned to not trust outsiders. All the more reason this request of ours is odd, even more so for us than you, I believe. However, Juliet is our leader's daughter and is at an age where she would normally seek out some adventure and then come home to us. It seems your group may be an answer to this. So, not only would you be fulfilling something she would be required to do anyway, but she is also the chieftain's daughter and, as such, is precious to us."

Louquintas laughed. "Well, now, I would be responsible for a chieftain's daughter? This does not help your case, my friend; I don't need that added responsibility!"

Weelay shook his head. "There is no responsibility on your part. Our custom dictates that she must make it on her own, that meaning no help from us. If she seeks to partner with others not of our race, we see that as part of the growing process. If something should happen to her, it is all on her, and we would not think anything of you, your party, or your race. It would be as it shall be."

Louquintas appeared to mull it over, then looked to Trealine, who shrugged his shoulders and grunted, "Don't look at me!"

Juliet had stayed silent and unmoving during this exchange, but seeing Louquintas hesitate, she stepped toward him and said, "Have no fear. I will do as you ask and follow your lead. If your wish is that I should leave the party, then that's what I would do."

Kalend also stepped forward and looked at Louquintas. "I think she could be a valuable person to have along." Everyone turned their attention to him as he spoke; he noticed but kept his focus on Louquintas. They stood looking at each other for what seemed like a terminally long time before Louquintas nodded and replied dryly, "ok," then turned to Juliet, "It seems you may join us. Kalend will fill you in on what you need to know after he and I chat, and he will then be responsible for you." Kalend felt his heart skip a beat but managed to keep his composure and nodded his head to Juliet.

Weelay's men had brought to him several items he passed over to Juliet, which included a backpack, sword, bow, and a quiver; as he handed over the last item, he said, "I shall tell your parents what has happened to you. Good luck, and come home when you're ready."

Juliet moved to the railing, leaned against it, and replied, "Tell them not to fret; I will be back soon and that I love them."

Weelay bowed. "I shall do as you ask. Be careful."

Kalend watched the goodbyes as the realization of the responsibility he had just been handed crept up on him. He looked over to Louquintas, who stood off to the side watching him. Kalend straightened his back and made his way over to stand beside his teacher. They stood looking at each other for several moments before Louquintas looked away and asked in a quiet voice, "Do you know one of the reasons I agreed to this?"

Kalend turned, shook his head, and said, "No, I don't."

Louquintas looked at his apprentice, noticed the tall stance, head held high, and felt proud as he responded, "Because it's time for you to take more of a role and say in your life. You stood up and spoke your mind at the correct time after letting me and Weelay discuss it first. And now she is your responsibility."

Kalend, humbled by his words, nodded and said, "Thank you."

Louquintas laughed and put his hand on Kalend's shoulder. "Don't thank me yet. Just take care of her. You need to inform her of what we are about, but I caution against telling her all. Just enough so that she can stay out of trouble. Who knows; maybe she will be some help after all."

CHAPTER ELEVEN

Juliet proved an interesting and fun companion. First, she was about Kalend's age and had a free spirit. It also became evident early on that she was looking forward to this journey they were on, even after Kalend had filled her in on what she was getting herself into. In fact, this seemed to make her more eager about the whole trip. He only told her what he thought was need-to-know information, like the Panes, Twork, and his brother, and some other tidbits. He avoided the whole reason of why and his parentage. She accepted it all at face value and did not ask any prying questions, for which he was grateful.

Over the course of the following two weeks, the barge floated, peacefully and without any further incidents, down the Hessporr river. The time was used to get to know Juliet, meditation, and Kalend's favorite, weapons practice. They would clear a spot in the front of the barge; it was a little cramped, but as Louquintas would repeatedly say, "It's good to learn to fight in close quarters." At first, it was just the two of them. But after one less than stellar performance on Kalend's part, which ended with Kalend planted face-first into the wood planks, Juliet, who had not been able to contain her laughter, asked if she could take a turn. With a bruised ego that matched his face, Kalend peeled himself off the hardwood, moved to the side, and waved for her to give a try at Louquintas.

She placed her bow and quiver to the side and drew her sword to stand before Louquintas; she bowed respectfully and assumed the ready position. Louquintas had watched all this with his usual smirk but bowed in response to Juliet. With both hands on his sword's hilt, he also took a ready position. Juliet moved fast and with purpose right at him; he parried, stepped backward, and slid to the right. She followed up with several quick and efficient blows; Louquintas blocked them all. They continued for several minutes, with Louquintas doing nothing but blocking, parrying, and dodging. At some point, he became pressed up against the railing, and that is when he changed from defense to offense, and he quickly had her in a position of locked swords and hands. Then, using his superior strength against her, he let one hand slip from the hilt of his sword, reached out and pulled her close by the hip, leaned in, and gave her a quick kiss on the cheek. With glaring eyes, she growled and struggled to break free, but to no avail. Louquintas released her and used his sword against hers to push her away. He said, "You are very skilled, but get too close to a stronger opponent, and you will be in trouble." He lowered his sword and continued, "However, even that can be changed. I will teach you how to win even if you get into the same situation again. If you would like?"

Juliet continued her angry glare.

Louquintas shrugged. "My only intent is to help."

Shaking her head and with a long sigh, Juliet said, "Thank you for that. I apologize for my anger."

"Anger can be a good thing if used properly."

Juliet bowed and asked humbly, "Will you teach me?"

"Of course," Louquintas responded with a sincere look before breaking out in a mischievous grin.

Kalend had felt a mild flash of jealousy when his mentor kissed Juliet, but he quickly suppressed it. He knew Louquintas was only making a point, that it was part of the training. That Louquintas was a much more flamboyant version of Tosrayner and meant no harm. Besides, Kalend hardly knew this young woman; why should he be jealous? He shook it off as just a passing moment and told himself not to let it happen again.

The three of them often practiced over the following days, with much cursing but also laughter as they learned more about each other. It was during this time that a strong bond of friendship and respect emerged, forming what would become a lasting partnership. No matter what happened later in their lives, the three of them would look back at these days and understand that this was the time they coalesced into something special.

***** *****

They arrived at Quasar on a warm spring day, full of sunshine and the smell of trees starting to blossom. There was, however, another smell that was not at all pleasant. Kalend could not put his finger on what it was and asked a barge workman, who stood close by poling them along, "That would be the marshes, sir."

Kalend took a closer look around and could not really see much of a difference with the land that slid by on either side. The workman noticed the look and said, "No need to fret, sir. Quasar is not actually in the marshes but just on the edge."

Kalend nodded his head. "Thank you."

The barge came to a halt along a patchy, dark sandy beach. A few derelict barges had been tied down amongst the reeds and left to rot. The shoreline looked like it was being used infrequently; large clumps of river grass threatened to overrun the landing, and only a few tracks from previous landings marred the sand.

Louquintas and Trealine led the horses off the ramp that had been put in place for them. Once the entire company was safely on the sand, Louquintas turned to the captain, graciously thanked him for the ride, and wished him a safe journey. The captain, who had not gotten off the barge, grunted in reply and immediately began bellowing orders for the crew to get them out into the open river and head back the way they had come.

Louquintas mockingly shook his head and glanced over to his companions. "That's just rude, not even a proper goodbye!"

They mounted their horses, with Juliet getting behind Kalend, Whistler having won the duty of carrying them both since she was under Kalend's care. He did not appear to mind. Louquintas remarked that they would need to find more horses, as it was not practical or safe for them to be doubled up on the two horses for a long time. Where they would find two more, Kalend had no idea.

In short order, they found themselves before the town's entrance, and it was not much to look at. The entrance or the town. Kalend was not sure which was more run down. The entrance consisted of two broad wooden beams thrusting up from the ground at odd angles on either side of the road. A wide, weathered board hung precariously between them, and red squiggles ran along its length; Kalend thought they may have formed words at one time but now were lost to times ravages. The whole warped mess swayed with the rank breeze that swept in from the marshes beyond the town. Kalend hurried under it lest it decided to crash down upon them, thereby ending its pathetic existence in this forlorn place.

The road meandered through the town with no clear reason or purpose. Most of the buildings were marginally standing, and stumpy decrepit trees were mixed in between them, giving the whole village an eerie air of desolation. If it weren't for the occasional bundled-up person hurrying from place to place, he would have thought the town was abandoned long ago.

Louquintas stopped one of the hunched-over villagers by riding his horse directly in front of the person. The startled villager looked up, and Kalend could see that it was a man with a worn and beaten face and a ruddy red nose that spoke of heavy drinking.

"Kind sir, do you know if there is an inn here about?" Louquintas asked.

The beaten old man blinked at him with rheumy eyes and responded, "Yes. It ain't much, but it's all we got. Stay on this street till it ends; it will be on your right."

"Thank you," Louquintas said as he dropped a few coins into hastily cupped hands.

The villager furtively glanced around, then peered up at them and whispered, "Some advice for free. This place ain't so safe for good seeming folk as yourselves. Get your business done and leave as fast as you can." And after that cryptic remark, he shambled away with a speed that surprised Kalend.

Trealine hopped off the back of the horse he shared with Louquintas and grunted, "Well, that's auspicious." He proceeded up the street without looking to see if they followed.

Louquintas frowned at Kalend and Juliet and shrugged his shoulders, then hopped off his horse and followed after Trealine.

They found the inn on the right, as the old man had said, but half the roof had caved in, and what was left did not seem very promising. Louquintas told them to wait outside as he shoved open the beaten door and went to find the Innkeeper.

He quickly emerged back onto the street with a disgusted expression and shook his head. "This whole town is much worse than I feared. I don't think we should stay at this inn or anywhere in town."

Trealine, who had been fondling his axe and keeping an eye out all around them, said, "Good choice, I think."

"It's still early, and we can put some distance from this place. I would feel better about that," Louquintas said as he mounted his horse and gave Trealine a hand up. He turned his horse and pushed it into a fast walk down the road leading away from town. Kalend and Juliet quickly mounted Whistler and followed. Juliet whispered into Kalend's ear as they rode away from the inn, "I had the feeling someone was watching us back there." Kalend glanced backward and could not see anyone, but he was not about to argue; the whole place made his skin crawl; there was something off about it. But he could not put his finger on what. He urged Whistler on, eager to catch up with Louquintas, who had put his horse to a canter. Kalend figured the farther they got from the town, the better.

*****   *****

Several hours after having left Quasar, they made camp on the edge of the swamp; Kalend had drawn the first watch and stood off to the side, away from the fire. It was an excellent position to see the camp but yet far enough that the firelight would not interfere with his eyesight. It had been decided to risk the fire as Louquintas did not believe anyone would live this close to the swamp, and even if they did, they wouldn't want to tangle with such a well-armed group.

Kalend leaned against a short, scruffy tree and touched his bracelet, calling out to Hollilea in his mind. He realized he had not heard from her in quite some time and wanted to catch up. She responded quickly within his head, *"Hello there, my wayward brother."*

Kalend smiled. *"Hello to you, too."*

"Where are you, and what have I missed?" Hollilea asked without any preamble.

"We passed through Quasar today and are heading toward Frok camp. It's been an interesting journey," Kalend said cryptically. He realized he was unsure how to tell his sister about Juliet since his feelings on the matter were a little suspect. He enjoyed having Juliet as part of their group and was willing to concede his feelings went even deeper than that; however, this did not mean he was ready to speak with his sister about them.

"Hmmm, What exactly do you mean by interesting?" Hollilea asked.

With a sigh of resignation, knowing full well that he couldn't hide it. While also not fully understanding why he was hesitant to tell his sister, he decided the best course was to just tell her and get it over with, *"....we have another person in our party now. Her name is Juliet."*

Hollilea laughed. *"Do tell! A woman!...and from your tone, this is someone you have taken a liking to?"*

Kalend blushed and, with a little cough, continued, *"Sure....she is an interesting companion and fits in easily."*

Hollilea laughed again, and it sounded like a silver bell within his head.

"Don't laugh," Kalend said sheepishly.

"Well, brother, that is a fine deal; you are off on an adventure and find love while I am stuck with the witches. I should be with you." Hollilea finished with a more serious tone.

Kalend laughed softly aloud, decided to ignore the love comment, and said, *"I know how you feel; I would be happier if you were here as well."*

Kalend proceeded to fill her in on all that had transpired over the last few weeks, including how they came to have Juliet in their group. He did not leave out many details, not necessarily by design, as his sister was very adept at asking probing questions. In short order, he had her up to date on their doings, and she seemed satisfied, or at least enough to quell the questions.

"Sounds like you did indeed have an interesting time so far. But now I need to get some sleep. Call for me again soon, and I'll fill you in on the fun we have been having," Hollilea said in mid-yawn.

Kalend let out a little growl. *"Fine. But I'll keep you to that."*

With the connection severed, Kalend went back to keeping an eye on their camp. All stayed silent and still, except for the occasional rustle deep within the swamp as some creature moved about. A short time later, Trealine came over to relieve him, and he was able to curl up in his sleeping roll and find the sleep he needed.

That sleep did not last long. Kalend was awoken by shouting and cursing and the ring of steel on steel. Kalend reached for his ever-present sword, jumped up, looked around in confusion, and tried to get his bearings on what was happening. His attention landed on Trealine and two men; the three were engaged in a deadly dance of death. It appeared that Trealine was holding his own and seemed to be pushing his attackers back.

To his right side, Kalend saw Louquintas engaged with two other attackers, who did not appear to be faring any better than their comrades.

Out of the corner of his eye, he noticed another man standing to the side. He was jumping up and down while shouting in fury at another group of men to enter the fray from the other side. As they moved to obey, the first one halted with a grunt and surprised expression as an arrow suddenly quivered from his chest. Kalend spun to see Juliet knocking another arrow to her bow. Thinking to help her, he drew his sword with a bright steely rasp, raised it high, and shouted in defiance. As he strode toward the onrushing party, he felt a hard whack to the side of his head. The world spun; he stumbled, felt another blow, and then all went black.

CHAPTER TWELVE

The light was blinding; it pierced his skull and made his already considerable headache that much more severe. He kept trying to open his eyes, but the pain was too much. He decided that keeping them closed was the best option. Other senses picked up clues as to what was going on around him; the smell of food and smoke led him to believe someone close by cooked over an open fire. His ears picked up the sounds of people speaking, but in the hushed tones some men use when it's still morning. He felt his hands tied tightly behind him and could feel them grind painfully with the slightest movement against the rough bark of some sort of tree to which he was bound. And again, the light that found its way to his closed eyes was there but not as bright now; he surmised that the blow to his head made him more sensitive to all light, and as he gained consciousness, it became more tolerable.

Kalend thought of his friends and what had happened to them. Did they make it out? Were they alive? These were the thoughts that drove him to finally open his eyes, even at the cost of the pain. He blinked to dull the edge of that pain, and the light slowly became bearable as his vision cleared; he could then make out the rising sun and white sand that surrounded him. Even with the near-blinding glare of the sand, he was able to make out a fire ahead of him with five men standing around it, three of which were eating from wooden bowls, slurping between soft laughter from jests their fellows made.

He shook his head slightly to clear his vision more, blinked away pain-induced tears, and noticed Trealine and Louquintas tied to other trees nearby. They appeared to be unconscious but alive and none the worse for wear, considering they must have lost their fights. His gaze could find no trace of Juliet, and that concerned him; he hoped that she was alright and just out of his field of view. The horses were picketed to other trees nearby, and Whistler was calmly munching on the small scraggly brush that dotted the area. He grimaced; mostly good news, he thought, but Juliet's absence worried him.

Pulling his attention back to his own state, he found that his hands were tied with rough cordage, and another looped around his chest, holding him to the tree. He realized that "tree" was an overstatement. All the "trees" he saw, and the one he was tied to, were just large bushes with small scaly barked trunks. This, combined with all the sand, led him to surmise he was in the desert, the Ikara Desert if he remembered his geography lessons correctly. This made him smile sadly at the memory of his teacher telling him that the knowledge he had learned would prove useful someday. What a time to remember that.

He tried to wiggle his hands and feel how much slack there was in the bindings but quickly realized there was not nearly enough to try and get them free. He glanced at his captors, who did not seem to have noticed he was awake. Wiggling his upper body against the second cord, he found that that cord was also too tight to move much and that breathing in too deep was an issue due to its constricting nature. Getting free from the rope without some sort of assistance seemed unlikely.

Kalend saw that Louquintas had awoken and was looking around, apparently taking in the situation. When his gaze fell on Kalend, he mouthed, "Are you ok?"

Kalend nodded his head slightly and mouthed back, "Yes. What do we do now?"

Defenders of Myth

"Sit still and wait," Louquintas replied and, after a glance at their captors, put his head back as if to sleep.

That was not the answer Kalend had hoped for, but since he could not see any other option, he leaned back and waited.

With eyes open and head pressed against his bushy jailor, his thoughts turned to Juliet and his hope that she was alive and not hurt somewhere. Why she was not with them was something Kalend did not understand, and try as he might, the only reasons that came to mind were dark ones. Lowering his head, he tried to think of other things, but every time his mind wandered off, it came right back to the fate of Juliet.

It was not too long before the men at the fire finished with breakfast, and two of them came over to check on their prisoners. This was Kalend's first good look at their captors, and his first impression was of men of low means and a hardness distilled from a rough life. They both wore ripped and shredded hose with doublets stained from food and drink and other things best not thought about. Sporting scared faces from previous encounters, the only real difference he noticed was one was tall and wiry while the other was short and stocky. With the swagger and arrogance of men used to having their way, they approached the prisoners with matching sneers.

Reaching Louquintas first, they kicked him on the thigh to wake him up. Pretending to be startled, Louquintas looked up and around, then cursed the two men. That made them laugh, and they moved over to Trealine and repeated the same process, which garnered similar results. Once they reached Kalend, they found him awake and glaring with defiance, his anger over the unknown fate of Juliet, a fire that radiated from his eyes. This resulted in more laughter from the two men, and they kicked him anyway.

Louquintas spat into the sand and asked, "What do you want with us?"

They both laughed some more, "It's not what WE want with you," joked the tall and wiry one.

"Then who?"

"Ohh, we can't be givin' that away, my boy; no, we can't!"

The shorter captor made his way back over to Louquintas, bent down, and with his face thrust close to Louquintas, said, "Have no worries. I am sure he means you no harm," then he poked him in the chest.

"Then you are both nothing but lackeys and only do as you are told; no better than common street thugs!" Louquintas exclaimed.

The tall one grunted at this and replied, "Yes, that mighten be so, but we are paid well, and you can insult us all you want. It won't get you nowhere."

"Well, when are we to meet this person?"

"Soon, boyo, soon. First, we have a little journey to take." They both laughed at this remark and moved to join their companions by the fire.

***** *****

The little journey ended up not being so little. They had been traveling for days; how many, Kalend had no idea, but it felt like a lot as he trudged through the seemingly unending desert. It was all becoming a blinding white blur. He found the heat to be an oppressive mistress, one that beat down on him from above without mercy. An old dirty shirt had been thrown over his head; he guessed it was some form of pity, but it did not feel like it helped much, if at all. The ground upon which they slogged made the miles feel longer, the sand sliding with his every step, moving back half a pace with each planted foot. It was hard to know how long or far they traveled; he had been told it would be a two-day trek, but so far, it felt considerably longer. His hands were secured in front of him, and they were tied to a rope wrapped around his waist, which drooped out before him four feet and wrapped around the waist of Louquintas. This same rope, in the same manner but from Kalend's backside, connected him to Trealine, who stumbled along in their wake. Overall, it was an unpleasant experience, and Kalend looked forward to reaching their destination. No matter who or what was waiting for them, if there was some relief at the end, he felt it had to be better than this.

Eventually, their journey ended, and they came upon a large rock formation that jutted out from the sand. Like some prehistoric mountain that had been partially engulfed by sand and time, it rose above the sand, cacti, and dunes to dominate the surrounding area. Huge boulders were heaped on top of each other, forming a giant mound with scrub brush dotting the land around it. Three of their captors led them off to the right side to a shadowy area that appeared to be an entrance into the mound; the other ruffians led the horses around the left side.

Two smooth rectangular stones thrust up from the sand and angled inward, their tops resting against each other to form a triangle; a narrow-rutted pathway led under them and into the mound. Kalend felt immediate relief as they passed under the triangles and into its shade. A cool breeze wafted over him from inside, and he closed his eyes in pleasure as he took several long, deep breaths of the refreshing air. When he opened his eyes, he gave a little half-smile as his mind cleared, then straightened his posture as he felt strength flow back into his body.

The light faded as they moved deeper within the passage. As they rounded a narrow curve, the light from the entrance dwindled down so that Kalend could not even see his hands by his waist. He felt vulnerable in the darkness and stretched his hands out as far as the rope allowed to give himself some measure of reassurance. After a few more turns and a few swear words mumbled as they stumbled blindly into the clammy walls at each bend, the company found themselves in a large, dimly lit cavern. Small braziers inset into the walls gave off a soft glow, filling the room with just enough light to once again see where they were going.

People moved about the cavern as shadowy figures, with heads bowed; they moved with a singular purpose, not bothering to pause or look up, nor to look at the prisoners or at each other. The shadows glided about in an otherworldly, detached silence. Everyone wore robes of dark color with hoods that kept their heads and faces buried in darkness.

Kalend found the place eerie and unsettling. His instincts were yelling at him to get out, that this was an unholy place. He wished he could follow those instincts, but all he could do was follow his captors and hope. That is when a scream shattered the deep silence. The sound bounced off the rough stone walls, and it rose into a shrill, high-pitched wail that hovered in the air, then abruptly went silent. Kalend shivered at the pain he heard in that voice.

They came to a stumbling halt as their captors stood and, in quiet but animated voices, discussed something amongst themselves. Kalend took the opportunity to look back at Trealine, who looked at him with steely eyes, gave him a small nod, and grunted, "Hang in there, laddie." Kalend turned his gaze to the side of the cavern, and he was able to get a better look at the braziers that provided the barely adequate light. Some type of sand or dirt inside gave off a soft glow that radiated outward, illuminating curved walls that disappeared in the darkness above.

Some decision must have been made, as he felt a tug on the rope, and they were back on the move. They paused as they reached a rough wooden door on their right, at which point one of the ruffians mumbled something to his compatriots. Then, the door opened with a slight screech from rusty hinges, and the companions were herded down a new avenue. Every few feet, they passed grey cloth that hung from ceiling to floor; these appeared on both walls at regularly spaced intervals. Kalend could, on occasion, hear the hushed tones of people talking behind the curtains. He surmised that these were living quarters for those who lived within the cave, but he shook his head slightly; who would want to live like this?

The corridor abruptly ended at a black iron door with red etchings carved deeply into its surface. As they were gruffly told to wait outside, the lead captor pulled on the loop embedded in the center of the door, and he slipped inside as it opened. A few uneasy moments passed before the man reappeared, and with a heavy push, the door creaked open all the way, and they were ushered within.

Kalend found himself standing in a rectangular room with a round table situated in the middle and empty, plain seats encircling it. At the other end of the room, a black-robed man with his hood pushed back stood looking at them. Kalend could not put his finger on why, but he sensed something familiar about him.

"Welcome, friends," the man said in a sniveling voice. "Louquintas, Trealine, and the prodigal son Kalend, so good of you to join us!"

Trealine took a step forward and gave the man a chilling smile. "Since you know who we be, then who might you be?"

The man pointed to himself, "I? I am the man who holds your future in my hands. Which may not be much of one." He laughed and continued, "My name is Lusstail."

Louquintas cleared his throat, grasped Trealine on the shoulder, gave a quick squeeze, and stepped beside him; the whole time, his gaze never left the man at the other end of the room. "Well, I see that our chance meeting in Quasar was not chance at all. Who do you work for?"

The man cocked his head to the side. "That is the big question, is it not? You may know them, Twork and Pouluk?"

"Yes, we are familiar with them," Louquintas replied casually.

"That is good. You shall be getting more familiar with them when they arrive. They are eager to meet you," Lusstail said as he gave them an oily smirk.

Kalend's mind had lit up when he heard the answer to Louquintas's first question. Taking a closer inspection of their captor, it slowly dawned on him where they had met before. This was the hunched-over villager that Louquintas had stopped and asked about an inn's location. Then he felt a shiver course through his body as he heard the response to Louquintas's last question; his mind went numb with all the implications of this meeting.

Lusstail motioned for the guards to take them out and said, "Take them to the cells and be sure they are fed, watered, and treated well. We want them in good shape for when our masters arrive."

The guards nodded their heads and led the dejected companions from the room.

As they moved through the complex, Kalend's thoughts wandered, and he asked himself how Lusstail could know who they were and even by name? He could not believe it was a coincidence they had stumbled upon the man in Quasar, which would indicate he had known they were coming; how was that possible? Kalend grimaced; he had many more questions, but he suspected few answers would be forthcoming.

After several sharp turns and down many similar corridors, all with the same grey stone appearance, they arrived at the dungeons. The cells' doors were stout oak with a small slit at the bottom that Kalend surmised the guards passed food and other items through. They each were set free from their bindings and shoved into individual cells. As he stumbled into his cell, Kalend felt his knees go weak, and he kneeled on the ground as what little light there had been was closed off with the thud of the door sealing shut behind him.

CHAPTER THIRTEEN

Time stretched on, seeming without end. Kalend thought the trip through the desert had been challenging, but this was proving altogether different and, in some ways, worse. In his cell, all he had for company was darkness and questions, with the only respite in the form of food being delivered at regular intervals. At least, he thought it was regular. All he had to go by was his stomach, and he was not too sure about its ability to tell time. Hunger seemed to be his new friend; they fed him, but it consisted of a bowl half-filled with some watery substance best not thought of while choking it down. The guards, who delivered the food through the small slot at the bottom of the cell door, never spoke, and no one came to see him. He was all alone, with just his thoughts for company.

Where was Juliet? That was one of the first. He thought so much about it that he finally decided he had to assume she had escaped because the alternative would drive him mad, especially in a place like this. So, he fervently hoped she lived and was out there somewhere, waiting for them to get free.

He had then tried reaching out to his sister, touching and turning the bracelet, trying to get in touch with her with his mind. It had been to no avail, and he did not understand why it would not work, so he had eventually given up.

He forlornly sat there in the dark, fighting off despair and hoping that they had not forgotten about him. He deliberated with himself over various ways to escape, each more dangerous and desperate than the last. Then, knowing he was starting to lose his mind, he focused on his sister and Juliet. The good times they had shared together, however brief they may have been. During one of those cycles of desperation and joy, he heard the grinding of metal on metal at the door, and then, after a loud clank, the door groaned open.

He flinched back and away from the harsh light that abruptly silhouetted two heavily armed guards. One of the guards grunted, "Get up, boy. Time to go."

He scrambled shakily to his feet and asked, "Go where?"

"Tworg and Pouluk wish to speak with you. Now come along."

He was roughly pushed from the cell before he could ask any more questions. Then he shuffled along the best he could as they prodded him. As his reeling mind began to calm, they arrived before the same heavy door where they met Lusstail. After a quick, perfunctory knock, the guards ushered Kalend inside. Once again, he found Lusstail waiting on him; however, he was not alone this time.

Two men towered over and flanked Lusstail as he waved his hand toward the table. "Please be seated, Kalend," he stated in a deceptively welcoming voice.

Kalend moved to the table, plopped onto the hard oak chair, and stared at the men looming over Lusstail. They both sported long dark purple robes that covered them from head to toe, and hoods drooped over their faces. They stood menacingly with arms crossed and hands buried in the opposite sleeves' folds.

"Well, my young friend, this would be Pouluk," Lusstail said as he introduced the man on his left. Then he turned and gestured to his right, "And this would be Tworg."

As each warlock's name was called, they pushed back their hoods, and Kalend was able to finally see who had hunted him and driven him from his home. They both were bald and clean-shaven, with piercing green eyes that glowed in the dim light of the cavern room, giving an appearance of cat eyes at night in the light of a fire.

Twork addressed him, "You led us on a merry chase, Kalend. But that is all over now. We have some questions for you, and you may either end this easily or not. The choice is yours." His voice was smooth, and the words seemed to ooze like thick mud sliding down a hill.

Kalend thought of all the fear and anger he had been holding since he had first taken flight from the monastery, trying to feed off that, let it all pour through him, then out. Allowing that stream of fear and anger to stiffen his resolve while not letting the rage control him, using it to face his attackers with honor and dignity as his mentors would expect of him. He glared at Tworg with a half-smile.

Pouluk laughed and stepped forward and, with an almost identical oily voice as Twork said, "It seems the young one has some backbone after all. It will do you little good. Answer our questions, and we shall go easy on you. You may even find that we can be good friends."

Kalend stiffened at that and snapped, "The killers of my parents, I doubt that!"

"Now, now, young one, that was a long time ago, and you never even knew them. Besides, I not only refer to you to go easy on. This could also be advantageous to your friends," Tworg paused, cocked his head, "Or maybe your sister."

Kalend felt a chill crawl down his spine at the mention of his sister. The control over his anger and fear slipped, and he involuntarily gasped in some air.

Pouluk placed both his hands on the table and leaned ominously toward Kalend. "We would love to know where your sister is so that we can speak with her as well. Do you know where she can be found?" he asked in a deceptively calm and quiet voice.

"No, I do not," Kalend responded between gritted teeth. He was glad that he did not actually know, so no matter what they did to him, he could not tell them.

"That is too bad. We had so hoped you would be reasonable about this," Pouluk replied. Then he grinned at Tworg, "Didn't we, brother?"

Tworg gave an answering grin. "Yes, yes, we did. Now we shall have to ask your friends, and if they are as uncooperative as you, then we shall cease the easy route and proceed to the....more unpleasant options."

With matched mocking smiles, they gazed down at him as they waited for either an answer or a reaction. Kalend felt his blood boil and felt the need to lash out to prove he was not cowed by them. He pointed toward Pouluk's forearm and the scales peeking out from under the folds of his cloak and asked snidely, "Does that hurt?"

Pouluk laughed, shook his arm free from the sleeve, and held it up so Kalend could get a better look. "No. It doesn't. Do you like it? I am rather proud of it. In the coming days, maybe I shall tell you the tale. Not sure you will be able to focus on the story so well since you will be preoccupied......with other things," and he laughed even harder.

Kalend felt his face flush at the taunting, but he could get a better look at the arm. It wasn't really scaly but mottled and waxy like it had been burned, and the skin had healed over itself in folds.

"Your defiance is commendable but pointless," Tworg said as his brother put his arm down and stepped back.

Lusstail snapped his fingers, and the two waiting guards opened the door and stood at attention before them. "Please take our young guest back to his room."

As he was led from the room, Pouluk called out to the guards and said, "No need to make him too comfortable. As long as he is alive and can speak next time, that's all we really need."

Kalend's blood chilled with despair as laughter floated out the door and followed him down the hall.

***** *****

There was a scratching at the door, and Kalend moved further into the dank cell and pressed his back against the cool, rough wall. Unsure what this new torment might be, he was reluctant to get too close to the noise. All things considered, he felt lucky; the guards had only come a time or two and slapped him around, nothing that caused any serious harm. He figured that in the last day or so since he met with the warlocks, they must have told the guards not to rough him up too much, contrary to what they had said earlier. This did not comfort him much as it was just a guess, and the guards did seem to enjoy dishing out the roughing up.

The scratching suddenly ceased. After a short pause, he heard a muffled curse come from the other side, then a loud click, and the door slowly swung open. "Come on, we don't have much time!" a female voice whispered from the hallway.

"Go away; I am not interested in talking," Kalend replied defiantly.

"Sshhhh, not so loud, you clod!" The voice answered.

"What do you want with me?"

"To get you out of here! You do want to leave, do you not?" the voice answered a little more loudly this time.

"Juliet?" he asked.

"Yes, it's me. Now, come out of there!" She replied in exasperation.

"How do I know it's you? Get in the doorway so I can see you."

"Oohh, I forgot," she said sheepishly, and then Juliet materialized before him.

Kalend's jaw dropped. "How did you do that?"

"I have the ability to go invisible when I want. It's one of the few advantages of this curse we have. It comes in handy on occasion. Now let's get out of here!"

Kalend swallowed any questions he had and followed her down the dimly lit hall. They quickly came before a dark wooden door with a small, closed peephole embedded in it. A guard slumped haphazardly against the side wall, and Kalend noticed a large purple contusion along the left-hand side of the man's face. After a loud snort, the body began to snore. Juliet shrugged. "Louquintas's handy work. I found him and Trealine first and got them free, but it took us a while to locate you."

Juliet opened the door, and they found their friends waiting for them on the other side. It was a quick, quiet, and joyful reunion, and Kalend was relieved to see his friends in relatively good health. Somehow, Juliet had also managed to procure their weapons, and Kalend felt even more relief once he had his sword hanging from his hip again.

Louquintas motioned for them to follow as he took the lead and led the group away from the cells. With Juliet behind him giving whispered directions, they quickly made their way down deserted hallways. Kalend could not keep up with the twists and turns and soon realized that even if he had wanted to return to his cell, he would never have been able to find it. After another sharp right turn and down another seemingly identical corridor, they abruptly halted before a stone wall. Juliet slipped before Louquintas and ran her hands across the face of the smooth rock as if feeling for something; then, she gave a slight hiss and pushed on a specific spot. A section of the rock slid to the side with a skin-crawling grating noise, and a dull white light poured in from the opening.

They stumbled outside, and Kalend felt relief flow through him as he looked up at the night sky. It was cold, and the moon shone brightly, filling the night with its luminous beauty. He breathed in the air and heaved a long sigh. Louquintas stood beside him, reached out, and squeezed his shoulder in reassurance.

Juliet let out a soft whistle that was quickly answered from the darkness ahead. She looked at the party and said, "We need to move on; this place is about to get very unpleasant for those inside. And don't worry about the men passing us."

Before Kalend could ask about that comment, man-shaped shadows bubbled up from the ground around them and flowed stealthily toward the doorway they had just left. With blackened swords in hand, the shadows penetrated the complex.

Another group of shadows approached them directly from their right. Kalend perceived they were also men but covered in desert-colored garb that blended well with the surroundings. Armored and armed, with the strut that spoke of professional soldiers, they came to an abrupt halt before his group. The apparent leader raised his hand, then bowed toward Juliet and said mildly, "Well done. We will take it from here."

Juliet nodded and replied, "Thank you, Sergeant Galland."

Sergeant Galland looked at the group and grinned in the moonlight. "Greetings!"

They each happily shook the Sergeant's hand and thanked him for their rescue. Kalend's curiosity got the best of him, and he blurted, "Where did you come from, and what is going on?"

"Well, that is a long tale that would be better told away from here. Once we reach our camp, all will be explained."

CHAPTER FOURTEEN

The group followed the Sergeant and the men under his command through the starry night, stopping only once for rest and a quick drink of lukewarm water. Kalend was burning to hear how Juliet had come to know these men and how they had found the compound. He also worried about Whistler and hoped the rescue party had found him. When he tried to ask some questions, he was sharply hushed by the stern Sergeant. With lips firmly closed, he trudged along and once again found himself having to wait for answers.

The dawn light was just cresting the desert dunes with its promise of oppressive sultriness when they came to the edge of the camp, and guards hailed them. Sergeant Galland spoke with them briefly, then waved the party forward.

A familiar whistle greeted them as they entered the camp, and Kalend looked over to find Whistler peering over the edge of a broad stockade. Other horses gathered in tight groups within the fencing but largely ignored the group as they munched on bales of hay. He seemed in good spirits and snorted as Kalend waved to him and called out, "I will see you soon, my friend; have patience." The horse snorted again, pawed the ground, and then whirled away as if telling Kalend what he thought of having to wait. Kalend laughed and followed his friends.

Making their way through the camp, Kalend observed a sprawling complex of small grey tents lined up in neat rows mixed with bulkier but still uniformly grey, pavilion-style tents placed at regular intervals. Men gathered around equally spaced fire pits and quietly conversed while eating breakfast. They were dressed in matching armor with weapons at their hips, and most ignored them as they marched past. Kalend was impressed as the entire camp displayed efficiency and precision. A few soldiers did call out to Sergeant Galland with some form of morning pleasantry, and his usual response was a quick wave as he continued to lead them unwaveringly toward their destination.

That destination ended at the heart of the camp, a much larger pavilion than any they had previously passed. Still made with that washed-out grey canvas, this one had bright, colorful pinions fluttering in the slight breeze at three different points above it. Armed guards stood at its entrance. They saluted the Sergeant, and he returned it; then, he opened the flaps and held them to the side as he gestured for the group to enter. With Louquintas leading, they went inside, where they found a cozy room with rugs strewn about the hard-packed sandy floor. A long table stood in the middle with chairs around it, and divans lined the side walls. The back wall had more flaps, which Kalend assumed acted as doorways to other rooms, for the space they were currently in was not nearly large enough for how big the tent appeared from the outside. They were alone, and Sergeant Galland motioned for them to have a seat at the table as he exited through the back flaps.

They sat quietly, and Louquintas winked at them, relieving some of the tension they felt.

A man soon sauntered into the room from where the Sergeant had disappeared. The first thing that struck Kalend was how incredibly tall he was; by far, he was the tallest person he had ever seen. The man had to bow to enter, and when he straightened, he towered over everyone in the room. A large, infectious smile split his face as he surveyed those sitting at the table. "Welcome, my friends," he boomed in a deep, cheerful voice while he raised his hands palms up and toward them in greeting.

Louquintas stood, and the rest of the group hastily followed. The tall man took two great strides and stood before Louquintas, then extended his hand and said, "Well met Louquintas, it is with much happiness that we found you in these troubled times."

Shaking the man's hand, Louquintas smiled and replied, "We are happy to find you, King Dathmoot. We were in a predicament, and the help was much appreciated."

At hearing the name Louquintas called the man, Kalend felt his body give a slight jerk in recognition, as he recognized the name from his studies as that of the King of Touser.

The king turned to each of them and shook their hands in greeting. When he came to Juliet, he bowed extravagantly and said, "Well done, girl. You were true to your word, and here they are!"

Juliet blushed, and her multicolored skin turned a slight tinge of red. "Thank you, your highness. They are my friends, and all I did was do what they would have done for me."

The king laughed. "Be that as it may, I am thinking they also do not have the same....ummm talents you do. Which are quite remarkable, my dear lady."

Louquintas grunted and looked at Juliet with a raised eyebrow. "Yes, her talent was a fair surprise for sure."

Juliet bowed her head and stammered, "I am sorry I kept my abilities from you; it is something our race does not speak much of, and we have found it wise not to discuss it."

Louquintas smiled reassuringly. "Do not worry. It was a good surprise, and I thank you for it!" Turning more serious and back to King Dathmoot, he asked, "I have many questions, like how did you find us? Why are you out here?"

King Dathmoot gently settled into the end seat and motioned for them to sit. "To begin, I shall start with your last question. We are here because I was asked to come, and I agreed to meet some other like-minded people who believe something must be done about Odethane and its current leadership. The supposed King, Kourkourant, and his lackeys, the warlock twins, have been stirring up trouble all over, even into my kingdom. It seems many things are in motion, and so I believe the time is ripe for some change."

The front flaps rustled open, and Sergeant Galland coughed politely. "Pardon me, sire, but those you have asked for…have been sent for."

The king nodded his head. "Good. Please find my steward and ask him to bring our guests and myself some refreshments. Then return here and join us."

The Sergeant saluted and slipped out of the pavilion. Turning his attention back to the company, the king continued, "So that answers why I am here. Now, do not get me wrong; normally, what happens in another man's kingdom is his own, but this whole business with Odethane affects everyone. Besides, the last king was friends with my father, and I think I owe their legacy this."

Again, the entry flaps opened, but this time, an ancient man hobbled in, precariously balancing a large tray between his bony hands. Kalend suddenly found that he was famished when he noticed that an assortment of bread, cheeses, and fruit graced the platter as it was gently placed in the middle of the table. Two more much younger men followed, carrying a large, stained cask, which they plopped in one corner, pried the lid off, and then quickly exited. The old man had shuffled his way through the back flap but soon returned with mugs for each of them.

The King had gone silent during this, and as the mugs were handed out, he said, "Thank you, Fortan, that was very.... expedient of you."

The old man bowed and grunted, "You're welcome, my liege. No need to send the Sergeant after me; I know what I am about."

The King laughed and said, "Yes, yes, you do. Thank you, my friend. Please keep everyone out but the Sergeant and yourself for a while."

Fortan bowed again, and as he exited, he shuffled past Sergeant Galland coming in, who winked at Kalend as he sat down by his side.

The King waved expansively toward the food and keg. "Please, help yourself as we talk. I do not stand much for formality when in my own tent. The cask contains an excellent ale brewed in the mountains of my home."

After a pregnant pause, Louquintas was the first to act; he stood, strolled over to the keg, and dipped his mug. He took a hearty swallow, and as he lowered the mug from his foam-covered lips, he grinned like a cat that had gotten into the cream. This released everyone to either reach for food or follow Louquintas's example to the ale. The king raised his voice slightly to be heard over the gluttonous sounds and continued, "So, as to how we found you? Well, that was pure luck! This remarkable young woman with you is the cause." Dathmoot looked to Juliet and asked, "Would you like to tell your tale now?"

Juliet inclined her head, "Yes, and thank you." Still looking at the King, she continued, "I would also like to thank you for your hospitality. It is not often that those of my race are welcomed with such kindness and warmth as you have shown."

"My dear, it has been my pleasure."

Glancing around the room nervously, Juliet began her tale. "When we were attacked that night, I saw Kalend get hit over the head and knocked out. Two men then picked him up and shouted at Louquintas and Trealine to stop, or they would cut his throat. I was off to the side some, and they did not take much notice of me, so that is when I used my innate ability to blend in. I moved further away and watched as Louquintas and Trealine dropped their weapons, and all of you were tied up." She stopped, took a shaky sip from her cup, and after a deep, calming draw of breath, continued, "I followed them to that cave they brought you to. On the way, the men discussed some camp that they desperately wanted to stay away from as they traveled. They talked about its location and how close it was to the cave, and they were not too happy about it. So, once you were in the cave, I figured they would hold you there for a while, and my best bet was to find help, which meant the camp they had been discussing. If I could not find help at the camp, then I would try to rescue you on my own."

The King leaned in and roughly chuckled. "Yes, they had been talking about our little camp here, and they had every right to be leery of it."

Juliet swallowed some cheese and continued, "Well, that's when I came here. I snuck around some, listened to the people, and realized they were waiting for our group. So, I took the risk and showed myself to the exterior guard. He was quite surprised and didn't know what to do with me, so he tied me up and led me to Sergeant Galland."

Sergeant Galland cut in, "Once she told me what had happened, I informed the King."

The King stood up and went to the cask for a refill and said, "And that is when we hatched a plan of rescue, and I also figured we could wipe out that vile nest of murderers at the same time. So, here we all are at Camp Frok."

Louquintas munched on some bread and asked, "What exactly was that nest of?"

The king motioned for Sergeant Galland to answer, "Our understanding is that it was a jail and torturing facility for the twins. One of our spies in King Kourkourant's court had come across the plans for it. A place to take political prisoners and extract information. We knew of its existence but were not sure where it was. We had conflicting reports on that."

Darthmoot laughed harshly. "It was luck that led us to them, bad for them but good for us. If they hadn't taken you and if this young lady," he pointed to Juliet, "had not escaped, we may have never known of their fortress so close to us."

Sergeant Galland took up the story again, "When we raided it and got you out, the twins were already gone. My guess is that at the first sign of trouble, they ran. They probably knew we had a small army at our back and did not want to risk taking us on. Everyone else in that place either fought to the death or committed suicide."

Louquintas grunted. "Suicide. They were a committed bunch."

"Yes, they were; try as we might, we couldn't save any of them."

The steward reentered and told the King, "Your guests that you asked for are outside."

Motioning that they should be allowed in, he looked directly at Kalend and said, "I know you have been through a lot, boy, and I know all about your parentage and such." He smiled gently. "I also know it's been many a shock over the last month or so, but we have one more for you."

Two people entered as he finished. One was a middle-aged man with short-cropped, silver hair, well dressed, and carried himself with dignity. The second person was a woman, also of middle years, but with long dark hair tinged with silver. She glided toward the table intently, unheeding the stares upon her, for her dark green eyes had immediately locked onto Kalends and, like an arrow, pierced Kalend where he sat. A stabbing shock of recognition coursed through him. He trembled and wobbled to his feet to gawk at her. She started to tear up, covered her mouth with her hands, and stopped before him.

The King had quietly come over to stand beside him. Kalend felt the King's hand lightly land on his shoulder as he gravely pronounced, "Kalend, I am happy to introduce your mother, the Countess Rashana."

Kalend felt his head swim and, for a second time, felt his world shift as he found yet another relative that he never thought he would know, and this time, it was his mother.

The Countess Rashana stood still for another moment and then grabbed him by the shoulders; she pulled him in close, wrapped her arms around him, and whispered his name… "Kalend." He hesitated for a moment, then fiercely hugged her back as he whispered, "Mother."

After a too-brief of a moment, his mother pushed him away at arm's length and took a long, close look at him. "I am ever so happy to finally meet you," she said, then smiled warmly, "You look like your father."

Kalend's mind was a whirling chaos of thoughts and emotions, and all he could summon was to stammer, "How?"

Laughing lightly, the King interjected, "Part of that tale will be told here and now for all to hear. However, we have pressing matters to attend to, and some of them shall have to wait until later. Do not fret, young man; time will be had tonight for you both to get acquainted."

Rashana quickly tidied herself and grimly nodded as she replied, "You are quite right, my lord." She moved gracefully to the table and motioned Kalend to sit beside her.

Kalend numbly stumbled to the chair beside his mother. His mind would not properly focus on the task of walking; putting one foot in front of the other suddenly seemed beyond his abilities. He laughed inwardly and a bit hysterically as a random thought floated by. Was this how babies felt when they took their first steps? But then it washed over him again; his mother was alive! That became his only thought as he sat down. His mother was alive! The King moved back to the head of the table and stayed standing while he addressed everyone again. Kalend did not hear the following few sentences as his mind was still reeling in shock....his mother was alive!

CHAPTER FIFTEEN

The morning air was brisk, the sun was just making its appearance, and a low buzz of voices and noise surrounded the camp as people woke to greet the new day. Kalend sat in a camp chair at the edge of the encampment. He wanted and needed a chance to relax. To unwind, in relative peace, from all that had transpired the day before. He gazed about in contentment; he had never been in a desert, but this was different than he had imagined. There was much more life than he expected. More scrub brush and palm trees, more creatures, like the lizard that crawled out from under a small clump of cacti to his left. He had been told he was on the edge of an oasis, where a small pond off to his right and a large grouping of palms and brush stood tall and healthy. An actual oasis, he had thought they were fairy tales, but here he was admiring one.

The promised chat with his mother had not happened; the meeting with the King lasted long into the afternoon, and then his mother had been called away on some urgent matter by the man who had accompanied her into the King's tent. That man, he had found out, was her personal guard by the name of Havlock, and he saw to her protection, but there seemed to be some other connection he could not put his finger on. He figured that would have to wait for another time.

What he learned yesterday was that his mother had been in hiding since he had been delivered to the monastery, and she has been under the protection of King Darthmoot ever since. A few months ago, King Darthmoot informed her about all that was going on with King Kourkourant and the twins, so she and the King decided the time was right for her to come out of hiding and strike back. The King had been in contact with several dukes of Odethane, who had reached out to him for help, and they had decided to meet at the edge of the desert. But so far, he and Kalend's mother were the only ones to arrive; they expected representatives of the dukes any day.

This meeting place had been chosen for its remoteness, and being in the heart of the Quillick Federation was helpful. The Federation was a loose group of self-governing states with a small central government that oversaw the protection and commerce between those states. The whole thing was relatively new. For only a few decades, they remained weak and isolationist in general. Their primary contact with the other kingdoms, such that it was, had been strictly economic in nature while they refrained from the neighboring kingdoms' politics. Throw in a desert, and you have a recipe for an excellent place to hide a small army.

It still amazed him how life was turning out. There were so many things he never thought he would see. His sister and mother alive, being hunted by a king and warlocks, and finding a remarkable woman he was attracted to in Juliet. When things slowed down, like now, he tried to reflect on it all and make sense of it. He wanted to reach out to his sister and tell her the wonderful news about their mother, but he did not know how to approach it with her. He knew she would ask a few questions, ok...many questions, he thought with a grin. Since he could not answer most of those questions, he felt he should wait until he was able to.

Kalend noticed two people break away from the bustling camp and make their way in his direction; he quickly recognized them as Juliet and his mother, Rashana. In short order, they hovered before him like two angels, with the glow of the morning sun illuminating them from behind as they smiled radiantly down upon him.

Juliet broke the warm silence gently. "Good morning Kalend."

"Good morning to you both," he responded humbly.

Juliet laughed gaily, flung her hair to the side, and turned to Rashana. "See, I told you he has good manners."

His mother grinned and replied, "Yes, it seems that he does." She looked to Kalend and continued, "We missed you at breakfast."

Kalend bowed his head and said, "My mind has been a whirlwind; I didn't sleep much last night and needed to get away to let it cool down." He looked up at her and smiled. "I am so happy to meet you; I have thought about you and father often over the years but always figured my imagination of who you were would have to do. Yet here you are, and I am overwhelmed with emotions, thoughts, and questions."

Rashana leaned over and cupped his face with her hand. "I love you, my son; I always have, never doubt that. It was that love, your father's too, and our need to keep you safe that overrode all other concerns and compelled us to send you away, however much we wanted to be with you."

Kalend clasped her hand on his face and squeezed. "I know and understand that....now. Louquintas has explained it over this journey, and I have come to terms with what you did; the events I have been a party to are a testament to all I have heard. Please know this: I love you too…mother." He smiled at her, brought her hand to his lips, and kissed it.

Juliet gasped and wiped a tear from her eye. "You two are going to make me cry and break down right here!"

Rashana laughed and stood straight. "We can't have that now, can we. Besides, if you start crying, then I will, and we will both end up a mess."

Kalend shook his head sadly and said, "Women, all these waterworks and then worrying about how you look."

With her hands on her hips, Juliet sternly replied, "You, sir, have been spending too much time with Louquintas!" She paused a moment dramatically, then placed a hand over her mouth as she stifled a giggle.

Kalend scowled as the two ladies sat in the sand in front of him. Rashana adjusted her pale blue dress to cover her legs while Juliet, who wore dark green leggings, shifted the sand beneath her for a more comfortable position.

The three sat there for some time and talked. That is, Kalend talked and told them of his life at the monastery and growing up learning the warrior's art; he also spoke of his journey and how he ended up at their current location. For their part, the women remained solemn and quiet, letting him spill out what he needed to. Juliet added a few bits and pieces of her portion of his tale, but otherwise, it was his to tell. Some of this was new to Juliet, but he figured it was time she knew the whole story and the reasons for what they were doing. He found it refreshing and cathartic to put order to his thoughts and then weave it out as if it were someone else's story.

As Kalend wound down, Rashana smiled lightly. "It sounds like a wonderful journey with mentors and friends who helped you along the way. I am grateful for them…and envious."

Kalend nodded. "I am lucky for all of them."

Rashana then asked intently, "So, how is your sister, my daughter?"

Kalend grinned and replied, "She is doing well; last I spoke with her." He then told them both about his bracer and his ability to speak with her. They asked several questions and were intrigued by it but seemed much less surprised than Kalend would have thought they should have been.

Rashana hesitantly asked, "Would I be able to speak with her through it?"

Kalend shook his head. "I am not sure, but I doubt it." He sighed and continued, "I have not even told her that you live or that I have met you. I do not know how to go about telling her."

"There is no need to be scared; this should be happy news!" Rashana exclaimed.

"I know, but she is already unhappy to not be with me; when she finds out that you are here as well, I am afraid she may do something rash, like leave the witches and come here by herself."

After a moment, his mother nodded and sternly said, "As much as I want to meet her. We can't let that happen; it's far too dangerous."

"Agreed."

"But I still think you need to speak with her; the sooner, the better. We shall just have to figure out the best time," Rashana grinned, "and who knows, we may meet sooner than we realize."

Kalend cocked his head and asked, "What do you mean by that?"

Rashana pointedly ignored the question and looked at Juliet.

Juliet stood, brushed the sand from her clothes, and asked Kalend, "Why don't we get you some breakfast?"

Kalend gazed at them both in irritation, sighed, and then gaily replied, "Juliet, that is an excellent idea regarding breakfast!" He figured he could play along with their game, for now, as he stood and offered a hand to help his mother up.

The three made their way back to camp, and just as they passed the guards, something caught the corner of Kalend's right eye. He slid to a halt in the sand, swiveled his head quickly, and saw the swirl of the bottom back end of a dark blue cloak dart around a tent. The ladies also stopped when they noticed he had not kept up and quizzically asked if everything was okay. He motioned for them to continue and said he would be there shortly; they looked at each other, then at him with raised eyebrows. He reassured them that everything was fine and that he just wanted to check on something for a moment and would be along shortly. The two hesitated briefly but then told him they would meet after breakfast.

As his mother and Juliet moved off towards the kings' pavilion, Kalend turned his full attention towards the tent, which housed the guards and scouts as it lay at the edge of the encampment. It was one of the larger tents in the compound and stood about twelve feet long and nine feet wide. Unsure precisely what he saw or the cause for him to look in that direction in the first place, or even why it piqued his interest, he just knew he wanted to find out. Two guards casually stood fifty or more feet to his right; they looked out and away from the camp, and no one else appeared nearby. He shrugged his shoulders and strode over to the tent. He crept up to the corner, peeked around, and saw nothing but sand and dunes beyond it. Thinking that perhaps the cloaked person had slipped inside, Kalend edged around to the front, pulled the tent flaps open, and peered inside. Again, he found no one. How did the person disappear?

Maybe he imagined the whole thing. Even if it had been someone, why should he care? There were many people in this camp, and it was not a crime to be walking around it. But a small alarm inside his head had been set off, and he could not shake the feeling something was not right. Determined not to let this go but not knowing what else to do, he set off to find some breakfast and decided to be more vigilant around camp. Just wait and see if anything else sets off more alarms in his head.

Finding the mess tent had not been hard; he asked a couple of questions to a passing soldier, and he found it centrally located, not too far from the King's pavilion. While he sat and ate a large plate of steaming porridge and sausage, the thought occurred that maybe he should tell someone. The problem was, what would he tell them? He maybe, perhaps, saw someone…that he could not find when he searched? Or that his mind was telling him the whole situation was wrong somehow, but he did not know how? No, he could not tell anyone; he would look foolish, and his young pride could not handle that.

His dilemma resolved itself shortly after breakfast. Having decided to check on Whistler after eating, he ended up on the other end of camp where the horses were kept, which happened to be close to another scout and guard tent. He noticed a man furtively duck behind it as he put Whistler's rear hoof down after inspecting it for damage. His suspicions aroused from his earlier experience; he quietly and quickly made his way over to the tent and put his back along its side. He had a couple anxious thoughts as his back touched the canvas siding. One was that if anyone saw him right now, they would have some awkward questions for him, and the second and more unsettling thought was that eavesdropping was not a very noble quality. He quickly dismissed both as he heard two men speaking in low voices; he crouched down low against the canvas and listened.

The first man's voice was whiny and high-pitched, "Why were you not at the first approved meeting spot?"

The second voice was gruff and hoarse like he had been yelling all day, "Because I had seen that young whelp headed in that direction this morning. He passed right by that tent. I didn't want to risk him coming back and seeing us."

The winy man replied, "I ain't seen no one when I went to meet you there. I waited a while on the side of that tent."

The gruff-voiced man grunted, "Good for you, but I wasn't willing to risk it."

And that answered Kalend's question about why he could not find the man in the other tent. The man must have gone to the other side of the tent, and Kalend realized he had only checked the back but not the other side. Shaking his head ruefully and trying not to audibly swear, he vowed to be more careful and deliberate when investigating strange men creeping around tents.

The whiny man continued, "Alright, never mind that. No guards are within; now, let's get on with this. What do you have for our Lord? Any news of these strangers who came in yesterday?"

"Yes, that young whelp appears to be Rashana's son, so it would appear the rumors are true. They also had a few runs-in with the warlock twins but somehow managed to escape."

The whiny man gave a weak laugh. "I bet that didn't make them happy. And I doubt they have reported any of this to our Lord."

"I would bet not. But someone needs to, and I pick you!"

"Alright, don't get all huffy about it. Luckily, it's not too far, and I should be able to return with none the wiser. I could use a horse; can you procure me one?"

The Gruff voice responded sourly, "Maybe, meet me at dusk at the horse pens. By then, I may have been able to make an excuse for a horse, and we can get you out of here."

Kalend had heard enough and realized that he must now tell someone and that if he did not leave the side of the tent fast, he would be discovered. Looking around, he did not see much in the way of cover close by, nothing but sand and the horse pens—too much sand…and not enough time. So, he decided that ducking inside the tent would be his best option, and he darted around to the front and slipped inside, just in time to hear them say goodbye and leave. After waiting nervously for several minutes to be sure they would not see him come out, he exited and made his way to the King's pavilion. It was time to tell Louquintas what he had witnessed; he would know what to do, or so he hoped.

***** *****

There was much debate as to how to handle the spy situation. Kalend had told Louquintas, who had immediately informed the King, who then brought in some advisors and Rashana, her guard Havlock, Juliet, and Trealine. They all sat around the King's table, well -most sat, some stood as they argued the merits of their thoughts. The prevailing wisdom from the King's advisors seemed to be that they should entrap the men at the horse pen and then see what kind of information they could wring out of them; there was, however, some dissent from this course. A few believed they should follow the spy and see where he went and find out who this "Lord" was that he was to report to. It was Kalend's friends who thought along this latter line of action.

Louquintas stood across from the advisor he was debating with. "It does matter who this Lord could be. If we know who he is, then we can isolate them and maybe even gain more intelligence."

The advisor, Falcon, who wore an elaborate doublet of all black, tight black hose, and short-cropped slicked-back hair, stood with hands on his hips as he glared at Louquintas. "The more important matter is to stop the spy and make sure he doesn't deliver his message. Most likely, he reports to someone within Kourkourant's Court," he replied dismissably.

"We can't be sure that it's someone within his court. We know the twins are working with Kourkourant but also playing some game of their own. And it's this other game that has me worried."

Kalend spoke up. "The spy did mention he didn't think the warlocks had reported their failure of keeping us imprisoned in that cave. Almost made it sound like he thought they were afraid to do so."

Louquintas replied with relish, "Aha...see, that's what I am talking about," as he pointed to Kalend. "I doubt they fear Kourkourant, so who is this Lord?"

The King, after hearing both sides speak their minds and having grown tired of the debate as it seemed they were now repeating themselves, expressed in his deep voice, "I have to side with Louquintas on this. We are at a point where even if the spy slips away and delivers his message, by the time he does, I doubt it will matter much....and that's assuming Kourkourant hasn't already been informed by the warlocks. We will be on the move shortly, and our intentions will be made clear to all soon anyway. So, I say let's try and get to the bottom of the Lord and the warlocks' dilemma. Kourkourant, I know how to deal with, but what we don't need is another player in this mess, especially one we don't have knowledge about."

Everyone else sat back down as the King stood, and they all focused their attention on him. He moved to the corner of the room, dipped himself a mug of ale from the ever-present cask, and then addressed those before him. "We must now make a plan to follow this spy and see what we may learn. I am open to any suggestions on how best to proceed with this."

Louquintas grunted and said, "I will volunteer to follow him, Your Majesty."

The King smiled. "I am not surprised. You do know, your reputation proceeds you, my friend; I would imagine you would find this little adventure fun?"

Nodding his head, Louquintas said, "Yes, I would. But there is more to it than that; everyone here at camp you will need as you prepare for your next move. Let's face it: I am expendable. And I have some small experience with this type of thing."

Juliet quietly coughed and said, "I would like to join you, for I think my abilities would come in handy."

Kalend blurted out, "I will join as well!"

Louquintas looked over at Trealine and asked, "What say you?"

Trealine nodded his head. "Sure, what would you all do without me?"

Dathmoot looked them each in the eye, then said, "Well then, it's been the four of you for a while now; it may as well be the four of you who continue this. However, I am a little concerned about Kalend's part in this, as we know they are looking for him."

Kalend stood up to protest, but the King motioned him to sit back down as he did. "No worries, lad, I have concerns, but this whole thing involves you, and I believe it's time you started to meet these challenges head-on. Besides, you made it this far and have what seems to be excellent companions who will look out for you. So now the only issue is how do we go about getting your group to follow a man in the desert without being seen?"

Louquintas tapped his fingers thoughtfully on the oak table and said, "I think I have a few ideas on that. With Juliet's abilities, that should give us an edge. We can use her as the forward scout, and the rest of us can use those cloaks that your majesties men wore to hide themselves when they rescued us. Could we borrow a few of them?"

King Dathmoot nodded his head. "Yes, of course." He then looked over at Sergeant Galland, who was acting as one of the King's advisors. "How effective are those cloaks of ours?"

Sergeant Galland shrugged. "They are most effective when sitting or standing still. The more you move, the less concealment they will offer, so using Juliet in this way and the rest staying farther back should help, but it won't be foolproof. I would also like to suggest that we stop all horses from leaving the pens; I can make up some excuse and pass it along. If he manages to get a horse, then I can't see the cloaks being any use."

"Can you do this without arousing the traitor or spy's suspicion?" the King asked.

"Shouldn't be a problem. This desert has been creating havoc with the horses and their tack, so I can think of a couple reasons. I will make sure the consequences are dire enough that the traitor will not be willing to risk it for this spy." Sergeant Galland replied with a grim smile.

"Good; please see to it and get some of those cloaks for our guests."

Sergeant Galland stood up, bowed to King Dathmoot, and quickly left the tent.

Louquintas looked to Juliet with a raised eyebrow. "Sure you are up for this?"

Juliet nodded and replied, "Yes. It should be easy enough. I can even signal to you and hide this from the spy; as long as I know where he is, I can have that side of me blend in, but you would be able to see all of me or any part I choose."

Louquintas shook his head in admiration. "That is a remarkable gift you have. Thank you for your help. I know this isn't your fight, and it would be perfectly reasonable for you to get out anytime you want, and we would not think less of you."

"It is my fight now. All of you have become my friends.....and more," she replied with a slight blush.

Rashana chuckled, and this made Juliet blush even deeper. Kalend looked at his mother, then Juliet, and shook his head, knowing he missed something…..but had no idea what.

Louquintas continued, "We should be all set then."

Kalend had a thought and asked, "What of our horses?"

The King responded, "No need to fret about them. They can stay with us, and we shall care for them until your return."

"Thank you," Kalend replied with a frown. He was not too happy about leaving Whistler behind; there was something odd about that horse, and he needed to get to the bottom of it, but he guessed that would have to wait. This also made him think about his sister; he really needed to get in touch with her and let her know what was going on. The longer the wait, the harsher the scolding; he sighed and vowed to contact her as soon as he could.

CHAPTER SIXTEEN

Juliet motioned for them to stop. Kalend, Louquintas, and Trealine did as she bid and hunkered down, groveling as low into the sand as they could while keeping their heads high enough to make out Juliet about ten yards away. Kalend thought the plan had been working remarkably well. They had followed the spy from the horse's pen, where the exchange with the spy's counterpart had not gone well for him; he had not been happy to hear he would not have the use of a horse. The spy's unhappiness had made their stalking much easier. Once he had gotten out of earshot of the camp, he had stumped along irritably, grumbling to himself for most of the way. A side part of the plan had been for some of the King's hand-selected men to watch the horses and the meeting area. Then, once Kalend's party had left, the gruff man was to be rounded up and hauled before the King. Kalend smiled at the image that was produced.

Dusk was deeply upon them, and the little light they had was rapidly dissipating. Straining to see Juliet in the dimness, the three waited on her signal, which came shortly and was for them to stay low and come toward her. They slithered slowly through the sand until they were beside her. She pointed straight ahead and motioned for them to remain quiet. Kalend looked forward and down; he and his friends were lying on top of the crest of a dune; he saw shadowy shapes that looked to be walls or ruins of some sort. The dim light prohibited his gaze from seeing many details. He looked at Louquintas and mouthed if he could see anything; a shake of the head no was his answer, but he did motion for them to continue crawling down the crest toward whatever lay below. With his crossbow in hand, Trealine remained on top of the ridge, keeping watch over their progress.

The companions crawled to a halt as they came to an ancient broken wall, with fallen blocks littering and half-buried in the sand around them. It stood about four feet high with a jagged, uneven top; the mortar between the stones had turned to dust long ago, leaving gaps between many of the blocks. They each peered through separate holes to see what lay beyond. At first, all they could make out were dim, shadowy figures, but light suddenly flared to life from the one shade, briefly blinding Kalend and his friends. As their sight adjusted, they clearly made out two men standing beside a well, the whiny spy hunched over, with his head bowed toward a man with a glowing staff. The man was wearing odd clothes that Kalend had never seen before, dark-colored pants with a shirt with buttons all down it, all of which were buttoned up except the last two near his neck; the pants and shirt were unfamiliar material. Without bothering to look up, the spy said, "Hello, Master. I have news," in a different but familiar voice.

Kalend jerked his head and looked questioningly at Louquintas; this was the same man who had captured them, Lusstail! How could that be? He sounded so different when he heard him conspiring at the King's camp. Even though he had never seen the spy's face, he felt sure he would have noticed some similarity to Lusstail. Kalend had trouble believing it.

The man with the staff nodded his head and said, "Look at me, Lusstail."

Lusstail looked up but still maintained a submissive posture. "Yes, Master," he said in the more whiny voice Kalend had heard behind the tent, but now with a touch of a tremble.

"That is better. Now tell me, what news do you bring?" The Master's voice was clear, deep, and very masculine.

Lusstail told a surprisingly detailed account of the happenings of Kalend's party, which made Louquintas look at them both with raised eyebrows. As they sat there and listened to the trembling whinny voice drone on, it became ever more apparent that the spy had been able to get very close to the King's tent and those in attendance at their meetings. He told of Kalend's parentage and of his mother; the parties run-in with the twin warlocks, even some of their long journey to the King's encampment.

There were a few moments of silence when Lusstail stopped, and the Master pondered all he had heard, then he asked, "Is that all of it?"

"Yes, Master," Lusstail mumbled as he bowed his head.

"Good. You have done well. I have another mission for you. I want you to go to Pleus and wait for more instructions there."

"What of the twins, Master? Have they reported in?"

"That is no longer a matter for you. I shall deal with them appropriately."

"Yes, Master," Lusstail said submissively.

"I do have a couple of companions for you to take along. They will be useful for your next assignment," the Master said as he gestured to the well with the glowing staff.

A thick, chalky mist wafted into the air above the well, as white light slowly emanated from within its confines. The light and mist continued to spew until it filled the darkness directly above; the brume then dissipated into the night air, leaving only a column of light thrusting into the star-filled sky.

As the fog cleared, two ghostly figures slowly emerged. The hair on Kalend's neck began to rise, and a shiver ran down his spine as he watched and realized he recognized the forms appearing before him. It was not a matter of knowing who they were; it was a matter of knowing what they were, for he had seen their like not that long ago. Panes, the creatures that had chased and hunted him and Louquintas in Pleus.

The Panes lept from the beam of light to land before the Master, then they bowed their heads and spoke in a language unfamiliar to Kalend. The Master responded in what seemed the same language and motioned toward Lusstail. They were like the ones Kalend had seen before, but now he could get a clearer view of them, unobstructed from running for his life. Each had horns protruding about one foot from their heads and curled slightly back. The goat-hooved legs they stood on were muscular and hairy; both were heavy in the torso with long arms that reached their knees. Their faces sported long beards, and that is where he noticed a difference between them. Each wore their beard in different styles; one was bushy and unkempt; the other was neatly groomed and forked into two braided ends.

The Master addressed Lusstail, "They are all your's now. They will do as you ask and follow your commands. Beware; however, they shall only follow commands that do not contradict any I have already given them."

"How will I know which commands those are?" Lusstail asked.

"You will know when it happens. Now take them and go; wait for further instructions in Pleus."

Lusstail barked a command to the Panes, and the three of them quickly disappeared into the night in the opposite direction from where the three friends hunkered down.

The Master's steady gaze followed them until they were swallowed by the dark. Then he imperiously gestured to the well, and with a spry leap, he jumped in. The waiting mist and light winked out of existence, leaving the watchers in darkness.

Louquintas was the first to regain his senses; he looked at his companions and dryly said, "Well, that was interesting."

Juliet cocked her head and replied, "What was all that?"

Louquintas frowned. "I don't know, but it worries me. It seems we may have been wrong all along regarding who is running this operation. That "Master," for lack of a better name at this point, appears to have our spy, Lusstail, and the warlock twins under his control."

Kalend asked, "Then who does the Master report to? King Kourkourant? Or is it the other way around?"

"That is one of the many things that worries me. We have more questions than answers, and those questions are of more importance than ever."

All three spun around at a noise behind them, but they visibly relaxed as they heard Trealine's voice right before he appeared out of the darkness. "We got ourselves a good mystery, alright," he gruffly stated.

"Yes, we do. I think it's time we head back and consult with everyone."

"Harrumph...... let's get movin' then," Trealine responded as he stumped back up the hill.

***** *****

They arrived back at camp in the early morning, tired and in need of sleep, and found the base in a state of mobilization. Everywhere they looked, people scurried about, gathering things together, taking down tents, and packing everything on horses or wagons. The wagons were not being overly packed, for they were in the desert, even if the part they were in was hard-packed and not loose sand; it was sand all the same, and the risk of getting bogged down was ever-present.

Trealine, who was sourly watching all this as they moved towards the King's tent, mumbled, "Sure hope they leave at least one tent up. I need some sleep, or I will get grumpy."

Louquintas smiled at the Othurean and responded, "We can't have that! Don't want to disrupt your normal sunny disposition."

Trealine grumbled under his breath, but no one caught what he said.

They found King Darthmoot and a few of his counselors near where the King's pavilion was being dismantled, in a smaller tent sitting around a smaller table. They quickly informed the King of all they had heard and seen, to which he responded sarcastically, "Great, looks like we have another player to deal with, one that is a warlock himself and has the twins as his lackeys."

Louquintas shrugged and replied, "Seems so. Add him to the list."

Kalend asked, "What about Lusstail? How did he escape the lair?"

The King grimaced. "Not sure how he escaped, but it seems he is a master of disguise and sneaky. Men like him are survivors. From what you have told me, it would appear likely that his true master is the one you saw him with last night. Most likely, he had been under orders to spy on the twins. He is one more to keep an eye out for."

Louquintas eased himself down into a nearby chair with a sigh. "We never seem to run out of questions." He picked up a nearby mug of ale before continuing, "My main concern is still the identity of this Master."

"We shall have to figure that out a little later. We have word from the dukes of Odethane; they will not be able to make it. It seems that Kourkourant has raised a small army and kept it hidden in the mountains but is now mobilizing to move over them toward my border with him, near Pleus. The dukes have fielded some small groups of men and are also on the way to Pleus; they are not under their colors, so hopefully, they will go unnoticed." He paused to draw from his mug of ale, then continued, "So, now the plan is for me to send the two cavalry units I have here toward Pleus to meet up with the dukes. All will then move on toward the mountain border. In the meantime, I will head back to the capital and see about raising the full legions, just in case."

Louquintas looked to his companions, then to the King, and said, "I think it best if we go with the cohorts to Pleus."

The King grinned and replied, "That would be good; I was going to ask if you would lead them. Once there, I will have other officers sent from the capital to take over."

Louquintas nodded in reply, "I will be happy too. Besides, I will most likely know some of these dukes and can help smooth the way between your people and ours."

"That was one of my reasons, yes."

"Which dukes shall I be dealing with?" Louquintas asked as he grabbed a date from a bowl on the table.

"Dukes Torano, Curswana, and Thumack"

"That's good, Torano, and I go way back."

Kalend spoke up and asked, "Why is Kourkourant going to Pleus?"

King Darthmoot sighed and replied to Kalend, "They know I have been speaking with the dukes; the spy and his master have done their work well. I believe they are trying to strike first by taking the city. However, I still feel in my gut this is a diversion and meant to delay us or make us look away. I am hoping one or two of the dukes will have more answers."

Trealine grunted and asked, "Any word from the witches or my people? They may have some idea what this is all about."

"No, we haven't heard anything, but you make an excellent point. Much of this involves those who use magic; we need to get in touch with them."

Kalend was about to speak up about his sister and that he could ask her, and therefore the witches, but he caught a slight firm shake of the head from Louquintas. He clamped closed his already opened mouth—the fewer people who know about his ability to talk with his sister, the better.

Louquintas strolled over to replenish his now empty mug. Even with the mobilization and a smaller tent, King Darthmoot made sure to have ale close by for everyone. "I can send someone to inquire about the witches when we get to Pleus," Louquintas declared as he returned to his seat.

"Good, do that. As for getting all my men to Pleus, I am thinking you get to Quasar and find whatever boats you can. Load them up and take them to Renthar Village. Then, send those boats back upriver to any soldiers left behind. They can follow the river until they are picked up. I hate to split my forces up, but I think this will be the fastest way. Once at Renthar, you can evaluate the situation and decide to wait for the rest of the troops or head to Pleus with what you have and leave instructions for the rest to follow. Sergeant Galland will be with you and will be your second in command. The troops know him and have their respect, but they do not know you, and you are not even from their country. That should not be an issue with him at your side. Any questions?"

Louquintas bowed his head, "No, sire, sounds like a reasonable plan, and I shall do my best." He glanced at Kalend and gave a quick wink.

The King caught the exchange and forcefully proclaimed, "Get my men killed over something silly, and you and I will have words."

Louquintas, with a sincere voice, said, "I will behave while in command of your troops."

"Hmmm, you better. Oh, and pick out a couple horses for Trealine and Juliet." The King looked each member of Kalend's party in the eye, nodded, and said, "Now, let's see about the final camp breakdown and get you all on your way."

The King and Louquintas headed off to see how things stood with the camp's mobilization while the rest of Kalend's companions split up to prepare for the journey. Which involved either getting food, a quick nap somewhere, or both.

Kalend went in search of his mother. He found her amidst crates and canvas bags strewn about her tent as she packed up the last of her belongings before it, too, was to be dismantled. She warmly embraced him and said she was happy he was back and unharmed.

Kalend promptly filled his mother in on all that transpired and that he would be traveling to Pleus. She paused, then gravely announced, "I think I will join you. With the dukes on their way, it would be good for me to speak with them. I will send Havlock to handle my affairs back home."

"I hate to take you into harm's way, mother," Kalend responded reluctantly. His desire to see her kept safe ran counter to his need to keep her close; now that he knew she was alive, he had no wish to part from her again.

"I won't hear any of that. I have been in harm's way since you were born. Always looking over my shoulder and staying hidden, it's time to stand up to Kourkourant," she replied with hands on her hips and steel in her voice.

Kalend sighed. "I am glad in a way; I want to keep you close and learn about the mother I never knew."

"We shall have time as we journey to Pleus," Rashana said as she reached up and gently brushed his cheek.

Kalend shook his head to clear the tears forming in his eyes and gruffly said, "Well, looks like things are handled here; I need to check on Whistler and get what little stuff I have together."

His mother smiled knowingly, "Go then, and we will talk later."

"Yes, mother."

"Ohh and Kalend," she said as he headed out of the tent, "I love you."

Kalend stood still for a moment and let that phrase, what he had always wanted to hear from his mother, soak in....then he replied with a tremor in his voice, "I love you too, mother."

As he plodded through the camp to find Whistler, Kalend reflected on what he had just heard. His mother said I love you. His mother! It was still a fantastic thing, one he was pleased about, and he looked forward to learning more about her and telling her more about himself.

He was deep in those thoughts as he came upon the horse pens and found Whistler standing tall beside the nearby fence as if he had been waiting for him. Whistler gave his approval with a deep, loud whinny-whistle. Kalend's thoughts of his mom flew from his head as he noticed something odd. As if on cue, all the other horses in the pen looked at his horse. They stopped what they were doing, no matter if it was in the act of munching on hay or taking a long drought from the water trough; all turned their full attention to Whistler, each watching and waiting. Whistler then shook his head and gave another whinny whistle, and all the horses turned away and went back to their eating, sleeping, or whatever it was they had been doing before Kalend had shown up.

He reached out a trembling hand and stroked Whistler's nose; all the while, his mind raced. Did he see that, or had it been his imagination? He couldn't wrap his mind around the image of all those horses staring at Whistler at the same time; he shook his head and mumbled unconvincingly to himself, "It's been a long night and morning. I just need sleep, is all."

The Horse Master had ambled over and asked if he needed anything. Kalend responded that he did not and said he would return shortly to pick up Whistler. Kalend decided not to ask about what he saw; he did not want confirmation that he was seeing things or going crazy.

Kalend moved off to find a tent that was still up to try and get at least a couple hours of sleep before they headed out. Luckily, he found one that still had a cot in it and asked the soldiers, who were about to take it out and the tent down, if they could wait and let him get a couple hours of sleep. They looked at him with slight consternation and hesitated, so Kalend said, "I know you have your orders, but if anyone says anything, tell them that Sergeant Galland said it was ok for me; my name is Kalend."

"Yes, sir." They glanced at each other and then saluted smartly and moved off. Figuring if this young man would throw Sergeant Galland's name around, then that was his business. Besides, they had seen him in the company of Countess Rashana many times, all of which was good enough for them.

Kalend was too tired to care what anyone thought. He wasn't sure if using the Sergeant's name like that was a good idea, but he had more important matters to attend to, like getting some much-needed shut-eye. He fell into the cot with a sigh, closed his eyes, and remembered nothing else until he awoke.

CHAPTER SEVENTEEN

The conversation with Hollilea was a crazy, twisted, mixed bag of emotions for them both. Kalend had reached out to his sister to inform her of all that had transpired. This included finally telling her about their mother. There was much crying, laughing, and a little anger at some of their friends for keeping this a secret, but overall, Kalend thought he was handling his sister's outbursts well.

In Quasar, they had found a few boats for hire and had loaded up as many soldiers as they could, and the companions were now traveling lazily down the river on a cloudless, bright blue morning to Renthar Village. It had been decided to make only one trip by boat. The horses were left behind to follow along with the rest of the troops; by changing horses often along the way, they would travel a little faster. Louquintas wanted to get to Renthar Village as soon as possible to gather information, and there were not enough boats to ferry both troops and horses in only two trips.

"*Are you listening to me?*" Hollilea exclaimed loudly inside Kalend's head.

"*Yes, yes, of course, sis,*" Kalend responded sheepishly.

"*You better; I haven't heard from you...in I don't know how long, and then you spring all this on me!*"

"I know. It's still all so new for me as well. I can't wait until you meet mother!"

"Me too.....Sure hope she likes me." Hollilea trailed off into silence.

Kalend laughed. *"Wouldn't worry about that; I like you, so therefore she will as well."*

"I hope you're right...Is she close by now?"

"She is talking with a couple of the soldiers."

Kalend heard his sister sigh inside his head and decided to change the topic. *"Everything I told you about the spy......can you ask Yarguri about it and see if she knows anything about this Master?"*

"Yes, I will see what I can find out. It almost sounds like this Lusstail met with a Wiccenda..."

"No, I don't think it was; this guy was much more substantial. In that, he was physically there, or at least he sure seemed to be, unlike the Wiccenda I saw the witches with before."

Hollilea grunted, *"You know they don't like that term."*

"Then don't tell them I said it," he replied impishly.

"Anyway, we are on the other side of the mountains and closer to Pleus than before. I will let them know all we have spoken of and find out what our plans are. I do know I want to see mother...and soon!"

Kalend sucked in his breath and slowly let it out before responding, *"I know you do, but please don't do anything rash."*

"Rash?" she asked with a slight shrill bite to her voice.

"Yes, rash. Mother doesn't want you rushing out to find us. We will all meet in due time, and the safest place for you is with the witches right now. Don't worry; we are coming your way."

"That's all fine and good for you; you're with her!" She paused and continued, *"My powers have grown considerably, and Yarguri thinks I will be the strongest sorceress in a millennium; I can handle myself now."*

Kalend kept his voice level and tried his best to keep it even. *"That is excellent, dear sister, but please stay with the witches. Besides, do you want to get me in trouble? I told mother I wouldn't tell you yet."*

Hollilea sighed again exasperatingly and said, *"Ok, for you, I will....but you better hurry."*

"Thank you," Kalend responded with relief.

"I had better go for now. Talk with you soon......and take care of mother!"

Her voice faded out, and Kalend was alone with his thoughts again. His mother had made her way over to him and stood waiting for him to notice her; he did and said, "I told her what's going on and to see if she can find out anything on her end."

"Good, we need all the information we can gather," she nodded as she peered out past the rail of the barge at the passing dense foliage.

Trealine, Juliet, and Louquintas joined them, and they all stood and spoke of things to come and their plans once they reached Renthar Village, which they expected to do later that day. The boat slowly rocked as the guides polled them along and helped them past the more treacherous parts. Trealine, who had been looking at the sky to their west, pointed and said, "Looks like some unfriendly weather is headed our way."

Juliet squinted in the sunny sky and said, "Yes....but those sure seem to be some odd clouds."

Trealine replied, "Yep, and moving fast."

Louquintas called the captain over and asked, while gesturing upward, "Are those clouds normal for this time of year?"

After the captain watched the clouds intently for a moment, he replied, "No....they ain't," then shook his head. "No, in fact, they are damn right peculiar."

Trealine frowned. "I have a bad feeling.....they are closing on us very fast."

The captain grunted, "I think we should head to the shore....." he trailed off as the first leading gusts of wind hit, knocking them all back a little as they were forced to widen their stances to stay on their feet. "Make for shore!" the captain shouted above the wind as it tossed the boat uncomfortably.

The wind quickly grew into a howling gale, and the clouds engulfed them as lighting tore open the sky. Thunder boomed and crashed above them. The company found themselves stunned and pressed up against the rails, which they grasped with shaky white-knuckled hands, as they stared in open-mouthed shock at the savagery of nature that had manifested around them. The clouds opened, and rain cascaded down in blinding sheets, soaking them within minutes. Rock-sized hail soon followed, which pummeled everyone on board in equal portions, leaving welts and lumps on exposed skin. The captain and crew were left defenseless, and they lost all control of the craft.

Kalend tried to peer beyond the turbulence and caught a brief glimpse of the shore. He made out a cloaked figure standing, seemingly immune to the raging weather, with his arms upraised to the heavens. However, his attention was quickly diverted as the boat made several disturbing and loud snapping noises beneath his feet. The railing twisted and turned in his grip as if it had become some living thing seeking release. With a loud pop, everything lurched backward and then heaved downward as several of the wide wooden planks in the middle of the craft gave way. Water rushed in to fill the space, and Kalend was suddenly submerged in shockingly cold water. He clawed his way to the surface, and as his head cleared the waves, he heard screams come from everywhere at once. Several of the boats had all come apart at the same time and dumped their occupants into the raging waters.

Kalend's sight was obscured by the roiling waters and waves that kept crashing over him, threatening to take him back under as he searched for land. Quickly, he decided to head in the last direction he thought land to be and where he had seen the figure on the shore. Kalend was convinced that the strange apparition had something to do with this unnatural storm. As he struggled against the waves, wind, and hail, he came across flailing arms splashing the water; he reached out and pulled them in close. "Stop struggling; I have you!" he yelled. He found his mother's determined face staring back as she clung to him with one arm and tried to help them stay afloat with the other.

"Brother, what is happening?" Kalend recognized his sister as her voice crashed into his mind

"I don't know...bad weather...think it's an attack of some sort..." he managed to mentally gasp when a wave gushed water into his mouth.

"Hold on....stretch out your arm with the bracer and put your palm facing outward," she replied.

Kalend battled to do what she asked as he juggled his mother and fought the crashing waters around him. Then, with his palm outstretched, a narrow tunnel of calm pierced the wind and rain. He could shift the tunnel with slight movements of his hand and palm and, with only a few sweeps, found what appeared to be a suitable landing. Telling his mother to hold on, he plowed toward the shore. With his arms burning from the strain, he finally hauled his mother up a slick muddy bank onto solid ground.

Once Kalend had captured his breath, he took in the madness surrounding them. Holding up his arm, he felt relief; the tunnel vision still worked. He quickly scanned the shore and found the figure he was looking for twenty yards away. The eerier figure still had his arms and face raised toward the sky as he mouthed words lost to the gale. His head was shaved, and Kalend recognized him as one of the warlocks, Tworg, he guessed from the look of his arms.

Sliding his sword from its sheath, he headed toward his enemy and, with his other hand outstretched before him, kept the tunnel trained on Tworg, *"Sister!"* he yelled into his mind.

Hollilea promptly responded, *"I am here, brother."*

"I see the bastard making this storm through the tunnel; can he see me from his end of it?"

"No, it is one way only. I can also see what you see. I am not sure how much help I will be with him; it is taking a lot of energy to keep the vision stable."

"Not a problem. I will handle this scum myself!" Kalend growled.

"Be careful! He is very powerful; he has to be to make a storm like this."

Kalend leaned into the driving rain, angling his trajectory to help minimize any chance of discovery. When he was about ten feet away, another figure popped into being behind Tworg.

It was Juliet, her sword pointed low toward the unsuspecting warlock's back, and with a hasty thrust, she struck at him. Tworg twisted at the last second, and the blade sliced into his side; he brought his hand down and slapped the blade away. Juliet's sword was knocked from her grasp as she stumbled forward.

The rain, wind, and hail stopped at once when his hands came down. Kalend moved quickly to finish the warlock, but as he did, Tworg looked up with a grimace, winked at Kalend, then clapped his hands together and vanished.

"Damnit, how does he keep doing that?" Kalend shouted in the sudden silence surrounding them.

"I have a theory and will ask Yarguri," Hollilea responded.

"Please do that; it makes it hard to kill him when he can hop away like that."

Juliet, who had recovered and wiped her sword on her wet clothes, asked, "Hollilea?"

"Yes, she saved mother and me."

Juliet nodded her head and looked around. "We need to look for survivors."

They encountered several surviving soldiers on their way back to his mother. Kalend had them all gather along the shore and made sure they would stay together to create a rallying point for other survivors to find.

Louquintas ambled into the gathering, bedraggled and grumpy. He gave Kalend a nod, quickly took stock of the situation, and began barking out orders. Trealine followed not far behind, and Kalend heaved a sigh of relief that all his friends were safe and that Louquintas was back in charge. It quickly became apparent that even though most of the boats had fallen apart in the river, their casualties were exceptionally light. Only a couple of soldiers were missing. Luckily for them, Kalend thought, the storm had not lasted long.

Most of the survivors had landed on the same shoreline, and those on the other side were quickly ferried over by the few remaining floating craft. The barges still afloat were in ill repair and could not hope to carry all the survivors the rest of the way. As it was only a half-day journey by land, Louquintas decided they would carry on by walking.

CHAPTER EIGHTEEN

After making camp outside Renthar Village, it had been decided that they would wait there for the horses and the rest of the troops. The horses would make the next stage of their journey faster and easier over the hills and grasslands between the village and Pleus. Louquintas also decided he wanted to go into town the following morning and see if any information could be found. With the dukes on the march and King Kourkourant on the move, he figured news may have already reached even a sleepy village such as Renthar.

Kalend was busy making other plans. Unfortunately for Juliet, she lost her bow in the plunge into the river and the subsequent fight for the shore. The bow was specially made for her by her people and unlike any Kalend had seen before, so he understood the desire to replace it. The plan was to go to her people and get a new one; they were camped only a half day's journey from where the Barnasea usually lived this time of year. Kalend planned to accompany her, along with Trealine. Their goal was to leave at first light and return just after dusk. The only problem he could foresee was how his mentor would respond to all this.

Louquintas had listened quietly and nodded his head in approval as the pair told him their plan. Kalend was mildly surprised by his mentor's quick acquiescence.

Louquintas noticed the surprised look, cocked his head to the side, and said, "The way I see it, she should have a bow. I have seen her in action with it and believe it would come in handy. She should also inform her parents of all that is going on, this is for two reasons. First, so that her parents know she is still safe and plans to stay with us a while longer. The second is for them to decide if they need to take any precautions to protect their own people."

Kalend looked down and mumbled, "Guess I should have realized all that myself."

Louquintas laughed and then smiled kindly at Kalend. "It's alright. You have come a long way in a short amount of time, my young friend. Much has been thrown at you, and you have handled yourself well."

"Thank you."

"Still, you are correct; you should have thought the whole mission through, BUT this is a step forward. You are young, have learned much, and will continue to grow."

Kalend bowed and continued, "We shouldn't be long."

"I am glad, however, that you're taking Trealine with you."

Now, it was Kalend's turn to laugh. "I at least knew you probably wouldn't have allowed us to go alone."

Louquintas snorted. "AND... with that, you are correct. Now go get some sleep and get ready to leave at first light. I expect you back by tomorrow evening."

Kalend and his friends were up and on the move the following morning before dawn. They wanted to get an early start to give them time to return; Kalend knew Louquintas would send others after them if he was not back at a reasonable hour. He did not want that to happen.

The first couple of hours slid by peacefully as they journeyed west along the riverbank. Juliet led the way with Kalend beside her; Trealine followed behind and kept a watchful eye. They felt secure enough to speak in normal tones and discuss the upcoming reunion with Juliet's family and people.

"My parents are not so much kings or queens, but rather, they are leaders of the community," she explained. "Everyone has a place and duty to help each other; we are a very tight group."

"How many of you are there?" Kalend asked.

"Only about one hundred or so."

Kalend reflected on this a moment and asked, "How did you get your abilities?" then quickly realized that that might not be a polite question. "I don't mean to pry, and you don't need to answer."

Juliet laughed quietly. "No, no. It's ok. My understanding is that many years before I was born, everyone had been part of a village. Two outsiders, magicians, showed up one day and got into a fight. The resulting release of energies leveled the town; many died, and those that survived ended up as we are. We call it the time of The Change."

"What were the magicians fighting over?"

Juliet shook her head. "I don't know; I have never heard. After the changes, many went off to find their way in the world and lick their wounds. Some stayed and tried to rebuild. Neither option went well. Some of those who had gone off…came back, for the outside world did not trust them and mistreated them. Those who had stayed behind found they could no longer trade or deal with other villages for the same reason. So, it was decided to leave the village life and wander in search of a new home away from anyone else."

Trealine spoke up from behind them, "Sensible choice. We have found it best to stay away from others. Keeping to ourselves has kept my people safe."

"Yes, it has worked out well."

Kalend nodded in understanding; from the suspicion he had seen from the boat captain when they had found her, it made sense.

"Eventually, my people settled among the forest and hills along this river. We have a few places we call home now; we have worked with our abilities and can blend in with our surroundings."

Juliet stopped and looked around. "We need to turn South; it shouldn't be far now."

They trekked into the thick woods along a narrow game trail; tall pines mingled with broad, venerable oaks created a green leafy canopy that blocked the sky. The sighing of a slight breeze wafted amongst the boles, making them sway and creak; they continued in silence, each wrapped in their own thoughts. Kalend shook his head about the sad tale Juliet had told. It made him angry that people could be so suspicious and treat others who had gone through so much with such vileness. And what could the magicians have been fighting over to release so much energy? He guessed he may never know.

Juliet suddenly stopped along the trail. She appeared to listen with a cocked head and motioned for them to stand still and be quiet. Kalend heard nothing and, after a few moments, was about to ask why they had stopped when three figures stealthily materialized from the trees ahead.

All were dressed in forest-colored garb with hoods pushed back and falling locks of hair that framed their faces, revealing similar features that marked them as kin to Juliet.

"Welcome home, Juliet," the lead figure said solemnly.

Kalend peered closer at the one who spoke and realized it was the same Barnasea that had led Juliet's rescue on the barge. He tried to remember a name as he moved to shake the offered hand.

"Well met, Weelay." Kalend smiled inwardly; the name had popped into his head just in time. "It is a pleasure to see you again under much less stressful circumstances." He said with confidence. He shook hands and looked Weelay in the eye.

"Tally..hoo, the young sapling that saved our Juliet!" Weelay exclaimed. "It appears the sapling has grown much in the short time since our last encounter," Weelay continued with a broad smile.

Trealine grunted, shook his head, and said, "Maybe, but he still has a ways to go till he becomes an oak."

Juliet giggled.

Kalend frowned and was at first annoyed but then laughed aloud, a little too loudly, in appreciation of the quip.

Juliet briefly informed Weelay of their mission, who nodded and motioned for them to follow as he slipped back into the forest. They followed silently, sliding among the trees like ghosts; they made quick time on their way to the home of the Barnasea. The camp, or home, was nestled in a small clearing of small trees and brush, made of an organized and neat set of structures. The living quarters consisted of heavy canvas coverings over a shell of upright wooden poles that fanned out to form a low dome. Smoke rose lazily in tiny tendrils through holes at the center of each. The structures blended in with the forest as the canvas was painted to melt into the greenery around it. They were big enough for a family of four or five but small enough to break down and move when needed. When Kalend inquired about the shell when they moved, he was told those were left behind. They had four or five locations they called home, and each had the bare bones for the canvas tents. When they moved to the following site, each structure would be evaluated to find if any poles needed replacing.

Weelay guided them along a beaten path that meandered around a couple acres and ended at a larger but similar domed hut. He pulled back the entry flaps and bade them enter.

Taking a moment for his eyes to adjust to the dimness inside, Kalend found a cozy circular space with a large brazier at its center; though not cold out, a few coals glowed within and radiated a comfortable heat. A long polished pine table ran along the right canvas wall, two unlit candelabra graced its top, and several low-backed chairs were pulled in tight to each side—groups of rich brown leather couches and chairs on his left formed seating areas. Hanging from the ceiling were several globes from which a soothing light emanated and filled the room; Kalend had never seen their like and could not fathom what powered them.

A man and woman stately approached from the far side with warm smiles. Juliet squealed and rushed to embrace them. She was engulfed in a bear hug by both, and the three stood holding each other, silently reconnecting, as Kalend glanced around the room in some embarrassment. Trealine stood stoically off to the side and intently studied one of the globes of light.

After several long minutes, the three disentangled themselves, and with Juliet between them, they turned to Kalend and Trealine. The man stepped forward with a frown and said in an ominous voice, "So, you are the ones who took my child away from me."

Kalend grimaced and opened his mouth to angrily respond, but Trealine beat him to it, "Nah, look at me. Do I look big enough to steal anyone?" he said with a calm air.

Kalend's mouth fell open at the uncharacteristic jovial response from his friend.

Juliet's voice rang out in laughter at both the audacious question and the look on Kalend's face. Once she regained her composure, she introduced the man as her father, Saarphis, who was now smiling warmly with no hint of anger. He shook Kalend's hand vigorously. "Welcome! It is good to meet you all."

The party was quickly introduced to Saarphis and Juliet's mother, Charree. Kalend smiled and felt grateful he had been saved from embarrassment by Trealine's quick reaction to their host's opening remarks. His hasty anger could have led to an uncomfortable situation over a comment he should have seen as a jest.

They all sank into seats in one of the pods of couches and proceeded to talk amicably about the group's adventures. Juliet led the chat and provided a fair account of all that had transpired since she had left her people.

Kalend took stock of his hosts as the story unfolded. Saarphis had short salt and pepper hair and deep blue eyes that seemed to change depending on how the light was hitting his face, and he wore a loose-fitting white robe. His wife had long reddish hair, which shimmered in the odd lighting from the globes, and wore a long blue gown that matched her eyes.

Overall, they both seemed easygoing and clearly enjoyed seeing and hearing from their daughter.

As Juliet was wrapping up, a guard dressed in curious leather armor that seemed to heighten his natural camouflage came in and whispered into Saarphis ear. Who then nodded and loudly proclaimed so those around could hear, "By all means, please let him in." The guard walked back to the opening flaps, held them open, and motioned for someone to come in.

The light from outside was considerably brighter and bathed the new person from behind, making it difficult for the companions to see who came through the entrance. The silhouette strolled forward, and as the flaps of the doorway fluttered close, cutting off the backlight, Kalend gave a startled grunt of recognition. Jarlwo stood before them, ginning with mirth at the looks on their faces.

***** *****

Kalend was in a reflective mood as the group made their way back to Renthar Village. They had already reached the Hessporr, and the steady sound of its water rushing along beside them made him feel a sense of contentment. The day was quickly morphing into dusk, and small dusty colored clouds filled the darkening sky as his mind turned to all that he had learned in the short time with Juliet's parents. He wished he could have stayed longer, but the day had been drawing on, and he was not about to be late getting back. Their main goal had been accomplished; Juliet had a new bow. His thirst to hear more from Jarlwo would have to wait for another time.

Jarlwo, what an enigma, Kalend thought with a grimace. He shows up out of the blue and in unexpected places. First to save his life and those of his companions. And now at Juliet's parents' hut. Then he proceeded to tell a fantastic tale, where his disfigurement and the Barnaseas' camouflage abilities are all connected and his fault. Kalend could scarcely believe the account.

As Jarlwo had told it, he had had several encounters with the twins over the years. One such incident had been near a small village forty years ago; that village happened to have been Juliet's people before the time of The Change. Kalend tried not to think that Jarlwo did not look nearly old enough for this to have taken place that long ago. Kalend had to believe him; he had seen and heard too many things in the last few months he once would have considered outlandish but now seemed normal. So Jarlwo, looking like he is thirty years old, even with the scars, but who was around fighting the twins forty years ago, should not really bother him.

The incident landed Juliet's people in the middle of a wizard's duel, which unleashed powers that changed the ones involved and the innocents in the village. Jarlwo had been tracking and following the twins for some time, believing that they had been the cause of many deaths over the years, but no one had any proof. He had taken it upon himself to discover their secrets. With a brashness of youth, he had thought himself beyond his opponents' powers; he learned otherwise, to his and many others' detriment. Kalend had been surprised to hear the heartfelt remorse in the ordinarily stoic man as he had told that part of the story.

Jarlwo had not known, but the twins had been on to him, lured him out to the field by the village, and attacked him. Working in tandem, the twins timed their spells so that they came at him one after the other. Powerful as Jarlwo was, it was still two versus one. In a desperate bid to obliterate the twins, he gathered his remaining strength and hurled a powerful spell toward them. The twins had sensed the desperation before the power was unleashed and hoped to destroy their opponent with quick, powerful magic of their own. Together, and at the same time, they sent a wave of energy at Jarlwo. They were not fast enough. The two spells collided in front of Jarlwo and exploded, sending magical shockwaves coursing through the village and land around them. The warlocks, people in the town, houses, and trees were all knocked down; the blast should have killed everyone. The twins and Jarlwo still had their defensive spells wrapped around them, and as tattered as the shielding was, it had held enough to allow them to survive.

It did leave Tworg with his arm mangled, twisted, and deformed and Jarlwo's face in its current condition.

The people of the village, on the other hand, had no such protection. The blast should have meant their end. Jarlwo still did not know what allowed them to survive; he had some theories but did not share them. Nevertheless, it had left the people bruised, battered, and in shock.

It was not until a few days later that the people found out that something had changed about themselves. They would talk and work together in groups to repair the damage done to their homes when one of them suddenly disappeared. The others could still hear them talking but could not see the person with the voice. Over many days, this continued, and they grew scared that they were all cursed. Jarlwo had still been at the village, recovering from his injuries in a makeshift shelter, for even though they had been mad at him, the villagers had taken pity and nursed him back to health. The elders came to him and told him about the occurrences, hoping for some answers. The magician detected the changes and told them to view it as a gift, but deep down, he was distraught and saddened that he had caused this.

In time, the people learned to hone their new abilities and use them to help themselves. Eventually, it became a part of who they were, and they accepted the changes. Jarlwo felt responsible and kept in touch with them, giving aide and guidance when he could. Kalend and his friends had just happened to visit during one of those times. His other responsibility, he felt, was to keep the Barnasea updated on the news occurring out in the wider world, which he then proceeded with before the companions left.

After hearing all that Jarlwo and Kalend's group told him, Saarphis said that his people would be on the move shortly, but if there was any way they could aid them, he would. Trealine had thanked him for his gracious offer and said they would keep in touch.

Kalend was still mulling over all he had heard as they passed the guards stationed on the outskirts of their camp. It was immediately apparent that the rest of the troops had arrived, and recently. Soldiers hurried about with various tasks while Sergeant Galland barked orders and managed the settling of the new troopers. Without pausing or lowering his bellowing, he had taken note of Kalend's party arriving and made his way over to them. "Welcome back, laddie," he gravely greeted them.

"Thanks, looks like we have a full company again," Kalend remarked.

Sergeant Galland nodded. "Yes, I will get them all settled soon; tomorrow morning, we will have the full force ready to ride."

Kalend looked about and asked, "Is Louquintas back yet?"

"Not that I have seen, but this lot has kept me busy the last hour or so."

"Ok, thanks. I shall look for him at his tent."

Sergeant Galland waved goodbye to them and stumped off, snapping out more orders as he went.

CHAPTER NINETEEN

With evening in full swing and darkness closing in fast, they came to a halt about two miles outside the city of Pleus. Louquintas directed that camp be set up behind a couple of the more significant hills, and preparations were made to stay for a few days. He also dispatched a few scouts to find provisions for the horses and men; they were to do so quietly and with limited contact with the city. There were plenty of farms scattered about that should house enough for their needs without the risk of alarming the town.

The trip through the grasslands and hills from Renthar Village had been uneventful. Slower going than his last time through the area, Kalend thought, but that was to be expected since he was returning with a much larger group and no longer fleeing for his life. His life was still in danger; of that, he was still assured. The big difference on his return trip was that he was coming to confront that danger -and end it, or so he hoped.

With the wind gently blowing his unruly hair into his face, Kalend stood beside Juliet, and they discussed, with some disagreement, the possibility of making a trip to Pleus. Both wanted to find Lusstail and see what he was up to, thinking that it could not be anything good and would be helpful to know what. Juliet shook her head. "It is too dangerous; he knows what you look like and has most likely given your description out to everyone he knows. The best thing for you to do…is wait here. I can blend in and not be seen if needed."

Kalend sighed and mumbled, "I knew you were going to say something like that."

"Can't say I am wrong, can you?" Juliet replied with her hands on her hips.

"No. But that doesn't mean I like it."

Louquintas strolled up in time to catch that last remark and asked, "Don't like what?"

Juliet poked Kalend in the chest, saying, "He wants to go into Pleus and find Lusstail; I told him I was the better choice."

"Hmm, yes, you would be…but I say we all go," Louquintas replied with a grin.

"Now that's a plan I like!" Kalend responded with a wink to Juliet.

"Don't get too excited; we will be going after dark and straight to the Punchers Inn to talk with Jacob," Louquintas warned them both.

"What about Lusstail?" Juliet asked.

"That's why we will speak with Jacob at the inn. He will know things, and we can tell him to keep his ears open for us. Since I wasn't able to get much information while in Renthar, it's become more important to find out what's going on while we have been out of touch. So, both of you go get ready and wear dark clothes. I will meet you at the edge of the camp in one hour."

The group parted ways with assurances to meet back at the appointed time. Kalend went to find his mother. He had a favor to ask regarding something that had bothered him of late. He quickly found her in her tent, sipping tea and nibbling on a biscuit. After filling her in on the companions' plans, he changed subjects and asked, "Could you keep an eye on Whistler while I am gone?"

"Yes, but wouldn't the soldiers in charge of the horse pens be a better choice?"

"They would be fine. But there is something peculiar about that horse, and I need to know what. Please just check in on him and see if he acts weird."

"Weird? How does a horse act weird?"

"I am not sure, but you will know if you see it.....Please?"

She nodded and gravely answered, "I will look in on him, my son, and report if he acts unusually in any way."

Kalend sighed with relief. "Thank you."

*****   *****

Night had fallen. Flickering shadows danced over the dirt and leaf-covered earth between the evenly lit fires placed around the camp. Soldiers sat huddled around them as they settled in with their drinking horns and loudly boasted tales of past glory. A cloaked shade moved sedately among them, and with head bowed and buried under a think wool hood, it strode stealthily to the edge of the camp. Staying clear of the guards, it furtively glanced both right and left before gliding in the direction of the horse pens. Arriving at the temporary fence, the shadowy form silently observed the horses for several moments. Then, a delicate hand slid out from a billowing sleeve and made a small gesture toward the animals. A lean black and brown horse looked up curiously before making its stately way to the fence, where it stuck its head over the wooden rail and gave a low whinny whistle. The small hand rested atop his head and gently stroked his falling mane.

"It is almost time," the figure said in a quiet voice.

The horse responded with another low whinny-whistle.

"You must protect him; there is much that rides on his shoulders."

The horse nuzzled the cloaked hand a moment, then turned away to join the others of its kind. The shadow's gaze lingered admiringly on the horse, then bowed its head and started to shake as if crying. The horse looked up one more time and gave a louder whistle, to which the figure responded, "I know, I know."

*****   *****

Pleus was quiet as darkness, and a light fog enveloped the sleeping city. Not all was as serene as it first appeared, Kalend thought, as he heard a sharp skittering reverberate from a side alley. It could have been an animal, but he knew better; those who lived on the less legal side of life prowled the evening.

His group had been left alone; they were only three but heavily armed, and Louquintas led the way with a confidence and swagger that would scare off all but the most foolhardy or desperate.

Having already visited Jacob at the Punchers Inn, they were on their way to see another man Jacob had recommended they speak with. This person supposedly knew much of what went on in the city and the surrounding area and had ears everywhere. The hope was that he might have some information on how to find Lusstail or at least find out what he was up to.

They turned down another alleyway, which came out to the main thoroughfare. Louquintas stopped to peer around and then led them to the left. Shuttered shops lined both sides of the street, and a small sliver of light peeked out from a few windows and door frames, which, combined with the close quarters and fog, produced an eerie tunneling effect that made Kalend shiver as he crept ahead.

A blob of hazy light emanated at the end of the foggy tunnel, gradually revealing a three-story building with elegant oil lamps blazing from posts on either side of double oaken doors. As they crept closer, Kalend made out the broad face of a lion embossed into the wood. It covered the center of the two doors, and a seam ran down the middle of the face where the doors met. Underneath the lion was written, in stark black paint, "Lion Head Den of Enlightenment."

Louquintas paused outside the doors, glanced back at his companions, and whispered, "Stay together in here. Let me do the talking and keep your eyes open." He then pulled the right door open just enough to allow entry into the building.

"Welcome, gentlemen, to the Lion Head Den." A pleasant, baritone voice greeted them right as they entered.

Louquintas turned in the direction of the voice and evenly replied, "Hello and greetings."

A tall, slim man stood before them; he was smartly dressed in what Kalend knew to be high fashion for the city. A white buttoned-down silk shirt covered by a dark brown vest enveloped his torso while tight-fitting black pants clung to his legs. He had black hair, cut short and cleanly kept, and looked freshly combed. He had seen others dressed accordingly, and they always seemed to have a high opinion of themselves; he frowned as his first impression of the man before them was not high.

"I am Parseen, and I am this evening's greeter and host. In what way may I assist you, gentlemen?" He looked to Juliet and bowed. "And lady, of course."

Juliet smiled broadly and bowed in return.

Louquintas stepped forward and asked, "We are looking for a storyteller, one who is known to spend much of his time here."

Parseen pursed his lips. "We have many gentlemen here. Most do not like to be bothered by those they do not know. I have worked here many years and must say that you three are unfamiliar. My other unofficial duty is as gatekeeper; only those who are members or guests of members are allowed entry to the rooms beyond."

"We were told to say that we come from Jacob at the inn and to ask for the ol' story-tellin' hack," Louquintas replied with a grin.

Parseen grimaced. "That is most unseemly. Wait here, and I will be back shortly." He turned smartly toward a corridor to their left, and with a stiff back and haughty air, he walked away from the trio.

Louquintas chuckled. "Guess I upset the poor fellow."

Kalend shook his head in irritation. He then looked around the small room and decided it must be a waiting area. One richly appointed chair sat off to the side, and dimly lit corridors fed into the waiting room from each direction. He moved over to a wall and, with arms crossed, calmly leaned against it to await the gatekeeper's return.

As time passed, Kalend became nervous over the wait. His mind started wandering, and he came up with several ugly possibilities for why it took so long. He looked over to Louquintas for some reassurance but found him seated in the chair with eyes closed; he looked like he did not have a care in the world. Sometimes, his mentor's casual demeanor really irritated him, Kalend thought as he sighed audibly.

"Now, now, my dear boy, you must learn to not fret so. Relax, calm your mind, let go of the ugly thoughts," Louquintas said with his eyes still closed.

"I know. I know," Kalend grumbled and sighed again, but this time to release pent-up tension.

"We have been through much, my young friend, and you have grown, but you must keep up with your meditation. The deeper calmness you reach through meditation, you will then be able to call upon whenever you need it."

Humbled by his mentor's words, Kalend nodded and responded, "You are right….and I need to be more like you."

Louquintas shook with laughter as he peeked over at his apprentice. "You don't need to be exactly like me. Just the good parts."

With a raised eyebrow, Juliet teasingly murmured, "What good parts."

Before Louquintas could respond, Parseen sashayed back into the waiting room and curtly informed them that they should accompany him to the library room. Then he turned his back on them and, not bothering to check if his guests followed, strode back down the corridor he had just come from.

As they hurried down the corridor after their guide, Juliet stopped abruptly beside a non-descript door on their left. She cocked her head as if listening to something and stood there a moment as Kalend and Louquintas looked at her questioningly. She raised a finger to her mouth for them to stay mute. Then, after a few moments, she shook her head, moved close beside them, and whispered, "I thought I sensed or felt something for a moment. It was there briefly, then gone."

Louquintas gazed at her intently momentarily and asked, "What do you think it was?"

"I am not sure. Some Barnasea can sense or feel when magic is around, usually only when it is either strong or related to our gift. But it is hit or miss with each person. I usually do not have the ability to sense anything. So maybe I imagined it."

Louquintas paused thoughtfully, then replied, "If you sense it again, let us know immediately."

Parseen was waiting for them before a door further up on their right and did not say a word as they caught up with him. With a stern look of disapproval, he opened the door for them to enter and then swiftly closed it on their backs, leaving them on their own on the other side.

The library room was exactly that, a room filled from floor to ceiling with bookshelves built into the walls and filled with books and scrolls. A spacious fire crackled within a fireplace that dominated half the wall straight ahead of the group. Leather couches and chairs filled most of the room, clustered into pods with end tables between each seating and oil lamps that radiated a pleasant glow; Kalend thought the setting was ideal for a place of contemplation and learning. Other tables, shorter and square, sat before the couches, and most of those held an array of disheveled books.

Hazy smoke filled the room as the pungent odor of tobacco flooded the companions' nostrils. A few patrons lounging about the room held cigars of varying sizes and colors; they filled the room with many different aromas with each exhale. Kalend had only seen a couple people smoke in his life, and none of them were people he knew well. His mentors had always frowned on the practice, and he had never been given a satisfactory answer as to why they disliked the practice. However, despite his teacher's nay-saying, he enjoyed the smell that wafted from the burning sticks and thought he might want to try a cigar in the future.

Defenders of Myth

Louquintas motioned for them to follow as he strolled over to a group of couches that held three men, one of whom appeared ancient to Kalend's young eyes. The ancient one beckoned them to sit down as he spoke in a gravelly voice for those sitting with him to leave. All of whom hastily stood and bowed respectfully to the elderly man and walked away without a word.

"What may I do for you, my young friends?" the gravelly-voiced old man asked. His voice matched his appearance, bald-headed and wrinkled skin, and a long beak of a nose; Kalend noted his facial features resembled a hawk. Dressed in a flowing black robe, he sat with one leg crossed over the other as he easily assessed each of them. Old he was, ancient even, but there was a vital spark of life behind his dark blue eyes. His hand held a smoldering cigar between two fingers, which he puffed on frequently. Kalend noticed a deceptive strength in how he held that cigar and moved it from his lips to the armrest beside him. That simple act, done with efficiency, assurance, and nary a tremor, betrayed that all was not as it seemed, no matter how old he otherwise looked. There was more to this ancient man than one may think Kalend thought, and he figured it would be best to not let their guard down.

The friends settled amongst the couches and looked to Louquintas to answer for them, "We are looking for any information you are willing to share...Jacob sent us."

The old one laughed coarsely. "Ahhh....Jacob! He is an acquaintance from years gone by." He shook his head and continued, "I am known as the storyteller around these parts, and I have much information, so the question is, what information do you need?"

Louquintas glanced around the room and asked quietly, "Have you heard of anyone named Lusstail?"

Taking a long drag from his cigar and exhaling a prodigious amount of smoke, the Storyteller hesitated before responding somberly, "Yes, I have. He goes by many names and is a weaselly sort of fellow. What is your business with him?"

"We need to know what he has been up to in town. Has he been in contact with others outside? Any general things you can tell us about his movements?"

"Well now, that is a fair amount you wish to know."

Louquintas shrugged. "Anything you can help with would be greatly appreciated."

The Storyteller laughed briefly. "I am sure it would! No matter, I shall tell you what I know, and I can tell you he has been up to nothing good. It seems he has amassed an army on the other side of the Hestur Mountains. Which is now heading through them by way of the Norry Pass. The armies' purpose is not completely clear to me, but I believe it may have something to do with the movements of King Darthmoot and the dukes of Odethane."

Louquintas grunted, "You are well informed, it appears."

The Storyteller winked at him, drew another puff from his cigar, and continued, "It's kind of my business to know. Anyway, Lusstail has been gathering info about all kinds of things and passing it along to…I am not sure who."

As Louquintas started to ask another question, Juliet lept from her seat and swept the room with a glare. She paused for a moment, then whispered in a quivering voice, "Something.....is wrong!"

Kalend cautiously scanned the room, and his eyes came to a halt at three men sitting behind Louquintas in a semi-circle facing his party. They were blatantly scowling at Kalend. Chills raced down his spine as a shimmering haze began to surround them. The three stood up together, and their eyes never left his. He sat rooted in place, unable to move, as their foul gaze bored into his mind. Raging with the need for release, his mind fought back, and deep within himself, he felt a jolt as his instincts won out, breaking any hold the three had over him. A shockwave rippled through his body, forcing him to his feet and his hand to reach for his sword. He knew what the shimmering meant. As his sword cleared his sheath, he cried out, "Panes!"

His companions surged from their seats and into action. Louquintas spun about to face the threat with his sword pointed low as Juliet slipped to the side in a defensive posture. But the Storyteller was faster still. Kalend never saw anyone move so quickly, even when Louquintas fought his mentor Tosrayner all those months ago at the monastery. The old Storyteller had vaulted over the couch and engaged the Panes before they could take even one step in the companions' direction. Kalend and his companions froze in their tracks with shock and a reasonable degree of awe; they watched the old man incapacitate the first Pane he encountered. A couple strikes with his hands, a blurred movement they could not follow, and the creature was down and unmoving. Dead or alive, Kalend could not tell.

The other two Panes paused for a moment, confusion written across their faces as to what had just happened to their fellow. Shaking his bearded head, the Pane to the old man's right came to his senses first, raised his sword with both arms and struck downward at the Storyteller with a fierce cry. The Storyteller slid to the side just enough to allow the blade to whistle past, and as it did, he reached out with both hands and followed the strike to its most downward point, where he trapped the hands of the Pane onto the hilt. With a swift turn of his whole body, his arms staying in front of him, and the Panes hands still trapped onto the hilt, the Storyteller twisted the Pane around. They now faced the opposite direction, and in a quick motion downward, the Pane flipped over his own sword to land in a pile beside the Storyteller. Kalend heard several bones crack. The Storyteller easily stripped the sword from the Pane and threw it off to the side.

The third and last Pane paused for a brief panicked moment and then frantically dashed toward the door. The Storyteller was quicker. He caught the beast before it reached the exit and, with a couple well-placed blows to the head, sent it flying into the door, which had been left slightly ajar but closed with a bang as the body slammed into it headfirst.

Silence descended over the room as the Storyteller casually turned to them and, with a raised left eyebrow, asked, "You let him get away?"

In confusion, Kalend blurted out, "Who?"

"Lusstail."

CHAPTER TWENTY

As he waited for everyone to get settled again, Louquintas leaned deeply back into a couch while he slowly lit a cigar he had pilfered from a nearby table. The sofas and tables knocked over in the fight had been righted while other staff of the Lion Den had come in and dragged the three unconscious Panes from the room. After a stern look at Kalend and his friends, Parseen escorted the other patrons of the library out, with many a humble apology, and then shut the door firmly behind them.

"That's irritating," Louquintas proclaimed as he sent a cloud of rich white smoke wafting into the air. "Not sure how Lusstail keeps getting into our business, but he seems to have a knack for it, and we can't underestimate that little weasel anymore."

Kalend leaned forward on the opposite couch and asked in an annoyed voice, "Now what?"

"First, I finish this fine cigar, maybe even have a whiskey to go along with it," Louquintas replied with a grin. "Then, we need to head back to camp and get everyone moving."

"But where do we go?"

"The Norry Pass. If we can bottle up that army coming through, then we can wait for the troops that King Darthmoot is bringing and squash this thing before it gets out of hand."

Juliet, who sat next to Kalend, asked in a worried voice, "What about Lusstail? He knows we are here, most likely heard about our camp.... and if he gets to that army first...." she trailed off and shook her head.

Louquintas took another drag from his cigar, paused, and replied, "We can't do anything about that at this point. Trying to chase him down would take too much time. We need to get our forces moving. Don't worry; that army won't be going anywhere. The pass will have them hemmed in; in the worst case, they will try and move faster through it. So, we need to hurry and be in position before they come out."

Kalend focused on Juliet and asked in puzzlement, "How did you know those Panes were in the room? Was it that feeling you had in the hallway?"

She hesitated as if trying to find the words before answering, "Yes. It was odd, but it was as if some part of my mind felt their disguises. I just couldn't figure out where in the room it came from." She sighed and continued, "Good thing you saw them."

Kalend reflected on all that had transpired, and something seemed to click, "I think what you felt was them starting to change. They had been looking at me, but I only noticed it when you yelled. The more I think about it -the more I am convinced they had already started to change; maybe that is what you felt, the changing?"

"Could be," she said with a shrug. "Just glad I did."

"Me too," Kalend responded with a nervous laugh.

"But how did we overlook Lusstail?"

Kalend shook his head. "Not sure. He must have been in the room somewhere else and bolted out when the fighting started."

Louquintas, who had been sitting quietly, letting the two work it all out, declared with an approving voice, "Well done. Both of you."

Kalend bowed his head and abashedly replied, "Thank you. But we still missed so much."

Louquintas laughed. "When dealing with magic, all you can do is respond the best you can. You did that, and well." He sent another cloud of smoke into the air. "I am also proud of how your mind works, trying to figure out how everything happened and why. Looking back and analyzing the situation, trying to work through what worked and what can be changed. All of that is the mark of a good leader."

"Leader? Me?" Kalend asked with a nervous laugh.

"Stranger things have happened," Louquintas said with a shrug.

"I can't see that happening anytime soon."

"You never know when you may be called upon to do more than follow. Besides, you do hail from a family of leaders."

Kalend sighed and changed the subject. "The other question I have is, the Storyteller. He is not what he seems -at all."

Louquintas nodded his head toward the Storyteller as he entered back into the library and came up to the group, then asked him directly, "It appears there is more to you than just being a storyteller?"

Sitting down, the Storyteller removed a cigar from his robes and looked at Parseen, who had followed closely behind. "May we get some drinks, my good man?"

Parseen smiled and replied, "Of course. I shall have some whiskey brought out for each of you."

"Thank you," the old man replied politely but dismissively. Parseen bowed respectfully, glided over to the door, went through it, and softly closed it behind him.

Looking at the rest of the group, The Storyteller addressed them as he cut his cigar. "Yes, I have been many things in my life. The Lion Head Den is a place for powerful people to meet and plan their escapades. But also, to socialize." He paused and lit the cigar. "And I? Well, let's just say I am just an old storyteller who has lived an...interesting life. And now I sit back and listen to others who need an ear."

Louquintas smiled. "With the skills you have just shown and the respect being given to you by the staff around here, you're being just an 'old storyteller' -my arse. Jacob is a trusted friend, and since he has vouched for you, that goes a long way. But… there are too many unknowns about you for us to trust fully. Hope you can understand."

The old man nodded in understanding. "I do. We live in perilous times with much chaos swirling around. Know this: the twins are playing a much bigger game than would first appear, bigger than the kings involved so far. This goes to the essence of all magic and where it comes from. In order to get to the bottom of it, you must find who is behind them."

Louquintas waited to respond as a server unobtrusively entered the room and delivered glasses of whiskey to each of them. Once the man left, he raised his glass and watched the contents intently as he swirled the dark liquid around. Putting his nose over the edge of the glass, he inhaled the aroma. And with a slow, drawn-out sip, he savored the contents, then raised the drink and proclaimed, "Ahh…. now this is a fine way to wet one's palate."

Kalend tried his without all the pageantry of Louquintas and had difficulty swallowing the drink without having a coughing fit. He mentally shrugged and figured it must be an acquired taste.

"Finding who the head of the snake is will be challenging, I believe. We did see him once, we think, but that was of little help other than to know he seems to have the warlocks under his control." Louquintas finally responded to the Storyteller.

"Finding out who is the head is a must. Or this will end badly for all the people of the lands," the Storyteller cryptically said as he stood up, went over to the fireplace, and grabbed a fire poker to light his cigar.

With some irritation, Juliet asked, "How? And what do you mean all the people?"

"What I mean, my dear lady, is that there is much more at stake than Kalend and his heritage. And yes, I know all about that as well."

Louquintas grunted sourly. "Why am I not surprised!"

Kalend took another cautious swig of his whiskey and grimaced, "Can you tell us anything more about who may be behind it all?"

The Storyteller exhaled a ring of smoke that expanded as it rose lazily toward the ceiling. "No. But I would advise keeping your eyes and ears open for who and what their ultimate purpose is. That is all I can give you. I would also advise that you should get going and get your troops in place fast, stop that army, and then hunt down what is really going on. If you stop them at the pass and even if you defeat them -that will not be the end of it."

Kalend had another thought, "What about the dukes of Odethane? Have you heard of any movement from them?"

"Not really; there had been some speculation that they were gathering an army, but no one has heard or seen anything of the sort. This does not mean it's not happening; they may be pulling men from somewhere else. I would guess they would want to keep their movements secret from King Kourkourant."

Louquintas finished his drink with one long pull, put out his cigar in the ashtray on the table, and abruptly stood. "It's been a pleasure, but it's time to go!"

***** *****

Exiting the city had been relatively easy, with some help from the Lion Head Den. The Storyteller arranged it so they could leave the city without hassles or too many prying eyes. It was late at night, and therefore, there was little traffic in or out of the gates. The group quickly passed through them as the guards were too distracted by several men who had been sent ahead for that purpose. Kalend was not sure how they had been distracted, be it bribery or some other method, but the results were what counted. They walked cleanly through without seeing a soul and were soon on the way back to camp.

Kalend ambled bemusedly behind his friends as moonlight bathed the three of them. He found the effect quite fetching on Juliet, as her bluish-white hair seemed to glow, which framed her tanned multi-hued complexion and gave her a majestic look. His emotions toward her had changed over time, and he realized his nervousness around her had faded long ago. He knew that he had feelings for this woman, who was now such a big part of his life, feelings that were more than just friendship, more than lust, but actual feelings of affection. The question he was now facing was what to do about it?

He laughed sheepishly at his predicament. Falling for a young lady while dealing with all the other craziness in his life is great timing.

Louquintas glanced back at his apprentice and asked, "What's funny?"

Kalend blushed and hoped the low moonlight hid the redness in his face. "Nothing. Just thinking about something."

"Heh...ok," Louquintas said with a knowing smile as he turned back to the path they followed.

Kalend blushed some more and sighed inwardly; one more thing to worry about. What was he going to do about his feelings for Juliet? His little experience with women had primarily been with family; he did not count Francine at the brothel in Pleus; that had been an altogether different matter. Asking for advice from his sister was out of the question. He was not sure he could handle the teasing he would receive. So, what was he to do?

As they approached the outskirts of the camp, he still had not made any decisions but decided it would have to wait, at least for a little while longer.

***** *****

First light found the force led by Louquintas and his companions on the march towards the Norry Pass. The day had dawned with plentiful sunlight, small puffy white clouds gently roamed the blue sky above, and the earth gave off a warm, moist smell of fresh grass and things starting to bud, all of which gave the promise of warmth and good weather for the trip ahead. Spring was at its peak and would soon be transitioning into summer. Kalend hoped the beautiful spring weather was a harbinger of things to come as he rode Whistler past the scattering of giant oaks, tall pines, and wide willows that dotted the land around them.

The last time he had been headed towards these mountains, it had been winter, and running for his life. But now he returned, with a small army at his back, and heading towards the trouble. He had never participated in or seen an army on a march toward war, and he found the experience both nerve-racking and exciting. What a difference a few months and weeks had made.

At midday, Louquintas called a halt to give the troops some rest and food, and he gathered the companions together along with Rashana and Sergeant Galland. Under the broad canopy of a nearby willow and as a breeze gently shook its gnarled limbs, they sat down beneath its shade to discuss their plans going forward.

"I figure it will take four or five days to reach the pass. Would you agree, Sergeant Galland?" Louquintas asked as he munched on some jerky that had been delivered by a conscientious soldier.

"Yes, with the horses burdened as they are with both rider and supplies, that sounds about right. If the weather holds." Sergeant Galland responded after taking a sip from a water skin.

"Let's assume it does. We will be outnumbered vastly, at least from what we know. Let's assume that as well."

"I hate assumptions," Trealine rumbled.

"I do, too, but I don't see what else we can do. If we are wrong, then hopefully, we will be wrong in such a way that we will be in a better position. I'd rather err on the side of caution. We do not have much room for error."

Sergeant Galland replied, "Either way, we need a plan. If my memory serves me, that Pass narrows down before it ends. And it ends with high cliffs on either side; their force should be bottled in tight. I suggest we send out a couple riders to scout the Pass and see if we can find out how far in they still are."

"I like it. Kourkourant's plan hinges on getting through before we get there, but we have no idea exactly when he left." Louquintas approved.

Trealine nodded. "I'll volunteer to go with a couple others. We can move much quicker than this horde and should make the pass in a day or so. I may not ride a horse well, but well enough, and I know more about those mountains than anyone else you send. Once I get an idea of their progress, I can send the fastest rider back to you. I can then find my people; maybe they can send some help."

Louquintas swallowed the last of his jerky. "Any help would be greatly appreciated."

"Don't expect too much; my people are not warriors and usually stay out of the big folk's business." Trealine cautioned.

"All you can do is try; if you can at least find out what that army is up to, that will be help enough."

Trealine stood and gathered his stuff together. "I will leave now if that is ok."

Louquintas waved him on. "That leaves the rest of us. We need to hurry but not so much that our force is too tired by the time we get there. Sergeant Galland, you're best equipped and experienced to dictate our pace, so please do."

"Understood," The Sergeant agreed. "And I think we need to send out another pair of scouts to find out where King Darthmoot's army is. Especially now that there is some question if the dukes are even involved or are mobilizing at all. It would be helpful to know how far away the king is and from what direction they come. And we can let them know of the urgency that is needed and what we are planning."

"Ok, do that as well, please," Louquintas said as Sergeant Galland stood and quickly left the group.

Looking back at Kalend and the ladies, Louquintas smiled. "What shall we do with you three troublemakers?" he asked with a laugh. With his mustache aquiver, he continued before they could reply, "don't answer that.....You three shall remain by my side at all times; do not stray. You are all too important."

Kalend sighed. "I assume that means I am to be left out of the fighting?"

"Yes, you are, my young apprentice. If I can help it, all three of you will remain out of it. In fact, I want all of you to be ready to flee if things turn badly. I want your word on that," Louquintas said seriously, brooking little argument.

Kalend felt slightly resentful and irritated at still being considered the "young" one. Regardless of his mentor's tone, he wanted to rebel and opened his mouth to strongly object, but as he did, his mother and Juliet reached out and touched his legs from either side. He looked to one and then the other and noted their solemn looks. With another sigh, he closed his mouth and nodded in agreement.

Wordlessly, Louquintas watched the exchange between the women and his apprentice and then proclaimed, "Time to get moving."

*****   *****

Late the next day, as Kalend contemplated all that was about to happen, he realized he should contact his sister. He wanted to know she was safe and fill her in all they had planned. Touching his bracer, he reached out to her in his mind. Several moments of silence passed, and he called her name again.

"Hello, dear brother," Hollilea responded quietly within his head.

"Hi sis, how are you?" Kalend asked in an equally quiet voice.

"We are all well here." There was a pause before she continued, *"Much has happened since you left me all those weeks ago."*

"Hopefully, all good things?" Kalend asked worriedly.

"For the most part. My powers have grown, and I have gained more control over them. It is a little scary the things I can do....sometimes, I worry about having this power. How and when to use it? What if I hurt someone I care for?" she asked meekly.

"Sister, we have only known each other a short time, but I believe in you. We are both lucky to have the mentors we do; the witches and Louquintas would not lead us wrong. We both need to believe in that and ourselves."

"Thank you for the kind words." She sighed. *"It would be helpful to actually be with you and learn together."*

Kalend led his horse behind Louquintas as the column began moving along the dusty road through the fields and trees. He was unsure where his sister's hesitation came from, but he realized they were going through similar things. It seemed as if they were both being groomed, for what he was not sure.

"Our destinies have not been our own for most of our lives, but I believe it will lead to where we need to be." Kalend then laughed at his own vagueness. *"Not sure what that means."*

Hollilea laughed with him. *"Oh brother, how serious you are!"*

Kalend's tone became earnest. *"I have much to tell you....but first, where are you?"*

"Deep in the Hestur Mountains. The one twin keeps trying to find us. Luckily, Yarguri has usually been able to sense him before he finds our exact location. But this has meant we are now very deep and much removed from the part of the mountains you had found us in."

Anxiously, Kalend blurted out, *"Be careful! There is a whole army on the move through the Norry Pass."*

"The Norry Pass? Are you sure?" Hollilea asked in a worried tone.

"Yes, it's a long story, but we found out that the Twins of Evil and King Kourkourant are all on the move. They know about you and me and that King Darthmoot has been protecting our mother."

"I will let Yarguri know right away. We are not that close to the pass, so we should be safe," Hollilea said in reassurance.

"Good. I am with a small group of troops headed that way; we hope to trap them in the Pass and defeat them there."

"Please be careful, my brother; I would hate to lose you!"

Laughing out loud, he responded, *"I will be."*

There was a pause before Hollilea continued, *"If you need me, don't hesitate to call out."*

"I won't. But don't worry, Louquintas plans to keep me away from any fighting," Kalend responded ruefully.

"By the way, I like the name you gave the twins...the Twins of Evil," Hollilea giggled in his head.

Laughing out loud again, for which he received a backward questioning look from Louquintas. He motioned to his bracer, and his mentor nodded understanding. *"Thank you, it just popped into my head."*

Hollilea sighed. *"I need to go now. Yarguri is waiting for me, and she hates to be kept waiting."*

"Then you better go. I will let you know if anything else happens along the way. Hopefully, we will be together soon."

"Goodbye, dear brother, be careful!" admonished Hollilea in parting.

The connection was lost; Kalend looked at the beautiful scenery rolling past him and wondered how so much beauty could lead him to so much that was not. Everyone was worried about his safety, which he understood, maybe, but he was not sure that he could keep all those promises of staying that way. Too many were after him with bad intentions. And those intentions were for reasons that were not completely clear to him. He understood his parents had been powerful, "had" being the operative word, so how much danger could he still pose? To either the twins or the king? There had to be more to all this than he had been told. More about who was behind it all but also more about why. He would not feel safe until he found out the answers to those questions.

CHAPTER TWENTY-ONE

A gentle breeze blew through the mountain trees; the pines creaked and swayed with its passage as it gently nudged Hollilea along the narrow game trail. She was excited to hear from her brother and worried at the same time. He was headed into danger while she was hiding out in the woods, and she wished she could be more help. Her powers were growing stronger, not as fast as she wanted, but Yarguri kept giving assurance that things were moving along as quickly as they may and not to fret over the pace. The couple times she had come to her brother's aid had given her a sense of purpose and reason for all the hard training; she could see and feel the results, and each time, it came easier. But still, there was a sense that more could be done. Only so much could be channeled through him, and she knew if she could be with him, her true power could be unleashed in his defense. If only the witches would allow her to join him.

Yarguri sat simply upon a fallen log beside the slender creek that flowed through that part of the forest. Its cool, clear waters sprang from an unknown source higher up the mountain, providing them a clean drinking source back at their camp. As Hollilea hurried to her teacher's side beside the burbling brook, she could tell something was amiss; she was unsure what it could be, but she hoped it was not her tardiness.

"Have you heard from your brother?" Yarguri asked in a tone indicating she already knew the answer to her question.

Hollilea sighed with relief and then told her teacher all that she knew. After a grunt and a few moments of reflection, Yarguri responded with a grimace, "I think your training for today needs to be postponed; let's talk with my sisters and see what they have to say."

Yarguri rose and hurriedly led north along the creek bed until they came to their campsite, which held a waterfall cascading down over jagged rocks into a shallow pool. The sound of the falling water surrounded and enveloped the whole glen in its peaceful song, which usually soothed Hollilea, but this time, it did little to diminish her anxiety.

Hollilea stuck close to her teacher as she stumped over to the other two witches, who were huddled around a small fire beside the water and appeared to be in a deep discussion. To Hollilea, it sounded like they were seriously discussing the best way to cook frogs! Yarguri determinedly interrupted, "Have you sensed anything unusual from our enemy, Queshan?"

"Yes," Queshan replied as she looked up at the two of them. "There has been something, a couple things, but I cannot pinpoint the source of either of them. Why?"

Yarguri quickly updated them on all that Hollilea had told her.

"What are you thinking?" Queshan asked with a frown.

"That it is time to move. Things seem to be coming to a head, and our help will be needed."

Queshan and Yootuk firmly shook their heads negatively as they confronted Yarguri. Hollilea's blood had quickened at the thought of rejoining her brother, and she blurted out, "I know I can be of help to my brother. Look at all I have been able to do for him from a distance; imagine all that I can do by his side!"

All three swiveled their heads toward her, and she shrank from their piercing gaze. She had overstepped her place and knew it; all the long years of training, all the years she had been with them, she had always known her place. But this was different; she could feel it deep within her. Kalend needed her, needed them, and she was determined to help her brother. She straightened her back, put her hands on her hips, and stared right back at them.

Several excruciating moments passed as the crones' steely gaze bored into Hollilea. Just as Hollilea felt she may falter, Yarguri nodded, turned to the other two, and coarsely laughed, "It seems our little sparrow has grown into a fierce eagle."

Yootuk maintained her intense gaze on Hollilea for a moment more and then burst out in a deep cackle. "It would seem so. But now, what to do with our war eagle?"

Hollilea blushed from the teasing and felt some slight remorse for the defiance she had shown. She opened her mouth to apologize, but Yootuk raised a hand to forestall her and, with a shake of her head, admonished, "No child. Apologize not. We have trained you well and have dedicated the last few years to raising you to become a leader. One whom we knew would one day rejoin the world as a force for good. If that time is now, is yet to be seen, but you have earned the right to speak your mind and be one of us."

All three witches stood smiling at her, and Hollilea was humbled by the uncharacteristic, kind words from these mentors who had been a part of her life since she was a babe. She bowed to them and said in a quiet voice, "Thank you for all you have done on my account and the training you have provided."

The three bowed back to her in a smooth unison that belied their ages. Yarguri straightened and lost her smile in doing so. "Now, since that is out of the way, let's get back to the business at hand, shall we?"

Hollilea smiled inwardly; it would figure that Yarguri would quickly change the mood. Still, the recognition she had received had boosted her spirits; praise from these three was something not to be overlooked. For the first time, she felt a part of a larger world and that her destiny would eventually reveal itself.

While Hollilea had been reflecting on all that had just transpired and her new role within the group, a decision appeared to have been reached. Queshan was speaking of the need to get things together and break camp if they were to find another place of refuge. Hollilea hung her head in dejection as she realized their course of action. She desperately wanted to go to her brother but knew that the decision had been made, and there was no more persuading the witches otherwise. She then looked around and asked, "What of Karl? Is he still out scouting and hunting?"

"Yes, we will need to wait for him to return; he should be back by nightfall. We can leave at first light," Yarguri answered.

Since they had never built a large camp, they quickly had the essentials packed and ready to move. Hollilea had just finished taking down the last tent and had stowed it in a backpack that Karl would carry when she felt a cold chill crawl down her spine. She felt that something was off and out of place, and she noticed a coldness had settled over the camp. Cautiously, she looked around the glen, trying to pinpoint what was wrong. But she saw nothing except woods, the waterfall, and the wind gently rustling the trees. Then the chill came again, but more potent this time; it washed over her in waves, and she involuntarily cried out with fear. Her head jerked to the left as she caught something vaguely humanoid but bulky and slow, lumbering among the boles of the trees. Too far away for her to clearly make out, Hollilea stood rooted in place and watched in fear and fascination as it plodded steadily toward their camp. Yarguri and the other witches had heard her yell and now stood beside Hollilea, where they peered through the mid-morning light into the woods.

Yootuk grimaced. "Whatever that is, it cannot be good. Someone hides their approach from me; I sense nothing."

Queshan pointed further to their left. "Another comes from there. I, too, cannot sense what they are; it's as if someone has dampened our ability…and I would guess it's one of the warlocks."

Yootuk took a determined stance and said, "Whatever they are, it may be time to confront them and end this."

The other two witches quickly agreed and barked at Hollilea to get behind them, to stay close to the water, and to stay out of the fight. Hollilea pleaded to help but was roughly cut off and ordered to find Karl and get to her brother if things went badly.

Hollilea retreated to the waterline and readied herself for a flight across the stream, but she promised herself she would not leave until the last possible moment. The thought of fleeing and abandoning her teaches for a second time made her nauseous. And she was determined not to let that happen again if she could help it. Her three teachers spread out and created a perimeter around their student; waiting patiently, calmly, and with no emotion, they watched the trees.

The creatures ambled and stumped among the brush and trees, angling toward their camp; neither one had little care for what stood before it as smaller brush and saplings were crushed in their wake. They moved with a slow, plodding pace, drawing inexorably closer. Then, the one on the right moved around a tree too large to bowl over and came into clear view. It was large and must have stood close to eight feet tall. Hollilea grimaced with revulsion as she noticed it was covered in some type of hairy fungi, green and brown all mixed together; it covered the being like the slick coating of moss one would find covering boulders in the stream behind her. It oozed and dripped as it shambled closer.

The other also strolled into view, and it appeared to be of similar size and shape as the first but was dry, craggy, and fissured as if a mound of rocks all mashed together could walk. Both their faces had dour expressions that lacked intelligence but spoke of brutal power and strength.

Yarguri grunted, "Golems. The left is Rock, and the right is Earth."

The golems took note of their prey, and with a fearsome, almost smile, as if eager to crush and maim, they picked up their pace toward the companions. Yarguri thrust out her hand,

and a ball of fire blossomed within her palm. She waved it toward the rock golem, and as the fireball streaked from her fingers, it expanded to thoroughly engulf its target when it struck. Fire lit up the glen and forest, but the creature strolled through the flames, unhurt or thrown off its pace.

The other two witches also engaged the creatures, each hurling lightning, fire, and ice. Yarguri and Yootuk concentrated their efforts on the rock golem as Queshan kept a steady stream of energy magics towards the one made of Earth. Hollilea stood in awe at the display her teachers poured forth. So much power from seemingly frail and ancient women was stunning. They had never used this kind of power while teaching her. She had known or at least suspected a hidden might within them, but this was more than she would have thought possible.

The combined effect and steady flow of power eventually slowed them both down, the rock golem more so as two witches were striking it at once. Slowed but not stopped or seemingly hurt in any fashion, they continued their relentless approach. The earth golem reached Queshan, and she stumbled back from its searching hands while hurling pure bolts of lightning into its torso, trying, with limited success, to stop or hurt the shaggy brut. Without looking back to Hollilea, she shouted, "Go, child, get to your brother, NOW!" As she finished yelling for Hollilea to run, one of the golems' huge hands struck her a glancing blow to the head and sent her spinning to the ground. She did not move to get up.

Hollilea froze in indecision; she knew that to run was what her mentors expected of her, but she felt equal parts shame and anger. Why should she always run? Her mentors were in harm's way due to her. She wanted to lash out and destroy, to finally get back at those who hunted her and her brother. That indecision cost her any choice she may have had.

The golem clumsily stepped over Queshan and reached for Hollilea before she could make up her mind. All she could do was lash out with a scream and a raised hand that sent waves of power toward the creature. The surge of energy smashed into the being and spun it past her as its grasping hands narrowly missed her shoulder. It stumbled into the stream, where it stopped, and looked around in confusion, unsure where its prey had gone.

Hollilea took advantage of the golem's disorientation and sent waves of red-orange fire into its back, pushing it toward the waterfall. The creature made a moaning sound, turned toward its attacker, and started toward her once again. She kept up the fire, hoping to burn it to the waterline. It grimaced but kept its plodding pace toward her. Her mind blazed in fear and anger, but she took a deep breath and shut out her feelings. Remaining calm is what was needed, not emotions that would cloud her mind and slow her reflexes. When her mind reached a deeper state of peace, she noticed the waterfall behind the stumbling thing, and something clicked.

Without fully thinking about it, she let her instincts take over. She stood up straighter and extended both hands, then hurled waves of fire and lighting, one from each hand, directly into the chest of the golem. It slowed to a crawl and bent into the forces slamming into it. Hollilea's mind sunk into a profound core of relaxation, and more power burst forth as she pummeled the creature, halting its approach.

They stood facing each other in a grueling stalemate for several agonizing moments, the stream and forest alive with the energies that bounced off and cascaded over the golem. Then, it stumbled backward. Hollilea reacted instantly with a thrust of both hands, sending pulsing waves of fire crashing into the beast, forcing it back a few more steps. Slowly but steadily, Hollilea pushed the unsteady monster until it stood beneath the waterfall.

Hollilea switched to lightning, attempting to keep the beast in place under the deluge that tumbled over it. The lightning and water mixed, sending sparks flying out from the waterfall. The creature thrashed and bucked as chunks of moss and dirt flew from its arms and hands. Its body began to sag while its head and face became distorted as it dissolved under the cascade of water. With one last desperate heave, it attempted to stand upright from the flowing water, but another barrage from Hollilea kept it from doing so. Suddenly, it collapsed within itself with an eerie, bubbly moan and melted into the stream. Hollilea found herself staring at muddy water as it washed the last vestiges of the golem into the forest; with a sigh, she lowered her arms in exhaustion. Then she turned to see how her mentors fared.

The witches had succeeded in slowing the rock golem—each taking a turn at sending streamers of fire and ice slamming into its body. Alternating the bursts, the combination of heat and cold seemed to momentarily confuse the creature, but still, it lumbered closer. The crones backed up, giving them space from the rocky horror. Unsure how to help, Hollilea realized that this golem would be much harder to take down, water would most likely have little effect on rock, and the stream was on the wrong side of them. She was exhausted from her fight, utterly drained, so she backed up as far as she could to give them room.

From the forest came a loud yell, and three more figures appeared. Hollilea gasped and prepared to take flight across the stream but stopped as she recognized Karl in the lead. With his staff raised above his head, he ran and screamed at the golem as he tried to get its attention. Two others sprinted behind him, another human and an Othurean, and both joined in with the yelling.

Karl came at the beast from behind and struck a hard-downward blow to the top of its head. The staff bounced and slid sideways; Karl moved with the glancing impact to stand to one side. The other two figures took up stances on the other side and back, so each stood on three sides of the creature while the witches kept up their torrent of fire and ice from the front.

They took turns attacking. With sword, axe, and staff, they disoriented and kept the golem from fully committing to attacking any one of them. Their weapons, at first, seemed to have little effect, but Hollilea noticed that chunks of rock would fly with each blow. As time wore on, the fragments became more significant, and the missing pieces of arms, torso, and legs began to hinder its movement. Hollilea realized that the fire and ice blasts were making the rock brittle and, thus, the strikes more effective.

With a powerful overhand blow of his sword, the human Hollilea did not know, managed to sever one whole arm at the shoulder. Then the Othurean struck a blow from behind at the creature's left knee, which sent the lower portion flying into the forest. The golem tumbled to the ground. The witches ceased their magical attack, and Yarguri gruffly shouted, "Finish it!"

The three newcomers quickly rained blows upon the hapless creature and soon had it dismantled into chunks that littered the ground around them. Hollilea shuddered in revulsion as she watched the pieces continue to twitch where they lay.

Karl leaned on his staff, breathing heavily, and said, "I see I can't leave you ladies alone for long without some sort of excitement."

Yarguri ignored the remark, gestured to the others, and asked, "Who are your friends?"

Karl responded with a grave voice, "They are friends of Louquintas and bring troubling news."

CHAPTER TWENTY-TWO

Three days and nights passed without incident for Kalend and company as they continued their travels toward the Norry Pass. As the sun sunk low into the late afternoon sky on the fourth day, Louquintas called a halt. He pointed to a thin trail of dust coming toward them along the road ahead. Sergeant Galland barked out orders for the troops to get themselves ready, just in case. In short order, they could make out a single rider coming fast at a gallop.

The rider rode directly up to Louquintas and reigned in his heaving and puffing horse. Kalend, who had been riding beside his friend, recognized him as one of the scouts dispatched with Trealine.

"What news?" Louquintas asked.

In a breathless voice, the scout saluted and reported, "We found the army. They have just entered the pass and should reach its end in about four days' time."

Louquintas mulled this over for a minute. "What are their numbers?" he asked.

"About five thousand infantry and three hundred cavalry."

"We only have about five hundred cavalry with us!" Kalend exclaimed in shock.

Louquintas pursed his lips. "They have us outnumbered by more than I had anticipated. Anything you can tell us about the opening to that pass?"

The scout took a swallow from a water skin that had been provided by Sergeant Galland before he answered, "That pass gets real narrow. I believe we can bottle it up with fortifications made from trees from the forest before it."

Sergeant Galland added, "We should reach it tomorrow and be able to fortify our position to some degree within three days. After that, it will be a race for which king reaches us first. We should be able to hold it for a couple of days if needed. Then again, until we see it, I won't know for sure."

Louquintas sighed. "Looks like it will be a race after all." Shaking his head, he grumbled, "Sure wish I knew where King Darthmoot is or whatever happened to the dukes and their men they were supposedly raising."

Kalend looked to the scout and asked, "What of Trealine? Any word from him?"

"No. The last I saw, he was headed up into the mountains with Marc, the other scout."

Louquintas dismissed the scout with a word to get some rest and food. "We must get to that pass tomorrow, gentlemen," he told Kalend and Sergeant Galland with a serious look.

Sergeant Galland frowned. "We are not in a good position. We must be ready to flee if we cannot hold that pass. King Darthmoot will need to be told the pass is lost. And I am skeptical he will reach us in time; the capital city of Thurmacia in just too far away."

A soldier trotted up to the Sergeant from the back of the company, saluted, and said, "Sir, someone approaches from our flank."

"Now who? and how many?" The Sergeant urgently asked as he turned his horse to follow the cavalryman to the back of the formation.

"Not sure, sir. Looks to be only a few, but riding fast directly for us," the soldier responded as he led the way.

The troops parted to allow the four to pass, and as they did, they could see ahead to their left a group of riders coming down a smaller, rarely used trail that intersected the main road they were on.

Louquintas squinted and shook his head. "You're right. It's not many; I am thinking thirty or so. But I can't tell if they are friend, foe, or neither. They are riding without colors."

"Could they be bandits?" Kalend asked anxiously.

"Doubtful, bandits would not be so bold to directly attack such a large force like ours."

The company waited nervously as the riders rode closer. When they came within range and faces could clearly be seen, Louquintas laughed aloud and exclaimed, "Well, well, looks like help comes after all."

Kalend peered closer at the group, and his heart soared as he noted who rode in the fore. With a ponytail flying in the breeze behind him…was Tosrayner.

The Martial Master and his company reigned in their heaving horses before his old friend, and then he and Louquintas exchanged salutes. "Have we missed anything?" Tosrayner asked in a calm voice as if they had just recently parted.

Louquintas shrugged and replied just as nonchalantly, "Nope. All is quiet so far."

With a smile and a sideways wink at Kalend, the Martial Master responded, "Maybe we can help with that?"

Louquintas turned to the smiling Sergeant Galland and said, "Let's get some water for our new friends so that we can talk about how to make things more exciting."

As Sergeant Galland commanded that water be brought for their guests and horses, Kalend dismounted along with the rest of the group. He approached his old teacher and bowed with heartfelt relief. "Greetings, it is excellent to see you."

Tosrayner bowed in return and looked his former student up and down before responding, "It is pleasing to see you again. Looks like you have become the man I expected you would become."

Kalend hesitated while answering, "Maybe." Then, he shook his head. "So much has happened, and I am still unsure of it all."

With a laugh, Tosrayner clapped him on the shoulder. "That is to be expected, but I can see in how you hold yourself that you have grown and matured much since last we were together."

Sergeant Galland had camp chairs set up and food brought for the newcomers. Louquintas quickly filled Tosrayner in on all that had transpired since he and Kalend had left the monastery all those months ago. He gave a broad overview without going into specifics, and they kept their focus on their current situation and how best to move forward.

Tosrayner informed them that he led a group of about two thousand infantry that trailed a few leagues behind. His scouts had discovered Louquintas and his calvary, and Tosrayner had felt the need to come ahead to meet them and see how best he could help.

It was decided that they would wait for the infantry to catch up. Tosrayner ordered one of his group to go back and explain the situation and to hurry them along. Once the infantry caught up, they would, together, head to the pass and see about fortifying it.

Kalend gazed out upon sun-drenched fields during a lull in the conversation and its scattering of trees that dotted the landscape. He contemplated all he had been told. It felt good, it felt right, to have Tosyarner here, now, when help was needed the most. Between both of his mentors, he was confident a way would be found to stop the coming army.

After the group split up, Kalend spent some time catching up with his old mentor. He learned that Tosrayner had raised his forces over a couple months and that contingency plans had been put in motion at about the same time Kalend had left the monastery. Apparently, Louquintas knew of these plans all along, and yet, once again, Kalend had been left in the dark. He shook his head in irritation at the thought; when would he ever not be kept out of the dark? He turned to ask that very question when Tosrayner, who had watched his student digest all that he had been told, said, "It was necessary to keep you from knowing. You will find that there will be times when knowledge must be withheld. As you become a leader, finding when and who should know vital information will become a burden, but one that cannot be shirked."

Kaled sighed, shook his head, and said petulantly, "Still, it would have been nice to know that you were coming."

"That is unbecoming of you, Kalend," Tosrayner admonished.

Kalend hung his head and realized his old teacher was correct. "Yes, sir."

"Have no fear, lad. I predict at some point, you will relish these days of relative innocence. For in the not-too-distant future, you may be called upon to lead others, and then the choices will be yours. Along with the burden and responsibility."

Kalend recalled a previous conversation with Louquintas regarding his leading others in the future and wondered why both his mentors had now mentioned it. He thought it through and decided not to pursue the issue for now. He would just need to keep himself aware as best he could and learn from them both, and whatever happens, hope that he would be ready.

***** *****

Hollilea hurried along the rocky mountain trail. She was trying to keep up with the witches and wondered how they could move so quickly and with such stamina at such advanced ages. They stumped along, up and down the mountain, with hardly a hitch in their gait and with determined looks. At the front of their group strode Karl, who led the way with assurance and kept them on a steady course. Hollilea was in the middle, with the scout Marc right behind her and the Othurean, Trealine, taking up the rear position. The witches had decided that they would head toward her brother after all and offer what assistance they could. Between the golem attack and the information Marc had provided, Louquintas and his small army would be outnumbered; the thought was that they would need help.

She was excited about the prospect of rejoining her brother but apprehensive about the coming battle. Fighting a golem was one thing, but this would be something else entirely. The plan was to arrive at a high point above the Norry Pass; once at the pinnacle, the witches and Karl would go down and through the Norry Pass, then make their way up the other side. This assumed they could sneak across the pass without being seen by any lingering elements of the army passing through, but the witches seemed confident. Hollilea and the rest of the company would remain on the opposing peak and wait to see how the battle unfolded. In this way, each group would be above and on either side of the pass, allowing the witches to help in any way they could without risking Hollilea. In the strictest of terms, she had been told to observe but not get involved.

From what the scout Marc had told them, they knew they had about four days to reach the pass before the army arrived at its mouth. Their journey would take about that much time. Karl led them along a route he felt would keep them far enough from the pass to not be seen. Therefore, they followed the many small game trails that crisscrossed the mountains, and when there was no game trail, Karl would blaze the path for them. Hollilea did not know how he kept track of where they were in relation to the route the army took. She may have been raised in the mountains, but this level of forest mastery was beyond her.

The group came to a halt as Karl stood motionless in the middle of the narrow animal trail. He motioned for the witches to come forward, and as they did, Hollilea noticed that a Wiccenda stood silently waiting for them. Over the years, she had met all three of her mentors Wiccenda; she did not recognize this one. This one seemed different, and a small shiver of excitement ran through her for some unknown reason. The Wiccenda spoke briefly with the witches before nodding in Hollilea's direction, then Yarguri beckoned to

Hollilea, "Come here, child. It is time for you to meet someone."

Hollilea hesitantly walked forward. She took stock of the ethereal figure, noticed how the forest showed through her, and noted the long, lustrous black hair that hung to her hips. This was a woman who oozed confidence and commanded respect; it showed in how she held herself erect with a self-assurance that spoke of someone used to the trappings of power. She wore a full-length white gossamer dress cut low at the bosom that billowed about her ankles from a breeze that Hollilea did not feel.

She bowed before this powerful woman and said, "Greetings, my Wiccenda. It is a pleasure to finally meet you."

The Wiccenda bowed in return. "Hello, Hollilea, your instincts do you justice. My name is Morgne."

Hollilea smiled and replied, "I have had good teachers, but I feel I have known you my whole life."

"You have, in a way. I have watched you and felt your power grow. Or, more accurately, felt you draw more and more power. This is all good. Our relationship will grow and change over time. I wanted to meet you before you reached the pass and tell you that I am proud of what you are becoming. The connection between Wiccenda and Sorceress is a deep one, one that most will not understand. The deeper that connection, the deeper the well of power you will be able to draw from." Morgne paused, looked deep into Hollilea's eyes, and asked in a solemn tone, "Do you understand?"

"I believe so. There is much I still don't understand. But I have felt our connection grow each time I have used the magic."

Morgne nodded in satisfaction. "And grow it shall; it is ever-changing. Soon, your need may be great, and you will be tested, but do not fret; I shall be there. Buried within yourself, you will find a way to draw even more power through me."

Hollilea looked perplexed. "How will I be tested? How will I know when it happens?"

Morgne laughed. "That, unfortunately, is something I cannot tell you. I do not know the specifics, just that it will happen."

Hollilea hung her head for a moment, then looked up and changed tactics. "What of my brother? Is that connection like we have?"

"No. That is a different matter," Morgne said in a grave voice.

Yarguri, who had been standing with the others close by, grunted and said, "I do not mean to be rude, but we need to be moving. We do not have much time to get to the pass."

Morgne glanced at Yarguri with a patient smile and replied, "Yes, you are correct, Yarguri." Then she shook her head and laughed. "You have ever been one to speak your mind. I have often told your Wiccenda that she has been too lenient on you."

Yarguri grunted without responding.

Morgne laughed again and then turned her attention back to Hollilea. "Just remember your training and that I am here, and when the need is greatest, the power will be available. However, it will be up to you to access that power, harness it, and use it as you have been taught."

Hollilea nodded and replied with a determined look, "I will be ready."

***** *****

Kalend considered the pass and admired the beauty of the scenery before him. The sun was just coming up to kiss the sides of the mountain while leaving the pass deep in shadows. The trees were starting to bud, and bird songs filled the air. A sense of sadness washed over him as he realized that such a serene setting would soon be filled with violence that Kalend could not yet comprehend. He shook his head and frowned.

Louquintas quietly walked up to Kalend and took note of the grim continence his protégé wore while looking out at the beauty of the mountains. They stood still for several moments, side by side, taking in the view. And then Louquintas said in a calm voice, "The world is filled with remarkable things. Beauty and evil. Here is the beauty."

Kalend sighed. "Yes, it is a remarkable thing. But this same beauty will be marred by horrible deeds in the coming days."

"All we can do is try and stem the tide. What comes is not our doing; we do what we must to protect others. Whoever is behind this wants one thing: power. They then want to use that power to subjugate everyone. This is not about you. You have learned much about history from your teachers, but there is another history that is not talked about much and is only known to those who are part of it. You are now a part of this other history. Know that in this other history, there is a constant fight between those who would see freedom for all and those who want to dominate all life."

Kalend reflected on that a moment before responding, "I will do what I can. Hopefully, I can help in some way."

Louquintas clapped him on the shoulder. "In the end, I think we will find that your help has been more than any of us could know."

"You and Tosrayner keep talking as if I were a leader and a bigger part of this than I feel. What are you not telling me?"

"All shall be revealed in time. Until then, you will have to trust us. We each have a part to play, and for now, your part is to follow and help where you may."

Juliet approached and informed them that Tosrayner was gathering all the commanders to review their strategy for defending the pass. Louquintas squeezed Kalend's shoulder in assurance as he left to join the meeting.

Kalend looked to Juliet and asked, "You have been quiet lately. Is everything alright?"

Juliet gazed into the distance as she replied, "Yes. Things are moving rapidly, and I have been observing. This whole army business is beyond my experience. Plus, I am unsure how many of those traveling with us are comfortable with me being here. So, I thought it best to lay low and let things come as they may."

Kalend nodded in understanding. With all that was going on, he had forgotten that Juliet was often seen as different and would not be accepted in some quarters. He remembered how the barge captain had treated her when they had fished her out of the river. "Sorry, this must be hard on you. But I need you and have come to rely on your presence. It makes me feel more at ease when you are around."

Juliet smiled at him with appreciation. "Thank you for that."

They stood quietly for a bit, taking comfort in each other's company while reflecting on all that had happened and what was yet to come. With a nervous smile, Kalend clasped Juliet's hand and said, "Please stay close, and we will look out for one another."

Juliet returned his smile and gave his hand a reassuring squeeze. With an optimism Kalend had not had in a while, they moved together to find the others and see what their roles would be in the coming battle.

CHAPTER TWENTY-THREE

It was morning, and a cool breeze blew across the hastily fortified field. Stakes had been driven into the ground, creating a palisade along the length of the pass, with each stake ending with a sharpened tip. A series of shallow ditches were dug out front and resembled a maze in which the coming army would have to navigate to get to the barrier. Behind these fortifications resided the makeshift company of archers, infantry, and cavalry that would have to hold the pass once the fortifications were breached. For being breached, they would be, or so Kalend had been told. The goal was to slow them down and kill as many as possible with archery. They were outnumbered, and thus, much of their strategy relied on the archers' ability to hold the line and cause havoc.

Kalend sat atop Whistler on a small hill and pulled his cloak in tighter to ward off the chill as he watched the last of the preparations being made. He had become fidgety and unsure what to do with himself, so he had ridden out to watch and wait in a mix of fear and nervousness. When Louquintas noticed his protege's jitters, he told him that this was always the most challenging time, just before the battle was joined. Watching as the soldiers readied themselves, he noticed joking among some while others were uncharacteristically quiet. The feel of the whole encampment was one of breathless anticipation. He shifted his shoulders and attempted to alleviate the discomfort from the chain mail rings biting through the wool gambeson he wore beneath his new armor. Even though it was a more lightweight chain mail than most, to better go with his fighting style, he had been told, it still pinched him aggressively along the shoulders. Tosrayner had presented the armor as a gift to an astonished Kalend the evening before. He was pleased and happy with his present, but now, feeling it lay heavily upon his shoulders and seeing the camp make ready for a battle, he truly felt the burden of what was coming.

Louquintas and Tosrayner trotted to their student and, with plums of vapor snorting forth from their mounts, reined in beside him. Kalend nodded to them without saying a word, while Louquintas nodded back and asked, "How do things look?"

"From my inexperienced eye, as best they could be. I wish we had more time to prepare better," Kalend responded ruefully.

"That is always the case. Time. Usually, the need for more."

Tosrayner grunted in agreement, pointed to the other side of the fortifications, and said, "And I believe our time is almost up."

Kalend looked to where Tosrayner pointed and saw the creeping movement as soldiers slowly emerged from the mountains' shadows. Marching in unison, they soon filled the pass and then stopped two hundred yards out from the ditches. It seemed as if Kourkourant's army had arrived.

The three hastily rode to the tent that had been erected as their base of operations. The company's other leaders had already assembled and sat around a small camp table, impatiently waiting on them. Tosrayner made sure everyone was confident in their roles, and one by one, they nodded in assurance, then they were set loose to make ready to defend the pass. Kalend, Juliet, and his mother were all to stay close to Louquintas and, if they needed to, retreat to the tent. Several soldiers were being left to guard it and them.

Sergeant Galland came in as the others left and, without preamble, stated, "A messenger was sent from that army; they wave the white flag and wish to parley."

Tosrayner raised an eyebrow. "Wonder what that is all about? Surely they don't expect us to let them pass?"

Sergeant Galland shrugged his shoulders. "I do not know. And I don't trust them. I say ignore it and let them sit out there and eat crow."

Tosrayner grunted and looked to Louquintas. "Your thoughts?"

"As much as I like the idea of the good Sergeants, maybe we should at least see what they have to say. We may glean some more information from them."

Tosrayner mulled it over for a few moments, then said with a determined voice, "Let's hear them out. As you say, we may be able to gather some information. Besides, I would like to find out who exactly is with them."

*****   *****

Kalend sat atop Whistler beside Juliet, behind the palisade, and watched as his two mentors and three guards rode out to meet with the leaders of the opposing army. Slowly, they made their way around the ditches and, once past them, stopped to silently wait. It had been agreed upon that each side would send five to parley. Kalend was worried for his mentors; even though he had been assured that even the King would not disrespect a flag of truce, he did not trust this King. One thing he had learned since leaving the comfort of the monastery was that trust was a hard commodity to come by. And so, he had no trust for this King who had been trying to kill him all these months.

Five figures broke away from the front line and rode toward his friends. One man rode in the lead on a large, magnificent white horse with a gait of bold confidence, almost arrogant in its strut. It high stepped while the rider upon its back held himself stiffly with an air of superiority. A large garish crown adorned the man's head; its gold and encrusted jewels sparkled in the morning sunlight. Here, finally, was King

Kourkorant, the man who had changed so much of his life. Kalend knew that this show was meant to intimidate those who watched, but all he felt was disgust, and by the expressions of the soldiers around him, he knew his feelings were shared.

The parley began with Tosrayner and the King talking while their guards watched each other with wary unease. Kalen noted one hooded figure, who sat astride a speckled bay and kept his face hidden. For some reason, this person kept Kalend's attention, and he felt sure he knew him. The group wrapped up their discussion, and the King motioned to his companion that they were to turn about. When the hooded being reached out a scaly hand to signal the rest to move, Kalend grunted with recognition; it was Pouluk.

Once back within the relative safety behind the fortifications, Tosrayner filled in his student and Juliet on what had been discussed. The King had informed them that they should get out of the pass or be overrun. Kalend was taken aback by the brusque way the ultimatum had been delivered and inquired about it. Louquintas shrugged and said, "The King was not in a listening mood. Something was off about him; I can't put my finger on what, though. I have only met him a few times, long ago, and he was ever the arrogant bastard, but this was…something different. As if he wasn't all there."

Tosrayner shrugged. "In either case, we must be ready for what comes. They still outnumber us significantly, but luckily, the pass has them hemmed in so that only so many can come at us at once."

A deep, brassy horn rang out from the enemy lines and reverberated off the hills, sending a chill coursing through Kalends's body. The wait was over. The opposing force's front lines surged forward as the infantry marched its way to the edge of the ditches. Just before they entered the range of the archers, they halted in unison and quickly parted, creating a tunnel that ran like a wave deep into the pass.

A blue fire sprang into being at the end of the tunnel, and a hush fell over both sides of the standoff. The blue light grew into a blaze that illuminated two figures standing together on either side of it; both waved their hands before a large flaming staff planted into the ground. With each wave, the intensity of the flames grew and climbed high above the staff.

Louquintas led the way through the nervous troops lining the palisade and up the hill to the command tent; they stopped halfway, turned, and scrutinized the pass. He motioned for Kalend and Juliet to continue the rest of the way to the tent. They both hesitated, neither of them eager to leave before the battle was even joined.

Tosrayner gave them a stern look and barked, "Get moving, you two. Whatever devilry this is, I want you both clear of it!"

Kalend nodded his head in acquiescence and guided Whistler upward. With Juliet following closely behind, he made his way quickly up the hill, where he found his mother waiting outside the tent. She stood with her shawl drawn close about her as she peered intently out at the blue flames that had kept growing. It rose high above the tops of the tallest trees and illuminated the whole pass as it cracked and thrummed. A rainbow of colors mixed with lightning joined the flames, creating a vortex of sight and sound that rose high into the sky.

Then in one swift movement, the flames, lightning, and turbulence seemed to get sucked down into the staff, and a deathly silence descended over the pass. Kalend blinked and tried to shake the white spots that had clouded his sight by the sudden disappearance of the flames and light; he desperately wanted to see what had become of the staff. Just as his sight righted itself, a wave of purple and black power lashed out from the staff and swept down the avenue of soldiers. It slammed into the defenders; the palisade's wooden stakes burst into splinters as the men were thrown backward.

A gaping hole was created in their defenses, and soldiers' bodies littered the front of it, many of them unmoving, and many more rolled in agony, either from the blast itself or from wooden splinters that pierced their bodies. The whole line was in chaos as men scrambled to get up, and others looked about in confusion. The enemy's horn blasted another note loud and clear over the din of the defenders' shouts and cries.

Tosrayner had galloped down into the chaotic scene, yelling out orders to his commanders, attempting to regain control. With a booming voice, he yelled, "Archers at the ready! They come now, lads. Make'em pay!"

A rain of arrows shot out from behind the line of troops and looped over the battlefield. They fell indiscriminately among those charging, and many enemy soldiers were pierced. More cries of agony filled the air, and the charge faltered but quickly righted itself as more troops pressed forward to replace those fallen.

Kalend watched in dismay from the hilltop at the havoc created by the blast but noted how quickly Tosrayner took command of the situation, and some form of discipline was restored. Watching the arrows fall with a deathly hissing grace among the oncoming soldiers, he noted that by the time the archers had started to shoot, the enemy had already managed to weave its way past half the ditches and would quickly reach the breached barricade.

However, the steadily falling arrows did slow the incoming forces enough for Tosrayner to form a new defensive position along the broken barrier. Making quick decisions while barking orders, he reorganized and created a new line from which to repel the oncoming forces. Luckily, the men responded well, many of whom were seasoned veterans and been able to quickly recover from their shock.

Louquintas, meanwhile, had rushed over to the lines of archers to help galvanize their efforts. He knew what was on his friend's mind, so he worked toward the same purpose, giving the men time to reform in the front. He had the lines firing in alternating patterns; one line fired while the next pulled an arrow from their quiver, drew, and aimed. In this way, the incoming forces had to contend with a steady downpour of death.

Kalend watched in admiration as his teachers unconsciously worked in consort to stem the oncoming tide. He looked up and back into the pass; the two figures continued their undulations. A mist ebbed above the staff; it spilled out and down like fog until it grew into a broad cloud that hung low over the ground. Enemy infantry peeled off from forces nearby and approached two at a time; as they met the fog, Kalend saw a small flash of light, and they disappeared. Two by two, these troops entered, and each time was the same: a flash of light, and then they were gone.

A new commotion caught his attention; the steady flow of arrows had become jagged while shouts of fear reached his ears. Two enemy soldiers had materialized and were attacking from the rear, and several archers were down before anyone knew what was happening. As the others ceased firing to confront this new threat, two more appeared, and a few moments later, another two. Louquintas had been in the front of the line and was now trying to make his way to the back, but as more enemy soldiers popped into being, the cohesiveness of the archery unit splintered, and chaos took over. Archers either turned to escape or turned to confront the new threat. Those who chose to fight were ill-equipped as they had only their bows in hand and did not last long.

Witnessing that things were getting out of hand, Kalend stood on the hill and felt paralyzed by indecision. He now understood where those misty disappearing troopers were headed, to the back of the archers. With the arrows flow all but stopped, the enemy moved quickly around the ditches and pits. As he stood watching their carefully laid plans dissolve, he heard the horn call out yet again. This time, a low thunder arose from behind the infantry lines still waiting within the pass. Two rows of calvary burst forth, one peeled off to the left and the other to the right. In a single file, both groups skirted the narrow opening between the ditches and the sloped mountainside. They swept around them and then quickly brushed past the edge of the fortification and followed its curve to where Tosrayner's troops stood waiting in defense of the pass.

Kalend watched helplessly as his friends tried to confront the triple threats. He knew they were ill-prepared for this turn of events; they were outnumbered, and with the use of magic now involved, he knew it was just a matter of time before they were routed. Looking toward his mother, he grimly shook his head. Unless Tosrayner and Louquintas could find some miracle to turn this mess around, things did not look promising, and he knew it was almost time for them to flee.

One idea did spring to mind. With all the magic being used, he thought of his sister and reached out to her. *"Sister,"* he called into his mind, *"are you there?"*

After several desperate tries, only silence greeted him.

CHAPTER TWENTY-FOUR

Hollilea looked down upon the army of King Kourkourant as it assaulted the defenses spread before the pass. As she watched and worried, a stiff breeze made her white dress billow out around her lithe figure. The stone cliff they stood upon jutted over the end of the pass as if a large boulder had been deposited there long ago and now teetered out and over the mountainside. A craggy rock and dirt slope careened down and leveled off just as it reached the bottom. Marc, the scout, and Trealine flanked her on either side and stood quietly, all three lost in their thoughts.

Yesterday, Hollilea had said goodbye to the witches as they had split up. Having caught up to the army, they had waited until it passed; once it did, the witches headed up one side of the pass while Hollilea and her protectors the other. For that was what Marc and Trealine had become, her guardians. Yarguri had been clear and unrelenting on the issue; if anything untoward befell Hollilea, Marc, and Trealine would have to answer to all three of the witches. Both had solemnly nodded and agreed without hesitation.

Yarguri had also been insistent that Hollilea just watch, and under no circumstances was she to get involved. Queshan had informed them that she could sense the warlock brothers were close and that magic was already being used. In what way, she was unsure, only that it felt powerful and odd. It would be up to the three of them to deal with the warlocks and not her. Yarguri had also told Hollilea not to use the bracer to speak with Kalend; the warlocks may be able to hear what they said while this close to them, and it would be better to be safe. It had been impressed upon Hollilea that in the unlikely event they could hear, any advantage of surprise the witches had would be compromised. She had relented to this demand as well and had reluctantly agreed.

But now that she looked down upon the field before the pass and saw for herself the armies as they engaged each other, she was not so confident that she could keep that promise. She assumed her brother and mother were both in the opposing army somewhere. If she needed to do something to help keep them safe, she would. How exactly? She had no idea, but she knew she could not allow anything to happen to either of them.

As the three watched from above, a horn sounded for a third time, and cavalry rushed out of the pass. It split in two and flowed along the edges to attack the defenders from either side. Hollilea balled her hands into fists. She knew the battle had barely been joined, but already, things looked grim for those below. So far, the amount of magic unleashed was more incredible than anything Hollilea could have predicted. The cloud above the warlocks' staff continued sending soldiers behind the defenders' lines. It created havoc with the archers, limiting their ability to stop the oncoming infantry. She chewed on a fingernail in worry and wondered why her mentors had not countered the twins. She hoped nothing had happened to them as they had attempted to climb to the other side.

Marc nudged her shoulder and pointed toward the opposing side of the pass. High up, higher even than where they currently resided, a red glow lit up the trees, and three figures could be made out standing before a row of tall pine trees. At last, she thought, her teachers were about to enter the fray. The red spot of flaming light slowly spun; with each turn, it grew until it was big enough to draw the attention of those below. It pulsed once and then started to move downward; it gained tremendous speed as it hurtled down the mountain. While leaving a trail of fire in its wake, it streaked toward the twins and their staff.

Both the warlocks looked up and raised their hands together, and a shimmering green wall of energy burst forth that enclosed the two, along with the staff, just as the ball of fire reached them. The concussion from the collision of green and red energies could clearly be heard all the way up the mountainside. The flames wrapped around the green shield and engulfed it. A few moments passed before the fire slowly dissipated.

Once the flames winked out, the warlocks unleashed a barrage of mystical energies up toward the three witches, who defended themselves with their own pyrotechnics. Waves of power quickly flowed back and forth; the air was filled with crackling and thunder as each side tried to get the upper hand.

Hollilea looked down to see the defenders were engaged with the enemy troops and seemed unaware of the confrontation taking place deeper in the pass. She shook her head and said with a trembling voice, "I hope that without the warlocks' interference, our friends below can prevail."

Trealine gave his customary grunt while Marc remained silent. All three knew the odds still did not favor those defending the pass.

*****   *****

Some had noticed the side conflict taking place. Kalend stood with his mother and Juliet as they watched the war of energies streaking across the Norry Pass. "Looks like someone has engaged the warlocks," Juliet said quietly.

"I hope it is Yarguri. But since my sister has not responded, we can't know for sure," Kalend responded ruefully.

Shouts rose from the left and right sides of the defensive positions along the palisade as the incoming horseman crashed into the defenders. Kalend noted that the battle was now fully engaged on all fronts. The infantry had reached Tosayner, and his reformed troops were in the middle. The archers, who had finished off the enemies that had popped up behind them and with no more appearing, concentrated on slowing the troops still navigating the trenches. For a time, the defense held as the battle flowed back and forth.

Kalend was worried for his sister. If the witches were engaging the warlocks, where was she, and why did she not respond when he called out to her? He shook his head as his mother moved silently over and slipped her arm through his as they watched the fighting.

*****   *****

Tosrayner had moved back toward the archers, met with Louquintas, and said, "We need to get our cavalry over to the sides to help out. Right now, it's too narrow for those horses, but if enough get through, we will have a serious problem."

Louquintas nodded to their left. "It looks like Sergeant Galland has the same idea." The cavalry had split up and moved to support the infantry on both ends, with the Sergeant leading those headed to the right.

"It seems the warlock twins have their hands full. Let us hope whoever that is…can keep it up for a while. We can hold for a time, but the warlocks could quickly swing this back around."

Shortly after that statement, the archers were once again confronted with adversaries popping up among them. Their attention became diverted, and a full-scale fight now raged in the back of the formation as they ceased firing arrows to defend themselves. Louquintas quickly waded into the melee to lend support and shout guidance to the crucial archers.

*****   *****

Kalend noted the archers were under attack again and swiveled his head to peer toward the pyrotechnic battle deeper in the pass. From what he could see, it looked like the witches were still engaged, but the warlocks were now playing more defense, sending less energy back at their enemies. Only one twin was defending, while the other formed the cloud with the staff buried in the ground. The staff's stone continued to glow purple and pulse with life, and a new cloud of puffy greyness had formed off to the side, where troops lined up to go through.

The archers were becoming overwhelmed as more of the twin's forces appeared. Before the broken palisade, the defensive line was shoved backward, step by step. The calvary led by Sergeant Galland on the left was holding, but the right side was not faring as well; slowly, it was being pushed into the middle. Kalend helplessly watched as Tosrayner and Louquintas attempted to direct what they could, but three sides were folding inward, and the numbers were not in their favor.

Rashana reached over and touched Kalend's shoulder. "My son, we must leave while we can."

Kalend shook his head vehemently. "No, we must do something. I can't leave both Tosrayner and Louquintas."

"You must; that is what they would want. There is nothing we can do."

Kalend helplessly looked down at his friends as they struggled to hold the Norry Pass. He could not think of any way to help and knew his mother was correct; turning his torso upon Whistler, he looked at both his mother and Juliet and nodded in resignation. "We must leave."

Then Whistler stepped forward restlessly as he snorted and pawed at the ground. "What is it, my friend," Kalend asked as he patted his horse's side to comfort him.

Taking another firm step down the hill, Whistler looked back and let out a loud whistle-whinny while he dug up more earth with his hoof. Concerned now, Kalend pulled back on the reins in an attempt to turn Whistler around. The horse raised his head in irritation, clamped down on the bit, and fought against him.

Rashana moved her horse backward, gestured for Juliet to do the same, and quietly said, "Kalend, release his reins."

"Why?" Kalend looked back and asked in a puzzled voice.

"Just do it. Something is happening here; that horse is much more than you know. Release him, and let's see what he does."

Giving her a perplexed look but unwilling to defy his mother, he let go of the reins and grabbed Whistler's mane. As his hands grasped handfuls of dark hair, Whistler reared up, pawed into the air, and let loose a loud Whistle that reverberated off the mountainside.

Elation coursed through Kalend's mind as sudden understanding crashed over him; his horse was there to help, that this was his destiny. How or in what shape that was to take, Kalend knew not, only that this was right, and his fears and doubts suddenly vanished. Whistler's hooves hit the ground, and they rushed down the hill, quickly reaching a full gallop; Kalend drew his sword and leaned forward as the wind whipped past him. He urged his horse toward those below with a desperate need.

As he pounded down the uneven hill, irrational thoughts began to clog his mind; a madness seeped into his subconscious, threatening to overcome him. His peripheral vision caught shadowy shapes to either side, running with them. Figures formed, ghost-like and ragged around the edges, with two on either side, they solidified and took the shape of horses. The madness grew to a crescendo in his mind, but still, he noticed something was off about his new escorts. At first glance, they appeared normal, but now fully formed, he saw flames fly from their mouths and pointed teeth gnash the air. Their eyes glowed a deep red, radiating a sickening madness that matched the growing madness within him. The earth flew up behind the four as they rode in unison with Whistler, matching his stride and coming into formation around him.

The five plowed into the enemy troops that were slaughtering the archers. Kalend swung his sword to the left and right, his mind ablaze in a sea of red; he killed all those who stood in his way. All the hard training over the years coalesced, and he fought with a skill and strength that could not be matched by those he encountered. The four horses reared and bucked beside him, flesh and armor no match for the iron-hard hooves and flames that spewed forth from their mouths. Quickly, they mowed over the attackers, leaving a mess of bodies and burnt limbs in their wake. The remaining archers backed away in fright, unsure if this new threat of unholy creatures was friend or foe.

Once the archers were freed of attackers, Kalend swung Whistler about and plunged directly into the middle of the defenders, and Tosranyer's men hastily parted to let them pass. He waved his sword above his head and led his band of horror into the enemies poring through the palisade. Madness raged unchecked within his mind; he had but a singular thought...stop these enemies at any and all cost.

Then, from deep within his subconscious, a quiet bell of rebellion softly rang out in warning. A rebellion from the insanity raging within, and it tried to push through the ravening darkness that engulfed him. Another presence joined the struggle, and slowly, his mind cleared; the hazy red fog was shoved to the side. Not gone, but partitioned off, he could feel its seething mania as it fought to break free, but it was no longer steering him, and he regained some control over himself. As his sanity returned, he reached out to the other presence and inquired about who or what it was; the answer surprised him, but he realized it should not have. Whistler was that Other. It was not so much that his horse spoke in words but more in feelings and attitude. He understood that Whistler had brought him back from the madness-fueled void and that that void had come from the strange horses that rode beside him.

He had questions, but Whistler conveyed that now was not the time. Kalend suddenly could clearly see about himself, with only a slight red glow around the edges of his vision. He saw a bloody battle raging all around. With fire frothing from their mouths and madness shining through their eyes, the crazed horses used their bodies to form a protective ring around Whistler and Kalend. The enemy soldiers' swords sliced right through them but caused no harm. There was a slight flicker at the moment of contact; part of the animal turned to smoke, which reformed hard and substantially once the blade passed through. They were barely holding the enemy at bay; too many troops had pored through the defenses. While Kalend and his strange entourage had thrust forward, too far forward, he now realized Tosrayner and Louquintas had been pushed back and were retreating in a slow and organized manner. Kalend felt a new sickness well up from deep within his gut as he noted they were now effectively alone and surrounded.

*****   *****

Feelings of fear and anger threatened to overwhelm Hollilea. She had watched as those defending below had been pushed back. She had witnessed her brother and the four strange horses plunge into the melee and become surrounded. Her senses reeled with the emotions coursing through her body and mind. She wanted to help...needed to help.

She took a few tentative steps to the edge of the cliff. She knew what had to be done; not being involved was no longer an option. With hands thrust upward and head tilted back, she closed her eyes, letting all the fear, anger, and emotions sweep through her. Dark clouds gathered as a cold wind blew through the pass. Her white gown began to glow brightly, and her gleaming red hair waved behind her like a pennon flying above a castle. Power flowed and pulsed through her; it filled her with a glorious need to be unleashed, to punish those who dared to take her only family from her.

Hollilea opened her eyes and glared down at her brother, surrounded by enemies and the defenders in full retreat. The wind grew into a gale as lightning flashed across the sky, and heavy darkness fell over the pass. Those below ceased their struggles while they fearfully looked upward at the gleaming white figure with flaming red hair that seemed to tower over them while radiating raw power.

Hollilea dropped her left hand and pointed down toward the pass. There was a moment of silence as if the world stood still and ceased its movement among the heavens. Then, the skies burst open as multiple streaks of lightning dropped like hammers among the invaders. Explosions erupted wherever the lightning struck, and the battlefield was soon littered with bodies. The enemy troops cowered in fear, and many dropped their weapons and ran.

The defenders retreated further and reformed once they realized the damage was contained to the troops of King Kourkourant. They formed a new defensive line and struck down anyone that managed to escape the carnage, which was few.

The wind and lightning continued to grow; Hollilea dropped her right hand, and magic flew downward from her fingertips, leaving a trail of brightly colored lights that stretched from the mountain ledge to those it struck. Lightning continued its deadly dance from the sky as she sent waves of colored death at those it missed. Her body tingled, and she tried to draw more power; it was seductive, like a parched man in need of water; she needed more power.

An ethereal shade appeared to her right, and a woman soon stood beside her, yelling into the hurricane of wind. Ensnared in the power that flowed from her and filled with the need to punish those below, she barely recognized her Wiccenda. Morgne sagged to her knees and reached out as if pleading for help. Trealine moved forward, bent over into the wind, and tapped her on the shoulder.

The touch of Trealine and the look upon her Wiccenda's face, one of fear and distress, snapped her from the power-soaked rage she had been feeling. She clasped her hands together as she realized all she had done, and the lightning ceased, and the wind calmed. The death and destruction she had visited on those below came rushing in and filled her with sadness. What had she done? Morgne gingerly rose and looked her in the eye. "Never have I felt such power drawn so fast," she said as she tried to catch her breath.

"I am sorry. So very sorry," Hollilea replied in a tearful voice.

"Do not be my child. I am only glad you came to your senses when you did. You could have killed us both if you had continued. Altering the weather in such a manner and using it that way takes tremendous magic. Almost more than we can siphon from the True Source."

The dark clouds had scattered, and sunlight once more filled the pass and covered those still alive in the valley of the Norry Pass. Hollilea gazed at the swath of death and felt a keen sadness. But then she noticed her brother, riding Whistler among the bodies, as he slowly made his way back to his teachers. A smile lit her face, and some of the sadness passed. She had done what was needed to protect those she loved. After all, that had been her original intent, and the warlocks and King Kourkourant had brought this on themselves. She hardened her mind and realized that this was bigger than her and her brother; something more was at play. She now knew that she needed to find out what that was. There was no more hiding with her mentors; it was time for her to join her brother and finish this business.

Morgne nodded her head as she watched the play of emotions sweep across Hollilea's face and, as if she had read her mind, said, "You are now part of something bigger than yourself. Rejoin your brother, and in time, you will find out what that is." She sighed and wavered on her feet. "But for now, do not try and draw power from me; I need rest and time to heal. That was beyond my experience, and I can sense the power is distant for me."

*****   *****

Kalend had rejoined his teachers. He patiently sat upon Whistler while Louquintas and Tosrayner dispatched men to find any other survivors of the battle. The injured were to be brought to a medical tent for patching and healing, which was set up on the hillside beside the command tent. All were to be attended to, friend and foe alike. Tosrayner explained that those soldiers who had been enemies just a short while ago were only men, blinded by loyalty to a misguided King.

Scouts had been sent out to canvas the area in search of King Kourkourant and the warlocks, but no trace of them had been found. It was assumed they had once again used their magic to escape.

Kalend replayed it all in his head; so much had happened, he was unsure what to make of it. Whistler, the flaming-mouthed horses, his sister's power that had been unleashed, all of it made little sense. For he knew it had been her, had known as soon as the skies had changed. He had felt it deep in his bones. After it was over, they communicated with the bracer, and she confirmed his beliefs. It had been a quick discussion, and they had agreed to speak of it later. She was coming to him and would be there shortly, which made him smile in anticipation of the reunion.

Tosrayner glanced at Louquintas and Kalend. "Let's head back to the command post. We have some things to discuss, like our next steps."

Once they were all seated around the table in the command tent, there was much discussion on how to move forward. But few actual decisions were made. Sergeant Galland entered and was followed by the witches and Karl; all four looked weary and dusty.

Yarguri spoke without preamble, "Things are moving at a fast pace. We need to make some decisions and move quickly."

Tosrayner heartily responded, "Welcome, my friends."

Yarguri grunted. "You and Louquintas were ever the match."

Tosrayner laughed. "We were also your favorites."

Yarguri, again, grunted in response.

Tosrayner continued, "We were thinking we need to get into Odewin city. Their King is gone, and I doubt he went back there."

"We agree. I doubt the twins would take him there. We have had word that Jarlwo is in the city; you need to speak with him. He knows much and has learned more." Turning toward Kalend, Yarguri gave him a direct look. "Finding those warlocks is now your priority."

Kalend was taken aback and asked in a shocked voice, "Me? Why me?"

Shaking her head, Yarguri said, "It is what you are meant to do. We cannot do it; we are too old and do not have the stamina for such things. We plan to head back into our mountains and stay there. This must fall to others." She pointed a bony finger at him. "Those 'others' being you. I know you have more questions, but Jarlwo is the best to answer them."

Kalend sat back and muddled his way through it. He did want answers and knew the witches well enough to know if they would not provide them now, then no amount of badgering would get them to talk. And then a thought struck him. "What of Hollilea? Surely, now she can join me?" he blurted out.

"Yes, what of me?" Hollilea asked firmly from the tent flap doorway. She stood silhouetted by the light outside, and with her hands on her hips, she gave those in the room a determined look. "I believe it's time I help him with this. For it involves both of us."

Kalend rose to his feet, rushed over, and hugged her fiercely. They turned together, and while holding hands, they stared at everyone with a look that dared any to naysay them. Silence greeted them, but he noticed smiles on both his mentors' faces. The witches gave no hint of emotion, of course.

CHAPTER TWENTY-FIVE

The long, plodding march to Odewin City gave Kalend and his sister time to catch up with each other and their various escapades over the past few months. They each wanted and needed answers; so much had occurred recently and at such a fast pace that they both felt events outpaced their ability to process it. In a gentle and probing manner, they teased the information from each other, asking questions and then patiently listening to the replies. Although they each learned a great deal, much was left unanswered.

Watching his sister and mother meet for the first time had brought a tear to everyone's eye; even the gruffness of Trealine had been no match for the raw emotions of their first hug. Kalend still broke into a huge smile when he thought about it. Taking dinner together each evening and retiring to a tent left exclusively for them, mother and daughter quickly got acquainted. Kalend had watched as the bond they already shared by blood blossomed and grew into something much more profound. Something that only a mother and daughter could feel, and that also made him smile with happiness.

Kalend understood that, for now, Hollilea was powerless; she did not know when she would have access to the magic again. Her Wiccenda had warned her not to try, and she could feel a distance she had not felt since her very first awareness of the bond between Morgne and herself. Surrounded by the survivors of the Norry Pass and with the warlocks on the run with King Kourkourant, they felt safe enough, even without the use of her magic. Besides, he thought ruefully he did have other protection.

Shaking his head, he shuddered at the thought of the flaming-mouthed horses and the fury that had infected him. The horses had dissipated, turned to smoke, and wafted into the breeze immediately after Hollilea had ceased her pyrotechnics. All traces of the madness that had threatened to overwhelm him had scattered with them, for which he was immensely grateful. How much help their insanity-laced protection could provide was something that needed to be explored, but not anytime soon. It was still too recent and raw.

When asked, the witches had been vague with any answers. Shocked by that, he was not. They did provide that Jarlwo could be of some help, but that had done little to ease his mind. Their advice was to refrain from calling the horses forth until he received more information. And since he did not even know how to do that, all he could do was grumble under his breath about having to wait. Luckily for him, they had either ignored the grumbling or had not heard; he guessed the former.

Even Whistler had remained silent. Kalend could still sense the presence of the bond that had formed, but all attempts at communication were received with a cool stillness. He patted Whistler's side and told him he would be there when he was ready. So, all he could do was wait to speak with Jarlwo. He shook his head mockingly and thought how patience was not really his strongest asset.

Looking up at the towering walls of Odewin city, he was once again thankful for the knowledge imparted to him by his teachers at the monastery. The city straddled the Odessian River, which split into many fingers and formed a delta as it emerged from the sea beyond. It had the reputation of being one of the finest in the world, with renowned housing, streets, and inns. A place of vast commerce, the lure of the legendary deep coffers of Odewin kept a steady stream of traffic flowing through its streets. Merchants with caravans of thick wool carpets from as far away as Langgford, to exotic oils and dates from the Islands off Touser, all frequently passed beneath its gates. Known as the Sleepless City, with goods and services available at all hours, Kalend was eager to see if the descriptions matched reality.

Having reached the river three days ago, they had followed its burbling waters to the city walls. Tosrayner had the army camp further up the river and out of eyesight from those looking out from the crenels above. Twenty guards accompanied the group with the hope that a smaller force would be less provocative and, therefore, easier to pass into the city. One soldier rode in the lead with the flag of Touser fluttering on a pole in the gentle breeze. Sergeant Galland had pulled it out of his travel bags and advised them to enter under its banner, which should afford them some diplomatic license while also easing their passage through the gates.

A line of merchants and travelers snaked its way along the cobblestone path awaiting entry, but, at the approach of the heavily armored group and with fearful glances, most hastily stepped off into the brush and mud along the sides. Tosrayner and Sergeant Galland stood before the gate guards and requested access; after some heated words, they were reluctantly allowed to enter.

Kalend's first impression seemed to confirm what he had been taught. The streets were clean and wide, and the shops and inns were a colorful mix of sizes and shapes. Oil lamps stood at even intervals, unlit; they stood as a testament that even in the nighttime, the city would not sleep. The people were just as colorful in dress. He thought the difference between Pleus, the only other city he had ever visited, and this one was striking. Here, people moved more sedately but with an arrogance that said they had no need to hurry. More like the strut of a peacock he once saw, they walked about with heads held high and looks of disdain for those about them. Even their speech with each other was haughty, but none seemed to take exception since they all had the same attitude.

With Sergeant Galland leading the way, the group moved at a slow, deliberate march. Like at the gates, merchants, citizens, and travelers all parted to let them pass, many with open looks of disapproval. After a few turns, they entered a broader and more ornate boulevard, one lined on either side with tall oaks interspersed with elaborate statues. This opened to a grand view of the palace ahead.

Kalend stared and shook his head in wonder. The palace gleamed in the sunlight, a glowing vision, one that stood out, even in this city of opulence. The three-story walls were encased in blinding white marble, statues of people and animals filled niches regularly, and tall columns graced the entrance. It all spoke of unimaginable wealth.

Functionaries had been alerted to their presence on the promenade; they silently stood two rows deep and waited for them before the palace entrance. Tosrayner dismounted and addressed the crowd that stood apprehensively around them. "Hello from His Majesty King Darthmoot. We come bearing news and have no ill will toward the city or its people."

One colorfully robed, long-haired older gentleman stepped out of the gathering and, with a smile, said, "Good to see you, Tosrayner, my old friend. The years have been kind to you, it seems."

Returning the smile, Tosrayner replied, "Thank you. We have much to discuss, Duke Salasar."

"Why yes, I believe we do," Salasar replied solemnly.

***** *****

Their guards had been billeted, and the rest of the party sat in an airy covered alcove filled with an assortment of leather couches, velvet-covered divans, and high-backed chairs. Along the far wall stood tables groaning under an array of meats, cheeses, wines, and liquors, which permeated the air and made Kalend lick his lips in anticipation. The alcove formed a semi-circle in the back of the palace, which was ringed by tall granite columns that held up a light blue-tiled roof. The floor was covered in a colorful mosaic depicting a hunting scene with horsemen, hunting dogs, and a scared fox on the run. A cobblestone pathway led out into a garden of roses, lilies, daffodils, exotic bushes, and trees that looped around a three-foot stone wall that held a pond filled with koi. It was a serene setting, but Kalend noted that it was not as peaceful as it seemed on the first impression. Closer inspection found the gardens not particularly well kept, with weeds growing throughout, pathways littered with debris, and a pond so dirty that he could only tell fish resided in it by the tiny circles left behind after they broached the surface in search of food.

Duke Salasar lounged in a luxurious purple and gold chair, and with an artfully etched pewter cup in hand, he raised it to the group, "Greetings', again, to you! It is my pleasure to host my old friends Tosrayner and Louquintas, as well as their companions." Kalend raised his cup with the rest of the companions as they returned their host's greeting. The Duke nodded in appreciation and continued, "To business then. We need to make some decisions…and quickly. As you are now aware, the King is not here, and from your presence, I can assume things did not go his way at the Norry Pass?"

Tosrayner shook his head. "No, they did not. He and the warlocks disappeared right after they were routed. Do you have any idea of where they went?"

"No. Things have been unsettled around the palace for many years." He paused for a moment and took a deep breath before continuing, "And to be honest, for the kingdom, it is probably for the best that he stays gone. It is my head on a stake for saying that, but for too long have I been silent, and it looks like we may finally have some relief."

"Hopefully, we can help with that. Have you heard from any of the outlying dukes?"

"Yes, I have been in contact with them for the past few months, secretly, of course. We are all in agreement that change must happen for the kingdom to survive. I have been able to keep things from completely flying apart, but it has been getting harder. They are ready to send in troops once I give them the signal."

Louquintas had gone over to a table to help himself to another goblet of red wine and, as he returned, said, "Good. Luckily, as the ranking duke in the kingdom, you will have some pull with the palace and city guards. We need to secure them first."

Duke Salasar nodded in agreement. "I can make a proclamation that the King has left and abdicated the throne. That begs the question then of who takes over until we can convene the council to elect a new King, which has not been done in several generations."

Tosrayner looked over at Louquintas, and both grinned as they turned to the duke.

With a frown, the Duke shook his head and firmly said, "NO!"

"Oh yes," Louquintas replied. "We are here to serve YOU, my Lord Chancellor."

"Damnit. You know I don't want this. The only reason I have stayed for as long as I have was to help guide our King as he became more erratic. I was one of the few he trusted anymore. His paranoia had reached a point where he had surrounded himself with sycophants who only looked to enrich themselves at the expense of the Kingdom. Taking over was never my intention," the duke said emphatically.

Tosrayner nodded in understanding. "I know, but the kingdom needs the stability that you will bring. The other dukes respect you and will follow your lead. I will stay with our force and help to smooth things over until they arrive. Once they are here, the council can convene, and a new King can be crowned."

With a sigh, the duke smiled. "You two always were a pain in the ass. I remember when you both came up under the old King Olbert, always did as you were told, but also not afraid to speak your minds."

Tosrayner smiled. "Where did we learn that from?"

Duke Salasar snorted and took another draw from his wine.

"We need to move onto other matters." Tosrayner changed the subject with a reflective look. "It is my understanding that

Jarlwo is within the city, and we need to find him. Any ideas where he could be?"

The Duke smiled. "Most likely, at The Fox."

Tosrayner looked over at Louquintas. "I think it best that only your group goes: Kalend, Juliet, Hollilea, Trealine, and yourself. Sergeant Galland and I will stay here and focus on keeping things settled."

The meeting broke up, and Kalend stood off to the side while the rest of the group assembled to find Jarlwo. He was reviewing the meeting with Duke Salasar in his mind. He had stayed silent; this business was serious, the removal of a King. Even with his mentors' nonchalant words and demeanor, he had noticed an underlining tension; they were staying calm, but deep-down, currents flowed that said otherwise. Staying quiet and observing was for the best, he thought; besides, he had no rank here, no authority, and his main concern must be for what the twins were up to next.

When questioned, his mother had also chosen to remain silent and said she would stay here with Tosrayner and the Duke. Her voice could still carry weight with the other dukes, and she hoped to ease the transition. Besides, she said with a rueful smile, she was too old for galivanting about the world looking for trouble. Kalend had frowned but understood. At least she would be protected here, and he would not have to worry about her, for he suspected their search had the potential for much danger. With little hint of humor, he grimaced as he knew that last part to be an understatement.

Tosrayner and Louquintas had finished speaking with Duke Salasar about some last-minute details and now stood before Kalend and his friends. "Do whatever is necessary to track them down. If you need help from me, I will be here, and once the other dukes send troops, we can mount a posse to help. Keep an eye out for what or who is behind this," Tosrayner advised.

Louquintas looked to Kalend with a raised eyebrow. "Shall we get going?"

Kalend nodded. "Yes, where and what is The Fox?"

"You shall see."

*****   *****

Standing before the double oaken doors, Kalend stared at them momentarily as recognition teased his mind. There was a large fox head embossed into the door under which read the words "The Fox Head Den of Enlightenment," which looked eerily like the set of doors in Pleus, where they had found the Old Storyteller, but instead of a lion's head, it was that of a fox. He glanced at Louquintas with a raised eyebrow. Louquintas nodded in answer to the unspoken question as he shoved the right door open. Like at the Lion Head Den of Enlightenment, they were immediately greeted by a fastidious gentleman with slick-backed hair and an air of authority. "Welcome to The Fox. I am Murdock; how may I be of service?" He asked as his eyes ran over each of them, appraising their appearance and demeanor as if to decide how best to proceed once an answer was given.

Louquintas stood with his back straight and answered in an uncharacteristic sober tone, "We are looking for Jarlwo and wish an audience with him."

Without a pause, Murdock asked, "And who is seeking to meet with Jarlwo?"

"Louquintas and Kalend and their friends, he will know who we are."

With a nod, he motioned with a slim hand that glittered in the lamplight from elaborate golden rings upon his long fingers. "Please follow me. He has been expecting you."

They were led down a narrow hall with doors on either side, again, like the Lion Head Den. Kalend figured, at this point, this could not be a coincidence. Two similar buildings with similar names and similar greetings, too much similarity for him to believe this Den of Enlightenment was not somehow connected to the one in Pleus. They came to the end of the hallway to a door that Murdock silently opened and then stepped to the side to allow them to enter freely. The door was quickly shut behind them after they filed in, and they stood momentarily uncertain as they took in the room with its lone occupant. A rectangular mahogany table took up most of the room and pulled up close around it over a dozen tall forest green upholstered chairs. Several open boxes of cigars and a couple full glass decanters littered the middle of the table, and at its head sat Jarlwo, with his cowl pushed back and craggy face standing out for all to see. With a crystal tumbler in one hand, a quarter full of a rich dark liquid, he pulled a half-smoked cigar from his smiling lips with the other and said, "My friends, so good to see you again!"

Each member of the party nodded and said their hello's as they pulled out chairs to sit. Louquintas sat down on the left-hand side of the table and poured himself a generous helping from a decanter into a glass that awaited before each chair. Once settled in with his drink, he leaned back and replied, "Good to see you as well. Hope things have been going smoothly for you?"

With a snort and raised eyebrow, Jarlwo said, "Not sure smoothly would be the appropriate word; however, from what I hear from the witches about your exploits, maybe so. Things are moving apace and quicker than anyone could have known. So.... if you could hold off the questions, I would like to tell you what I have learned so far?"

With a tilt of his tumbler, Louquintas implied that he should continue.

Jarlwo sighed, took an extended pull from his cigar, and exhaled a generous cloud of white smoke before continuing, "You know at this point that the warlocks are working for someone else. Who that other is, I am still working on. My Wiccenda is also trying to find out information from his end and will relay what he knows when and if he finds anything. What I can tell you is that much more is at stake than just the fate of the Kingdom of Odewin."

Jarlwo smiled gently at Kalend, "And you, my young friend, are the key to much of what is going on."

Kalend nodded grimly. "I gathered that, but how and why?"

"It appears you have been prophesied about. That you and your sister have a destiny. This scares the warlocks and whoever their master is. However, I still do not have all the details on this prophecy, if there is one." Jarlwo shook his head and frowned. "There are secrets being kept even from me. For what purpose, I do not know."

Kalend nodded in understanding and said with a frown for those around him, "I know the feeling."

Jarlwo laughed at the exaggerated hurt look that Louquintas gave his protégé. Then, Jarlwo continued, "Yes, I believe you do. However, I can give you some help with other matters. Those horses that saved you at the pass for one, Yarguri told me of them. They are called the Horses of Diomede. They are led by Whistler and his rider, which is you. You can call them when in great need but can only control them for so long. They are an old magic and not seen in centuries and are quite mad. Your connection with Whistler will help shield you from their madness; powerful they are, but dangerous. Their madness has made them into flesh-eaters, and I would advise caution when employing them."

Kalend shuddered when he thought about their madness. "I am not sure I want anything to do with them."

Jarlwo nodded in understanding. "They are wedded to you now. Use them sparingly; in time, you will gain more confidence in how and when to call them forth. They are magic from another place and time. That is all I know; you will have to find out more as you use them."

After another long puff from his cigar, Jarlwo continued, "Now, as for the whereabouts of the evil twins and the king, I believe they are headed to the Isle of Frouth. That has been their base of operations and where they can regroup. I believe the witches have told you of the basis of our magic and the Wiccenda, but there are other sources that can be used. One of which is wells. These will look like normal watering holes, but they are focal points and gateways to where the Wiccenda come from. At these points, physical objects and beings can be called forth."

Louquintas chimed in, "We encountered one in the desert," and then he proceeded to tell the story of Lusstail and the mysterious master they had encountered.

Jarlwo grunted, "That sounds like one. This business of Panes is worrisome. The fact that they can bring them into our realm is something I would not have thought they were capable of until now. The warlocks have been given a staff with a stone of power, which in turn is tied to something else. This helps to amplify their powers. It is also how they can pop up from nowhere and disappear at will. But even that is something only used sparingly. You remember when we had that run-in with Tworg outside Renthar Village?" He received a few nods to the affirmative and continued. "That is how he escaped."

Louquintas said, "We saw them using that stone ourselves at the pass."

"I heard. We need to get the stone and staff away from them. One more thing that your group can look for."

Louquintas nodded. "It looks like we may need to get to that island."

"Yes, you do. Kalend and Hollilea, you are the only ones capable of stopping them. I cannot interfere," he raised a hand to stop any questions. "And no, I cannot tell you why at this point."

Kalend had taken a cigar, cut, and lit it like he had seen the others do while he listened intently. Then he took his first drag, inhaled deeply....and proceeded to cough excessively. Louquintas laughed and advised, "Try it without inhaling." He did and found the experience fascinating; a flood of different tastes flowed over his tongue and filled his mouth. Finding that he liked it, he exhaled and smiled sheepishly at the group that had stopped to watch him in amusement.

With a frown, Jarlwo addressed Kalend and Hollilea, "It is not due to your parents that they have hunted you. The twins have been trying to stop you from reaching your full powers. They fear what you are becoming. The King has been used all these years to find and kill you." He sighed and said with a faraway look, "Really, the King was just a pawn. They have control over him in some manner; it's a sad situation."

Hollilea shook her head and said sternly, "Maybe sad in a way, but he still killed our father and made us exiles. I will not be sad if something happens to him."

"When you find him, that may change. We will see. For now, I think it best that you go to that island and try and get to them before they cause more problems. We MUST find out what their real end game is. Whatever it is, I doubt it's good for any of us."

Louquintas peered at everyone around the table. "We have been through a lot and have a ways to go to see this business finished. I will stay till the end with Kalend and Hollilea, but others here who have been of great help now need to decide for themselves if they wish to continue."

Trealine sat back and grunted, "I got nothing better to do."

Juliet leaned forward and, in a firm voice, said, "I have not had many experiences with outsiders, but these past few months, I have come to count all of you as friends, and this business involves the whole world. My place is now with this group. You may count on me."

With a nod to each member of the group, Louquintas turned to Kalend. "Well lad, shall we go hunting for warlocks?"

Kalend stood and solemnly addressed everyone, "Thank you to everyone here. I appreciate all that you have done, and it warms me that each of you will continue and see this through with my sister and me."

CHAPTER TWENTY-SIX

It was nearing dusk as Kalend sat astride Whistler and followed Louquintas along the cobblestone road that led to Oeshland Port. The road was in good repair, with new cobblestones and drainage ditches lining either side; it was obvious that the palace's neglect did not extend everywhere. This was too vital of an artery for the city and kingdom. Plush rugs, silk clothing, perfume, and other luxury items poured in from the southern empire of Kulrung, which were gobbled up by Odewin City elite. The leftovers, those objects that did not meet the latest fashion trends or were outdated, were sent off to be sold abroad at exorbitant prices. More mundane items also flowed in and out of the port regularly. Iron ore, wood, and foodstuffs packed in salt, all of which filled the wagon beds of the merchant class as they plied their trade among the various kingdoms.

The friends made steady progress through the sparse forest as clouds flitted above them on warm, moist currents of air. After visiting the palace to retrieve their horses and get supplies, they now expected to make the port city in two days. A letter signed and sealed with Duke Salazar's signet should suffice to allow them entry into the port. From there, they would have to find passage aboard one of the trading vessels and entice the captain to cross over to the Island of Frouth.

The duke had warned them that the island was known to be rocky, with small mountains and few people living on it. It also had a reputation for strange events and creatures, but otherwise, not much was known about the isle's interior.

Louquintas planned to cross over to the only known village on the island. It resided along the coast diagonally across from Oeshland Port and should be only a day's journey. Jarlwo had told them that the twins had a camp in an abandoned keep somewhere within its depths, but that is all he knew of its location. The hope was to gather information at the village or, if they could get lucky, a guide. Otherwise, they would have to head into the interior blind and find their own way, which is not the best idea, Kalend thought.

Trealine moved his horse up past Kalend to ride along beside Louquintas. "We have someone following behind us." He said in a quiet voice. "They are staying far back, trying to disguise themselves, but I catch a glimpse of them here and there."

Louquintas nodded. "Are they trying to catch us or just follow, do you think?"

"Follow. They make no move to catch us. If anything, they are doing their best to stay as far back as possible and still keep us within sight."

The two rode in silence for a few minutes while Louquintas thought it through before replying, "Let's leave them be for now. If you lose sight of them or they move to catch us, then we will do something."

Trealine growled something that Kalend could not catch and moved back to his rear-guard position. Louquintas looked over his shoulder at Kalend and motioned him to come up front. "Did you hear that?" he asked as Kalend trotted up beside him.

"Yes. Seems we have unwanted company," Kalend replied.

"We only have two days until we reach the port. My guess is that it is Lusstail."

Kalend sighed. "You are probably right." Then he gave a fake laugh. "I had almost forgotten about that little snake."

"I have not. I would love to get my hands on him and see what all he knows. Bastard has dogged us for too long."

"Should we stop and deal with him then?"

"No. Let him flounder behind us, for now. It is no secret where we are headed. Too many saw us leave the city on this road."

A few hours later, they made camp atop damp ground while heavy moisture continued to hang in the air. The clouds that had dogged them all day had turned from white, puffy, and high flying to dark and low, threatening rain for the coming night. A small fire was lit for warmth and cooking, but otherwise, the companions found it to be a miserable evening to be outside. Trealine thought their following friend was still behind them but continued to keep their distance. Juliet offered to go have a look, but Louquintas shook his head and said to let whoever it was alone. However, they did post two guards that night instead of their usual one.

Kalend and Hollilea took the first watch and sat apprehensively, staring out into the darkness. The fire had been allowed to die down and go out shortly after eating. Leaving them in heavy darkness as the clouds obscured the night sky. All about them, condensation formed drops of water that fell off leaves and tree limbs, creating a steady patina of wet plops as they struck the ground. Occasionally, their eerie evening was broken up by the rustle of some animal that prowled the darkness in search of prey.

The hours slipped slowly by as the unnerving night kept the duo nervously awake. Once, Kalend thought he heard a voice in the distance, a human cry of pain, there, then quickly gone. He turned, leaned toward Hollilea, and, in a whisper, asked if she had heard it too. She shook her head in the negative. He nodded his head and swung his gaze back to the now silent forest to continue his watch, straining to capture the sound again, but nothing more was heard that resembled that pitiful cry. At last, they shook Trealine and Juliet awake to take the next watch. Then, both fell into a fitful slumber with dreams that haunted them until they awoke unrefreshed the following day.

The threatening rain had swept in while Kalend slept. Sitting astride Whistler, he grumpily endured a steady drizzle that managed to sneak its way down beneath his layers, making his undergarments cling coldly to his clammy skin. He pulled his oil-slicked coat tighter about him, which did little but send another current of rain slithering down his back. Whistler, of course, did not seem to mind and trotted along happily, and for some reason, that irritated Kalend even more.

Just around noon, Trealine informed them that he believed their guest had ceased following but that something new was now on their trail. He could not tell what it was, but he was sure there was more than one. And whatever it was, it was not content just to follow. He estimated they would catch the companions before evening.

Louquintas stopped, looked around at the dripping landscape, and said, "Not much in the way of cover here. Any chance we can outrun them?"

"No, not in this weather. They are moving fast and already closer than I like." Trealine grimaced. "I should have spotted them earlier, but they are good at concealing themselves."

Louquintas grunted and said, "Let's move along, and everyone keep their eyes out for cover or a good defensible spot."

Hollilea had trotted up, "I still do not have all my powers back; I just want everyone to know." She frowned at them. "Not sure how much help I will be."

"No need to fret. I am sure we can handle whatever it is," Kalend assured his sister with a cockiness he did not necessarily feel. His sister smiled nervously at him and nodded her head in thanks.

Louquintas led the way for an hour before Kalend called out and motioned for everyone to follow him to their left. The group fell in line behind him as he led them to the shore of a river, one of the tributaries that led from the sea to Odewin City. The water gurgled and burbled over rocky rapids that stretched over one hundred yards to the far side. The bank curved inward and created a U-shaped basin in which they had stopped.

Louquintas nodded in appreciation. "Good find. This is as best as we have seen. Hopefully, this river will protect our backside. We may not be able to escape that way, but at least they can't come at us from that way either."

Trealine grinned humorlessly. "Unless they can swim."

Louquintas gave the Othurean an irritated look, which made Trealine grin more broadly.

Kalend, who was used to this banter from his friends when things got tight, noticed Hollilea's horrified expression and bravely said, "Don't mind them. It's how they are." Hollilea shook her head silently and said she was not convinced by his act or theirs. Kalend grinned impudently at her in response.

Louquintas had them tie their horses to a couple of larger trees that lined the shoreline. He wanted them secured and away from any fighting; having them run in fright would cause them even more significant delay after the coming confrontation.

Now that they were no longer moving, Trealine thought their followers would reach them in about an hour. The group spent that time piling brush and dead limbs on either side of the basin, creating a narrow corridor through which they hoped to funnel their pursuers.

With less than an hour passed, grunting and hooting rose above the babbling river to reach their ears. Kalend, Louquintas, and Trealine reassembled at the base of the funnel while Juliet stood off to the right side with her bow, and Hollilea stood off to their left. The rain had ceased, and the small clearing was soon filled with the grunting of what approached.

Kalend's hand regripped his sword, and he tried to calm his mind with meditation. Using techniques he had been taught since childhood, his mind slowly cleared like from the lifting of the fog of fever, allowing him to clearly see around him. He could now almost sense the presence of those coming and feel them closing in. He also knew that Whistler was watching and wanted to help and that Kalend could, if needed, call forth the Horses of Diomede. But Kalend knew one other thing: he could not allow those demons to be called. The madness they brought was still too raw, too new, and he was not sure he could contain it. No, it was best to handle this threat themselves without the dubious help from the Diomede Horses. He relayed this to his horse; Whistler sighed but otherwise went silent within his mind.

The hooting stopped, and silent figures quickly filled the entrance of their makeshift funnel. Hollilea gasped as they got their first clear view of the creatures. Standing on two feet, close to eight feet tall and broad-shouldered, they towered like giants compared to Kalend's little band. They were covered in a thick carpet of white fur; their faces resembled those of apes that Kalend had seen drawn in books from his days of study. What made them significantly different from the apes in his books, however, were their arms; they had four of them. There were two on each side that ended in furry hands. They carried no weapons, but those rippling arms and massive hands gave the impression of immense strength.

Only two at a time could stand in the entrance of piled-up brush, but more could be seen eagerly lined up behind the lead pair. The group's plan was to keep them bottled up at the entrance and take them down before they could push their way through. Kalend grimaced, seeing what stood before them now; he was not confident he and his friends would survive the encounter if the apes managed to break through.

In the hopes of avoiding bloodshed, Louquintas made a hand gesture in friendship. Both the lead beasts snarled and beat their chests with all four of their meaty fists in response. Louquintas gestured again, but this time for the group to attack.

Juliet released her bow with a twang, and a second later, an arrow sprouted from the left ape's shoulder. With a furious look, the beast reached up and yanked the shaft out, and as blood spurted from the wound, threw it on the ground.

Louquintas, Kalend, and Trealine all reached the beasts at the same time. They fought to contain the behemoths; it was three on two, but the size, weight, and four arms of the ape beasts quickly proved to even the odds. Juliet turned her attention behind the two leading apes, attempting to slow them down while her friends tried to kill the ones in front. Trealine aimed low with his axe at the ape Juliet had struck first and took out its hamstring with a gush of blood. As it collapsed, Kalend darted in and sliced it across the neck. Gurgling out its lifeblood, it keeled over to its right while another jumped into its place.

The replacement ape had several bleeding arrow stubs protruding from its chest and shoulders, providing testimony that Juliet had been making those behind pay for standing back. Kalend attacked high; the beast deflected the blows with its arms, and chunks of fur and flesh soon littered the ground around them. The ape seemed not to notice the meat ripped from its body, and Kalend was pressed backward.

Louquintas had engaged the left ape with less success than his friends. He attacked alone and was strictly on the defensive as the four arms kept him constantly dodging and using his sword to block the beast's mighty fists.

The friends were shoved back as more apes flooded through the opening, and quickly, they found themselves under duress. Trealine took a blow to his right side, spun, and fell to the ground. He lay unmoving as Kalend rushed to help.

Two apes had spotted Hollilea and thundered toward her. She raised her arms in desperation, and with fingers spread wide, she hoped that some power could be found. There was an agonizing moment of stillness as nothing materialized, and she feared that her Wiccenda had not sufficiently recovered. Then lightning burst out and danced from her fingertips to strike the lead ape in the face. The clearing lit up with the energy, and the beasts stopped in mid-attack; they cried out as they all threw frightened expressions at Hollilea. Then they grabbed their dead and injured and quickly shambled back through the brush opening, and their grunts rapidly disappeared into the distance.

The friends stood with weapons still at the ready for several shocked moments as a sudden stillness lay heavily over the group. The quiet was broken by a low groan as Trealine rolled over in agony, and their attention turned to his needs.

Juliet tended to Trealine and reported that his wound would not be life-threatening. He had a bruised rib and would need to move with caution, but he would heal and be in fighting form with time. She bandaged him as best she could. To help ease his pain, she mixed some herbs and water into a foul-smelling elixir, then helped him choke it down from a wooden bowl. Kalend was unsure if the cure was worse than the bruised ribs from the expression on his face.

Louquintas thought they would remain free of the creatures from here on out but advised them that they would need to keep an eye out just in case.

Kalend was not so sure. "Why do you think they won't be back?"

Louquintas grinned mischievously. "I did not say they wouldn't be, just unlikely."

"Ok, why unlikely then?" Kalend asked in exasperation.

Louquintas threw another limb on the fire he had just started. "I believe they were frightened of your sister's magic, very frightened, and will stay well clear of it and, therefore, us."

"How can you know this?"

Trealine, who lounged against his pack and held his ribs lightly, said in a drowsy voice, "We Ortheans have many myths. One is of such creatures who attacked us; we call them Girillon. They are known for their ferocity, speed, and intelligence. I think Louquintas is right about this. The magic will keep them at bay; they are smart enough to know they have no defense against its use. But then again.....they are only known as myths to us. To see them in the flesh is a worrisome thing."

Kalend shrugged. "I hope they don't come back. But I wonder where they came from?"

Trealine responded with a deep snore as he fell asleep, a victim of the drink Juliet had provided.

Louquintas munched on some salted meat from his pack and said between bites, "That is a good question. One we may need to find an answer to...and soon. This whole business of Panes, and now these Girillon, has me wondering what other mythical horrors may pop up."

Juliet sat beside Trealine and tried to bundle up as best she could; the rain had ceased but left an unseasonable chill behind. "What do you mean 'mythical horrors'?"

Louquintas sighed. "These beasts and the Panes are not the only creatures that have been seen in the past few months. Tosrayner learned from Duke Salasar that he had been getting reports from the countryside all around Odewin City of sightings of various creatures. He had mentioned them to me, but we both figured it was nonsense since no one from the city had seen them, just some villagers scared from all the uncertainty of the King's irrational actions, or so we thought."

Kalend nodded thoughtfully. "Any reports from farther away?"

Louquintas shook his head. "No. Just around the city and between the city and the port."

"Could they be coming from the island?"

"That is a distinct possibility."

Kalend was slowly feeding the fire bigger sticks to create more heat as he looked up at Louquintas with an anxious expression. "We may be walking onto an island filled with beasts from another world. Beasts we have little knowledge of."

Louquintas leaned back against his pack, finished his snack, grinned at his protégé, and responded, "You see things clearly, my lad. Much more is going on here than a King under a spell and warlocks hunting you and your sister. Not to worry though, we are not without our own abilities to draw on."

They sat quietly and gazed into the fire for some time, contemplating all that Louquintas said. Reflecting on what they had been through so far and all that was to come, a solemnness settled over the group as they realized the daunting challenge that lay ahead. Kalend shook himself from his malaise, pulled a cigar from his pack, cut and lit it, and with his best Louquintas impersonation, quipped, "We are in for some interesting times."

The ladies looked up at him with startled expressions. Louquintas grinned, and Trealine mumbled gibberish in his sleep. They laughed together, and Kalend felt the atmosphere around the camp ease.

CHAPTER TWENTY-SEVEN

The group arrived at the city gates of Oeshland Port the following afternoon without any more incidents. Quickly, they had been allowed entry, the note from Duke Salasar having worked as expected, and they now found themselves down along the extensive wharf in search of a ship to give them passage across the sea. Louquintas led the way among the hovels and questionable drinking establishments that filled the Lower Wharf. He explained that there were two Wharves, the Lower and the Upper. The Upper was used primarily by the wealthy, merchants who brought in higher-end goods, and by the ruling classes. They currently passed by the homes of fishermen, merchants of low class, and smugglers. He assured them their best bet in finding a ship, and a captain that would not ask any questions they did not want to answer would be found here.

The salty sea air was mixed with the not-so-heady aroma of rotting fish. Dilapidated buildings seemed to be the norm, and quiet desperation hovered over the area. Kalend looked around in apprehension, and his hand never strayed far from his sword. The horses had been left behind at an inn they procured for themselves for the evening in a much nicer part of town, far removed from the squalor surrounding them now. And

Trealine had been settled into a bed to sleep as the rest of the party went about their search.

The tavern Louquintas chose to start their search was even more run-down than the surrounding buildings. He pushed open one of the double doors and entered with a confident swagger and a backward look that said to watch themselves. Kalend, his sister, and Juliet followed with poor imitations of that confident strut.

The interior was smoky and filled with patrons, most of whom slept with their heads on tables while snoring beside half-drunk tankards. Those not passed out filled the air with boisterous chatter and ignored the company as they made their way to the bar on the far side of the room. The fishy salty air permeated the building and hung over the room even though Kalend noticed incense braziers hanging from various points along the walls. They did little to ease the smell.

A barkeep with short, cropped hair and a stained white shirt shambled over, Louquintas quietly inquired about any captains they could hire for a trip. The barman took stock of the three with a practiced glance and then pointed to a table along the far wall. Three rugged seafaring men sat in a darkened corner and appeared more awake and less loud than the other customers. They sat speaking softly to each other with an air of wary caution that clung to them like well-tailored cloaks.

Louquintas thanked the barkeep, flipped him a bronze coin for his trouble, and jauntily led the way over to the dark corner. The men noticed their approach and silently eyed them as they slipped between the other tables and patrons. As Kalend's group stood before the ominous men, the middle figure looked them over with an appraising eye, leaned back in his chair, and asked in a cool, dry voice, "And how may we help you?"

Kalend could not help but stare at the speaker, from the long hair that hung down to his shoulders to the ridiculous curled mustache that shivered when he spoke. Even his mannerisms as he reclined with a jaunty air and asked his question…. all bore an uncanny resemblance to his mentor Louquintas. He was like a nautical, fish-smelling version and found the similarities disconcerting. By the expressions on the ladies' faces beside him, he knew they had the same thoughts.

Louquintas didn't seem to notice the similarity or the looks of his friends and responded, "We seek passage to the Island across the way. I understand you may be of some help?"

"We may be able to help. Then again, we may be unable to help," the Louquintas doppelganger responded with a smirk that gave Kalend a shuddering déjà vu.

The two on either side of the speaker snickered and, with arms crossed, leaned onto the table. Each had greasy hair tied back in ponytails, and scars lined their faces. They were the faces of men who lived hard and fast yet kept a cool calmness about them, even as brown eyes took everything in around them. The trio did not inspire confidence in Kalend that passage could be found with them.

Louquintas gave an easy smile as he pulled out a chair and sat. "Would coin work toward the able-to-help side of things?"

"First, I am known as Blunt, Captain Blunt. Second, yes indeed, coin may indeed help with your cause."

Over the course of the next several minutes, Captain Blunt and Louquintas bantered back and forth, but Kalend had a hard time following the exchange. He was unsure if they were negotiating, getting to know each other, or just seeing who could outwit the other—much of the chat involved insults, which was about the only thing Kalend understood. The rest was undecipherable; they spoke faster and faster as if each was attempting to be the last one to get a word in. Then Louquintas abruptly stood, bowed to the Captain, and said, "We shall see you tomorrow morning." He nodded to Kalend and the ladies, and they quickly found themselves back on the street.

A few moments after the shock of the sudden departure wore off, Juliet was the first to ask what the others were thinking, "What just happened back there? Did we book passage?"

Louquintas nodded without slowing his pace down the filthy street. "Yes, we did. You need to pay attention more."

Juliet frowned. "I did! None of that made any sense."

"Hmm, seems you may need to relearn how to hear then," Louquintas said nonchalantly.

Juliet started to snap back with a red face, but Kalend grabbed her shoulder with a firm grip and shook his head.

Louquintas noticed the exchanged and laughed. "What you saw there was smuggler speak. That is how they negotiate. We have booked passage, for a considerable sum, I might add, for tomorrow morning at first light. Luckily, the good Duke Salasar was kind enough to refill my coin purse for things such as this."

Juliet nodded with a frown but did not respond.

Kalend smiled at her in understanding and asked Louquintas, "Can we trust this captain?"

"As to that, we shall see. However, I believe we can. They may be smugglers, but from what I could tell, this captain Blunt is a man who has seen much and a man of his word. There is something about him that keeps me on my guard but equally tells me his word is good. I have known a few smugglers in my life, and this one appeals to me for some reason, but I can't put my finger on why."

Kalend exchanged glances with his sister and Juliet for a moment. Each shared the same thought that the appeal felt by Louquintas was easy for them to see and that they were surprised he completely missed it. They each contained their laughter with bowed heads as they walked briskly out of the Lower Warf and into the fairer part of town that held the inn they shared. If Louquintas noticed their silent amusement, he never let on.

*****   *****

Morning sunlight reflected off the rippling waters of the harbor, glittering like bright jewels; the beams of light filled the company's vision. They led their horses down the dirty and not-so-stable wood planks of the old pier where their ship waited. Kalend thought the beautiful sunlit morning versus the decrepit pier they traversed was a perfect metaphor for the coming foray onto an island known for its beauty and its many hidden treacheries. He hoped that more beauty would be found rather than the latter.

Bobbing and dipping with the small waves that gently slapped its hull, the smuggler ship Mistress Midnight stood out among the much smaller fishing boats that lined the pier. The name was clearly emblazoned on the hull in a deep red paint that looked to have been recently applied. Some paint had oozed down as if the letters had teared up at their application and left a bloody trail reaching halfway to the water.

Captain Blunt shouted a greeting to them from the deck and waved them to board. Once all were settled, the order was given to release the hawsers, and the Mistress Midnight quietly slid into the harbor. The Oeshland Port resided within a natural harbor surrounded by a narrow rocky slip of land with one opening at the far end that led to the open ocean. The wind was favorable, and they eased by the dock and past the few ships that roamed the waters as they slowly made their way to the waiting sea beyond the harbor's protection.

Captain Blunt sauntered up to the group as they stood at the bow. "We are on our way, my new friends!" he said enthusiastically. "We should make it to your island by tomorrow evening if the weather holds, and I believe it will."

Kalend was intoxicated by the smell of the sea and the thrill of his first sea voyage. He had never been on a ship such as this; it was exhilarating. His few other times aboard a boat had been on much smaller river craft, nothing as remarkable as this. The fresh sea air had him feeling like he floated above the ship; all his worries blew away with the salty tang of the slight breeze that hustled them along.

Looking forward to his first full view of the ocean, he leaned against the railing and took the whole experience in. He was finding that he liked new and different experiences and that they brought excitement and usually lifted his spirits.

He was not disappointed at first sight of the sprawling, deep green and blue ocean. And once out into the open sea, he quickly became accustomed to the ship's sway and movement as it rode the waves. Overall, he was incredibly pleased with the whole adventure; his sister, however, did not share those same feelings. Once past the protection of the harbor, she had ended up hugging the rail and leaning over it to relieve herself of that morning's breakfast. Pale and miserable, she stayed by that rail for the first hour. Kalend had quickly gone over to check on her, but she waved him away so he would not see her in such shape. Luckily, Juliet made a concoction from her ever-present herb bag that helped settle Hollilea's stomach. She was still sickly white but at least gained some control over herself.

Kalend was once again thankful for Juliet joining their little band. It was not just her companionship he was grateful for, but her abilities had been of much help to them all. From her fighting prowess with blade and bow to her knowledge of medicine, she had become a vital cog, and he was not sure if they could do as well without her.

Juliet joined Kalend at Mistress Midnight's bow as he stood, smiling and swaying with the ship as it rode the waves. She gazed at the glistening waters with him and quietly said, "Your sister will be ok. It's just seasickness."

"Thank you," he replied just as quietly. Then he smiled and hesitantly said, "I appreciate all that you have done for us."

Juliet grinned. "And I appreciate you appreciating me."

Kalend frowned, "There is more to it than that." He turned toward her, sighed, and blurted out, "I like you. What I mean is that…" he trailed off as he blushed and lowered his head.

Juliet laughed, and Kalend blushed some more. She reached out and touched his cheek tenderly, smiled, and said, "I like you as well. Growing up, I never had time for boys. I was always too busy learning to be a good fighter, leader, and other…less ladylike skills. My interests always lay in becoming a ranger and protector of my people." She shook her head ruefully. "And I believe my father was fine with it in the beginning; that way, he didn't have to worry about me getting into trouble with the boys of the village. Later on, I think he came to regret it as I became a woman and still did not show…what he considered proper interest in the men around me."

"You have become a fine fighter. And you are unlike other ladies I have met, but then, I have not met many. The monastery was not exactly bursting with girls or women."

Juliet laughed softly. "We are a pair. Whatever are we to do?"

Kalend smiled, cupped her chin in his hand, leaned down, and hesitantly kissed her on the lips. She wrapped her hand around his neck, pulled him in tighter, and passionately returned the kiss. After several heated moments, their lips parted, and Kalend stared at her in amazement, then grinned sheepishly. Juliet laughed gaily and leaned against him as he wrapped his arm around her.

The warm, pleasant weather held all that day as they swiftly glided over the gleaming waters. Louquintas and Captain Blunt spent much of that time together beside the tiller, laughing and telling long-drawn-out tales of glory. Each one was more extravagant than the last. The first mate had brought them skins of wine, which only encouraged them to tell more outrageous lies about themselves. Kalend was at least partially sure they were lies, for if not, then according to them, they had saved about every monarch in all the lands. But they did seem sure of themselves.

The company and sailors within earshot were greatly amused not just by the glorious deeds spoken of but by how neither teller of tall tales seemed aware of their resemblance to each other. It was as if they were long-lost brothers ignorant of their parentage in appearance and speech. Kalend smiled and laughed and, for a time, forgot what they were headed towards.

The following day dawned equally as beautiful, warm, and pleasant. However, the moderate weather only lasted until midafternoon, when dark clouds scudded in from the northeast, bringing with them cool dampness that spoke of wet weather that threatened to swallow them and the island they headed toward.

The island was spotted just as the beginning edges of rain caught them, enveloping them in a wet spray that mingled with the salty air; it stung their faces and forced the group of friends to seek shelter within the captain's cabin. The small ripples they had previously plowed through had turned into small swells that the Mistress Midnight now rode up one side and then down the other, making all those inside the cabin feel almost as bad as Hollilea had felt on her first hour aboard. All except Louquintas, of course, who indolently lounged in the chair he occupied. Swaying with the ship's movement, he lit a cigar and smiled knowingly at his less sea-experienced mates.

Luck was with them, or so Captain Blunt informed them a little while later when he came to check on his human cargo. He was confident this was just a small patch of rain and not the beginning of something more extensive like a hurricane. Kalend, already losing some of his enchantment with sea travel, asked nervously what a hurricane was. The answer he received unnerved him, and he was not sure if the good captain was toying with him or not.

They glided into the port an hour later, and the steady rain had become a drizzle that coated the pier and village in a hazy cloud of dampness. Getting the horses unloaded down the slick gangplanks was a slow process, but the experienced seamen managed it without much trouble. The group said their goodbyes to their captain, who assured them he would wait one week for them to return. Louquintas had managed to convince the roguish captain, with the help of more coins, to wait for them to finish up their business for one week, and if they did not return, he was free to keep the coins and move on.

It was a risk, but Kalend agreed with his mentor; they did not have much choice. From what they knew of the village and its lack of visitors, even if they did find another ship, they could not be sure how trustworthy another captain would be. They felt more secure putting their faith in Mistress Midnight and her captain. Only time would tell if that faith was well-placed or not. And that was if they even made it back to the village from their coming trials. Kalend shook his head with that thought and told himself, yes, yes, they would make it back; this would not be a one-way trip.

Michael Gisman

CHAPTER TWENTY-EIGHT

The village was not as run-down or decrepit as they had initially feared. In fact, it seemed to be thriving. Even with wetness clinging to everything and everyone, the streets bustled with the trappings and moving of people like that of any village or city on the mainland. The cobblestone avenues were clean and easy to traverse, and their horses' dull clopping reverberated off the sturdy two-storied buildings that lined both sides of the street they led them along.

The captain had given them one piece of advice they decided to follow: to find a one-armed man who ran the sheriff's office. Law and order were sketchy at best on the Island, but he was confident the one-armed man would deal with them fairly. And if they mentioned Captain Blunt's name, he may just prove to be of some help.

They halted at the boundary of a large square teeming with people and looked about in surprise. Canvas-covered stalls, busy with loud customers, lined the square's edges, while four other equally busy streets fed into the courtyard, creating a steady flow of people in and out. All manner of goods were displayed and shouted about by gaily dressed merchants. The sing-song voices rose above the clamor of the square; "perfumes for your sweetheart," "meat pies extraordinaire," "wine like the ambrosia of the gods!" From the stories of the island they had been told, they found this level of commerce and abundance of wares for sale unexpected.

Louquintas led the way to the closest vendor, who hawked bolts of plain linen in a booming voice. After denying the man a sale of cloth, which produced a sour look and a wave to move along, the vendor's expression rapidly morphed into a genuine smile when Louquintas dropped a few coins on the table. Coins that gave off the distinct tinkling noise of gold. After a brief exchange, they found themselves moving down the next street over, one upon which the vendor assured them they would find the Sheriff.

The standalone building holding the sheriff's office ended up being only a short distance from the bazaar. It was recognizable by the swinging sign above the doorway that simply read "Sheriff" in faded black lettering. Kalend tied Whistler to the hitching post before the stairs as his friends did the same, all except Trealine, who was still recovering from his wounds and wanted to minimize how many times he had to dismount. His horse was undersized and fitted him well, but the strain on his hurt ribs was more than he wanted to deal with. He told them he would await them outside.

The rest of the group climbed the stairs, and with a flourish, Kalend held the single solid oak door open for the others. A lean, tall man with short-cropped silver hair came out from a side room and greeted them warmly. He radiated an air of authority and shook each hand in a firm grasp as he looked them in the eye. Kalend was shocked at the feel of the man's grip and, when he looked down, was unnerved to find a hand that shimmered and shined in the pale light that shone through the large window facing the street. The hand was warm but did not feel to be made of flesh; it felt like some type of metal. Fine details were etched on each finger, even down to fingernails. Kalend looked up at the man in surprise as he released his grip and received a knowing smile.

Louquintas, in his usual way, took charge and asked who the Sheriff was and if he was available.

"I am the Sheriff, and my name is Nudd. How may I be of service?" The sheriff answered in a pleasant baritone voice.

Louquintas nodded. "I was told that you might be of some help," then hesitated as he looked meaningfully at both arms of the man before them.

With a laugh, the Sheriff said, "Yes, I have both arms. Some have known me as the one-armed Sheriff. That is not the most accurate of descriptions. I indeed have both arms; however, I, for a while, only had one hand." He held up his shimmering hand, and Kalend, now that he was no longer surprised, thought it looked to be made of silver. "That has been corrected, as you may have noticed."

"Well then, Captain Blunt says hello and is the one that sent us to you," Louquintas responded with a smile.

"Ahhh…. the good captain. If he has sent you to me, then we may can be friends. Again, I ask, how may I be of service?"

"We have business deeper onto the Island and have need of a guide," Louquintas replied smoothly.

Sheriff Nudd frowned and asked, "What business would that be? There is only trouble to be found at the center of this island. We live relatively free of it due to two things. First, we have a good-sized militia paired with a small wall not far from the town, and second…… we mind our own business."

Louquintas held up both hands in submission. "We do not mean to cause you trouble, but our business is our own. We will do what we can to keep your town free from it."

Nudd sat down in a leather chair along the far wall and motioned the others to join him in the other chairs that created a semi-circle before an unlit fireplace. Once seated, he continued his inquiry, "I will take your word at face value, and the recommendation of Captain Blunt helps, but you must understand my point of view. This town is my responsibility and all the lives herein. Surely you can provide more insight?"

Before Louquintas could respond, Kalend caught his eye and received a nod to go ahead. "Well, sir, we may be of some help. We know what and some of the why for your troubles, and our business may relieve your town of those headaches."

Nudd nodded and took his time while he appraised the group, then he shook his head and responded, "You may be able to do as you say. And that would be of great help, but if you were to fail…then what? We could see our problems escalate even more. What assurances do I have that you will not make things worse?"

Kalend learned forward, "Captain Blunt awaits us at the wharf, and we could sail away and land somewhere else on the island and still get to where we need to go." With a determined grimace, he looked the Sheriff in the eye. "We will do what we need to and WILL keep your town out of it."

"He is determined, isn't he?" Nudd asked Louquintas with a raised eyebrow, who smirked and shrugged his shoulders in response.

Kalend sat back with folded arms. He was determined to see this through. They had to, with or without the help of the Sheriff. Keeping the town safe may be the responsibility of this man, but what their group had to do would solve the town's problems in the long term. For if they failed in their mission, this town would be doomed; either way, it would just be a matter of time.

Sheriff Nudd pursed his lips and told the group, "I will tell you what. I think we can accomplish both our needs. There is a small smugglers' way station not far from here along the coast. I suggest you head there by horse; it is only a two-day ride. Once there, find the Bear Claw Tavern and ask for Husk. He should know of someone who can help."

Kalend nodded his thanks, stood, shook the Sheriff's hand, and gave one last assurance. "We will do what we can to keep your village safe and out of any trouble."

"For what it's worth, good luck to you all. Being rid of the deviltry on this island would be helpful, for it only seems to be growing by the day; creatures now roam the mountains and passes that most have never seen before. The deeper in, the worse the reports."

With that ominous warning floating in the air, Kalend led the group back outside to the waiting horses and Trealine.

Michael Gisman

*****   *****

As the good Sheriff had predicted, reaching the smugglers' way station took precisely two days. Though they had been on edge the first day out, with the last words from Nudd still lingering within their minds, they found little to fear and little that hindered them. They had decided to follow along the heavily wooded coast, keeping just enough trees between them and the water so as not to be easily seen by any passing ships but still able to navigate the coastline. Kalend's thoughts on the matter had been that they were less inclined to run into foul things this way, as the Sheriff had explicitly said the center of the island was where most of the creatures would be found. Louquintas had agreed, and along the ocean's edge, they traveled.

Later that afternoon, after the sun had peeked out from the clouds and mixed a heavy heat with the dampness leftover from the rain, Hollilea and Juliet walked their horses behind Kalend through the uncomfortable resulting humidity. The stone and tree-rooted path, such that it was, was too treacherous to ride along. Louquintas frequently used his sword to chop a clear way through the dense foliage, but still, they often found themselves dodging dangling vegetation that seemed determined to reach out and claw their faces. The ladies chatted amiably about various topics, such as the different foods they liked, weapons, and training they had received. Kalend found the chatter a blatant attempt at keeping the mood light.

His mind had wandered along a different path. He spent that afternoon trying to reconcile the growing nature of his leadership among the group with his youthful doubts. Who was he to lead people such as those he traveled with? Each had more experience and training than he, except for his sister, and even her training with the witches and Karl seemed to have prepared her better. His mind gnawed and circled around this. He realized he had a need at times to step in, such as with the Sheriff. Louquintas had nodded for him to proceed, which had given Kalend a shot of assurance. But was this need really the right thing? Was he taking liberties he should not? Ultimately, he decided it came down to trust. Trust in his teachers, that they had given him the tools needed to lead. He felt confident that Louquintas would step in and stop him from doing anything too foolish. He remembered Tosyrayner once saying that if he was given a task to do, then his teacher had already given Kalend his trust, and to question it was to question his teacher. With that in mind, Kalend decided he would need to become more comfortable with leadership; after all, who was he to question Tosrayner's judgment?

The next day, as the sun sank below the mountains, leaving a dusty, rosy hue, the companions found themselves walking the pathways that led up to the smuggler's way station. Not a village or town, Kalend thought; it more resembled a ramshackle collection of hovels. All were connected by dirt and gravel ruts worn into the lush mountain greenery to create a latticework of pathways interlinking the various huts, large tents, and the few questionable-looking free-standing buildings. All those various trails conjoined with one wider, almost-looking road that led to and from the beach.

Thinking an establishment called the Bear Claw Tavern would most likely be one of the more permanent seeming timber buildings, Louquintas led the group down the almost road onto a path toward the nearest and most prominent building. Which ended up being closed with boarded windows and a locked door. He turned with an apologetic shrug and looked around for another likely building to house a tavern. At that point, a burst of raucous laughter floated out from amongst the trees to their left. With a cocky swagger, like he had planned this all along, he confidently led them down a side path toward the now very discernable noise of revelry.

They came upon a towering oak tree, the largest Kalend had ever seen, with a sign nailed to it that proclaimed in large, bold lettering that the Bear Claw Tavern stood before them. The tavern was behind and yet a part of the tree. Massive branches forked out from the trunk above them. Kalend guessed the lowest to be fifteen feet off the ground, and a canopy of smaller branches reached out to cover what seemed to be a wide swath that disappeared into the night. Weathered green canvas sheets formed walls in a V shape leading out and away from the tree's base, one to each side; they reached up and were attached to the lowest level of branches. Welcoming light poured out from a gap in the hanging canvas on the right hand of the V. The companions tied their horses to nearby bushes, and then Louquintas led them through the portal.

As they entered, a riot of color, light, and sound assaulted the group. Lanterns hanging from the branches provided a dim light while four musicians played to their right. More beaten canvas covered the oak's hanging limbs above them to form a slightly slanted roof; with the peak somewhere ahead, it ran to the walled edges. Kalend could only guess at the size of the space as smoke filled the interior, and visibility was reduced to just a few yards around them.

Louquintas led them to a round table along the canvas wall and motioned them all to be seated. Juliet looked around in amazement and asked, "Louquintas, have you ever heard of such a place?"

With a nod to the negative, he replied, "No. This is all new to me."

Hollilea leaned forward and, in a quiet tone, said, "I can sense magic at work all around us. It's diffused, shapeless, and seems to encompass the whole tavern."

Louquintas gave her a penetrating look and asked, "Do you think it is anything we need to worry about?"

"I don't think so," she replied with a shrug, then continued, "but then again, anytime magic is at play, we should be cautious. I can't even tell what or where it comes from."

A tall, burly bearded man with a stained white apron approached their table and addressed them in a cheerful voice, "Welcome, welcome, to the Bear Claw Tavern. How may I be of service? Food? Drink? Information? All can be had here…..for a price, of course." He laughed loudly as he spoke the last words.

Louquintas grinned at the man and replied, "I believe we could use some ale and food, my good man. Do you happen to be the proprietor of this establishment?"

"Oh no. That I am not. I am a simple server of the bar. If you wish to speak to the owner, he is around somewhere and will most likely be by soon. You are obviously newcomers and strangers; the word is already spreading that you are here," he replied. Then, he continued when he noticed the worried look his words produced, "But do not worry, no harm shall come to you. While this place may be filled with all kinds of ruffians, scoundrels, and the like, no violence is tolerated at the Bear Claw Tavern. This goes for everyone." He said the last with a significant look at Kalend's well-armed group.

Louquintas laughed and grinned. "We shall abide by the customs and do not seek trouble. We just want some food and drinks."

With a smile and a nod, the server told them he would get some of each and quickly melted back among the many patrons that roamed the tavern.

Kalend began to ask what they should do next when another man, this one short, stocky, and bearded, approached them. He pulled up a chair from a nearby table and plopped down beside Kalend. He smiled and looked at them each before greeting them with a deep, calm, and relaxed voice.

"Welcome, strangers. It is seldom that we receive new folk here. My name is Husk, and I am the owner."

Kalend smiled back and replied, "Thank you for the warm welcome."

"My pleasure, young man. I saw a server was already by, and I assume he explained what I expect from our guests." He said it as a matter of fact as if it was standard procedure for his staff. "I am at your service. I will also assume, as you are new, that more than food and spirits are wanted?" he asked in the same matter-of-fact tone.

Kalend paused to organize his thoughts and gauge what he should reveal and what not. Husk sat patiently with the same smile and waited as if this was an everyday occurrence.

Remembering that the Sheriff had told them to ask for this exact person, Kalend decided that a moderate dose of information may be given. "We seek to head inland and would like to find a knowledgeable guide to aid us. We have spoken with Sheriff Nudd, and he suggested we speak with you."

With a nod, Husk replied, "Your business inland is your own, and since you have already spoken with the sheriff, I am betting you know what awaits you. I do know of a man who may be interested. He has recently returned from inland and has acted as a guide before. I caution, however, that you may need to give more details regarding your journey. He is cautious and private, and not much is known about him, but word is he is particularly good at what he does."

Kalend nodded his thanks and asked a few questions about the tavern; he was curious about the unusual establishment and wanted to know more. They learned that three large oaks formed a triangle of overlapping limbs used for the roof. The walls reached from tree to tree except for the door they had come through, all of which formed a large triangle. No fireplace was needed as each tree had an enchantment upon it to provide warmth or cooling, as needed, and kept the whole place at a steady temperature year-round. Husk also revealed that he had armed personnel secreted about to help ensure the peace.

The server was back with the promised food and drink in short order, and Husk bid them good day while saying he would find their potential guide and tell him about their needs. If he were interested at all, he would be by in a while. If not, then they were on their own to find someone.

The companions ate and drank with little discourse among themselves as each took in the scene around them. As their eyes slowly adjusted to the smoke-filled room, they realized that the tavern seemed more extensive than they had initially thought. The two canvas sides they could see reached out into the haze and disappeared from their gaze several tables away. Off to their right, at the edge of their view, played the musicians; they looked like ghosts undulating in the pale mist.

The melody that floated out from the ghostly figures was upbeat, fast-paced, and had lyrics that spoke of drinking, women, and adventure. With arms wrapped around their fellow drunk's shoulders, some patrons loudly and boisterously sang along, with much swaying and spilling of drink over themselves and each other. Though it sounded more like shouting than singing, everyone appeared to be enjoying themselves immensely. Besides the drinking and singing, many smoked pipes and cigars, enough at least to explain the smoky conditions.

Louquintas excused himself to explore the rest of the tavern. Kalend sat tapping his toes to the music; he was relaxed and realized he was enjoying himself to a degree he had not in a long time. The music set a fun atmosphere. They were on a dangerous mission, one that he was still unsure of why and what it was entirely about, but he felt newfound confidence in himself and now knew more than when he first set out from the monastery, much more. Along the way, he acquired a family he never knew he had, a new mentor, new friends, and a beautiful woman that, if he were honest with himself, held deep feelings for.

Kalend's good feelings quickly evaporated when a figure appeared out of the haze, approached their table, and stood before them. It was Lusstail. The party stood as one and reached for their weapons. A shout to stay their hands came from Husk as he and several armed men materialized from among the crowd and surrounded their table. The companions kept their hands cautiously on their weapons but did not unsheathe them.

Husk looked grimly from Lusstail to the companions. "There will be NO weapons drawn in my Tavern. Remember that," he growled to them all.

Lusstail raised his hands and addressed Husk innocently, "Not I. For I have no weapons."

Kalend motioned for his party to sit back down; he looked around for Louquintas but did not see him anywhere and hoped that his mentor would be back soon. He looked to

Husk. "We shall raise no weapons here….unless we are attacked," Kalend said that last with a meaningful glance to Lusstail, who stood with arms crossed and the oily smile plastered upon his face.

Husk grunted and motioned for his men to back off. However, they only moved far enough away to give the table privacy while keeping a close eye out for any shenanigans.

Lusstail lowered his arms and addressed Kalend. "It is good to see you again, boy. You and your friends have given me quite the chase. But alas, here we all are." He paused, cocked his head, and continued, "One seems to be missing, however. Where might your gallant leader be?"

Kalend opened his mouth to give a wise-ass remark, but the look and tone of Lusstail's question made his mind race. Where was Louquintas? It was doubtful that he could have missed the commotion. The tavern could not be that big. And that is when a nagging thought, combined with Lusstail's attitude, came crashing in.

Lusstail noticed all these thoughts play across Kalend's face and nodded. "Yes, that's right, my youngster. Louquintas is spending quality time with my associates. I know what you are about and believe you should leave this island and go back to your monastery. Or better yet, go into hiding. There is nothing you can do for your friend; soon, he will be spilling his secrets to my master."

Kalend's blood boiled, and he began a harsh retort when a soft whisper from directly behind him stopped his train of thought. He spun around to see what this new threat was and found an odd albino man towering over him. Tall, imposing, and with a steady gaze, the stranger stared directly at Lusstail. His soft voice belied the steel with which the man addressed their enemy, "Lusstail," he whispered again. "You should not be so quick to give commands. These are friends of mine. I would suggest you move along."

The smug smile had fallen from Lusstail's face, and he turned almost as white as the stranger, but he managed to croak, "Skalamar, what....what are you doing with these people?"

"That is no concern of yours. Now leave us." Skalamar responded with a dismissive wave of his hand.

The companions sat in shocked silence as Lusstail slunk away from the table and headed toward the tavern door. The stranger looked down at the friends and smiled good-naturedly as he greeted them. "Well, my new friends, it seems we have a journey to make and someone to rescue."

CHAPTER TWENTY-NINE

After each of the companions cautiously greeted him, Skalamar sat beside Kalend in the chair vacated by the Bear Claw Tavern's proprietor. Kalend leaned back and quickly looked over their new supposed friend. Finding someone who could scare off Lusstail so easily was good, but that did not mean they were all working towards the same ends. The man before him was imposing; he could admit to that, and he had never seen or met an albino before. Skalamar was lean, almost seven feet tall, and wore a deep black cloak that partially covered equally black leggings. He had snow-white hair that contrasted starkly with his clothing; it hung past his shoulders and framed his white face in such a manner that it was difficult to tell where his face ended and hair began. His eyebrows seemed to be missing, and Kalend was unsure if they were missing or if they were so white they blended in. However, the oddest part, which gave Kalend a shiver, was his eyes. They were black as the darkest night and had no irises. No color at all. The stranger seemed able to see perfectly fine, but when he looked over to Kalend, it felt as if that darkness penetrated him. As if they saw all the secrets he may be hiding.

Hollilea gave Kalend a worried look and asked, "What are we going to do about Louquintas? We must find him."

Kalend shook his head in despair. "I don't know."

Defenders of Myth

Skalamar leaned over the table, motioned the group to do the same, and said, "I can be of help." He continued in a raspy whisper. "Husk had informed me that you were looking for someone to act as a guide. At first, I had been undecided if I would even speak with you; however, I watched from the shadows to take your measure. Once I saw Lusstail approach and heard him speak, I knew I had to get involved. He and his masters are too embroiled in the doings on this island. They do much that is evil, and I fear they are bringing an even greater evil into this world."

"Those are cryptic words. To what are you referring?" Kalend whispered back in puzzlement. He was unsure about this stranger and wanted to know more about his purpose without giving away the group's own goal.

Skalamar smiled as if he understood the hesitation. "If you came to this Island and wished to go inland, then you must know some of what lay at its heart. An evil brews there, one brought about by two warlocks." He said this as if he did not surprise his audience. He looked meaningfully at Kalend before continuing, "I know this because I have had run-ins with them before." He paused and chuckled, "They have even tried to kill me."

Hollilea shook her head. "I am sorry, but we still know nothing about you; how can we trust what you say. Maybe scaring off Lusstail was a ruse to lure us away with you and directly back to him?"

Skalamar shrugged and looked at her. "That is something you will need to decide for yourselves. But remember, you have no friends on this island; treachery can be found around every corner, and now it seems as if your leader has been carried off. I do not believe you have many choices. All I can give is my word, which, if you were to ask around, you would find that it carries much weight."

Hollilea leaned back with an unconvinced, worried expression.

Skalamar stood up. "I will find Husk and settle up with him for you; let me at least do that. Talk amongst yourselves and decide if I speak the truth or not. When I return, you can decide, but I believe you have only one option...trust." He glided away and was quickly consumed by the roiling smoke.

Kalend led the group in a hasty and quiet discussion regarding what to do about Louquintas and Skalamar. Reluctantly, they concluded that they needed a guide, and Skalamar would be their best and only option. It crossed his mind, and not for the first time that since he had left the monastery, he kept putting his faith and trust in people he had barely met, let alone knew, on any real level. This was true, now, on the island, from the Captain of the ship that brought them here to this moment with Skalamar. Each name was always passed along, and either they had fantastic luck, as each time it had worked out, or fate was on his side. Kalend leaned toward the side of fate. He just hoped fate was on his side once again.

***** *****

The group spent the night a short distance in the woods from the tavern and got a fitful night's rest before waking with groggy heads, bloodshot eyes, and a tad grumpy. With the predawn light, Skalamar glided ahead while leading them on foot along a rocky trail through a narrow valley. A series of short mountains formed a ring around the center of the island; the valley was seldom used, and few knew of its existence. Skalamar assured them it was the best route. But they would still need to be cautious as the mountains were crawling with creatures and roving sentries that protected what lay within its depths.

After leaving the tavern, Skalamar argued and won a discussion on their next course of action. He had scouted the pub and found that Louquintas was most likely taken out a slit on the tavern's backside flap. A large group of Panes had been waiting and had quickly spirited off their friend. Panes could move swiftly and efficiently through a forest, such as on the island, much faster than their companions could on foot. Their horses would be of limited use, and they were unlikely to catch up with the kidnappers. The trail left behind in the Panes' wake had led inland, and that was going to have to be good enough for them all. So, he led them via a different route in hopes of finding their friend when they found the warlocks' camp.

Kalend heard a soft "kaw" from above and to their right. Skalamar had stopped and was gazing up toward a bushy pine tree slightly off the path. He cocked his head and gave a low whistle. A black crow lifted off its perch among the boughs and soared over Kalend's head before landing on Skalamar's outstretched arm. The two seemed to communicate in some manner. Skalamar nodded a few times as if listening, and then the bird launched itself back into the air and disappeared into the woods. Kalend had heard nothing and looked to Trealine, who shrugged and motioned that maybe their new guide was not right in the head. Kalend did not think that was it. He had seen too many odd things in the past months, not least his relationship with Whistler. That had opened his mind to most anything.

Skalamar looked to the group and solemnly said, "Morri tells me that your friend did indeed head inland with the Panes, but they have made camp. They are not far from us." He held up a hand in caution. "However, it seems they are setting a trap. They don't appear to know where we are, only that we didn't directly follow them. They are set up and using your friend as bait."

Juliet excitedly spoke first, "This is good; we can sneak up and get him."

Skalamar grimaced. "Did you not hear me, girl? They are purposely waiting on you."

Juliet put her hand on her hips and, with an impertinent look, responded with defiance, "I heard and don't care. We can take care of ourselves and can get him back."

Skalamar shook his head. "Fine, but answer me this: why do they want you so badly when Louquintas is the leader of the group?"

Kalend held up his hand to forestall anyone else answering, "All I am willing to say is that there is much going on here we can't reveal." He then paused to consider his next words and decided to trust this man at least a little more. "Let's just say that it is my sister and me they are really after. They know we would come for him, and this could be their chance to take us."

"If what you say is true, then would your friend want you to take the risk?"

"Probably not," Kalend laughed, "but then again, I am betting he knows we will anyway. And he will be ready for his chance to help."

Trealine grunted in agreement. "Yes, he will, and yes, he knows we would go after him. And now answer this, Skalamar, what is going on with that crow of yours? It ain't natural to talk with birds."

Skalamar whistled again into the forest, and the crow came swooping back to his arm, and he introduced them, "This is Morri." He gave them all a black look. "And I also have things I will not speak of. Just know that Morri is my companion and my eyes and ears when out in the wild."

Trealine grumbled something about too many secrets amongst them all but changed his tone when he saw the look Kalend gave him. "Fine then, let's make plans to get Louquintas. Seems like everyone knows we are on the island, so let's get this done and move on before the warlocks come for us themselves. Bad enough, we are going after them but would rather have them ahead of us and not behind us."

Hollilea looked to Kalend and motioned to his bracer, "That is still making it hard for anyone with magic to find us; I have been augmenting its powers to extend out to cover our group. It is not foolproof but seems to be working, for now."

Kalend nodded. "At least that is one less thing to worry about. Still, I would like to know how they keep finding us. But I think that answer lies with Lusstail. In fact, the more I think back, the more I believe he has been following us for some time. Back when we were attacked by the Girillion, I thought I heard someone cry out the night before the attack, and after the attack, our mysterious follower appeared to stop. I am betting Lusstail was attacked by them first and scared off."

Trealine nodded his head in approval. "Very good. I believe you are correct."

Skalamar had them gather around him as he cleared an area on the forest floor with his foot and drew a map of their location and the Panes' camp. He filled them in on his knowledge of the site, and they quickly put a plan together to rescue Louquintas. Kalend nodded his head when done, satisfied that it was about as good as they could make it with the knowledge they had. The rest of the group had followed his lead in the discussion, and he felt pride and confidence in their ability to pull it off. He was still unsure about Skalamar and his motivations for helping them, but he did not feel as though they had much choice. Skalamar's knowledge was the only thing that would make their plan work. They would not even have known the whereabouts of Louquintas without him and his crow. So, all Kalend could do was vow to covertly keep an eye on him and see what happened.

They left the horses in a small glade at the valley's edge, and Kalend communicated to Whistler to keep a watch over them and relay to him if any trouble came along. He and his horse had a much deeper connection ever since the battle outside Pleus. He may not have a complete understanding of that connection, but he knew he could count on it enough to leave the horses under Whistler's protection.

Skalamar led the way into the trees up the valley's west side; following an animal trail, they soon reached its top and continued along the ridge. Careful to stay hidden within the trees and making as little noise as possible, the companions strode along, each lost in their own thoughts of what lay ahead. The day passed swiftly, and night crept up on them when Skalamar finally halted to have them make camp. Staying hidden as best they could under low-hanging limbs and bushes, they settled in for the night. Morri kept a watchful eye above as the group went over their plans one more time; Skalamar assured them that by noon tomorrow, they would be in place to rescue Louquintas.

*****　　*****

Early the following morning, Juliet cloaked herself with her natural camouflage and then melted into the forest. Kalend sat on his knees with his buttocks planted on his heels as he impatiently waited for her return. With eyes closed, he was having only moderate success at meditation to calm his mind and spirit for the coming challenge. The companions had gotten as close to Lusstail's encampment as Skalamar deemed reasonable. Then Morri, with a couple hard flaps and a leap off Skalamar's arm, soared into the dappled sunlight and was quickly swallowed by the greenery above. Now, all the rest of the group could do was wait.

Time passed slowly as the sun slid by above. Enough gaps appeared among the leafy tree limbs above to allow shafts of sunlight to poke through and silently crawl atop the loam of the forest floor. After much difficulty, Kalend entered a calm state within his meditation. This calmness allowed him to hear and smell the air around him from a different perspective. He could almost feel the island, feel the pulse of life in and around it. It was tranquil. But as he headed deeper into the calm void of his mind, he noticed a tendril of darkness, a tiny wisp of blackness that seemed to seep out from the heart of the island. He attempted to reach out with his mind to clarify what he felt, but as he neared it, his mind suddenly lost focus, and his eyes jerked open.

Juliet had reappeared from the forest and was hurrying silently toward them. Kalend stood just as she stopped before him. "Did you find Louquintas and Lusstail?" he asked calmly.

With an affirmative nod, she smiled. "Yes, they have Louquintas hogtied and staked to the ground in a small clearing about three hundred yards away. I saw no sign of Lusstail."

Kalend grimaced. "Wonder where the snake is hiding?"

Juliet shrugged. "I couldn't find him anywhere. I circled around the camp in a wide arc and never found him."

With a thoughtful frown, Kalend paused before answering, "He is only one; if we move fast enough, we shouldn't have to worry about him."

Trealine ambled over and asked in his usual gruff voice, "How many Panes' are there?"

"I counted five. They were spread out and around Louquintas. A couple up in the trees. They were doing their best to stay hidden, but I still found them." Juliet answered.

"Five, that makes it even." Trealine shook his head. "Our plan of getting some of them away from Louquintas will help. Or else this maybe be a short rescue effort."

Skalamar hadn't bothered to get up from under the tree he lounged against but nodded in agreement. "I agree. But I think we will be fine. I can handle several myself if need be."

Kalend stared at Skalamar for a moment in consideration. The man was tall, lean, and moved with a hunter's assurance through the woods; he did not doubt his capabilities. His choice of weapons was odd. One-handed and crescent-shaped with gleaming blades on each end, leather wrapping around the middle made for a sure grip, while another smaller crescent that curved back across and below the blades acted as a crossguard. Skalamar called them Horn Knives and carried one on each hip. Kalend thought the name was somewhat misleading as they were much bigger than knives. But he had seen the guide whirl them around when Kalend had inquired about them, so he knew the albino handled them well. He just hoped their trust was not misplaced; this was not Skalamar's fight.

"It's up to you to lead some off," Kalend said to Skalamar.

"Yes, it is," Skalamar replied as he smoothly unwound himself from his prone position. "Give me a few minutes' head start." He motioned to Juliet, "Go and get into position on the far side." She nodded, then broke into a jog and once again allowed the forest to swallow her.

Kalend went over the plan with Skalamar one last time. "We will give you both a head start, then move in as close as we can. Once we hear the commotion of you drawing them off, Juliet attacks from among the trees with her bow while Trealine and I go in and free Louquintas. Taking out anyone we need to along the way. Then we all meet back at the horses."

Skalamar looked at Kalend with his dark eyes and nodded. "Morri keeps watch from above and will help guide you to them. Just follow her. I won't need her help." He then disappeared into the forest almost as smoothly as Juliet had.

Kalend looked to Trealine and Hollilea. "Now we wait. Hollilea, remember to stand back and hide while still being able to see. We may need your magic if anyone else there uses it. You are our only counter to that."

After Kalend thought an appropriate amount of time had passed, he led the trio into the woods. It had not been hard to spot Morri; she had patiently waited above them in an old gnarly oak. Once they started to move off, she took flight and flitted from tree to tree ahead of them, always staying within sight as she guided them toward their captured friend.

Gliding silently among the towering oaks, top-heavy pines, and occasional bushy spruce, they quickly came to a spot where Morri stopped and would go no further. They each found a batch of low shrubbery to hide in and kneeled to await the promised distraction from Skalamar. Morri sat on a low-hanging branch before them and stared directly to the east. That was where their friend would be, where they needed to head as soon as they heard the commotion. Kalend felt his blood start to race with anticipation.

The wait did not last long. Shouts and the ring of steel soon rang out through the forest. Kalend and his friends bounded up and followed the crow as it swooped from its perch and headed east. He was mindful of the bird and thankful. He was unsure from which direction the sounds of fighting came; it reverberated among the trees, making it hard to tell if it was before them or off to the side. If not for Skalamar's bird, he would not have known which direction to head.

Kalend burst out of a thicket of nettles, unheeding of the noise or scratches; speed was their best option now. He crashed into a small clearing and saw Louquintas staked to the ground in the middle, just as Juliet had said. Trealine burst through a moment behind him, cursing as the nettles hampered his short, stocky frame. The twang of a bow let them know that Juliet had engaged their enemies from the other side. They raced toward Louquintas unhindered, and Kalend quickly knelt and cut at the leather bands holding his friend down.

As Louquintas stood, he grinned at his protégé in a bizarre manner that made Kalend lose his smile and step back from him. Something was off; his demeanor and usual cockiness was missing. Darkness boiled within Louquintas's eyes, and waves of hatred radiated toward Kalend. He stood transfixed in shock and confusion as Louquintas shimmered. Within moments, his mentor evaporated, and, in his place, a thick goat-legged Pane smiled eerily.

The Pane unsheathed a long sword from his hip and, in one smooth motion, lunged at Kalend. Trealine was quicker than either Pane or Kalend. He had been unfazed by the transformation and swung his axe overhead and then down onto the Pane's thrusting blade, pushing it deep into the leafy ground. Before the Pane could pull his sword up, a bolt of lightning slammed into its side. The creature flew several feet and slammed into a wide oak with a thick, wet thud. It sat there, upright for a brief moment, then slumped onto its side with blood oozing from its mouth and wide-open lifeless eyes.

Kalend looked to Trealine with surprise still evident on his face, then over to the trees on his right, where his sister stood with an outstretched hand still pointed at the Louquintas-Pane.

"You must be prepared for anything, no matter how unexpected," Trealine solemnly advised.

Unable to verbally reply due to the shock, Kalend grimaced, and with a swallow, he nodded his head in acknowledgment. He recognized how close it had been and was thankful for his friends saving him. He took a long, deep breath, closed his eyes, and tried to soothe his mind, to find the relaxed place where his mind had been just a short while ago. The tension eased as he quickly found his center, and he realized two things: first, it was becoming easier to center himself, and the meditation was working. Second, if Louquintas was not here, then where was he?

Skalamar and Juliet entered the clearing from opposite sides and, with quick strides, came to stand beside Kalend as he stood looking over the carnage around them. They had managed to survive the encounter and killed all the Panes, but their primary objective remained unfulfilled. "Damnit, where is Louquintas?" Kalend asked in frustration.

Trealine shook his head. "I saw that creature change, but before it did, I would have sworn that was Louquintas. Fooled all of us."

"Yes, it did. But now we need to find him...again!"

Hollilea frowned. "I know we need to find him, but we also need to find the twins. At this point, finding them will probably mean finding Louquintas as well, as we first thought. This little excursion delayed us, giving Lusstail more of a lead on us."

Kalend grunted. Knowing his sister was right and glad for her insight, it did little to make him feel better about their path forward. There was too much uncertainty. "All right," he sighed. "Let's assume we can't catch Lusstail and Louquintas before he gets to the twins. That means we need to find this abandoned castle they are at."

Skalamar motioned for Morri to scout around, then looked at the group. "This castle you speak of is known to me. It is not so much a castle anymore as a collection of broken walls. The castle was built out and around a cave entrance. If they have fortified it, then gaining entrance will be difficult."

"We shall have to deal with it as we can," Kalend replied sternly.

Skalamar nodded. "That is fine. We still need to reach it, and stealth is still our best bet going forward. Too many creatures prowl the island. We should get a move on before any of them decide to come here and check out what all the noise was about." He looked around with his midnight eyes at the bodies strewn about and then evenly continued, "Or come to feed on the fallen."

CHAPTER THIRTY

Skalamar led the group and their horses down and into a narrow ravine. An old stream bed made for an easy path to follow. Made up of mostly dried dirt and pebbles, it looked to have been a repository for the mountain rain to funnel into from the steep mountainside on either side. In the not-so-distant past, something had changed, and now water only flowed occasionally. Kalend was not sure what could have changed, but he was glad for it. Maneuvering the horses was easier here than through some of the thick underbrush they had blazed to get into the gully several hours ago. Skalamar told them it would take close to two days travel to reach the twins' broken-down castle, which had been one day ago when they had left the clearing with the dead Panes. Kalend admired Skalamar; he was confident they would never have found this passage, such that it was, without him. Even Trealine had grunted with admiration when they were led into it, having missed it himself.

From above, Morri scouted ahead and occasionally reported back to Skalamar, who listened patiently and then would nod his head and send the crow back out.

Kalend probed Skalamar about what lay ahead; he wanted more information regarding the castle's remnants in which the twins were hiding. Skalamar was slow to engage and often answered in short, one-word, cryptic replies. Eventually, he either warmed up to Kalend, which Kalend doubted, or he realized the questioning would not end anytime soon. So, after half an hour of pestering, Skalamar opened up about what he knew regarding the castle's origins and replied in a resigned monotone voice, "The true origins are lost to time. The last time it had seen heavy use was by a smuggler who, being a smuggler, was very untrusting of others. He had used it as a hideaway and to keep his spoils. Eventually, he died off somewhere, and it lay abandoned ever since. Until the twins."

"What kind of defenses do you think could be there now?" Kalend asked with renewed vigor; he would not let Skalamar stop talking now.

Skalamar sighed and, with a resigned look, replied, "That depends on how many people and resources they have brought in. Inside that cave is a large cavern with a small lake at its center. Some have said it may be a magical lake. However, I have never seen it to have any magic."

"Then you have been inside?"

"Yes, a few times; the last time was several years ago. I never saw anything but normal-looking water. Other than that, there is not much to the place, but a few smaller rooms are used for storage. The lake is fed from deeper inside and makes for some clean drinking water. If the place is fortified, water will not be the issue for those hiding within."

Skalamar stopped speaking as Morri suddenly appeared and swooped down to land on his hastily outstretched arm. Skalamar motioned for everyone to stop as he cocked his head and stared at the bird for a few moments before quietly explaining, "There are two beings ahead; they appear to know we are here and are just sitting out in the open. Morri does not think it to be an ambush, but more likely, they are waiting on us. She also believes they do not mean us harm."

Trealine grunted, "We are to believe the word of a bird that they are not enemies?"

Skalamar coolly swiveled his head and gazed at Trealine. "She never said they were not enemies. Only that they do not appear to be ready to do us harm. There is a difference. And last, yes, I will believe her assessment of the situation. She is rarely wrong."

Morri gave a quiet squawk at that last part, but Skalamar just ginned at the bird without replying. He turned his attention to the group. "I suggest we openly, but cautiously, proceed and see what they want."

Kalend thought it through and decided they should do as Skalamar suggested but be prepared for anything. With Juliet and Hollilea in the rear, both ready to help from a distance if things turned poorly, the companions cautiously headed down the trail. Around a bend, the dry riverbed opened into a small clearing, and in the center squatted two of the oddest beings Kalend had ever seen. He thought they were statues at first sight, so calmly did they perch on their heels. They appeared human but were taller than any he had met, even Skalamar; he estimated each to be over nine feet tall. Broad and burly, they slowly stood from their kneeling positions and faced the group; closer to ten feet, he reconsidered as he peered upward at the beings. Then Kalend's mouth dropped open in astonishment as he fully noticed their faces. Each had only one eye, oblong and more prominent than any eye on a human; they were centered where two eyes should have been. Below those eyes were wide flaring nostrils, and below that, large mouths filled with mangled, stained teeth. A thick carpet of black hair covered their bare chests. Leggings made from animal hides and leather sandals were their only clothes; they casually held massive wooden clubs against their broad right shoulders and stood before the group in non-threatening but imposing postures.

After a moment of shock, Kalend strode forward. "Hello. We mean you no harm," he greeted them confidently and warmly.

The two laughed, a guttural, loud noise that filled the ravine and sent rivulets of perspiration down Kalend's back. They looked at each other, then back at Kalend. With a wide, lopsided grin, the one on the left pointed a giant hairy finger at Kalend and said, "No…..it is us that don't mean you harm."

Kalend and his friends stood still for several moments, each taking in the pair before them and weighing their options if the encounter turned ugly. Kalend felt the tension rise and eased himself into a relaxed state, telling himself that the odd pair would have already attempted an ambush if they had meant the group harm. He slowly held up his hands and laughed. "Yes, it seems we are all here peacefully. It also appears you have been waiting for us. How may we be of service?"

The two odd creatures lowered their clubs, leaned on them, and smiled back. It was the left one who spoke again, "Hello to you." He said in a quick fashion that sounded like he had marbles in his mouth. "We be here not from our doing. We need go home." It took Kalend a few moments to process what he was hearing. The fast speech and mumbled words made it hard to understand.

Kalend nodded cautiously and asked, "Where is home?"

"Home be under big earth." Was the quick, muddied reply.

Kalend looked to his friends to see if they understood what was being said. They either shook their heads or shrugged; none knew what "under big earth" meant. And each seemed content to let Kalend figure it out for himself. He gave them all an irritated look before turning back to the two behemoths.

Kalend tried another tact, "Who are you? Where do you come from?"

The creature slapped his meaty hand against his chest, "We be Cyclops." Then he pointed a hairy bent finger to the group, "You be Humans."

Kalend nodded in understanding and asked again, "But where are you from?"

They both growled and, with a speed that surprised the group, raised their clubs and smashed them onto the rocky ravine floor, pulverizing the peddles and sending up small clouds of dust. The companions took a hasty step backward, but Kalend held up his hand to stop them from drawing weapons. The two cyclops were now engaged in a fast, back-

and-forth chatter, which quickly escalated into a shoving match with their free hands. Kalend slowly began to comprehend the rapid speech, and he concluded that the right cyclops had insulted the left one, and now they were insulting each other with crude jokes. He shook his head in wonder at the strangeness of it all.

The companion's apprehension slowly turned to amusement as it became apparent that the two were now engaging in playful roughhousing. The oddness of the encounter and their playfulness was infectious, and soon, the group found themselves smiling at the pair's antics. Kalend smiled along with his friends and cringed at some of the more colorful insults. After several minutes, the pair seemed to realize they were being watched and stopped to beam at them with wide, open-mouth grins.

Kalend pointed to each member of his group and slowly said each by name.

"Me be Sha-bert," the lead Cyclops said before pointing to his friend, "He be Wil-bert."

Kalend had come to the realization that the two had been quarreling over how Sha-bert had answered his questions. Wil-bert had been less than impressed with his companion and teased Sha-bert regarding his accent, speech, and language use. Sha-bert had not taken kindly to the teasing and responded in kind. Kalend was not sure Wil-bert should be giving any advice in any of those areas, as neither spoke well; each was equally hard to decipher. It was not so much a matter of intelligence; they seemed to speak in their own language, one that may have started out similar to theirs' but had been altered. It was as if the two had been isolated, and over time, it had morphed into their own way of communicating.

He asked several more questions and received similar answers but with more detail. It seemed their two new friends wanted to go home, and the way home led back to the warlocks' encampment. However, they were afraid of the warlocks and unwilling to approach them. For the last few months, they had been wandering about the island in some hope of finding another way. Kalend was still unsure of where that home was. It became apparent that they had not actually lived in the cave, only that they came here from it. None of which made sense to him.

Hollilea stepped forward and asked a few quick, short questions, to which she received even shorter, faster answers. After a few moments, she turned to the companions. "I think the lake inside that cave might be magical after all. Our two stranded friends were whisked from their homeland and appeared above the lake. They managed to crawl out after falling in, then escaped out a rear entrance, and have been searching for a way back ever since."

Kalend shook his head and frowned. "How is that even possible? And we still don't know where they come from originally?"

"I believe the same magic that works the wells we know about also powers that lake. But on a larger level. Sha-bert claims that they have seen hundreds of beings coming out of that cave. Light and smog would come pouring out, and then the beings shortly after."

"Much like what we saw at that well in the desert," Juliet exclaimed.

Kalend stood still for several moments and thought it through; it made sense in a way. The Girillon were most likely not from this world, and with the other creatures seen and heard around Odewin City, he was getting the picture that the twins were doing more than hiding out on the island. But why these creatures, and why let them loose upon the world? He had more questions than answers, as usual. He grinned at that thought, not that it was anything new since he left the monastery. His life since leaving felt like a never-ending adventure of questions, one that was becoming more complicated each day. In a way, he missed the simpler times of his youth. But he also knew everyone had to grow up, and it seemed that the world had more prominent uses for him than sitting around a monastery every day. All he could do was move on and see it through; he did know he did not want to live in fear for himself or his family and friends.

Some more back and forth with the Cyclops, and Kalend learned that they would be willing to help the group if they could get them home. After a hasty consultation with Hollilea about the ability to send them back, he told them the best they could do was try to get them to the lake, and hopefully, Hollilea could figure out how to send them home. He also told them it would not come without considerable risk. They quickly agreed to his proposal, and the company now numbered two more.

Trealine had given his approval to the idea but asked what the plan was if the whole cave entrance was fortified and filled with an army of otherworld creatures. Kalend gave it some thought for a moment, then shrugged and, with his best Louquintas grin, answered, "We sneak up and see what happens."

Trealine gave him a cool look before replying, "Maybe you have spent too much time with Louquintas."

Kalend's grin widened, and then he said in a more serious tone, "We know we need to find out what the warlocks are up to, AND we need to get Louquintas back. We have already accomplished some of that; we know they are bringing over creatures but still don't know from where or why. This can't be all about my sister and me."

Hollilea sighed. "We may know from where—the home of the Wiccenda. I do not know much about the place, only that there are many different beings there. My guess is that is where they are coming from. But, then again, I can't be sure of that."

Kalend smiled reassuringly at his sister. "Don't worry, we will figure it out."

She smiled back and softly replied, "I know. Just wish the witches had told me more."

Kalend laughed, shook his head, and exclaimed, "Now that would have been something, our mentors not keeping things from us."

They both laughed together and gave each other knowing smiles. The rest of the companions stared at the two. They were deep in an unknown land, surrounded by enemies, and the two were laughing about how unfairly their mentors had treated them. Trealine grunted after a few moments. "If you two are done reminiscing, maybe we can get to saving Louquintas?"

*****   *****

With Sha-bert by his side, Kalend led the companions down the same old dry creek bed where they had encountered the pair. Sha-bert had told them he knew a "secret secret" route to the cave entrance, or at least to a small hill overlooking it. It seemed that the pair frequently went to look in hopes of finding the place unguarded. But each time, even if the site looked deserted, they had been too scared of the warlocks' magic to approach.

Morri flitted from tree to tree above them, keeping a look out as they made slow but steady progress. It all seemed too easy to Kalend, and when he mentioned his worries to Trealine, he received a grunt and reassurance that sometimes you should just be thankful when things were going your way. He pointed out that Skalamar also knew of this "secret secret" passage, and so far, he had turned out to be someone they could rely on. Trealine also mentioned that sometimes it was good to be lucky, which he said with a rare smile.

At a sharp curve, Sha-bert led them off the creek bed and uphill along a worn game trail between low-lying holly and mountain laurel. Kalend received a covert nod from Skalamar that this was correct; neither wanted to antagonize their new burly companions. Kalend's first look at the cave entrance did not inspire much hope. Across a wide swath of grass and low-lying bushes, the opening gaped from the side of the mountain. The mountainside above and around it was covered in greenery, towering oaks, and pines with smaller variations staggered between; the cave stared out like a ragged dark eye. An eye that sent an eerie chill coursing through the companions. It seemed to whisper to them from within its depths as if it were alive and knew they were coming. They shivered and let out slow breaths as they tried to convince themselves it was only a cave. All appeared affected except for Skalamar, who stood still like an unwavering oak. Kalend chalked this up to his having been here before; at least, that was what he hoped.

He shook off the dread and took stock of the situation before them. Not steep, the mountain looked more like a tall hill. For these were old mountain ranges, worn down by time and exposure to wind and rain, they did not reach the heights of the Hesture's he was more familiar with. A low crumbling wall that looked to have been recently shored up in a hasty, haphazard manner ran from one side of the mountain to the other in a horseshoe shape encompassing the cave. The only visible entrance to the compound came from a small opening in the wall between two broken-down watchtowers. A patch of land had been cleared from the gates to the woods below them, where a few mismatched tents and smokey fires resided. Kalend estimated the whole compound to be around fifty square yards. Except for a few guards at the gate, the compound appeared empty. There were at least one hundred open yards from the hill's base to the wall, making it unlikely they could sneak up on those guarding the gate.

Kalend looked at his friends and saw the same defeated look in their eyes. Knowing they had no choice and were determined to save Louquintas, he threw out any negative thoughts that crossed his mind and said, "Well, they may know we are coming, but they do not know how many of us there are now. We also have abilities they are unaware of. We have grown much. We will find a way in and out."

The ladies smiled in appreciation of his determined attitude, and Trealine nodded his head in understanding. Skalamar stared at him without emotion with his pupil-less eyes. The Cyclops…..grinned, shook their clubs at the cave, and grunted loudly. Much too loud for Kalend's liking, he attempted to calm them with a few words of caution, and they gave him an irritated look, but the warning seemed to seep in, and they smiled in anticipation. What they were anticipating gave Kalend pause; he was unsure if it was the anticipation of going home or the coming conflict. From the off-color comments they mumbled about smashing things, he guessed it was the latter. Keeping their new friends in line with any plan they developed would be a challenge, one he would need to keep in mind.

The group edged away from the hilltop and quickly trekked back down the game trail. Once Kalend felt they had put enough distance between the warlocks' compound and themselves, he moved off the track until he came upon a small clearing of knee-high grasses. They hitched the horses to some pines and set about preparing food and drink while they talked over their next steps. Morri quietly floated from tree to tree, safely keeping deep within their leafy embrace while also maintaining a wary eye out around them.

Kalend sipped on his waterskin as he addressed his companions. "I think we need to split up." He quickly raised his hand as several objections were immediately raised, "Whoa...let me at least finish explaining my plans."

Hollilea, who had been the loudest and quickest to object, grunted and shook her head as she waved to her brother to continue.

"As I see it, we need to harness all the abilities of this group. So, I propose we have the cyclops lead Juliet to the back entrance where the cyclops escaped from, and she can blend in and hopefully sneak past any guards and find Louquintas. I am betting the warlocks remain unaware of her ability, and that may give us an edge."

Juliet frowned. "What about when I snuck in and got you both out in the desert? They had to know someone got you out without them knowing. They may be ready for it this time."

Kalend smiled. "Yes, but this time there will be a distraction."

Trealine solemnly asked, "And how do we do that?"

Kalend looked around at his friends with a smirk and replied, "I turn myself in."

A stunned silence hung over the group as they each processed what he said; then, in one voice, they each began to harangue him about the foolishness of his plan. He stoically stood before their verbal assault and waited for them to get it out of their systems. Once they realized he was not fighting back or defending the idea but stood looking at them with a calm, determined gaze, one by one, they fell quiet.

Kalend paused a moment as silence settled around the clearing once again, then continued, "Yes, I know this idea isn't my best or one that you approve of, but it makes sense."

Hollilea huffed, angrily crossed her arms, and interrupted him, "It makes no sense! I will not let my newly found brother be subjected to those two."

"Yes, you will," he gently continued. "I will need you to stay and help out when the time is right. Remember, I can summon magic through you. Once they are focused on me, Juliet can free Louquintas, get back out, and get above the compound. From there, she can help cover me with her bow. Once she is clear, I can summon the magic and engage them. As I do that, Skalamar, Trealine, and the cyclops can rush in to help. And you, dear sister, can attack from the tree line."

Trealine grudgingly nodded his head. "That all sounds good, but I am not sure we are enough to defeat whatever may be hidden in that cave. We can see the outside of the compound but not in that cave. They may have troops hidden within."

Kalend sighed. "That is the risk we will need to take. If they had more troops of Panes or other creatures, I am sure they would have brought them to the Norry Pass. I think they used up what troops they had attacking those archers, and those were all killed. Besides, Sha-bert said he didn't think there were many guards inside. Remember, they have been worried about the warlocks, not troops." He knew each of his companions was probably thinking like he was, that Sha-bert was not the best source of information, but he could not think of any other alternatives. Besides, he did have one other trick to play…. if needed. He just hoped it would not come to that.

Michael Gisman

CHAPTER THIRTY-ONE

The group was not overly happy, but in the end, they grudgingly agreed with Kalend, and preparations began. One thought they all had in common was that waiting until dawn would be their best chance. This would give them all some time to get mentally prepared, eat, and obtain any sleep that they could find. Skalamar sent Morri off to scout the compound one last time and gather any last-minute details that may be of any help. Everyone else made themselves busy with small, mindless tasks intended to distract and help them to relax.

Kalend wandered off into the woods to gather firewood. He had agreed that a small fire could be risked; Skalamar was confident he could dig a pit that would burn the wood quickly, hot, and with minimal smoke. As he picked up loose, dry, dead limbs that littered the forest floor, Kalend thought through the plan one last time. It was not great, but he believed that Louquintas would be proud of him. It was just the type of daring deed his mentor would have devised. One that was aggressive but afforded them the best chances of success. Their options were limited, and they were few, but they had many powers that may prove the difference. He smiled, thinking of his mentor and what he would have thought of his leadership, something Kalend had not wanted but had grudgingly accepted. He gave a small laugh and mumbled out loud, "You bastard, bet you wanted to get caught. Force me into leading."

The evening was cool; clouds covered the sky like a grey blanket, and quiet darkness settled over the forest around them. They spoke in hushed tones beside the fire, wary that their adversaries would not hear them. But there was a grittiness in each voice, for they were determined to get their friend back and finally deal with the warlocks. The pent-up emotions from the whole day finally wore them down, and one by one, they drifted into slumber, all except Kalend, who had chosen to take the first watch.

He meditated and reminisced about his journey so far. All that he had accomplished, all he had gone through, and all those he had met and learned from to get to this point. Hours passed swiftly as his mind wandered down memory lane, keeping him from despair. He understood much of what was happening, but so many questions remained. Why were he and his sister so important, and who was behind the warlocks? He was impatient for those answers but knew none were forthcoming that evening. Shaking his head, he rose to poke Skalamar awake to take the next watch. He settled down with his head in the crook of his arm and drifted into a peaceful slumber, knowing those answers may come tomorrow.

Dawn arrived as the sun peaked out from above the mountains to the east and slowly spread its cheerful rays over the forest. A cheerfulness that was lost on most of those in the clearing. Each member of the group dealt with differing emotions; some were fearful yet passionately committed to the cause. Others, like Skalamar, went about their preparations dispassionately, only determined to help and yet survive. The Cyclops were the only ones that could have been considered cheerful, or at least that is how Kalend saw it. The two behemoths were almost giddy as they eagerly tramped around the camp while getting ready for their part in the great plan. Kalend unpacked his chainmail, and as he slipped on his gambeson, he went over the "Great Plan." That's how he thought of it now, and he hoped it would see them free their friend and themselves from the warlocks. Or it may just bring ruin to them all. He did not dwell on those dark thoughts. He knew he must stay positive; there was no room for doubt in his leadership.

Sha-bert and Juliet headed out first. A last-minute change made by Kalend, only the one Cyclops would lead her. Kalend had some concern that the two Cyclops together would not be able to remain silent enough to get her to the cave's rear entrance. One was noisy enough, but together, they were a loud, rowdy duo. Wil-bert had not been keen on the idea, but after much painful pervasive reassurance from Hollilea, he had grudgingly agreed to be separated from his friend.

The rest of the companions set out to the same overlook as the day before. The horses were left behind untethered in the clearing; Kalend did not have the heart to leave them tied up in case things did not go as planned. It was doubtful they would stray too far; they were trained for combat and knew to stay close. He had other reasons as well, but he did not feel the need to share those with the group at that time.

They quickly and quietly strode down the path leading to the clearing. Each focused on the mission, and any lingering doubts swept away with the cool breeze that ushered them along. Skalamar led the way with long, stealthy strides. Kalend followed closely, but without the same sure feet as their guide, he grimaced with each small snap of a twig or crunch of a dried leaf; his footfalls seemed to echo among the trees. He knew his mind was exaggerating the noise, that his noise was minuscule, that it was just his imagination, and that Skalamar was just that good. The best he had ever seen or -not heard. Even Trealine, who had grown up and lived his whole life in the forest, could not match him. None of that helped him feel better about his seemingly loud trampling. So, he followed the best he could and set his mind on the coming mission.

The glade had not changed much overnight. The big difference was their attitude. One of determination and single-minded focus, every member was ready to do their part. Kalend looked at the cave mouth once more, then at each of his companions; he felt grateful for their friendship and their faith in his plan. He nodded toward them one by one in a silent thank you. Kneeling onto the damp, leafy soil beneath the forest canopy, he motioned to his right, and Trealine and Skalamar melted into the trees. He then motioned to his left, and Hollilea and Wil-bert ambled, less stealthily but quietly enough, into the woods. Silently, he watched each group of his friends move off to get into a position to come to his aid when needed. For needed, it shall be. He was under no illusion that his plan would be safe for anyone, especially himself. Serving himself up on a platter like a side of mutton was not the safest place to be in this plan.

He stayed in his kneeling position on the plush carpet of the forest floor, feeling the cold dampness of the earth seep through his pants and settle into his knees as he stared out at the cave and the walled compound. Juliet and Sha-bert needed time to get around to the back of the hill before he gave himself up, so he waited and watched. Movement within the camp was limited; there still appeared to be few within its walls. The last sweeps that Morri had flown yesterday had revealed nothing new in the surrounding area. All was quiet and peaceful as if holding its breath and waiting for something, which he grudgingly guessed was most likely him. He knew his enemies were waiting on him, that he was coming and was not far away, but this level of inaction tickled his mind that all was not as it seemed. He sighed; there was nothing more he could do. He had to put his trust in the "Great Plan" and with his friends.

Time stretched, slow and implacable; Kalend closed his eyes and let his mind slow with its passage. He could once again feel a wisp of darkness from the island, like before, but now that whiff was more potent and felt much closer. He slid past it and eased himself into a deep well of calmness. He hoped to remain buried in that calmness no matter what happened. Like being in the eye of a Hurricane he once heard about, he needed to let any chaos rage around him as he stood within that well of calm and did what needed doing.

He calmly opened his eyes, rose noiselessly, and slid from the concealing brush out into the open field. He confidently strode toward the camp, shoulders square and head held high.

*****   *****

Juliet followed closely behind the towering form of Sha-bert. She was relieved to see and hear that he could move quietly when the Cyclops wanted. He was in no danger of anyone calling him a Ranger, but at least he maneuvered through the woods and around the small mountain with some level of skill. She now understood how the two beings had been able to remain undetected for so long and manage to scout out the cave and camp.

Juliet urged Sha-bert to set a faster pace. She knew that speed would be required, even if it meant taking some risks; they had to be in position once Kalend gave himself up. With that last thought, Juliet grimaced and wondered how their group had been convinced so easily of this reckless plan. Reckless, that is what she thought of Kalend giving himself over to the two warlocks. She knew he was tired of running, tired of the unanswered questions, and just wanted more control over his life, but to turn himself over to them? She shook her head in irritation.

But now, as she flitted among the trees and brush, she wondered why she had given in so easily. And it came to her as she hopped over a fallen half-decayed log. Kalend was becoming a leader, someone who could be counted on and willing to make the hard decisions. He no longer exuded the same puppy-dog earnestness as he had when he saved her all those months ago on the river. He had become more. At first, she thought it was the absence of Louquintas, his mentor and teacher, that had precipitated the change, but looking back, she realized that it had been a process that had been ongoing for some time. They had all agreed because of the air about him, the trust his demeanor instilled in them, and the calm he displayed when deciding what course of action to take. Couple that with his reasoned approach to explaining his plan, and they all collapsed to the mad plan. She still thought the idea of turning himself in was reckless. But she shook her head again, this time with a wide, eager smile; if he could manipulate them that easily, maybe he had some small hope against the warlocks.

Sha-bert came to a halt behind the bole of a towering oak that spread its massive canopy of limbs over a boulder and shrub-covered clearing. Juliet came up beside him and studied the open space; the tree limbs provided a large shaded area where other trees could not grow, or much else for that matter. Once past that shade, the forest sloped upward, quickly becoming steep enough that traversing the hill would not be easy.

Sha-bert pointed at the base of the hill, just at the end of the canopy's protection, to an extensive mass of bristling hawthorn bushes. He indicated that just behind those thorny leaves lay the cave entrance. Juliet patted him on his bicep and whispered, "Good job."

Sha-bert grinned and clapped her on the back hard enough that she stumbled a few steps. She turned to give him an angry retort, but when she saw his happy grin, she shook her head instead and said, "Stay here; it's time to do my job now."

Juliet cautiously approached the wall of hawthorns and pushed apart two of the bushes where their leaves just kissed each other. Being mindful of their thorns, she noted that both plants were beginning to bloom. Summer was coming to an end, she realized with some shock. How had that happened? How had she missed the turning of the seasons? And how odd that was where her mind turned while trying to sneak into a cave of warlocks. But then a thorn jabbed into her shoulder as she passed through and forced her mind back to the task at hand.

The entrance was a round shaft bored into the hill. Not man-made, but then not wholly natural either, Juliet thought. It looked as if a giant worm had burrowed its way through the earth and then found its escape. Or maybe it was the reverse;

something had burrowed into the mountainside. She paused at that idea; what if something still waited within. Then, it struck her that the hawthorn was old and surely would have been crushed by the creature before or after making the tunnel. Plus, the Cyclops had made their initial escape through it. The tunnel was large, but she would have to stoop to get through, which meant her giant companion would have had to crawl. She bent and examined the floor around the entrance. A single footprint had made an indentation to the left of the hole; it led away from the tunnel and was big enough to be a Cyclops. From what she could tell, they had crawled through and then stood once they had exited.

More secure in her belief that no creature waited for her just within its confines, she took two steps into the dark shaft. Then she set her thoughts to her surroundings, letting the image of the rocks, dirt, and sand flow into her mind and then on into her body. She felt a slight vibration run along the length of her limbs that signaled her camouflage ability had taken hold. A few more quick strides, and she was swallowed by the darkness of the tunnel.

***** *****

The two Pane guards noticed Kalend's approach and signaled into the interior of the camp. Good, Kalend grimaced in relief, better than a hail of arrows as a greeting. He was betting on the guards having orders to take anyone they found alive. He knew his enemies wanted him breathing at least, so hopefully, he would have a chance to talk before any unpleasantness occurred.

Once within twenty feet, Kalend stopped as the guards simultaneously drew their swords and, with a steely-sounding ring, crossed them before the entrance. "No further now. What is it you want," the left Pane demanded in a raspy voice.

Kalend eased his hands up above his head in a sign of peace. "I wish to speak with your masters."

"Do you now? And who is that comes a calling?" The same Pane asked.

Before Kalend could respond, four figures swaggered up to the entrance, and a loud familiar voice rang out, "No need for that, Darjin. He is a welcome guest!"

As his gaze came to rest on the approaching foursome, Kalend noted that it was Tworg's voice he had heard. His two adversaries stopped a few feet from him, just out of the range of his sword, while two personal guards ranged out on either side of them. They had not changed much; each wore violet velvet robes like his last encounter with them. However, the robes appeared worn and dingy now, as if they had been thoroughly abused. Tworg carried a staff of dark wood, and etched along its entire length were softly glowing purple glyphs unknown to Kalend. The warlocks wore unsavory and arrogant smirks on their faces as they looked him over. He kept his mind calm as he responded in a neutral tone, "I do not come as a guest, but I do come in peace."

"Either way, it does not matter to us. What matters is that you are here now." Tworg responded and then asked, "And where are your friends? Eeh? Perhaps hiding in the trees waiting to ambush us?" He looked out to the forest and gave it a dismissive wave.

Kalend stayed deep within his calm void. He needed to keep them talking, keep them right here, and give Juliet more time. "I have more friends now, and we do not fear your magic," he said defiantly.

"Yes, yes, we are aware of your friends. But you have now entered our home and base. Your sister's power cannot match ours here in this place," Tworg said as he gestured toward the cave.

Kalend smiled and paused, responding indifferently, "I do not wish to trade threats; we hope to end this peacefully. Why risk the chance that we can match you? Leave peacefully, and do not come after my sister and me anymore, and we will leave you alone."

Pouluk, who had been giving Kalend a steady stare of contempt, snorted in derision. "You would ask us to leave you alone?" he asked, then quickly continued in a low, even deep voice. "No. It is you who needs to come with us, peacefully, so that your friends may live. You may even keep your sword, for we already have your leader, Louquintas."

A coldness slid down Kalend's spine, but he did not let it penetrate his void as he asked, "What have you done with him?"

"Let us just say he is alive and well, but that could always change."

Kalend contemplated what was said and wished he could confer with his sister. That was not an option, though; they had discussed using their abilities to speak with each other, but Hollilea did not think it wise so close to the warlocks. Hollilea was unsure of what their powers were capable of and did not want to risk being overheard. She had risked it before, but that had been in an emergency; this needed subtlety. All he could do was rely on Juliet and give her enough time to search the cave. So, he asked, "What exactly is it that you want with me?"

"It's not just a matter of what we want so much as who else wants something from you," Tworg grunted.

"Ahh, you mean the master you both serve?" Kalend asked with a small, knowing smile.

Pouluk nodded. "Good....it is good that you already know of him. For soon, you shall be answering his questions. The sooner you give yourself over, the easier it will go."

"I shall never do anything easy," Kalend responded defiantly.

"We shall find out.......and very soon."

***** *****

At least Shar-bert had been correct in that there were few troops within the cave itself. Juliet had snuck around most of the complex and found only two Panes wandering around, which she had steered clear of, and they, in turn, never noticed her camouflaged form. A semi-circular lake took up most of the cave's back end, its emerald surface still and clear, with no sign of magic, at least none that Juliet saw. As she peered into its crystalline depths, she could make out blurry water welling up from deep within its depths that hardly disturbed the surface. A natural spring lurked at the lake's center and fed a continuous supply of fresh water, while a jagged opening several feet under the surface at the back wall suggested the water continued on into the hill. Flickering torches held by iron brackets bolted into the walls cast pale shadows that danced among the surrounding stone and provided a patchwork rosy glow over the water. Two narrow pebble-strewn paths lined either side of the lake, and both led to a few spacious rooms, all of which she had investigated, and all found either empty or moderately filled with an assortment of foodstuffs, weapons, and armor.

There was considerable space between the sandy lakeshore and the cave entrance. The worn grey stone floor had scuff marks that indicated much traffic had passed between the lake and the opening to the outside. Juliet was unsure which way the traffic had flowed, but she was sure that there had been a sizeable amount of it over time.

A jingle and creaking of leather warned of the approach of two more Panes making their rounds. Juliet silently glided into a small fissure within the nearby wall; she slowed her breathing and crouched down as she waited for them to pass. Her gaze followed their hairy backs as their hooved feet clicked along the stone floor. As they disappeared around a bend, she cocked her head as an oddly flickering torch along the far wall caught her attention. The flame danced and leaned to the side. The other torch fires along the same wall stood tall and straight; with a smile, she moved quickly but stealthily toward the dancing torch.

She found a passage partially hidden in a crevice; dank air wafted out and caused the torches odd capering. She slipped in and groped her way forward in the confining slip; it took a sharp turn, and she stumbled into a rectangular room. Small, softly glowing braziers lay on the floor along the walls, illuminating three cells built into the stone walls, each with closed wrought iron doors. The first two she glanced in held nothing but dust; the third and last held Louquintas. He lay on a moldy bed of straw with his hands clasped behind his head; with eyes closed, he appeared to be asleep.

CHAPTER THIRTY-TWO

Juliet led Louquintas along the lake's shore at a fast pace. She could not lead while camouflaged, so she was plainly visible and felt vulnerable. Getting Louquintas free of the cell had been relatively easy; the keys had been hanging on the far wall as if to taunt him. After a brief reunion and debriefing on the plan and some salty words of displeasure regarding those plans from Louquintas, they had gotten on the move. They followed the left lane around the lake, heading toward a storage area and the hidden opening Juliet had used to breach the complex. She stopped again at the corner of the lake. Juliet motioned Louquintas to slide into the same crevasse she had vacated earlier, then blurred into their surroundings and scouted ahead.

As she strode back from finding the way clear, a disturbance at the center of the lake's sparkling waters caught the corner of her eye. She slowed, then stopped, pressed herself against the rough, cold stone wall, and watched as the bubbling disturbance grew and a familiar mist rose above the lake.

The mist reached a hazy peak of around six feet before dissipating into nothingness. A figure emerged, and with a cocky swagger, it marched along the top of the water as if that were the most natural thing to do. It came to a stop at the edge of the shoreline, and with a dull thud, its right hand planted a wooden staff onto the pebble flooring. The tip of the staff glowed an ominous dark purple that reflected angrily off the lake's water. Juliet stifled a gasp as she recognized the man. He still wore an outlandish buttoned-down blue shirt of unknown material, and his slacks were a shiny black with a crease that ran down both legs. It was the Master from the well in the desert.

Juliet frowned; his presence could not be good for her or the plan that Kalend had laid out. With the cold stone pressed against her back, she quickly ran through her options; she did not have many, and all of them were risky. This Master was an unknown; she did not want to rely on her camouflage ability too much, but she was not sure she had much choice. Getting herself and Louquintas free was their best bet for helping Kalend.

The Master turned to the lake, raised his staff upward, and with his head bowed, began to chant; low and raspy, his voice quickly filled the cave. She could not make out the words, but they sent a cold shiver racing down her spine. Panes came bubbling out and poured onto the shoreline. Row after row, they smartly marched out from the mist to surround the Master, and with an eerie silence, they patiently waited. Then, all at once, the flow of the creatures ceased. The Master began to swing his staff in a circular pattern, his chanting becoming a guttural, unnatural growl. The staff swirled faster, and the growling cadence increased with it. Juliet slouched down and tried to sink into the ungiving stone behind her as what emerged next was a nightmare. A three-headed monstrosity on four legs, not unlike a huge wolf, she thought. But one with three slavering heads, each with deathless eyes like endless dark voids and a pitch-black coat of fur that seemed to inhale all light around it. Never had she seen a wolf so large or had one garner such fear from her. It towered over the Master and stood with an obedient posture toward him, all while radiating malice for everything else around it as if life itself was deemed unworthy. Even the Panes' were not immune from its dreadful presence, as they, as one unit, clopped back a pace.

Frozen in shock and overrun with fear, Juliet tried to calm herself and think clearly. All that popped into her head was that she had to warn Kalend. But hard on that flash of thought was Louquintas; he still hid within the stone wall.... and could not come out without being seen. She did not want to leave her friend and Kalend's mentor behind, and indecision gnawed at her.

The Master turned and guided his fearsome beast and small army to the front of the cave, where he stood silent and still while gazing outward. Acting instinctively, Juliet rushed over to where Louquintas hid; she allowed her camouflage to melt away and motioned for him to be silent and follow her. They rounded the last bend of the path and just reached the entrance to the storage rooms beyond when a wild shout rang out. Twisting her head, Juliet slowed and saw that a few Panes had broken off from the back row and were sprinting toward them. She noted how quickly they ate up the ground, and with a shout to Louquintas that he should go on, she winked out from everyone's sight. Running full speed, she winked in and out, each time a little closer to the Panes as she headed toward the entrance, trying to draw their attention away from Louquintas. They skidded to a halt, and after a brief pause, they gave chase. She noticed Louquintas swear, hesitate, and then sprint toward the back rooms. She hoped that either she got lucky and could escape, or at least Louquintas could, and he would find a way to warn Kalend.

***** *****

There had been snide deliberations and many disparaging remarks by the warlocks, but Kalend had eventually agreed to follow them back to the cave where they would release Louquintas. He just hoped he had bought enough time for Juliet to find his friend, for he knew the odds of the warlocks releasing him were slim, very slim. He walked slowly behind the evil brothers and scanned the forest above the cave entrance; he saw no one and heard nothing. He stared forward and contemplated what to do next. Luckily, the Pane guards had stayed behind to keep watch, which relieved him of one worry. He had been vague to his friends regarding this part of his plan, and that was because he did not have a good grasp of what would come next. If Juliet had been able to secure Louquintas's release, he had hoped to have gotten some sign by now. But it seemed he was going to have to improvise. His current working plan was to secure his mentor's location, if he could, then surprise the warlocks with his sister's power channeled through him. Hopefully, they still did not know the depth of his and his sister's abilities. Then, if that worked, he escaped back outside where his friends could help. There were many "if's" in this part of the plan, but it was all he had.

As the cave mouth loomed larger, Kalend noted the silhouettes of familiar figures at its entrance; his heart sank. A small army of Panes stood within the shadow of the cave. An army they had not counted on. Either the Cyclops had lied, or somehow, the warlocks had been able to sneak in reinforcements. If the strange creatures had lied, that meant that Juliet was in grave danger and dashed any hope that she could free Louquintas. He continued forward with a heavy heart, fearful for what would come next for his friends.

"HELLO DOWN THERE!" a voice gaily rang through the still air.

Kalend stumbled to avoid bumping into the backs of the warlocks as they came to an abrupt halt. He lifted his head to follow their startled gaze and found a man standing arrogantly atop a pockmarked boulder that rested on the lip of the cave's entrance. When Kalend's shocked stare fell upon the odd man, the man gave a jaunty wave.

"So, how is everyone today?" the man asked with an air of whimsy that set his mustache quivering. With an almost audible click, Kalend's mind finally caught up with his sight, and a thrill of hope cascaded through his body. Louquintas was alive and free!

Pouluk raised his scaly arm and, with an angry scowl, sent spurts of flame toward Louquintas from his fingertips. The fire washed over the boulder as man and stone disappeared in a sea of red. Kalend held his breath, but as the flames flickered out, he sighed in relief as a voice floated out over the entrance "....any time now, Kalend."

Kalend belatedly realized what his mentor had been really doing with that stunt. While his enemies were still distracted, he reached out to his sister, pulled in what power he could, and sent a mental shove at the backs of the warlocks. As they stumbled forward, Kalend spun and sprinted for the makeshift opening leading in and out of the camp. Knowing this was risky, he counted on his friends to react and give him cover. He was also still holding onto his sister's power, and he used it to fashion a wall of hardened air that he mentally thrust behind him to block any projectiles sent his way.

He heard shouts ring out from the enemy behind while metallic thuds and small explosions gave evidence that the shield he had erected was working. He pounded on while Trealine and Skalamar frantically motioned him to hurry over the blood-stained corpses of the Panes that had been left to guard the entrance of the camp. Just as he reached them, something vast and pitch-black swarmed in from his left, and he suddenly felt his feet leave the ground as a crushing blow hit his whole body at once. After several terrifying, weightless moments, he crashed into the ground with a painful grunt. Instinctively, he rolled away from this new menace and felt a wave of crackling energy sweep over his rolling form.

The acidic stench of burnt hair reached his nostrils while he rolled upright and whirled to face his attacker with a drawn sword. Kalend felt his body lock in place at the horror before him; it reeked of death and sent a spike of despair tearing through his mind. Like a wolfhound, Kalend thought, one he had seen with a visiting hunter at the monastery, except twice the size and with three snarling and snapping heads. The heads spit drool from open mouths while hungry eyes devoured him; it crouched before him. He mentally shivered and warily held his sword in a defensive posture, unsure how to handle such a beast.

And then his sister was there, like a radiant star; she stood beside him, and together they stared defiantly at the horror before them. Her hair blazed a vibrant red as she stretched forth her hands, sending another wave of blinding electrical energy blasting into the beast as it prepared to leap at Kalend. Forced to dig deep furrows into the earth with long black claws, the beast held its ground and stared back at them with a burning hunger. Then it eagerly sprang at them, and this time, it anticipated Hollilea's burst of magic and managed to swerve past her and her lightning to pounce at Kalend. Hollilea took several steps to the side, giving Kalend room to maneuver. He avoided the initial attack using his sword to block and his natural agility to evade, and they settled into a wary dance. Kalend dodged and blocked while looking for openings to strike but found few. The beast was quicker and stronger, and Kalend grimaced as he realized that it hid an intelligent mind behind those baleful eyes. After another furious round of attacks, the beast paused. Each head cocked to the right, and with tongues lolled out past pointed fangs, it seemed to contemplate its next line of attack. Kalend's eyes quickly swept the camp to find out why his sister had stopped her blistering attack.

Hollilea had stepped even further away and was now fully engaged with the warlocks, trading torrents of colorful but deadly raw power between them. He then found Skalamar and Trealine being pushed back under the assault of the Panes that had rushed out of the cave. While both Cyclops had entered the fray and swung their clubs like they were harvesting wheat, they, too, were slowly forced to retreat. And behind them all, Kalend saw someone staying out of the fight. He recognized the Master, who stood with arms crossed just before the darkened cave entrance as he grimly surveyed the battle before him.

Three heads darted in and snapped at Kalend when his gaze fell on the Master. Kalend belatedly realized the pause itself had been a diversion. Cursing himself for a fool, he felt their drool spray onto his right arm as he rolled to escape; a long cut that dribbled a thin line of blood down his shin proved how close it had been. Realizing they were all now in trouble, he cursed again. There were too many Panes, too many users of magic, and the beast before him. Deep down, Kalend knew it was more than his little band could handle.

Whatever plan they had was now useless. Kalend could not form a new one; the three heads kept his constant attention, and he had already learned the hard way not to let his mind wander too much. Kalend heard the flapping of wings before he saw Morri's streaking form strike with outstretched talons at the left head of the beast. Drawing a deep red gash on its snout, the bird pivoted, rose out of the reach of the snarling jaws, flapped back around, and landed between Kalend and the beast. Kalend watched in amazement as the bird shimmered in the air, and a woman emerged from the same space the bird had just occupied. Skeleton skinny, clad in shiny black leather breeches and a black shirt overlaid by a black vest, she crouched with a short blade in each hand. Long limp dark hair framed a sunken and hollow face, which gave her the appearance of a corpse, Kalend thought as she turned to snap at him with a gruff gravelly voice, "Call your horse!"

Still mentally reeling from the sudden appearance of the Morri bird-woman, Kalend was shocked again that she would know about Whistler and his connection with his horse. Before he could puzzle it out, the bird-woman quickly thrust with both weapons, forcing the three heads back. He decided to save the why for later. Not wanting to reach back into the madness but knowing the Diomede Horses were their best hope, he sent a probing thought out to Whistler. Quickly, he established a connection and received, to his chagrin, an overly enthusiastic response. With a resigned grin, he also noted that Whistler was already swiftly galloping toward them as if his horse had anticipated this moment, and he was almost upon them. Now that he was aware of what they were, he hoped that with Whistler's help, he could evade the worst of the madness that would ensue.

Morri, the bird-woman, held her own, but even her cat-like reflexes and wiry strength were no match against three heads and equally quick reactions, and she grudgingly gave ground.

Kalend raised his sword, bided his time, and melded his attack with hers at the right moment. They swarmed around the ravening beast like two bees, dodging and yet harassing the three heads; they formed a stalemate. Neither side could gain a sizeable advantage; Kalend felt time crawl, and minor wounds appeared on them all. He knew it was only a matter of time before he or his companion made that fatal error that would end them. He hurried Whistler on.

Morri, the bird-woman, slipped to one knee on a bloody patch of weeds, and two heads darted in to finish her off; Kalend allowed a missed strike from the third head to whisk him into position to fend them off. He gritted his teeth with exertion as sweat stung his many wounds, but he managed to keep his blade a blur of motion that kept the heads at bay. Then, a familiar sickening madness flooded his mind, and his defense began to crumble. He tumbled unceremoniously over the still kneeling bird-woman to land on his back; with the breath knocked from his lungs, he fought for air as the red mist threatened to consume his mind.

Whistler quickly joined him in corralling the madness, and his sanity returned easier than the first time. Rushing into place, his thoughts became his again; the madness was still there, but now was a dull ache, an ache he could endure. With a gasp, he rolled to his knees, stood shakily, and took in the scene around him.

Skalamar appeared as Kalend had crashed onto the hard-packed earth. With slashes of his crescent blades, Skalamar scored deep groves into the hairy hide of the beast, leaving gaping gashes that streamed blood down its side. All three heads whimpered in unnerving unison, and it slunk backward warily from this newest threat. As Kalend helped the Morri bird-woman upright, he watched as the demon horses swept through the Panes like wildfire. They plowed straight ahead, and when they ran out of Panes, they spun around to blaze another path of death.

The warlocks had been driven back beside their master, who raised his staff, and, as sparks flew from the angry purple stone at its tip, brought the butt sharply down onto the pebbled ground. A crack of thunder split the air as the ground roiled beneath them; Kalend, his friends, and his enemies all stumbled to catch their footing. A booming voice rang out and commanded, "Stop this, now!"

All fighting ceased. The few remaining Panes moved into the cave to stand behind the Master as the three-headed beast slunk off to the side and gazed at the companions with hungry eyes as it paced. With weapons held at the ready, the companions sauntered up to either side of Kalend, and grim-faced, they awaited his lead. Whistler led the Diomede Horses in a methodical strut around the company, creating a circle of iron-hoofed defiance while their blazing eyes cast a warning to those before the cave to keep their distance. Kalend smiled as he glanced from side to side; drinking in his companions' determination and resolve, he squared his shoulders and faced his enemies with new hope.

The Master surveyed the determined group, shook his head, and laughed mirthlessly. As Kalend mulled his response, Louquintas strolled into the camp and calmly answered the laugh, "I am glad I can bring some laughter to this unholy scene," and then asked, "Do you wish to surrender now?"

Kalend thought their situation was a little too complicated to ask for surrender, and he grimaced at Louquintas, who just winked gaily in response.

The Master grimly shot back, "Not all is as it seems, my friend, but first, I wish to speak with young Kalend." He gestured to Kalend, "You know not who you truly are or are destined to become. I have seen that possible future and will not allow it to unfold; what you bring is death and destruction." He paused and continued in a softer voice but still with a hint of menace, "But that course can be unmade, this unseemly future, with your help......or your destruction. The choice can be yours."

Kalend swallowed and let out a long, slow breath, calming his mind and body. The words made no sense. How was he the bringer of death and destruction? All that he had witnessed and experienced marked this to be a lie. But the Master seemed sure of his words; even with the menacing tone, they rang with a note of truth. How could he reconcile the two versions?

Kalend responded in a cool voice, "You had my father killed and have tried to kill me, my sister, and my friends. Using others, killing others, all in that cause. Your words are hollow and nothing but lies."

"You will see in time," the Master responded evenly. "I do what is needed. You and your sister cannot be allowed to fulfill your destinies." He paused and grudgingly said, "However, you have been much harder to stamp out than I realized."

"Sorry to disappoint you," Kalend responded with his best imitation of a Louquintas smirk.

The Master sighed. "Maybe, in time, once you have seen what is to come, you will join me instead of having to be eliminated." He gestured to the darkened right side of the cave. "Until then, I think it is time for other measures." Lusstail emerged from the shadow of the cave while dragging a stumbling and struggling Juliet toward his master. With hands bound tightly behind her back, her steely eyes found Kalend's stunned gaze and silently implored him not to give up.

Kalend shook off his shock just as the Master, again, raised his staff and struck the pebbles beneath him. The ground heaved once more, rippling outward towards the companions and knocking them all to their knees. The Master gestured, and his minions spun as one and fled deeper into the cave, yanking Juliet with them.

Kalend surged to his feet and hastily sprinted after; he heard his friends follow a step behind him. They slid to a halt in the grey gravel at the lake's edge and silently took in the view of an empty cave. Only the rapidly dissipating mist over the placid waters marked the disappearance of their enemies.

***** *****

The companions sat around the flickering flames of the crackling fire with an air of dejection; they stared into the heart of the blaze, each lost in their own thoughts. All except Kalend, who stood before the cave entrance and glared at the lake inside as he moodily contemplated all that had happened and what was to come. After hauling off the Panes' bodies into the woods and burying them in a shallow pit, they returned to the cave entrance to rest and recoup. They had explored the whole cave, finding nothing but some food, drink, and an assortment of supplies in a back room, with no sign of the warlocks or Juliet. Now, he wondered what was to come next. He felt the loss of Juliet keenly and knew he had to go after her, which was precisely what the evil warlocks wanted. He shook his head grimly and knew it would not stop him, could not stop him.

Kalend glanced at his friends and noticed his sister looking at him with her bright eyes, which saw his pain and resolve. He could not ask his friends for more. They had already risked enough on his behalf.

Hollilea stood, quietly approached him, and firmly said, "Dear brother, you are obvious to me. I, at least, shall go with you. And I will not argue this; just know that I am going." She smiled and continued, "It will be easier for you to just accept that fact."

Kalend exhaled slowly and softly responded, "I wish that I could argue, but I know that it would be futile." Then he smiled wanly. "Besides, we have had others dictate how we're to live for long enough. Time for each of us to decide on our own."

Hollilea reached out and firmly grasped his hands in hers and smiled warmly at him. "We WILL get her back…." she trailed off, and the smile faded from her lips as she peered at the lake; a mist had once again started to gather above it.

Kalend gasped as the mist bubbled upward, and with a steely ring, he whisked his sword from its scabbard. But as he started to hurl a warning to his friends, Hollilea shushed him and then firmly snapped at him to lower his weapon.

The companions had seen Kalend's reaction and, with weapons drawn, hurried over to investigate. Hollilea saw them come and stayed their hands with a gesture and said, "She who comes is a friend." She paused, inhaled sharply, and with an awed voice gasped, "My Wiccenda arrives….in person and not as a spirit. The witches said this could not be done!"

A black-robed woman strode from within the mist and walked calmly over the water to stand before Hollilea. "And right they are, my dear!" she beamed at her apprentice.

Hollilea bowed and greeted her Wiccened with a respectful hello before asking, "But how?"

"If you have the right friends and access to enough magic, the right magic, it can be done." The Wiccenda motioned back to the lake, "And I happen to bring such a person with me."

The old man who walked over the water toward them did so with a grace that oozed power. The companions felt that power wash over them, and each was humbled into falling to their knees. The old man stood before them and bade them arise. "No, no, no, this will not do. I am just an old man. None of you should bow to anyone. I mean that, ANYONE," he soundly admonished them.

Kalend rose and admired the air of command the old man wielded; old but spry, he thought. The man had a wavy grey beard that reached his waist and matching grey shoulder-length hair. A wrinkled, leathery face with piercing green eyes that alternately drank in all before them but also gave the impression of a deep sea of knowledge. His robe was snowy white, and he glimmered as he moved. A green braided cord belted around his waist complimented his eyes, and threadbare sandals adorned his feet. Kalend felt relaxation ripple over the group as the old man smiled, enticing them to be at ease.

The Wiccenda smiled at the companions as she introduced the old man, "This is Merlyyne. He is a Wiccenda from my homeland and the head of our order." She then bowed to the group before continuing, "And I am Morgne, Wiccenda to Hollilea."

Kalend stepped forward and shook hands with both, welcoming them to their camp. He invited them to their fire, and Louquintas moved to the barrel of ale they had rolled out from the storeroom. Then proceeded to hand out frothy mugs of the dark drink to those who wanted. Merlyyne tipped his mug and drained it with one swallow; he thanked Louquintas and handed the cup back for another. As Merlyyne sipped from the second helping, he greeted the group formally, "Hello…. it is with pleasure I meet you all." He gathered his robe about his skinny frame and settled cross-legged before them before continuing, "I have followed your activities for some time. You have all done well in helping Kalend and Hollilea. They are on a dangerous path, one that has been foreseen. One which is of vital importance to many peoples."

Kalend, who sat to the old man's left, leaned forward and breathlessly asked, "What people are you talking about? What path are you talking about? And why us?"

Merlyyne laughed gently and held up his hand. "Patience, my young friend. I will endeavor to answer those questions the best I can. Or at least the ones I am allowed."

Kalend opened his mouth to ask another question, but the old man gave him a stern look that made Kalend rock back and clamp his mouth shut.

With a smile once again upon his face, Merlyyne continued, "There are things afoot that affect both our peoples, along with many others. I come from a different time and place; this may be hard to believe, but believe you must. All of you have seen what Hollilea is capable of, her powers and magic, so please stretch your imagination just a bit further. This other place is home to myself, Morgne, and all the other Wiccenda. This would also include the one you call the Master." He paused, took another deep swallow from his tankard, and sighed with contentment.

Morgne shook her head in distaste. "You know you shouldn't drink that."

Merlyyne grinned impishly at her as he lifted the brew to his lips and drained the remains in one gulp. He then waved for more, "Maybe," he responded to Morgne, "but it sure tastes good; besides, how often do I get this chance?"

With a scowl, Morgne just shook her head and did not bother to respond.

Merlyyne accepted another full drink from Louquintas, thanked him, and once again continued, "As I was saying, you must put aside any skepticism you harbor. The Master, as you call him, is indeed from our world, but he comes from another part of it. One which rarely mingles with ours. He managed to sneak into our secret grove and steal a piece of the Lia Fail, or stone of destiny. That piece is what sits on top of his staff and gives him his powers; this staff is also connected to the one the warlocks carry. However, theirs is not nearly as powerful as the Master's."

Trealine grunted, "Powerful enough."

"Yes, it is," Merlyyne responded somberly.

Hollilea gestured to the cave and asked, "Then that staff allows them to open a portal at the cave lake and wells? Is that why they had that camp in the desert; it was not far from a well?"

Merlyyne nodded. "Yes, it is, on both counts. Even a piece of the Lia Fail can do this. For the Lia Fail is directly connected to the True Source, from which our magic springs forth. All the Wiccenda draw their power from the True Source, but what we can draw is a small sliver compared to the stone. Luckily, the Master and warlocks have little idea of how to use what they have stolen."

Trealine grunted louder this time and said, "Not lucky enough."

Merlyyne grinned back at him. "Maybe my grumpy fellow. But if they had full control and use over what they have, none of you would be here now." He paused, then looked to Kalend and Hollilea. "You two are the key. Both of you have a destiny laid on you, one that will shape both our worlds...and others. For the time is fast approaching, which will change all that we know. On our world, the True Source reigned supreme for many eons, but slowly, man moved away from it and toward science. So as not to be forgotten, the True Source was sent out to other lands and worlds in the form of artifacts, each different and hard to find. The Wiccenda were created from this, as another way to spread, allowing others across worlds to access the True Source."

Hollilea interrupted and asked, "If the True Source was spread to our world, why can't we directly access it here?"

"The power needs time to settle in, like a tree as it grows and sends its roots throughout the soil, so must the True Source spread. But like a sapling, it needs protection…and that my young friends are you!" Merlyyne said with a flourish of his hands toward the brother and sister.

The stunned companions sat silently as the fire crackled and popped in the cool night air, each lost in wonder at all that had been shared and the final revelation about Kalend and Hollilea. Kalend broke the silence and solemnly asked, "But why us?"

Merlyyne raised his hands palms upward and shrugged his shoulders. "No idea. But you are the ones chosen for this. Look at the mischief that The Master has caused with just one piece of the stone. Imagine those with evil within their heart gaining access to the other artifacts?"

"Even if we accept all that you have told us, my first priority is to get Juliet back," Kalend said with a grimly determined voice.

Merlyyne nodded. "I expected as much. The Master plays a game deeper than we know; I feel something else pulling the strings. The True Source is what we call where our powers come from, but there are deeper, darker powers long forgotten laying out there for the right…or the wrong person to come along. Over the eons, the True Source has tamped out much of this evil, but still, it abides, weaker but still there, hiding and waiting."

Louquintas took the old man's cup for another refill. Both pretended not to see the frown from Morgne and asked as he returned, "It sounds like there is a mind or conscience behind the True Source and this evil. Each striving for control."

Merlyyne stared deep into the flames before him for several seconds before responding quietly, "Very perceptive, and you are correct. There are. We do not speak their names often, and I will not utter them here. They usually do not get directly involved in the doings of mortals, and I hope they are not now."

Kalend stared at the old man and whispered, "You worry the Master is connected to this…..evil god?"

Merlyyne nodded. "Yes. But we do not know for sure. If it were so, I would have thought we would have had a sign or contact from the True Source's maker, which we have not."

Hollilea gestured to herself and Kalend, "Maybe we are that sign?"

Merlyyne smirked at Kalend and Hollilea. "Maybe. When I told you I had no idea why you were chosen, that is not precisely true. I know some of the why, just not all of it. You and your sister have a bond, a strong one with each other. But also a bond with others, like Kalend and his horse Whistler. And Hollilea has a bond through her Wiccenda, which is stronger than most. These bonds will give you the strength to defend the True Source. Whoever is behind the True Source chose you for those bonds; they knew you would manifest them and that they would be needed."

Morgne abruptly stood and said, "We need to leave; our time here is limited."

Merlyyne rose to stand beside her. "We thank you for your hospitality, but yes, we must be on our way. It is harmful to us to be here too long; the longer we are physically away from our world, the weaker our bond with the True Source becomes."

Kalend jumped up and asked, "But what are we to do now? I will not abandon Juliet."

Merlyyne grinned and pointed to the bird perched on Skalamar's shoulder, "Ask the bird!"

As the shocked group looked at the bird Morri, Morgne quickly herded Merlyyne from the fire towards the cave. Kalend turned back in time to see the old man wave his hands at the lake and mumble some unknown words, and then both disappeared within the mist hovering over the water.

Silence descended among the group as each processed the sudden departure of the Wiccenda. Their internal reflection was interrupted by the flapping of wings as the blackbird Morri flew from Skalamar's shoulder to hover before the fire. Then the bird briefly blurred, and the skeletal woman that had saved Kalend stood before them all and, with a raspy voice, commented, "I guess it's time...."

......The End

Book two follows the companions as they decide Juliet's fate and their own.

Michael Gisman

THANK YOU

Dear Reader,

Thank you for reading Defenders of Myth. I hope you enjoyed the journey as much as I did writing it.

If you enjoyed Defenders of Myth and have a few moments to spare, I would greatly appreciate it if you could leave a review on Amazon. For self-published authors, reviews are vital because online retailers use them as a factor in showing a book to other readers.

Are you signed up to receive advanced notice and free excerpts of my work? If not, please do so at: michaelgismanauthor.com/join-email. I promise not to share your email or flood it with useless drivel.

For a more social experience:

Please like my facebook page(michaelgismanauthor) or Instagram(michael_gisman_author).

For my website: michaelgismanauthor.com

And though this book has been edited and proofed, if you do find a typo, please email me at michaelgisman@gmail.com

Thank you again for reading, and please let your friends know about it!

Gratefully yours,
Michael Gisman

Michael Gisman

ABOUT THE AUTHOR

Michael Gisman lives in South Carolina with his wife under the Carolina blue skies.

An avid reader since grade school, he started with adventure stories and quickly moved into fantasy and science fiction. As a kid, one of his first favorite books was "My side of the Mountain" by Jean George. He enjoys sports, both playing and watching. He earned the rank of Sandan (3rd-degree black belt) in Shinshin Toitsu Aikido. He also enjoys Southern BBQ and is a certified BBQ judge for the SC BBQ Association.

Some of his passions are collecting fantasy books, music, and the great outdoors. He also enjoys attending Renaissance festivals. Rush is his favorite band. He loves camping and sitting by the fire while looking at the stars.

...and at the end of the day, he enjoys relaxing on his deck while listening to music.

Made in the USA
Las Vegas, NV
16 March 2025

19670969R00189